MERLYN'S HEIR

MERLYN'S HEIR

Marion Athorne and Osbert Norman-Walter

Other titles in the Merlyn's Legacy Trilogy

  Book 1: Wizard's Woe
  Book 2: Merlyn's Heir
  Book 3: Arthur's Ark

Also by Marion Athorne
The Glass Slipper

© Marion Athorne

Published by Green Dragon Books

ISBN 978-0-9565563-0-1

All rights reserved. No part of this book may be reproduced, adapted, stored in a retrieval system or transmitted by any means, electronic, mechanical, photocopying, or otherwise without the prior written permission of the author.

The right of Marion Athorne and Osbert Norman-Walter to be identified as the authors of this work has been asserted by them in accordance with the Copyright, Designs and Patents Act 1988.

Cover illustration by Imogen Hallam

Prepared and printed by:

York Publishing Services Ltd
64 Hallfield Road
Layerthorpe
York YO31 7ZQ
Tel: 01904 431213

Website: www.yps-publishing.co.uk

To my father
The greatest weaver of tales I ever knew

ACKNOWLEDGEMENTS

There are a number of people whose help and encouragement I would like to acknowledge, but especially my sister Sheila, whose unfailing enthusiasm nerved me to take the apparently presumptuous step of rewriting someone else's story. I would also like to thank my Wise Readers: grandson Edward, friends Alan, Peggy and Susan with the initial efforts, and pay tribute to all my family's patience. Also to editor Jenny Sanders for her encouragement, and again acknowledge my indebtedness to Dave Haslett of ideas4writers, whose help and unflagging attention to detail has taught me so much, and now to the expert and professional help of Cathi Poole and Clare Brayshaw of York Publishing Services. Finally, and not least, my thanks to Imogen Hallam, artist and illustrator, for creating yet another great cover for this second book of the trilogy Merlyn's Legacy.

ABOUT THE AUTHORS

Osbert Norman-Walter, writer, playwright, journalist, and Astrological Consultant of the "News of the World" (1937—39) conceived Book One, in his twenties around 80 years ago but could find no publisher. On his death in 1974, his daughter Marion Athorne inherited an unfinished trilogy.

Now widowed with three children, ten grandchildren and three great grandchildren, Marion has only recently had the necessary time to commit to working on a manuscript that comprised more than a million words. She enrolled with the Writers Bureau early in 2004, and studied the new writing techniques. The publication of two articles and a win in a short story competition, gave her confidence to author the revised, edited, and abridged version of the now complete trilogy. She sincerely hopes that Book Two will fulfil the expectations that so many have looked forward to enjoying after reading Wizard's Woe.

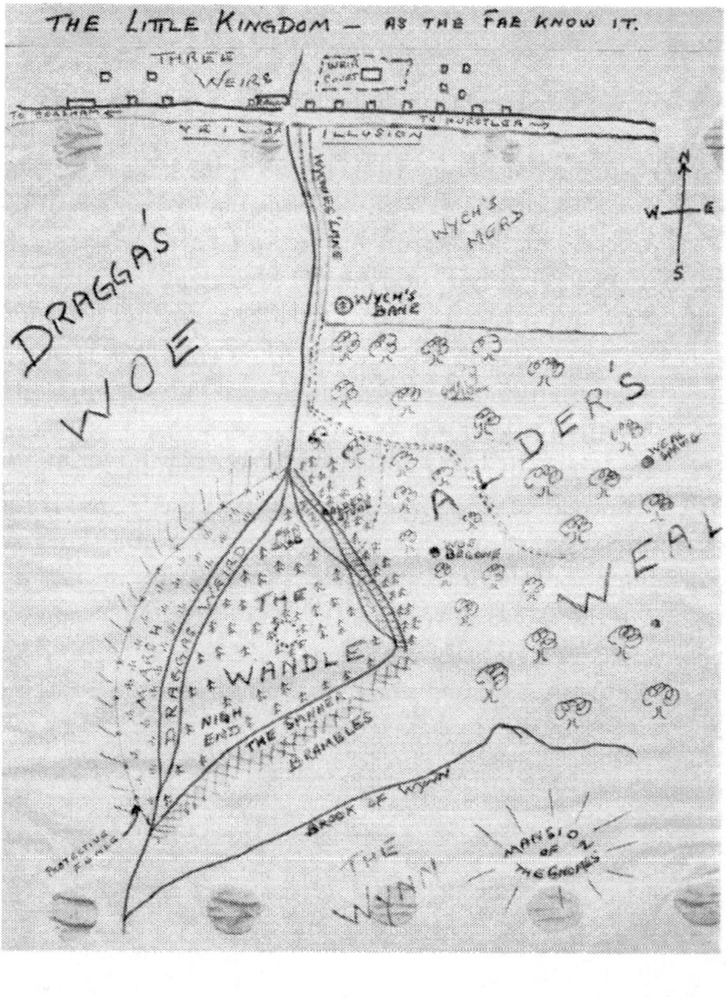
THE LITTLE KINGDOM — AS THE FAE KNOW IT.
THREE WEIRS
ILLUSION
TO HURSTLEA
N
W
E
S
WYCH'S MERS
WYCH'S BANE
DRAGGA'S WOE
ALDER'S WEAL
THE WANDLE
NIGH END
THE SNAKER
BRAMBLES
BROOK OF WYNN
THE WYNN
MANSION OF THE GNOMES
PROTECTIVE FENCE

CONTENTS

1	THE WEANING OF WHITE WAND	1
2	KING NEBUCHADNEZZAR	15
3	AM-MAR-EL-LYN	29
4	THE LORD OF THE HEAVENS	42
5	CHILD ROYAL TO ORDER	54
6	THE SILVER BOX	67
7	WITLESS WIZARD	77
8	MERLYN'S DECEPTION	84
9	WHITE WAND FEELS WATCHED	94
10	SLEEPING BEAUTY	105
11	MORE WAYWARD THAN WEIRDLY	112
12	A NEW KIND OF MAGIC	122
13	ALDER GOES SAILING	131
14	DRAGGA'S TEETH	140
15	SAVED FROM THE BANE	147
16	WHITE WAND'S VISIONS	157
17	THE BOOK OF AMARANTHUS	167
18	A COURT APPEARANCE	178
19	MERGYN REGINA	187
20	NYZOR	197
21	'AND SO BETWEEN US ...'	205
22	WYCH'S WEAL	214
23	THE GREEN DRAGON OF THE SOUTH	223
24	THE BIRTH OF ARTHUR	234
25	EXCALIBUR	245
26	GARETH AND THE HOLY GRAIL	258
27	THE WOLVES OF WAR	271

28	THE WEALSPRING	282
29	THROWN TO THE WOLVES	290
30	THE SAGE AVENGES HIS MOTHER	300
31	THE SAVING OF DRAGGA	307
32	A NEW WAND AND A NEW BEGINNING	316

CHAPTER 1

THE WEANING OF WHITE WAND

Why the immortal Merlyn's mortal guise should be a six-foot-tall, angular-looking monk with ginger hair, green eyes and large hands, Myrddin the elfin wizard didn't know. But a skim through the great Enchanter's treatise *Upon the Engendering and Nurture of Humanoids* showed that it appeared to involve some tricky procedures with human ova and spermatozoa. It had, he guessed, to be down to the luck of the draw from the gene cells available to the ancient wizard at the time. The skin also had a grey-blue tinge – a giveaway that its veins ran with ichor, the fluid said to run in the veins of the Greek gods instead of blood.

Since Myrddin's own height was just nine inches, the real magic for him was Merlyn's amethyst thumb-ring by which the humanoid body could be put on or off as desired, and allow Myrddin the best of both worlds – including the use of an electric typewriter. He had added a prologue to the manuscript of *Wizard's Woe* that he had sent Ann, plus an account of what had happened after she received it. All that had just been handed to the new Warden of Weir Forest, Sir Humphrey We'ard. The next manuscript lay in a pile of mounting sheets beside him.

To find that eighteen mortal years had passed since he had typed the original document impressed him now to keep better track of mortal time. He had just told Sir Humphrey that the Forest of Weir would be 'gone' before the next new moon, now only a fortnight away. He hadn't said how this would happen, because he couldn't. All he could have said, but didn't, was that nearly three mortal months previously, he and Ann, his partner White Wand, had experienced a sudden and unexpected vision of a solar eclipse, the effect of which was nearly as catastrophic as the promised doom it foretold. Myrddin reflected that it was just as well that the revelation had come while he, in his Office of Black Wand, was still alert at the water's edge of Dragga's lair, or their enemy would have caught them unawares. When neither sun nor moon were above the horizon, Dragga's usual gaseous form, a poisonous miasma known as the Scathe, would float like pallid green tentacles through the undergrowth all over the Weal, feeling around for any fay who had not found cover before losing consciousness. Conversely, when the dark moon rose their enemy's materialisation was stronger and more deadly, and the fae would cower down in their hiding places, terrified by what it would mean to be caught by the Wreak and annihilated. The only other protection they had was the combined power of their two guardians, Black Wand and White Wand, to hold it at bay.

Myrddin remembered the mind-numbing astonishment he had felt on seeing the black bite-sized chunk that suddenly appeared at the sun's rim and the cries of panic from the fae as they fled back to their shelters. The two Wychies barely had time to throw up their defence before their enemy's terrible form surged up through the water and towered over them like some giant hydra, its hungry jaws lunging towards them. It seemed appropriate that the second part of his manuscript should begin with his partner's reaction when she confessed to him afterwards that, as the darkness deepened, she had never felt as worried and afraid as when she lost all sight of his black-mantled figure, leaving her apparently alone to fight the menace.

'... In all the wonderful time we have been together, beloved Wychy, there has never been a moment of not knowing where you were, or not being aware of your love and strength supporting me,' she had said. She hadn't known then that he had been so loath to lose the innocence of her uncomplicated love that he had deliberately and literally kept her in the dark, preventing her from maturing into the full stature of a true Wych.

Then was not the time for confession, nor the place to rue his selfishness. He had known she would be unable to see him during those minutes of total eclipse, but dared not speak to reassure her. Any sign of a weakness like that would have given the enemy all it needed to devastate them both. He had been fully occupied keeping his own balance while Dragga sucked hungrily at the densely packed fir trees that formed The Wandle, its abruptly reinforced power threatening to overwhelm everything and everyone.

Ann had told him that she might have failed the trial had it not been for the unexpected light of a pale gold star in the circle of sky overhead, and a voice that was not a voice saying:

Behold Merlyn's Heir and Mergyn's daughter and Dragga also. Before Mona's light thrice more has waned, there shall be a passing and a coming, and a desolation within your lands unknown since their beginnings, and Wands all three divided one-and-one-and-one, and Dragga, too, undone, 'til the One who comes is seen and known by all.

Even Dragga had frozen, while Ann had stood transfixed by an icy dread, unable to understand the words but seizing hope from the small golden star that seemed to promise some great and ultimate triumph.

Then the dark moon had vanished and the sun's brilliance was burning into the Wreak with the ferocity of a sword thrust.

Baulked and venomous, Dragga drained a hasty retreat to the waters of his lake, his coils snaking back through the trees, waspish with pain but still trying to strike.

The two remained vigilant, however; their Wands stinging the last errant wisps of his Scathe on its way.

Ann turned quickly to Black Wand's once more sun-illumined figure, saying: 'O beloved Wychy, did you hear it?'

'I heard, dear Wych,' he answered, taking her in his arms. 'I don't know what it means, but I think we soon will – and wish we didn't.'

'Even Dragga heard it,' she said. 'How are we to continue without him, if he is undone?'

'Hush.' He silenced her with a kiss. 'Our people have been badly frightened. They're already gathering above Wandleside awaiting our welcome. Until their celebrations at Sunné's return are over, we can't begin to think about what it all means, let alone show our fears …'

*

After the general rejoicing, and sun and moon both set, Myrddin was thankful for a long interregnum in which to sit and think in his black crystal Retreat, while the unconscious fae lay safely under cover in the Weal.

His first priority was to hunt through the large book of accumulated lore and wisdom that he had inherited from his predecessor. He searched, without much hope, for some overlooked clue to guide him with an interpretation of the prophecy. There were records of all major eclipses, but no prophesies. Following the first eclipse ever recorded, a tremendous storm and an earthquake had nearly devastated Weal and Woe. He supposed that *'A desolation within thy lands'* and *'Dragga, too'* could mean another earthquake. The British Isles had a history of such tremors; though it would take a large one to dislocate the forest, the island of The Wandle and its three surrounding lakes.

He sprang up and began pacing back and forth, considering what precautions he could possibly take to ensure the safety and unity of his charges, without exciting their fear. He was still rejecting various ideas when King Alder's voice came to his mind:

O Wise One, my spirit is uplifted yet depressed. Come to me, beloved Wychy; I would have counsel of you.

Myrddin froze. The King had only ever communicated with him via Kye, the Royal Herald. He had never summoned either of the Wychies into his presence before.

Beloved Liege, I come, he responded.

He wondered whether to advise his Wych of the call, and decided against it. The message had been for him and, until he knew more, it seemed better to keep it that way.

He cleared his mind of all concerns and half-made plans and set off for Alder's Stede, wondering if the Queen would also be present. Thinking about Queen Gwen, however, raised questions he never liked to think about. From all accounts and references, it seemed that Alder had been content to live for all time in a state of single bliss, and was so other-worldly and remote that Myrddin doubted even a fully born fay could meet and mingle with such perfection, let alone a half-born like Gwen.

Strangely enough, Gwen had appeared less than enthused by her elevation. He remembered her somewhat wistful comment: 'You know I really believe I would have been accepted by the Wand if that terrible thunderbolt hadn't blasted everything.' And how his reply: 'Indeed, my Lady, but now you wear a worthier Weird,' had been met with only a rather doubtful sigh of agreement.

He wondered how she would have whiled away the time in her new home. The only occasion she ever appeared was when everyone gathered on The Wandle in celebration of the full moon. She would acknowledge Black Wand with a smile that no one else received; a peculiar smile that had grown more confident with the passage of time. It seemed to say that she was content to await her true destiny, which was to be his Wych, because she knew her time would come. Since this directly threatened his essential unity with Ann, he always veiled his eyes in response. She had never gleaned from him that his answer would be *over my dead body*.

On the path ahead, Myrddin became aware of two stone chairs facing each other. On the furthest sat Alder, as 'plainly' attired as any wicca in the Weal, while across his lap lay the golden Wand of Power. The Wychy went down on one knee before him, his shining mantle splaying gracefully from his shoulders. The King acknowledged him gravely, indicated the opposite chair and Myrddin sat and waited, his own black Wand across his knees.

Alder spoke to the point and seriously: 'O Black One, beloved of us all, at the time of Sunné's eclipse it came to me that I must pass from this place. Therefore, how say you, Wychy? What is to become of our people without their King?'

It was a moment before Myrddin could speak. Separation from their King was unimaginable. 'My Liege, how am I to answer? I have no words – and my Wand is silent. I have always understood that the ageless destiny of our race rests here in you. My Sister Wand and I are guardians only of the welfare of our people. Surely without you we will perish?'

'This is why I ask of your wisdom, my Wychy. How shall our people be saved?'

Myrddin groaned silently and wondered where he was supposed to find an answer. He took a deep breath: 'If I had the wit, wisdom and skill of the great Merlyn himself, my Liege, I might know. But all the knowledge that any Black One has had since Merlyn's time has been what each has learnt and added to the Book of Wisdom, which then passes to his successor.'

'Wychy, I had no idea.'

'Sire, how should you?' Myrddin said quickly. 'You have no need of the written word. It is because of our mortal cycle that each Black Wand needs a record of what each of his predecessors learnt before they went to pay their debt to Dragga.'

'So you know of no way to provide against my passing?'

'I do not say that, my Liege. No riddle exists that cannot be resolved in some manner or other – and I shall find the answer to this one.' He paused before asking tentatively, 'How was it with you, my Liege? How and when did *you* first come here?'

'I became and was in a land far distant, near to the beginning of all things at the time of Merlyn and Mergyn,' Alder replied. 'But of the manner of my coming, I do not know. I came with them to Britain, where Merlyn made The Wandle and Weirds. Here the first Wands took up their duties, and I mine, to guide and rule our people. I cannot tell you more, Black One; the vision wanes even as I begin to wane myself.'

'Then it seems, Sire, that our only hope is to seek the help of great Merlyn himself,' Myrddin answered slowly and heavily. '*If* his spirit is still within reach ...'

*

The puzzled Wychy thought hard on his way back to The Wandle. The King's words had explained that the 'Passing' would be Alder's. It was logical, therefore, that the 'Coming' should mean the arrival of his successor in the same mysterious way as Alder had said of himself: '*I became and was ...*' If that was happening then what was there to worry about? Which was when he realised why he felt so galled: Alder, the all-wise, all-knowing King, had asked him, Merlyn's Heir, for advice; and the Wychy, despite his title, had none to give him.

He became aware of Ann waiting for him at the meeting of the Weirds. From her look of guilt, knew at once that she had been up to something that she thought so awful that she was scared he would be angry about it.

'Black Wand!' she cried as he came up to her. 'Beloved, I have done the worst thing any Wych has ever done. I went looking for you at *your* end of The Wandle.'

He should have realised that his disappearance might cause distress. She must have seen the bright star of his whereabouts in her Wych ball, and watched in amazement as it glided across the narrows between King's Weird and Wychies' Weird – and then vanish. How afraid she must have felt! Wherever he went in the Weal, his star was always visible. She would have remembered the terrible words of prophecy, that, if it wasn't a remarkable exhibition of magic, then some darker thing must be at work and, in panic and against all Wychie protocol, gone looking for him at Far End without his permission. She would not have found his Retreat but had soon sensed his return, and castigated herself for not realising the simple and obvious – even if unprecedented – visit to the royal Stede.

He drew her close, smiling at her explanation and marvelling how fortunate he was to have a Wych more concerned with owning up and begging his forgiveness than with discovering the reason for his break with tradition. He laughed and covered her face with forgiving kisses before accounting for where he had been.

'Sweet One, our Liege summoned me privately to understand the prophecy. I could not forewarn you until I knew his purpose.'

'He heard it too?'

'Not in quite the same way as you and I, I think. His wisdom is of a different kind.'

'And have you, beloved magician, have you found out how and when this prophecy will happen?'

'In part,' he answered carefully. 'I know something of the Passing, which is Alder's, a little of the Coming, which will be his successor, but the manner of the Desolation is still beyond me. Nevertheless, our Liege has charged me with finding an answer …' He became silent as he thought: *if I assume it's possible to reach the spirit of the great Merlyn, then where do I begin?* All he knew for certain was that Merlyn had had a Retreat, but when the enchanter had vanished, so had all knowledge of the whereabouts of his dwelling, and anything it might have held.

*

In his own Retreat, he re-read the first passages ever written in his volume of Wisdom. Surprisingly, Alder's statement that Merlyn had created the three great lakes of the Weirds and the island of The Wandle was not on record, although the lost books were. It confirmed that the magician had placed his *Perfect Writings* in his Mount, although no one, it seemed, had ever recorded where the thing was. Yet Alder had spoken of the first Wands' arrival with the great Enchanter in Britain, and Britain was where the main legends of Merlyn abounded. Wasn't it reasonable therefore to assume that Merlin's Mount was somewhere in the British Isles?

He felt his Weird abruptly disturbed. Ann, who had dutifully returned to her vigil, was calling him urgently. *Brother Wand. The Lord of the Weirs* is walking the Weal.

Like his Wych, the Wychy was also surprised. Of all people, Sir Edward We'ard knew the time-honoured warning that every villager of Three Weirs learns from infancy about their forest: *Never go nigh it at night; never go nigh it alone.*

He looked out through the jet crystal walls of his Retreat. They cleared before his gaze to show the aging man's slow approach along Wychies' Lane. To the Wychies, it appeared far slower than it actually was in mortal terms. Their perception of time made everything physical appear to move with the speed of a slow-motion film since they themselves moved so quickly.

The Weir Lord in fact was walking as fast as his strength allowed, but starlight was not enough to prevent him from stumbling with only his walking stick to save him from falling.

I do not like this, beloved, Ann called. *It seems our dear Weir Ward labours in body and in mind.*

We will watch, dear Wych, she was counselled. *I do not want to wandle him unless he is in danger. He will probably speak to us from above Wandleside knowing we will hear even though we don't reply.*

But Sir Edward didn't go to the high cliff of Wandleside that rose above the two great lakes of King's Weird and Wychies' Weird at its foot. Instead, he turned off the track and went through the trees in such darkness that he had to cautiously swing his stick before him. An unseen branch swept the hat from his head, but he hurried on without pausing to pick it up, stooping and swinging his stick and breathing heavily as he dragged his feet out of the brambles. At last he stopped, panting, and looked around for some familiar outline. It was clear that the ancient Weir Ward was lost in a forest that he thought he knew well.

Please, Black One, my love, Ann pleaded. *He is looking for the Meeting of Ways. Can't we guide him?*

No, came her partner's reply. *It is his weird he wears and the doom he brings must weave its own pattern without our help. Whether he succeeds or fails in his mission, he must do it.*

They both knew that the wandling of mortals was not good magic, and Sir Edward had only to open his mouth and call for their help – as he above all should know. Ever since Ann had left him the book Myrddin had written as the mortal August Autrey, the Weir Lord would have known that the fae inhabitants of Weir Forest were real.

The man stumbled on again until a boulder brought him to his knees. But he recognised a landmark; he had reached the glade in which stood the blackened shell of a huge tree, once known as Great Oak. Examining the top of its splintered trunk, he drew an envelope from his pocket, secured it firmly in one of the uneven cracks, and spoke for the first time, his voice hoarse and breathless:

'Black Wand, Black Wand. Wyn me your wisdom, Wand.'

Both Wands became like carved images in their Retreats. The poignant words lifted from their Song of Longing made his appeal a wish they had to grant. Yet Myrddin did not answer or send any sign, for he knew that if Sir Edward had expected one he would not have written whatever was in the envelope.

After a short rest, leaning gratefully against the shattered tree for support, the old man pulled himself together and retraced his steps. The two watchers waited until he was safely on the open way of Wych's lane with the starlight easing his progress. Then Myrddin sent the instruction: *We will go together, my Love.*

*

At the Meeting of the two Weirds, they glided hand-in-hand across the waters, lightly ascended Windaway's path, and reached the top of Wandleside. They went silently to the stricken oak, whisking the snakelike wisps of the deadly Scathe from their path. Mortals were immune to these probing tentacles of Dragga – unless they fell asleep in the forest, where the evil could enter their minds and drag them towards the Woe. Any fay not under cover between moonset and sunrise could meet the same fate. But the Wands' vigilant guardianship ensured that no one ever perished in the Weal.

It needed quite a leap for the nine-inch wizard to reach the crack and retrieve the letter. Jumping down, he stood the envelope, two thirds his own height, on its end and slipped his Wand of Office under the flap to open it. Pulling out a typewritten page, he unfolded it and held spread against the tree trunk so that both of them could read its message.

The letter was dated and, to their amazement they learnt for the first time that a full eighteen years had passed since August had died as a mortal. Mortals moved slowly, time was therefore assumed to pass slowly to accommodate them. Myrddin's own perception of time since he had died had possessed a dreamlike and eternal quality – that now appeared to have sped at break-neck speed under the fluctuation of uncounted phases of the moon. The letter ran:

Knowing no other means of communicating with you, mighty Black Wand, I use this simple device in the assurance that nothing concerning our beloved forest can remain unknown to you.

It may be that you already know the nature of the news I have to tell. If this be so, you will know that for some years now the Planning Authorities of this realm have been considering the building of a Dormitory Town in Weir Forest. I have diligently contested the threat with every means in my power, but it has recently become clear that our forest is irretrievably committed to this end.

In an initial effort, I petitioned the Queen (of Great Britain) for her royal ratification of the provisions of my ancient Charter protecting the Forest from all such intrusions. Alas, the law lords have ruled that the Monarch no longer enjoys the right to exercise such personal intervention. I have also now learnt that the Ministry of Town and Country Planning are moving ahead with their schedule.

The only alternative I can see is for the forest to be taken over by the National Trust. But even this, although I shall fight for it, is doubtful of success, and is certainly not an ideal solution since the forest would be open to public invasion. Therefore I can only advise you of this tragedy in order to warn you.

O Wychy, I am sorely grieved. The blackness of this cloud appals me beyond endurance, for am I not in spirit at one with you? I long to depart and surrender the struggle to the younger and more virile hands of my son Humphrey, in whose loyalty I have abundant faith. Yet how and where shall I find my people if my demise is delayed, the forest destroyed and its faerie scattered – even annihilated?

The Wychy removed his Wand, allowing the paper to fall to the ground. So this was the promised Desolation; not the natural cataclysm he had expected. Overall, he felt, the latter would have been a better fate.

Ann was in despair. 'O Brother Wand, what are we to do?'

Her cry made him take her protectively into his embrace, realising how unprepared she was for the news. As he comforted her, he was aware of drifts of Scathe stirring in alarm around them without attempting their usual assault; telling him that Dragga's evil intelligence was also alive to the threat. For a moment, he felt a fleeting kinship with their ancient enemy. For countless years, they had dealt with each other, in their opposing ways, to provide an indispensable balance to their existence. The prospect of a drained and uprooted Dragga, his power annulled with scientific thoroughness, made Myrddin realise that he not only had to find a way of saving his people, but a way of rescuing Dragga too.

He lowered his Wand to a corner of the paper and the letter flared, its flames illuminating their motionless figures as it burned.

CHAPTER 2

KING NEBUCHADNEZZAR

Now that Myrddin knew the meaning of the three dooms facing the little kingdom and the forest, finding Merlin's Mount became his priority. He was sure the Mount and the lost Books of Wisdom had to exist, or his Book would never have mentioned them.

According to the mortal rendering of the Arthurian legend by Sir Thomas Mallory, both Merlin and Morgan le Fay had been deeply concerned with the faerie world – though neither, if the scandals were true, had quite acted in harmony with the loving principles that inspired the little people of Weir Forest. Mallory's legend also told of Merlin being enticed into a cave by a witch and left there to die. But was that possible? Surely Merlyn would have escaped in his elfin form … or would he? If the enchanter hadn't had his Wand with him, or some other faerie talisman, would he have made any impression on solid rock?

This line of reasoning brought forth a startling idea: suppose Merlyn was still imprisoned in that same cave, inhabiting his wraith?

As if to confirm this, the words of Mallory's tale came to his mind:

… And so in time it happed that Merlin showed to her (Nemway) a rock whereas was a great wonder, and wrought by enchantment that went under a great stone. So by her subtle working she made Merlin to go under that stone to

let her wit of the marvels there, but she wrought so there for him so that he came never out for all the craft he could do. And so she departed and left Merlin.

It was at this point that he remembered the Eye of Mona; the one oracle he should have consulted as soon as he had left the King's presence. He could have kicked himself; *why, oh why, had he wasted so much time?* He would go immediately to where the eye lay hidden in the great crystal cube of Alder's throne.

Then an instruction in his book came to mind: *Never disclose the purpose of any act to your Wych – even if you have no serious object therein.* He had to distract Ann's attention from what he was about to do. Both Wands overlooked the Circle of Rejoicing at the centre of the island from their Retreats – his Wych through her Wych ball, and he through the black crystal walls of his dwelling. He had to get Ann away from The Wandle and into the Weal where she couldn't see where he was going.

The gnomes had discovered that White Wand had an interest in runic inscriptions. Now, every time they found a piece of bone, or a metal fragment with a runic character, they would come running to present it to her. Ann, who had not yet become as awesome as the Wych before her, would never hurt their feelings by refusing to discuss their find. Fortunately, with the early rising sun, the fae were already awake. So he wandled a group of gnomes into finding a flint arrowhead, which sent them racing from their Mansion in the Wynn to the Glade of White Bluebells in the Weal, crying for White Wand's immediate attention.

*

In the Circle of Rejoicing, he reverently removed the heavy red and golden fabric that covered the block throne of crystal. He then cleared his mind of everything except the question he needed to ask: *Where is Merlin's Mount?* The Eye, invisible at first, gradually appeared and then faded, and in its place he saw a line of wedge-shaped characters, which he recognised as an ancient form of writing. He couldn't read them, but committed them to memory. When they eventually faded, he asked another question: *Where is great Merlyn himself?*

The crystal remained clear; no Eye, nothing. Dead question.

He carefully replaced the cover and left the Circle, pondering. He had only consulted the Eye once before, when he had needed its power to prevent the White Wand rising to Queen Gwen's hand, and his book had warned him that the Oracle did not always give an answer.

Back in his Retreat, he wrote down the characters he had memorised and stood staring at them. He knew that the wedge-shaped form of writing had originated in the ancient kingdom of the Chaldeans, but he had no idea how he might interpret their meaning, which he presumed was the direction to Merlin's Mount.

Did the characters represent the name of some city in Mesopotamia, like Ur of the Chaldees? Nineveh? Or ... Babylon? He shook his head irritably as an impossible suggestion came to mind. But then thought again. *Is it really so impossible? Aren't the Chaldeans reputed to have been the finest astrologers, necromancers and magicians in the ancient world? And wouldn't the immortal wraith of Merlyn have known these ancient civilisations? Most of them would have turned to dust before he ever came to Britain.*

Yet even if he ever discovered which city the characters stood for, how was he to get there? And even if he could, what chance would he, a nine-inch-high amateur archaeologist, have of excavating enormous clay tablets and transporting them back to The Wandle? Add to that the amount of time it would take, when he couldn't leave The Wandle for more than two weeks at a time between the dark and full moons. *No*, he decided. *It is too ridiculous.*

He was tempted then to think he had asked the wrong question, although if it *had* been the wrong question in the first place, then the Eye would have shown him nothing at all – as had happened with his second question. It simply meant he had to find a translation.

In theory, he thought, there should be books on the subject in the Public Library at Corsham. Perhaps he could get there somehow and investigate the matter invisibly, although he could hardly expect to find all he needed on a single visit. He would also need a Chaldean grammar guide and dictionary, which was not the sort of thing the local Public Library would have on hand.

Setting that problem aside, he pondered again the news contained in the Weir Ward's letter. The fae would need to be prepared and somehow hardened, to cope with the shocks that were coming. News of a general exodus from the forest couldn't be rushed. It called for the careful embedding of new ideas; the introduction of new things into their surroundings, and the kind of activities that, when the time came, would enable them to embark on a completely new existence with assurance and excitement.

And he had less than three full moons in which to do it.

Working out the details meant he was actively *doing* something – even if it didn't help with translating the Chaldean script. *Or did it?* An idea suddenly struck him on how he could kill two birds with one stone. What if Sir Edward were to wake up one morning and discover the inscription – say, impressed on a leaf of fairy gold – at his bedside? The Weir Ward would be bound to act on it if he believed it had anything to do with his letter to Black Wand, and his obvious reaction would be to get it translated.

Myrddin felt he could give himself a pat on the back for craftiness. A pinch of suggestion here, and a smidgeon of bewilderment there ... and hey presto, a huge task accomplished with a minimum of effort – which, after all, is the essence of all true magic ...

*

The following morning, the entire population of the forest came running in a state of high excitement to the clearing around the Wychy's half hollowed beech tree home of *Woe Begone!*. The word had spread like magic – which it was – that Black Wand was going to tell them a new story.

It seemed eras since their Wychy had delighted them in this way, so it was a gala occasion. Even the hard-working gnomes took the morning off. Only Ann, who respected ancient tradition, didn't appear. Myrddin knew she was happy to watch and listen from The Wandle.

Unfortunately, her innocent joy was short lived.

Queen Gwen, also on the receiving end of everything that happened in the forest, remarked to Alder how much she would dearly love to hear Black Wand's story in person. For some moments Alder hadn't replied, and she looked into his unreadable eyes with misgiving. Then the ethereal features lightened, and he granted her wish.

Alder then conveyed the news telepathically to his Wychy, who acknowledged the advice with outward and dutiful joy. Inwardly, however, he was aware of the possible trouble caused by, of all things, the placement of chairs.

In recognition of Omric, the Master of Gnomes, it was Black Wand's custom to provide a golden chair from his Weal Retreat of *Woe Begone!*. He could scarcely do less for Alder's Queen, and that meant she would be sitting at his side; something she had not done since Alder had taken her to be his Queen. The fae would receive her unprecedented appearance with wild enthusiasm, he was sure, but he doubted Ann would be so happy.

Common sense dictated that he should explain the position to her in advance. And he would have done, if it hadn't been for that long-departed Wychy's advice: *Never disclose the purpose of any act to your Wych, even if you have no serious object therein.*

He therefore waited inside *Woe Begone!* to give the Royal Coach time to arrive.

He knew that Ann, of course, would be aware of its destination as soon as it left the precincts of King's Weird. But the fae, who were dancing their way to the rendezvous, could hold only one marvel in their minds at a time. They even missed the approach of Rozyn's dray, which was trundling up from the Wynn in the wake of the racing gnomes.

Myrddin came out of *Woe Begone!* when all were nearly there, and raised his Wand in greeting. In the midst of the Wychy's tremendous reception, Smye ran forward to bring out the two chairs to place before the door. It was his privilege because, as he never tired of telling every new arrival, there had once been a terrible time when Black Wand had preserved him from the Scathe by covering him with his own magic cloak.

When Myrddin asked Smye to bring a third chair, Omric queried it. '*Three*, Black One?'

'Three is a magical number, beloved Master,' said Myrddin sagely. 'Two, as you doubtless know, is a negative number as they simply achieve balance, as with empty scales; whereas three is an active number since it can depress one or the other of the scales.'

The Master, though accustomed to handling scales, found the comparison confusing, nevertheless he nodded wisely, and replied: 'Indeed that is so, O Teller of Tales.'

Myrddin shot him a look, wondering if Omric was being miraculously guilty of sarcasm; but the reverberation of tiny hooves turned everyone's attention to the imminent arrival of a coach. The gathered fae and gnomes stood craning round, expecting to see Rozyn's dray.

"T'is the *Royal Coach!*' exclaimed Loy, who, being Master of the Queen's Barge, was someone to be believed.

The Royal Coachman brought the sparkling carriage to a halt and the crowd drew aside, leaving a lane for Black Wand to go and meet it.

You could hear a leaf drop as Gwen stepped out with the assistance of Black Wand's hand. Instead of the queenly attire she always wore at High Moon, she had on a diaphanous robe that made her look even more beautiful than usual. And no crown either; just a circlet of brilliants such as many of her wiccy subjects wore. In fact the only thing that was the same as her appearance at High Moon was the unmistakeable smile she gave to Black Wand – and to him alone. The crowd recognised it, sensed its meaning, loved it – and feared it – as they always did. They jumped up and capered and sang because it was such a marvellous thing to have Queen Gwen among them again. This was indeed a day of days.

Black Wand and Queen Gwen passed through the gathering, caressed by countless hands, to the chairs. The Master knelt to the Queen in delight before taking his seat beside the Wychy. However, Myrddin's seat was not a comfortable one. Somewhere in the background of his wyché understanding lay a pool of icy silence that held a reflection of his Wych as she looked sternly into her Wych ball. There was no time to think about that now though, for a wild cheer had gone up acclaiming the arrival of Rozyn and his dray of barrels and caskets.

The Royal Vintner halted his fauns, stood up, and gave the Wychy a huge wink before doffing his cap and bowing to the Queen. Then settled himself on one of his barrels, signifying that he was ready to dispense the contents when the Black One gave him the signal.

By tradition, Black Wand was quite incapable of telling a story unless he had an arm around each of two fae, and it was another tradition that they should be Dina and Sylvie. There had originally been a third – Leila – but she had departed with the Sickness into mortality, leaving the position at his feet vacant. It had remained like that ever since, although no one could ever remember why. It was a great surprise therefore when, in response to a barely perceptible flutter of an eyelid from the Wychy, Hetty ran over and took up the place, her arms on his knees and her head up-tilted in an expression of adoring love, while Sylvie and Dina nestled happily against each of his shoulders.

'I say, Barney, did you see that!' exclaimed Edmund, slightly shocked.

'Can't teach some people, can you?' answered Barnsley, who was still less fully born than any of his contemporaries. 'I'm surprised at Black Wand, though. It's like he's giving her a long-delayed death warrant – '

'Barney, *please* ...' implored nearby fae, shuddering at the awful word.

'I disagree,' said Baddenham. 'I think it's a cagey move on Black Wand's part because of the Queen.'

'Pack it in, the pair of you, can't you?' Simmonds said in a disgusted voice that had them all wondering what had come over them. They hadn't spoken in this way for a long time.

The Wychy sensed his sister Wand had registered the move. She would wonder whether her Black One was enticing Hetty as a warning to Gwen not to come too near – or was it his intention to mislead Ann herself, to cover some secret weakness he might have for the Queen? His loyal Wych would try not to think such thoughts, he knew, but it was clear that he had deliberately put himself in danger of becoming involved with one or the other of them, and that impression would stay with her.

Pushing the problem out of his mind, he began his story: 'Once upon a time there lived an all-powerful king who ruled over a mighty people in a land called Chaldea. His name was Nebuchadnezzar, and he was a great hunter and a fearless warrior. Everyone bowed to the earth whenever they heard his name. He had conquered all the peoples of the world, and now possessed everything that was in it – even the jewels and precious stones beneath it ...'

That had the Master of Gnomes stretching a pointed ear, which had been Myrddin's intention. It also caused Queen Gwen to give him an odd look, which had not been his intention. He was aware, too, that his opening was so new and strange and unexpected that he could follow it up with quite a bit of information before the inevitable interruptions. So he went on: 'There was just one thing that this mighty king did not have, and that was a son who would be king after him, and inherit all his power and possessions, and guide the destiny of the people, just as Nebuchadnezzar did. Now, one night this mighty ruler, King Nebuchadnezzar, had a dream –'

Hetty nudged his knee with an elbow – the interruptions had begun. 'Please, Black Wand, what is a dream? Is it a memory you have of something after you've forgotten it? Because if it is, I think I had one only yesterday.'

'No, Hetty, fae don't dream; it's something that only mortals do when they're asleep. It's like seeing and doing something, but when you wake up you know you haven't *really* seen or done it.'

'That sounds like magic,' said Smye.

'If it is, then Black Wand must have dreams, too,' said Baddenham.

'I never sleep, Baddy. I am awake all the time.'

'Well, that's magic in itself,' said Baddenham.

'Does Alder, our Liege, stay awake too?' Edmund asked.

This was more than Myrddin had bargained for.

'It is not a subject that I am privileged to question with our Liege,' he said courteously, as Smye's round eyes fastened on the Queen with curiosity. Black Wand's answer, however, had brought nods of approval from almost all his listeners, so he went on with his story: 'Now, in this dream King Nebuchadnezzar was told that his days of kingship were numbered because he had nearly worn his Weird. He must pass away, like all mortals. But unless he could find a successor to lead his people and tell them what to do, his entire and mighty kingdom would be overrun by thieves and robbers who would frighten everyone away. And that was too terrible to even think about.'

Everyone shivered. This wasn't at all like Black Wand's usual stories.

'Now, in this terrible dream,' the Wychy went on, 'there was also a very mysterious clay tablet engraved with signs –'

A gnome put his hand up. 'Please, Black Wand,' he said, and gnomes were not usually given to interrupting. 'Were these signs engraved in the same way that we engrave our gems?'

'Good question, Feldspar,' said the Wychy approvingly, 'because when King Nebuchadnezzar woke up in the morning, there on the crystal table beside him lay a sheet of purest gold, which he was quite sure hadn't been there when he went to sleep. And when he picked it up, he found to his amazement that it had written on it the same characters that had been on the clay tablet in his dream.'

'What kind of characters were these, O Wychy?' asked Gwen, with a look of keen interest.

'Simple yet passing strange, O Queen, and probably of magical meaning. But although King Nebuchadnezzar was a good scholar and recognised a lot of the words that the signs showed, he couldn't make sense of them –'

'Draw some,' demanded Hetty at his knee.

He smiled down at her fondly, guessing that her insistence sprang more from a desire to divert his attention from Gwen than to satisfy any real curiosity of her own.

'All writing is magic, dear one,' he hedged. 'It makes plain to others what is secret in one's own mind – '

'Magic! Magic! Magic!' chorused his listeners. 'Draw us some magic, Black Wand.'

So, of course, he obliged; it was what he had been working up to. And he took the showmanship a little further by closing his eyes with a concentrated expression before raising his Wand. But then Gwen interrupted him, leaning over and whispering in a most intimate chuckle: 'I dare you, O most inimitable wizard.'

He paused. *What in Mona's name did she mean by that?* he wondered. *Does she not believe that I can trace recognisable and meaningful characters in a long dead script?* It was a flash of the old Gwen, and confirmed his suspicion that she still had mortal memories that should have long since faded.

He raised the Wand once more, and inscribed in letters of fire an exact reproduction of the inscription he had seen in the Eye of the Moon. While the ideograms flamed in the air and the crowd gasped in awe, he saw an expression of utter disbelief on the Queen's face.

Dina, clinging closely to the Wychy with her cheek against his, exclaimed, 'O-o-oh, Black Wand. What do they mean, these wedge-shaped sticks of fire?'

He laughed, but glanced down at Hetty, who hadn't even turned around to look. 'Like King Nebuchadnezzar, I really have no idea. But I must try hard not to forget them, in case when I have made up my mind what they mean, I am unable to draw them properly again.'

'Forget them, Back Wand?' asked the Master in surprise. 'Never! Look!' He bent down and copied the signs faithfully on a bare patch of ground beside him. 'They shall be engraved on a scroll of gold which shall be set up for all to see when we gather for the next part of the story.'

It was exactly what he had been aiming for, and he extended a grateful hand to the Master, thanking him.

Gwen, still frowning at the fading outlines, was musing: 'Long, long ago, I knew such characters as these, Black Wand. They are cuneiform, a script only known in Chaldea. At least you are accurate in that.'

Myrddin replied with quick humour, 'Was that when I was a King in Babylon and you were a Christian slave?'

'O Wychy,' she said reproachfully, 'how could that be? Kings no longer lived in Babylon at the beginning of the Christian era. Henley's lines were poetic, but inaccurate, as surely you must know?'

He immediately sensed that Gwen's sweetly chastening reply had made Ann livid with anger. How dare the Queen put her beloved Wychy to shame in public like that!

'How could I *not* know, beloved Queen?' he replied gamely under his breath. 'So I am bound to ask if *you* know the meaning of these fearsome characters?'

'No, dear wizard,' Gwen laughed lightly. 'I am not now so wyché in this matter. And yet … perchance … who can say …?'

Seeing Gwen shrink from the counter-challenge, he felt Ann relax though remain angry. The Queen did *not* know. She was shamming, angling to get Black Wand on the hook, pretending to know something he didn't.

Returning to his waiting listeners, he manoeuvred them skilfully back to their favourite pastime of pestering the storyteller with endless questions on every side-issue. The questions and answers went on for some time before he signalled to the Royal Vintner that he could divert everyone's attention with his refreshment. During this, the crowd danced, sang songs and played pranks as they usually did at High Moon, except the Wychy and his principal guests remained on their golden chairs.

*

As she watched, Ann became more and more convinced that Queen Gwen was making a serious bid for her partner. She felt certain that her unprecedented visit to the Weal was just the beginning. Although she couldn't read Gwen as she could her wiccies, she could sense an anxiety behind the Queen's smiles at the wizard; a complexity of emotion that any wiccy would not have hesitated to tell him. Gwen, however, was repressing it – which struck her as quite ominous. Had Gwen been an ordinary fay, she would have wandled her attention away without a qualm for attempting to take on her Wychy out of turn. But she couldn't take liberties like that with Alder's Queen.

There was something else too. For the first time, she became aware of something alien about Gwen that she had never noticed before. *Possibly because I see so little of her*, she thought. The Queen now appeared strangely wyché – and, therefore, a potential Wych. *Could she really have known Chaldean texts in her mortality?* Ann wondered. She had certainly preserved some literary memory of her past, as she had demonstrated in her reply to the Wychy about Henley's poem.

*

Myrddin was wondering the same thing. He could have set his pride aside and asked Gwen about the matter there and then, if the Queen had not also made it clear that she wanted him on his own. When he escorted her back to the

Royal Coach, her last glance at him was one of such unfae-like despair and pleading that those near enough to see it shivered and turned away, embarrassed. Myrddin only bowed, keeping his eyes veiled as always.

But if one siren was gone, the second was still clinging to Myrddin's arm. And Hetty had certainly not missed Gwen's departing look.

'Beloved Black Wand,' she said, 'your story is so strange and foreboding about the passing of a king and a kingless land being overrun by robbers; I feel sorely beguiled. There is a memory somewhere in my mind – from somewhere long, long ago – and –'

He silenced her with a kiss. It was risky, but the quickest way to wandle her memories. Much as he wanted to toughen up a small coterie of fae, Hetty was returning to mortal thinking far too quickly.

Her arms at once came around his neck in eager response.

'Oh, Black Wand,' she sighed. 'How magic you are. With one kiss you have banished all the thoughts that threatened me so badly. Kiss me once more now, for your love and mine …'

'Oh-ho!' It was Rozyn, who came towards them bearing a golden cup filled with something of his own devising. He fell on one knee. 'Behold, I bear the most delicious, the most Mood-inspiring distillation. 'Tis named Enchantment.' He offered it first to Hetty, who took one sip and promptly fell asleep against the wizard's shoulder. Rozyn took the inert wiccy from him with a wink, while a soundless voice whispered a little sarcastically in the Wychy's ear: *Remember me …?*

And Myrddin sighed. His lovely, young and innocent Wych was beginning to wean her Weird fast.

CHAPTER 3

AM-MAR-EL-LYN

For three days, Gwen waited, hoping that the Wychy's need for a translation of the script would bring him to her. She had become resigned to what was little more than life imprisonment in a gold and marble palace underground. But her impatient longing for Black Wand had upset that hard-won harmony

She knew she had only herself to blame. If she had allowed herself to become absorbed in Alder, she would have been blissfully content. But the King was too perfect to be the kind of person she wanted as her lover. Only the Black One could meet that need, and Gwen, being wyché, knew she could have his love without taking the Mortal Sickness.

She felt that Alder understood her, even if he never spoke of her problem – for he seldom put anything into words. But he often looked sad, and that made her feel guilty and uneasy, so she tried to make up for it by being devoted to him.

Consequently, adoring her King, yet consumed with desire for the Wychy, she nourished her feelings by preserving many of her mortal interests and weaving them into her tapestries. Spinning gold and silver thread kept her fingers busy, but left her mind free to think – a very unfae-like occupation – and she had spent the time weaving stories concealed in Chaldean script that were borne of her longing for Black Wand. These she embellished into pictures of fulfilled desire, lovingly perfected and repeated over long periods, until each one glowed with an awesome beauty that surprised even her.

But now she had thrown aside that tradition, and walked out of her prison to visit the Weal and *Woe Begone!* to hear the Black One's story for herself, she realised that she could have done so any time she wished. She had been a prisoner of her own rigid thinking. It had taken the eclipse to make her realise that – and it was about the eclipse that she desperately needed the Wychy's advice.

After three days of waiting, during which she kept her dignity as proudly as she could, Gwen reached the end of her emotional tether and gave in. She *had* to see and speak to Black Wand. So she asked Alder if he would please summon the Master and the Pilot of her barge so she could spend the morning sailing on King's Weird.

She knew her request was an extraordinary one. The only time she ever used the vessel was in company with the King's barge at full moon each month. She gave no excuse, however, because excuses meant nothing to Alder. Indeed, his smile and nod of agreement seemed little different to those she had known before.

*

The Weal knew nothing about this; Loy – the Master of the Queen's Barge, Simmonds – her Pilot, and the Rowers didn't know themselves until they arrived at Alder's Stede in answer to the King's summons.

Ann, however, suspected what was afoot the moment she saw the little party of fae disappearing northwards from the bottom of Windaway.

When she called her partner to ask what he was going to do about it, there came no reply. She felt rightly indignant. He *had* to have heard her … unless he was at Alder's Stede. But he could hardly be there, since Gwen was clearly expecting to find him somewhere else. For the second time, she defied their protocol and walked purposefully to Black Wand's end of The Wandle where she could watch the approach of the barge. If her partner had any objection to her presence, he would need to do something about it. But, again, nothing happened.

When she stepped out of the trees into view, no one knew she was at the wrong end of The Wandle, since the fae had no idea where their Wychies lived on it. It was natural, then, that Loy should signal to Simmonds to draw the barge towards her, because it was hardly proper to sail on by without any acknowledgement. Loved as the Queen was, after the King, it was the two Wands whose law they lived by.

Ann noticed the look of annoyance that crossed Gwen's face, but she knew the Queen dared not forbid them. The fae must never know there was anything but glowing love between their Wychies and Alder's Queen. She smiled to herself at Gwen's ignorance. If the Queen had but known it, she could have commanded the Wych to wandle Loy, Simmonds and the Rowers into forgetting, and sail on by. But the barge touched ground, and Ann curtsied gracefully in salutation. She was being pointedly artful; the Queen on her own waters was one person, but once she set foot on The Wandle the boot was on the other foot.

Gwen acted as if everything had been prearranged – which was obviously not the case or Black Wand would also have been there to receive her. She rose, and accepted Loy's hand to step ashore and meet the White One's smiling welcome.

'I bring a message for Black Wand,' she said graciously, returning the smile.

'Alas,' the Wych deplored with a despairing gesture of her Wand, 'it would appear that my Brother Wand is absent, O Queen.'

This fact was so noticeable that it made the statement intentionally sarcastic, but Gwen treated it with dignity.

'Then with your permission, beloved Wych, I would await his return – unless you deem it unfitting to take me to his Retreat?'

'My apologies, again, beloved Queen – I have no idea where it is. My Brother Wand is free to visit my Retreat with my permission, but the law has always been that *his* must remain unknown.'

'I had forgotten, dear Wych, that Black Wand's Retreat must be like that of his master Merlyn, which has never been discovered.'

Ann was so surprised at the Queen's knowledge that she betrayed herself into showing it; which must have comforted Gwen, who still needed to save face.

'We could retire to my Retreat, O Queen,' said the Wych.

Gwen seemed taken aback, and suddenly wary. 'We could …' she answered, 'but not now. It will be enough to talk with you there when I come for the Bane, which only you can give me.'

It was novel for Ann to deal with a wiccy as self-possessed as Gwen – and even more alarming.

'If you will guide me to the Circle of Rejoicing,' Gwen went on, 'I think Black Wand will find us better there than anywhere else.'

The Wych bowed her head gracefully and they walked side-by-side to the meeting of the Weirds, with Loy and Simmonds keeping the barge floating slowly abreast of them.

In the Circle of Rejoicing they sat, by tacit agreement, on one of the large polished logs the fae usually used. It was clear that the Wych did not intend to allow her Queen to meet her Wychy unchaperoned.

Gwen looked up, as she always did, at the incredibly tall conifers, and sighed reminiscently: 'The trees go up forever and ever.'

'So you said on the night of Black Wand's choosing, O Queen.'

'How do you know that?' Gwen demanded. 'You did not come until the following High Moon.'

'A Wych has privileges,' said Ann lightly, remembering everything that her partner Wand – as the mortal – August, had written in the manuscript he had left for her. She could see that Gwen was impressed – and wondering what else might she know if she knew about such trivial incidents before she arrived.

Further questions remained unasked, as the next moment the glittering black magnificence of the Wychy himself took them both by surprise.

*

Myrddin knew full well that Ann was indignant he had dared to conceal his approach from her. But he was unrepentant; she had no business encroaching on his end of The Wandle.

He crossed the arena, smiling enigmatically, and went down on one knee before them. 'Hael and wyn, Beloved Queen and Wych.'

He held his Wand between the tips of his two middle fingers, which meant he was short-circuiting his thoughts and feelings, giving nothing away. After that, and with a flourish of his Weird, he sat cross-legged on the grass facing them, with the Wand across his knees. With eyes fully opened, he looked from one to the other with bright enquiry.

'Black Wand,' Gwen began, a little uncertainly. 'When you were telling your story the other morning, I said I might remember something of the meaning of the mysterious characters you scribed in the air with your Wand …'

'Apologies are unnecessary, dear Queen,' he answered, intentionally misunderstanding her. 'The matter is too small to be of any importance. And perhaps we were both a little flippant? I said they were beyond my comprehension; I did not intend that you should concern yourself with it.'

'But, Black Wand! I –' she began, and then subdued her outburst quickly. 'Perhaps you are not aware of a particular detail of my last mortal incarnation?' she went on more quietly.

'I recall only a chance reference of your own, long ago, my Queen, that your father had been a Canon of the Church, and –'

'To which, Brother Wand,' Ann quickly remarked, 'you yourself added the comment that Barney could also be described as being a "bit of warfare."'

It was so unexpected that Myrddin chuckled, but Gwen cried out 'This is preposterous!' and jumped angrily to her feet, bringing the Wands automatically to their own. 'It seems that even my innocent conversations have become the outworn banter of The Wandle. Take me back to my barge at once. At least the waters of My Lord the King do not mock me.'

Both Wychies were shocked into silent obedience.

They led the way back to the barge, and it was obvious that Gwen thought their silence could only mean they had plotted her discomfort between them.

Myrddin winced, thinking of what Alder would make of it when his Queen told him of such apparent disrespect. He bowed and Ann curtsied as Loy helped their visitor back onto the barge.

When the Wychies rose and looked aside at each other, Ann was clearly unrepentant at the harm she had done, while Myrddin had to veil his deep regret. But he understood the cause: his Wych was jealous, and weaning her Weird at an alarming rate.

As they turned, Ann said, 'Beloved, please explain the mystery of those strange characters of which our Queen spoke?'

'There is no mystery, beloved. I saw them in my mind's eye and drew them, and the Queen believed she understood their mortal meaning.'

'So the Queen, in her previous living, *could* understand the ancient characters?'

'Her father in mortality, the Canon, was well respected for his studies of ancient Sumeria and its long-dead form of Chaldean writing.'

He could see Ann was appalled to think that all Gwen had wanted was to give her interpretation of the ideograms. 'Brother Wand, I have wronged our Queen,' she said. 'Jealousy led me to wreck this meeting. How can I right the wrong I have done her?'

'It is not in my Weird to advise you, beloved,' he said, virtuously. 'You know very well that I have remained aloof from the first, fearing that no good would come of her coming here.'

His Wych looked so chastised that she forgot to ask him where he had been – and that suited him perfectly for he had been to Three Weirs village. The Master of the Gnomes had brought him the gold sheet, somewhat thicker and sturdier than gold leaf, inscribed with the characters. Myrddin had then shed his Weird, so his Wych wouldn't see him go, and journeyed out on the Woe-side of The Wandle – which wasn't dangerous while he had his Wand to keep Dragga in his place. But it was the first time he had gone beyond the bounds of the forest since his demise as August, and it had proved a steep learning curve.

It was finding a wall of white mist across his path in Wychies' Lane that reminded him of his first meeting with Barnsley. Their route to *Mens Sana* had taken them to a view of the Weal falling sharply away in the direction of the village of Three Weirs where they had clearly seen the tops of the trees marking Wisher's Barn and Wisher's Mead, but after that ... nothing! No highway. No village. The landscape had ended just as if a curtain of sky had encircled the forest. Barnsley had said: 'Funny that, isn't it? You'd swear there was nothing further, wouldn't you? Only a few of us new ones can remember there's a village with cottages, and a very good pub, and a road that hums all day long with cars and lorries and the good ol' stink of petrol fumes and dust an' all that ...'

With this in mind, Myrddin walked through the fog until it abruptly cleared and he could see the grassy-verged tarmacamed road that lay across his way ahead. He looked back. The curtain of mist had vanished. That had been a little worrying. Had his breaking through the barrier somehow destroyed it? He retraced his steps, turned and looked. No, there it was just as it had been. *A one way illusion!* he realised. Like a kindliness to help the fae forget the world of mortality on their door step, but not preventing other fae from finding their way back home. Now it presented another challenge for them to overcome – a Veil of Illusion.

He crossed through it again to the road which looked as wide as a football pitch but presented no problem despite the amount of traffic. He knew where he wanted to go, and moved with a speed that zigzagged around moving cars, lorries and village people until he reached his objective. He stopped only a few mortal seconds later in front of the huge building he remembered as Weir Court. All he had had to do then was climb the ivy to an open bedroom window – and that didn't take very long either.

He could have searched the whole house in as little time to find the person he was after, but one look at the still sleeping form in bed told him it was Sir Edward. All he had to do then was to charm a dream into the Weir Lord's mind, lay the small gold sheet on the bedside table and wake him.

Sitting up, and shaking his head, Sir Edward's eyes went straight to his bedside table to see the small sheet of gold. The dream that had woken him, told him it had it had come from Black Wand, and the Weir Ward thought hard – fortunately aloud, so the invisibly present wizard could hear his ponderings:

'Too early for the library ... they wouldn't have anything on Assyrian characters anyway ... have to go to London ... the British Museum should know ... but can't very well ask them to translate from a unique piece of gold ... too many questions ... Kinney! He'll have his father's old books! Why didn't I think of him in the first place ...?'

Then began a trial of patience for the wizard. After a gruelling wait for the Warden to slowly shave, wash and dress and have breakfast, Myrddin then endured a journey of fifteen miles in the back of a car, frustrated that he could have reached their destination in a fraction of the time if he had only known where they were going.

On arrival, however, he had no compunction in wandling the two men down to business. Even then, it threatened failure. Charles Kinney had inherited his father's books and manuscripts, but had little interest in the subject himself. Myrddin eventually got them to examine a grammar guide and dictionary, and kept them hard at it until at last Kinney declared:

'Well, that's about the best we can do, Sir Edward: AM-MAR-EL-LYN. I haven't the foggiest what it means, so the best of British to you. By the way, you haven't explained what all this archaeological bulldozing's in aid of? I thought your particular brand of insanity was preserving Weir Forest from the vandals in the Ministry ...?'

The letters meant nothing to Myrddin either. Having got them, though, and knowing his way back to the forest without having to wait for the car, meant Myrddin could leave and, swiftly back, he had arrived on Dragga's side of

The Wandle shortly after Gwen had stepped ashore from her barge. He remembered Charles Kinney had made a passing reference to his deceased sister's closeness to their father. That meant Gwen hadn't been bluffing when she'd hinted at possible help. To have his Wych present at such a conference, however, would not have been desirable.

*

The following day, Ann called him from her end of The Wandle. *Beloved Wychy, if it was against all tradition, but acceptable, that you visited Alder's Stede three nights ago, would it be acceptable for me to visit our Liege's Queen?*

I know of no reason why not, dear heart, he replied cautiously, and asked the King if the Queen would kindly grant White Wand an audience.

*

Alder arranged for the Wych to find Gwen sitting in the same chair that he had used when he had received Black Wand. His Queen's distress the previous day had prompted him to counsel her. She had bowed to his wisdom, and now received her rival on home ground with confidence.

White Wand, once more a genuine devotee, knelt at her feet and apologised humbly.

'Beloved Queen, I ask pardon for my woeful behaviour. I had no need to offend you when you wished to speak to my Brother Wand – although what I said was the truth because there are no secrets between Black Wand and myself. May I confide how I knew …?'

Gwen nodded, touched by her humility. She marvelled too at how the Wychy had so quickly and literally brought his Wych to her knees like this.

'When Black Wand returned to his mortal self as August Autrey,' Ann explained, 'I was still mortal. He wrote a book about all that had happened during his disappearance into the forest. Every act that he and others had done, every word that had been spoken, he wrote down without fear or favour. That is how I learnt all that was essential to my approaching Office, which left no time for the normal development of a new Wych.'

'A book!' Gwen exclaimed, looking at the delicate piece of tapestry in a hand frame that lay in her lap. What the Wych had just told her was far more important to her than the apology that came with it. She looked up at White Wand.

'I thank you sincerely for this explanation, dear Wych. But ...' and she gestured the chair opposite, '... please, be seated.'

Ann did as she was bid – although Gwen noticed, not before she had taken an inquisitive look at the tapestry's glowing threads in her hands.

'And what did Black Wand write of *me* in his book?' Gwen inquired.

'Only what he knew of your living in the forest at the time, and the help he received from you when the Mortal Sickness came upon the Wych-that-was.'

Gwen looked down again and smiled as she smoothed her work with a loving finger. 'Strangely,' she said, 'I have also devised a way of recording the same history as *I* remember it. Its most recent event is the extraordinary story of Nebuchadnezzar.' She held out the frame. 'What do you think, dear Wych? Do you find my tablet and inscriptions ingenious?'

Ann took the frame and Gwen saw her examine the work enviously, appreciating the hours it must have taken to achieve such perfection. The script however, wasn't Runic, which she could have read; it was Chaldean. Ann handed it back with an admiring smile, evidently impressed that the Queen should have kept alive such a vital thread of mortal interest.

'For many years I accompanied my father, the Canon …' she paused to smile reassuringly, '… on his expeditions. He was the leading Assyriologist of his day.'

'So you were able to recognise and read the symbols drawn by my Brother Wand?' said the Wych. 'I thought they were just a will-o'-the-wisp invention.'

'No, the characters made sense – and I had decided I should tell him. I hesitated though, in case he already knew. Do you know if he understands their meaning?'

'I have no idea, dear Queen. The Black One is far too wily to tell me anything he thinks unnecessary for me to know.'

'Wily, indeed,' Gwen agreed with feeling. 'But tell me,' she pleaded. 'If he doesn't know their meaning, and it's important to his story, do you think he would have asked me?'

'Nothing is unimportant to a wizard,' said Ann. 'Why else would he have wandled the Master into marking them on a sheet of gold to be displayed at the next session of his story?'

'But surely he wouldn't want to show his ignorance to the world? He has to explain the characters to the fae at some stage?'

'There is no reading the mind of a Wychy, O Queen. If he didn't know what they meant, he would undoubtedly invent something entirely plausible.'

*

By now, Ann was as perplexed and intrigued as much as it seemed was Gwen. Without admitting whether he knew the meaning of the characters or not, her partner had implied that Gwen *would* know. And that hint had been responsible for her remorse, and her desire to visit the Queen. It also meant that whatever game her lover was up to, she was helping him to play it with both hands. By coming here to make peace with Gwen, she was smoothing the way for further contact between the two of them. He was probably even relying on her to discover from Gwen what the inscription meant and pass it back to him. It struck her as so deceitfully clever that she became determined not to let him get away with it so easily.

She gave Gwen a smile that invited possible collusion between them. 'You said, O Queen, that the inscription made sense to you? Perhaps, if I heard its translation I might understand its meaning in the context of the story?'

Gwen returned the smile with understanding. 'Certainly, O Wych, but might I suggest caution? Let neither of us tell him something that he could now already know.'

Ann willingly agreed, and by the time Gwen gave her the lengthy explanation, the two of them were of one mind: White Wand would put Black Wand to the test in public – and leave him to wriggle out of it if he could.

CHAPTER 4

THE LORD OF THE HEAVENS

During her visit to Alder's Stede, the Wych was out of touch with the forest so she had no idea that Sir Edward had made another journey into it to hide the gold sheet, with a note, in the same crack of the stricken Great Oak where he had left the first letter.

The fae, being used to him, took little notice but when the cry *'Black Wand walks the Weal!'* went up to pinpoint attention to their Wychy, they came singing and dancing to meet him above Wandleside.

> *'Hael and wyn, Wychy, walking the Weal*
> *Bright is thy Wand! Be thy Weird in the wind*
> *Starry in moonlight, flashing in sun*
> *Wielder of wonders, weaver of fun!'*

The first to arrive cried: 'Black Wand! Black Wand!' You have come to tell us more of the story about King Nebuchadnezzar!'

'Soon, my People, and that is a promise. But first, I would like to walk alone in the Weal in order to arrange the story in my mind, for there is a lot to think about and I don't want to leave anything out.'

All respectfully agreed, and word went everywhere for Black Wand to be left alone with his magic thoughts while they started gathering by *Woe Begone!* reminding each other where the story had got to, and thinking up all the questions they still hadn't asked. This stopped anyone from seeing Myrddin going to the blackened oak himself to retrieve the huge envelope, which he destroyed after carefully removing the contents. Having secured the gold leaf 'banner' under his Weird, he read the note. It told him what he already knew of the Weir Lord's visit to Charles Kinney, after which it appeared that Sir Edward had telephoned the Curator at the British Museum and obtained the following translation:

... *AM-MAR-EL-LYN: Apparently an ancient Sumerian title meaning Behold the Lord of the Heavens. Doubtless the title of some famous Court Astrologer or Magician.*

Disposing of the note in the same way as he had the envelope, the Wychy pondered the significance of what he had learned while watching the flames consume the paper. He had asked Mona's Eye for the whereabouts of Merlin's Mount and of Merlyn himself, and been given what amounted to the title of some famous Court Astrologer or Magician, both of which Merlyn was – even at Arthur's Court as Merlin – and then it came to him.

'Am ... Mar ... El ... Lyn!' he whispered in astonishment. 'I *am* Merlyn!'

But does that mean the Eye of Mona itself, or is it a clue to something else? He wandered slowly on to the half-hollow beech of his Retreat in the Weal. The title did not tell him the whereabouts of Merlin's Mount, nor where the books were on which he was pinning his hopes. For all he knew both could still be somewhere in Mesopotamia. So the search had to go on and in the meantime he had promised a further instalment of the story. Well, at least he could now at least add a miraculous connection.

He had almost arrived at *Woe Begone!* when he heard the ether vibrating:

'White Wand is in the Weal at the foot of Windaway!'

It seldom happened that both Wands should be in the Weal at the same time and was so magical that a group sped away at once to greet her.

*

Ann found it faintly annoying that she would have to wait for her partner to return to The Wandle before she could speak to him, but as he would have no way of knowing what had passed between her and the Queen, she could hardly hold it against him. She would have gone back to her Retreat, except the little figures now hurrying down Windaway believed she had just crossed from The Wandle to be with them. When they arrived, they knelt at her feet, kissing the hem of her Weird, begging her to remain with them.

She caressed their happy faces with her fingers, which was the nearest she had ever gone to a kiss, so that they could kiss her hands in return. They called her the Fairest of the Fae because she was: her magic and her wisdom gave her a sweet dignity, which no wiccy could emulate even if one wanted to.

Her admirers begged her to come with them to *Woe Begone!* and hear the next instalment of the story Black Wand was about to tell.

'... Flying above him will be the marvellous golden banner the gnomes have made!' they cried excitedly. And begged: 'Please, White Wand, please let us hear it with both our Wychies side by side ...?'

Knowing her partner was already there; Ann agreed and followed as they capered ahead up the winding track shouting the glad news across the forest.

By the time she reached the top of Windaway, a throng of wiccas and wiccies were there in welcome. No sweetness could match the kind of happy affection that flowed from them to their Wych or from her for each of them.

Her partner rose to meet her, taking her in his arms and kissing her as naturally as he did in the privacy of The Wandle. Everyone laughed, cheered and turned somersaults, while Barnsley, Edmund, and the Master of Gnomes all shook hands at the unprecedented spectacle. Ann even extended a hand to the Master of Gnomes and kissed him too before she and Black Wand walked arm-in-arm to the golden chairs.

Omric was eager to explain the banner. 'Such a simple design, dear Wych, despite the curious formation of the symbols. I have no great love for them yet, not knowing their meaning.'

'Neither does my Brother Wand, dear Master!' replied the Wych, surprised at how soon the chance had come to test him. 'Didn't he say that they were just an airy invention?' She turned to her partner. 'Or are you guilty of deception, Brother Wand? Come, I challenge you, most artful of Wychies, do you know, or not know the meaning of these strange characters?'

'How well you know me, O Wych!' he answered. 'I did not intend to tell the secret so early but since you have thrown down the glove, I must pick it up. Just keep it to yourselves for the moment, please. The sounds of the symbols are ...' and he lowered his voice 'Am-Mar-El-Lyn.'

Ann was astonished. Before she could ask how he knew, the Master was whispering bewilderedly, 'Such sounds are strange to my ears, O Black One! And if I don't understand them, how shall our people?'

'Dear Omric, the language is long dead,' the Wychy said patiently, still keeping his voice down, 'but in our language the words mean, "Behold, the Lord of the Heavens."' Adding, with a look at his Wych, 'As well you know heart of my living!'

Ann was mortified, but covered her embarrassment. 'I was only teasing, beloved, for there is an alternative, isn't there?' And she went on as Gwen had taken care to explain to her. 'Aren't all dead languages known to possess the possibility of alternative prepositions – like, *of* the Heavens, or *from* the Heavens?' and waited for his reaction.

*

The alternatives hit Myrddin like a bolt of lightning. Behold The Lord *from* the Heavens – he who *was* to come: Alder's successor appropriately enthroned above the Eye of Mona. And wasn't The Lord *of* the Heavens – great Merlyn himself?

The whole thing astounded him. It still didn't help with the location of Merlin's Mount, but it did confirm the prophecy *and* that Gwen possessed a masterly grasp of ancient Chaldean script.

He invited Sylvie, Dina and Hetty to join them as soon as his Wych, Omric and he had taken their seats. Not even White Wand's presence could alter that tradition. They came at once, albeit kneeling to White Wand first before taking their time-honoured places. Not wanting her wiccas to feel neglected, White Wand signalled an invitation to Edmond, Baddenham and Loy for them to come and sit at her feet.

As fay and gnome quietened to listen, Myrddin's mind worked rapidly on twists and turns he had not had time to think about. He knew it meant making things up on the spot but he had to keep the theme moving. He also had to work in a meaning for Nebuchadnezzar's dream – something he hadn't even thought of up until then ...

The story left everyone stunned and breathless, although his larger audience looked a little uneasy. They could understand Black Wand's connection with his ancient counterpart, but was it right that he spoke so openly of such secret matters to them?

It was all part of Myrddin's overall plan, however, and with White Wand's loyal and nodding support at his side, as if it was only a small revelation so far as she was concerned, it helped reassure them that all must be well.

*

After this highlight came a time of relative inactivity, during which Gwen retired back to weaving her tapestries; White Wand to practice the kind of workmanship she had seen in them to perfect her own work; and Myrddin to gnaw his spiritual nails while he pondered the riddle of a name with two meanings. To his mind, it indicated a third pointer – somewhere. It came the day before High Moon, when he received an agitated call from the Master of Gnomes.

'Black Wand! The Rune reads true and the redes are riddled! Behold the banner of Am-Mar-El-Lyn no longer matters for a most sacred talisman of the Lord of the Heavens has been found –!'

Myrddin stopped him there. 'Be at peace, Master,' he said quietly, stilling his own excitement at the news. 'Calm your brothers, and let no word of what you have found be said to anyone until I come.'

'It shall be so, great Merlyn's Heir. I wait for you.'

It was one thing to get the Master to stay silent, but another to be sure that Myrddin himself drew no attention to his departure for the Gnomes' Mansion. It was an exquisite joy, however, to request a visit to his Wych before making for the Wynn. He could not confide in her, but he could reassure her how much he loved her.

Coming to his knees at her side, he kissed her hands. 'O Fairest of the Fae, behold a humble petitioner.'

She took his face between her hands and kissed him longingly, before gently teasing:

'And what plea can be so important that it needs such a formal request, O Most-Wily-of-Wizards that ever was?'

'If it was really important, Sister Wand, I would not need to kneel. It is your loveliness that commands it.' He kissed her. 'You know very well that to me you are the most beautiful and loveliest of fae, and for me no other more desirable.'

She dissolved into the kind of delighted laughter that he always loved to hear and said, 'If we were mortal, beloved, I might suspect your adoration but, being immortal, how can I argue with it?' She bent and kissed his forehead. 'What was it you wanted, beloved Wand?'

'A small thing. I need to take the banner that the Master made back to him for alteration, and then return it to *Woe Begone!*. I might be some time making sure he does exactly as I want, and I do not want you or our people worried by my absence.'

Ann thanked him for his thoughtfulness, and sent calming waves through her Wych ball over the forest so that nothing appeared out of the ordinary when he collected the banner, put it under his Weird, and walked purposefully to the Wynn without stopping.

The two gnomes he found waiting respectfully at the entrance into the Gnome's Mansion conducted him to the principal chamber at whirlwind speed. There the Master waited, and at his side an assistant stood holding a heavy hoop of gold more than a third of a wand across the centre and set with a square stone of amethyst

Recognising an ancient thumb ring of human size, the Wychy went straight towards it and looked down on the stone held uppermost for his inspection. He was not surprised to find it inscribed with the wedge-shaped characters that they all now knew to mean 'Behold the Lord of the Heavens'.

He stood looking at it for some time, holding his Wand at both ends between his fingers to conceal his overwhelming amazement. Here was the third pointer! Beyond doubt it was Merlyn's ring. It could only mean that Merlin's Mount must be wherever they had found the ring. He looked enquiringly at the Master.

''Twas found by accident, and not design, O Black One!' Omric said, as if excusing himself. 'He who found it – '

'Hold, Master!' said Myrddin. 'What else was found?'

'Nothing, Black Wand, because the instant the inscription was recognised, I stopped all further work. 'T'was too magical to proceed with until I had spoken with you.'

'You were wise, beloved Master!' Myrddin approved, but with such intensity in his voice that the gnomes trembled as he continued. 'Where was this ring found?'

'Near a place we know as The Mound, Black One – a place never worked because our records say it is wyché and unlucky.'

'Then how …?'

''Twas a half born gnome, Black One, one who returned to us just three mornings ago. Come, Sandstone!'

He turned and beckoned forward a wide-eyed gnome who, doffing his cap, fell to his knees at the feet of the awesome visitor.

'I knew nothing of the ban, Black Wand!' he pleaded fearfully. 'It is the custom that each newly arrived half born goes to find a stone described to him by our worthy Master to prove his worth and skill. I searched alone and unaided for three whole waking times to find a virgin spot most likely to hold the stone I was looking for, which was amethyst. The Mound, it seemed, was just the place, and so I dug. And then …'

'Enough,' said Myrddin kindly, halting him and holding out a hand. 'You have committed no crime, Sandstone – Mona herself inspired you to work there. Master,' he said, turning, 'please, can you accept this wonderful find as more than proof of Sandstone's worth and skill?'

'Most willingly, Black One!' Omric agreed with relief, whilst Sandstone kissed the wizard's hand in gratitude. 'Should I now lead you to the Mound? It is 915 wands distant from this spot.'

A wand being equal to three mortal inches, Myrddin calculated the distance to be a little over 76 mortal yards. He knew he would never cover a tenth of it without White Wand and the whole Weal becoming aware of the oddness of such a journey. He could wandle the fae into taking no notice, but not his Wych. 'In which direction?' he asked.

The Master pointed.

'How long would it take to excavate a tunnel of such length, O Master?'

Omric looked taken aback, but thought hard. 'Around eleven periods of waking time Wychy, remembering that the lengths available will grow shorter after High Moon with Mona's waning. There will be a lot of material to carry away, even cutting through solid rock in places, needing every one of us to work without rest. But it can be done.'

Myrddin wondered if he could live so long in such suspense. Well, he had survived to that moment without being aware that the newly-arrived Sandstone was working on the very thing the Wychy needed. He knew, too, that the excavation of the tunnel could and would proceed as quickly as possible. For the sake of the secrets stored at the other end, too precious to suffer the light of day – or night for that matter – it was worth the wait.

'Let the excavation begin immediately, Master! Our Liege commands your every effort!'

They had never heard Black Wand speak with such authority, and the sound of it made the gnomes shiver. They were further stunned when he looked around and added:

'There must be no word of this to anyone – not even among you. The Mound buries much woe. Only your silence can save you from it, and keep the rest of our people safe!'

Each nodded mutely, although looking aghast at the prospect. They would have done it for love simply because he had asked, but this last statement filled them with fear of the consequences if they didn't keep silent – and there was more.

'The ring must be hidden until I come again, Master. I need a secure place which I can seal so no one can disturb it.'

'There is a place here,' offered Omric, now as apprehensive as the rest of them. He drew aside the great tapestry of gold and silver and precious stones behind his great table and tapped on a square in the rock face behind. A stone door swung slowly open, and he stood back.

Myrddin placed the massive ring in the cavity, instructed the Master to close it and then traced the shape of an eye in fiery lines across the place of opening.

The gnomes began to breathe again when the tapestry fell back into place.

'Master, how big would you say the Mound is?' Myrddin asked thoughtfully

'Not great, Black Wand. Little more than nine and a half wands across and the same high. Its contours are uneven. Records say that fragments of a very hard and durable stone, not found anywhere else in Weal or Wynn, are nearby, as well as pieces of black crystal. They are still there because of the warning. I ordered it so myself from the beginning.'

'From the beginning …?'

From the beginning of our coming to the forest, Black Wand – ages after our Liege brought you, his people, here, and Merlyn made The Wandle and the Weirds.'

Myrddin's Book of Lore held no record of the gnomes' arrival but, as the Wychy realised, gnomes were another branch of the fae who kept their records independently, and Omric himself was another who had 'always been there'.

If he had not been so intent on his own secret, the Wychy might have inquired more deeply. As it was, he only just remembered in time to tell the Master how he needed the golden border to be indented before he left.

He returned to the Weal walking slowly, reflecting on all he had learned. A mound around little more than two mortal feet across and high – how could anyone of human stature fit into such a place? Yet they would have had to be a man's height to have left such a ring behind them. So what did it mean? Had the magician had the power to transform himself from fae to man and back again at will?

Yet why not? he asked himself *Wasn't I subjected to the same thing when I was turned from mortal into elf leaving no physical body behind? And later, didn't I regain my human form until I finally dispensed with it by drinking Wizard's Woe?* But as to how it been done, or where his body been in the interval, only the Wychy before him knew the answer to that one, and he had left no record. *But why would Merlyn have abandoned the ring near the Mount? Again, why not?* He knew Malory's legend asserted that the witch Nemway had shut Merlyn up in a cave *'so that he never came out for all the craft he could do'*. And if he had left the ring outside the Mount he must surely have been powerless to release himself – just as he, Myrddin, would be powerless if his Wand wasn't with him in a similar case. It made sense … or did it?

He was aware of Ann monitoring his thoughtful progress, and imagining he must be engrossed in thinking up some new twist to his story. He was aware that she wished he had not started on such a gloomy theme. The fae were now attending the sessions with quite mixed feelings, and she would be wondering if there was some way in which he could think of brightening things up.

*

The next day, Myrddin became aware that a pending death in the village was about to occur. Thirty-year-old Stella Mye was dying of a viral infection.

He looked out of the jet-black dome of his Retreat, and summoned mentally:

Rozyn! Rozyn-Who-Knows!

I hear you, Black Wand

Our Star Maiden will soon take her journey here for the last time. I would like to give you the joy of welcoming her. Be near the Veil of Illusion shortly before High Moon and bring her with you on your dray to the Circle of Rejoicing.

After that, and from afar, he informed Ann, whose protégé their Star Maiden was.

I suppose there's no prospect of making it a double event, O Wily One? she returned. *I thought our dear Weir Ward looked very near his end, too.*

His hour will come, Heart of my Desire, but not yet. He may still have things to do on our behalf.

But didn't he say in his letter that his son Humphrey would loyally continue his father's work?

He did; but Humphrey's soul has not been blessed with a faerie wraith, my sweet! It sounded grim, he knew. Seldom had a Weir Ward been without the wraith of a fae. At least one in every generation of the family had proved to be a Wychy-in-Waiting. It added yet another ominous cloud to the horizon.

His last message was to Omric, that the King's command did not mean that the gnomes should absent themselves from the revels at High Moon.

Their non-attendance would only raise questions, which was the last thing the Myrddin wanted.

CHAPTER 5

CHILD ROYAL TO ORDER

When the King and Queen disembarked onto The Wandle that evening and received the homage of the two Wands, Gwen's smile for Black Wand was more open, loving and intent than ever before. The instant she had had seen him waiting on the shore for them had awoken a new and alarmingly wilful desire in her, quite alien and completely replacing her previous feeling of hopeless resignation. She knew it was wrong – *But why shouldn't I have his love?* she thought rebelliously. *Every wiccy in the Forest has the right to seek it except, it seems, his Queen!* She therefore convinced herself that she did indeed have as much right as they – if not more – and so had no need to keep it a secret. Before the night was out, she would have him.

With the royal party's onward progress to the Circle of Rejoicing, Rozyn and his dray were first over the bridge, and beside him a radiant fay who sprang down and knelt before the Wands with arms wide open. The Star Maiden had come home to stay. She had been so many times before in her dreams that she was now almost as fully born as any returning fay could be, and White Wand welcomed her lovingly.

*

When the opening ceremonies were over, and the Wands wed, it became apparent that the gnomes were behaving with alarming weirdliness. There was nothing of their usual exuberance and robust sense of fun, and they took no further part in the celebrations but set themselves apart in a compact group, not communicating with anyone on the outside.

Myrddin hadn't foreseen this natural reaction to his instruction and Ann, who was mothering the Star Maiden, was sending inquiring looks in his direction that asked why he wasn't doing something about it, but Gwen had him fully occupied.

Ever since Alder had taken Gwen as his Queen, the King, Queen and the Wands had led the first dance in stately silence: Gwen because until that night she never dared speak, and Myrddin because he'd rather not; Alder because he spoke so little anyway and Ann because she was in downright awe of the King.

Tonight, however, was different for Gwen not only dared, but was challengingly direct.

As soon as he took her lightly in his arms, Myrddin knew she was possessed by some strange new, headstrong and stubborn spirit.

'Black Wand, I need and want to speak with you alone!'

How was he to put her off? He returned her gaze, and realised it was as if he had never looked at her properly before. He certainly couldn't remember ever seeing how deeply compelling her beauty was until that night. Even her hair seemed darker and had a rich sheen of reddish brightness about it.

'What strange fascination has my hair for you, beloved Wand?' she asked.

He seized on the lead, and answered without taking his eyes from her cascade of tresses. 'I find it a mirror I cannot read, O Queen, or maybe a veil – it's brightness and darkness are one.'

'Brightness and darkness as one ...?' she repeated, 'Surely that is describing the moment that the light of Sunne is wed with Mona's dark eclipse?'

'So ...?' he guessed, looking into her eyes again. 'You also had a vision?'

'Not a vision,' she said, drawing him closer, uncaring that every fae – and his Wych – were observing the embrace. 'A feeling. This is what I needed – and still need to speak to you about. It was like a revelation without words, without sight, simply of *knowing*.'

Myrddin had to return the embrace while they continued to move slowly, matching the measured tread of their steps, wondering if the eclipse had given the Queen some enlightenment that would help him with his own problems.

'Oh Black Wand – August – I love you!' she cried suddenly and passionately. 'I have loved you since you found me as an unlovely hag in the brambles. I was silly then, but even then, I wanted you.' Her voice held a breathless intensity as she went on, 'O Wychy! I love you, I love you, I love you!'

Alarmed, Myrddin took refuge in appearing as cool and wise as he possibly could. 'As all must do, dear Queen,' he reminded her mildly, with a smile that had always rescued him from trouble before.

But not this time. At the mercy of her emotions, Gwen hissed back: 'O Black One, I am no failing wiccy looking for obliteration! I want your love – '

'But are they not one and the same thing, O Queen?'

'Not for me, they're not! I love you, I want you, I will have you, and you will love me! It is ordained. It is something you can no more avoid than I can.'

The way she looked at that moment was everything that a fully-weaned Wych might be: imperious, supremely dominant and utterly beautiful. He came to a halt, appalled and fascinated.

'If I only had your understanding, O Queen!' he said quietly. 'For how can that be true? You know very well that my Wych is my one and only partner. It was ordained so from the beginning.'

'Beginnings have endings!' she said darkly. 'We are now at the door of new beginnings!'

There was no sidetracking her, and Myrddin needed inspiration. The vibrations of her passionate assertions were already disturbing the peace of The Wandle and everyone on it.

'Gwendolyn,' he said, changing tactics and speaking with genuine sincerity, 'it is obvious you are privileged to know more than I do about the woe that hangs over our forest ...'

'Woe?' she said sharply. 'I said nothing about woe – I spoke about love!'

He pressed on. 'It has been foretold there shall be a Passing, a Coming and a Desolation not known since our beginning here. Did your revelation have anything to say on this? I need you to tell me, because I need every clue I can find.'

Gwen looked taken aback. 'I have no idea what you are on about, beloved Wychy. All I knew was a torment of spirit without vision or help. It was as if something deeply loved but now lost beyond recall because of some wickedness that was once part of me. Yet there was light. There was light and love beyond measure that would redeem me. In that hour, I knew it was you, my Wychy, that it was *your* love that would redeem me.'

It seemed clear to Myrddin that Gwen had overlaid the mystery with some fond imagining of her own, and he saw no way that he should be compelled to give in to her.

'You don't believe me?' she accused him angrily, when he made no reply.

'Not so, my Queen,' he said bluntly. 'I hear what you say – but it is all about you. Such visions and feelings do not always mean what we would like them to mean, and I know nothing of *any* ruling that says that I shall love at your command!'

'Maybe not yet, Wychy. But you will!' she promised intensely. 'You will, whether you like it or not!'

They stood, facing each other like two adversaries: Gwen furious; he glaring a steely refusal'

*

Ann, who had been unable to hear a word, was nevertheless keenly aware of the mounting tension that was making everyone uncomfortable. She felt more than justified in taking advantage of the moment to sweep over to them.

'Brother Wand, the gnomes, our brothers, look woefully forlorn. What is the matter with them?'

'Stomach ulcers, I imagine!' he answered. 'I have one myself and can sympathise.'

It was rude, abrupt, and so unwyché, his shocked Wych, who had never seen him angry, thought the doom had come upon them there and then.

Her blanched expression, however, appeared to bring him to his senses. He calmed sufficiently to give a rueful smile. 'They have set me a conundrum, Sister Wand. If I can't solve the thing in time, it will make nonsense of the story I'm expected to continue tonight.'

Ann and Gwen had to accept the arm he was offering to each of them with the obvious intention of leading the Queen back to her throne. Ann was thankful to accept his lead, because the sight of all three of them arm-in-arm was all that could now restore the fae's peace of mind.

As soon as Gwen regained her throne, Ann wandled their Star Maiden into tripping lightly over to the Wychy. The train of wiccas that had clustered around her the moment White Wand left her unguarded, followed.

Stella, who was bubbling over with so much joy to have noticed any unrest, tugged gently at the Wychy's Weird. 'Black Wand!' she pleaded, 'Smye says you have started a new story, but I've missed its beginning. Please tell me how it began …?'

'Please, Black Wand?' chorused the surrounding fae. 'We'd love to hear it all over again.'

'And, *please*, Black Wand,' Dina wheedled, as she pressed against his free side, 'would you put something new in to make the gnomes happy? It's dreadful to see them looking so sad.'

Ann was thankful again to receive smile of approval from her partner that awarded her full marks on the way she had turned things round. While the newly-edged banner of gold was set up behind his seat, the fae came to sit or kneel closer, with Dina and Sylvie in their usual places and Stella, in whose honour the story was being re-told, taking Hetty's place at his knees.

The Wychy's revised story turned Nebuchadnezzar into a much more lovable character. He was still in search of a son and heir, but dreamed of an ancient buried temple in which the most beautiful queen in the world lay entombed, not dead but sleeping, and only waiting for the kiss of Nebuchadnezzar to revive her. So Nebuchadnezzar sent for his Court Astrologer, Am-Mar-El-Lyn – who, he reminded them, was their own legendary Merlyn – to discover the whereabouts of the buried temple and the hidden Queen. As it was obviously *under* the earth, and the Court Astrologer was able to find only what was above the earth and in the heavens, he did the sensible thing and called on the Spirits of the Earth who knew all the mysteries of its stones, minerals and secret caves to help him.

The effect on the gnomes was extraordinary. Jumping to their feet, they began to demonstrate the effort that they would put into the work.

Signalling for silence, Myrddin then told his audience that, of course, only the King, his Court Astrologer and the Spirits of the Earth, sworn to lifelong secrecy, knew about this high secret.

The gnomes took the hint with knowing winks and nudges as they subsided again to listen.

It was so well done that Ann missed the truth. She knew the gnomes identified themselves with any of Black Wand's creations that were anything like themselves, so was delighted to see them restored to their usual good humour. She glanced at the Queen and saw her frowning thoughtfully and regarding the Wychy suspiciously. Ann then realised that Gwen saw the Gnomes' conduct had confirmed for her that the wizard had a lot to do with their peculiar behaviour and was obviously wondering about the introduction of a Sleeping Beauty that had nothing to do with Biblical Assyrian Kings and Court Magicians, but possibly a lot to do with the argument that Ann had interrupted. She looked at Alder, but he was smiling at Black Wand as if assured his Wychy had just advised him that all would be well.

Ann smiled fondly across at her partner. *What an incomparable Wychy her partner was*, she thought.

*

None of this was apparent to Myrddin, however. He had tacked on the story of the sleeping queen to please the Gnomes and keep them silent with the reward that everything depended on their hard work, wisdom, skill and bravery. He thought he had done it rather well, until the inevitable questions started pouring in.

'You never said *why* Nebuchadnezzar was childless, Black Wand?' accused Baddenham. 'You said he had fourteen wives. Didn't they love him enough, or wasn't it in his Weird to have children?'

'And if they couldn't, or wouldn't give him children,' added Edmund, 'what made him think the Sleeping One would?'

Myrddin answered on reflex without giving himself time to think of possible consequences.

'For a very simple reason, both of you,' he said. 'His destiny or Weird was that he should have only one child, a very special child – a heavenly child, so it had to be a very special Queen who would be able to give him this.'

'How would she give it to him, Black Wand?' asked Clee who, like most of them, had long forgotten the mortal details. 'Where would she find it?'

But Barnsley had not forgotten. He laughed and answered. 'That's easy, Clee. I remember like it was yesterday. It's quite easy to understand because we're just the same as mortals as far as the works go. So first of all you get moody with a wiccy and disappear into the brambles for a loving session – '

'We know all about *that*, Barney!' said Baddenham. 'Which, if I may be a trifle personal, you don't! Just give us your theory and I promise to knock a hole in it large enough to drive Rozyn's dray through!'

'Think I don't know all about the birds and the bees!' said Barnsley. 'First of all a man has semen – '

'Which none of us has now!' interrupted Baddenham. 'We're fae, but do go on, dear Barney? Sorry I interrupted.'

Myrddin missed the look of distaste that Ann sent in his direction. He was enjoying a private joke with Stella, who was laughing up at him.

'That's true!' said Barnsley ruefully. 'We don't piss, either! So what the blazes do we do?'

'How would you know?' Hetty asked cuttingly. 'No wiccy's ever given you the chance to find out!'

That got Myrddin's attention. He knew Hetty was understandably jealous that he had not invited her to his knee that night, but it wouldn't do to allow more problems.

He looked at Smye, who was trying to attract his attention, and nodded. If he had realised what was in Smye's mind, he could have wandled the question away before Smye could ignite a trail of gunpowder.

'Please, Black Wand, why can't *we* have babies?'

When Smye had asked the same question earlier, Myrddin, as August, was able to refer him to the Wands. Now he was a Wand, he realised he must deal with the matter firmly and finally.

'Every fae must have a wraith, dear Smye,' the Wychy answered truthfully. 'There are never any more of us than there are.' He wasn't going to add the worrying thought that there were even less of them than there used to be. 'We take our wraith into mortality with us so that we may return to the little kingdom when that time is over. If we were to have babies, we would need new wraiths. But new wraiths cannot be fashioned even by magic. And even if they could be, there are no other little spirits like you to live in them.'

That made sense to them, but not to Smye. He continued to stare at Black Wand with an astonished look in his large elliptical eyes as if struck by a completely new idea – which it was. 'But Black Wand, suppose one of *our* little people's spirits agreed to be born again as a baby fay, instead of a mortal, wouldn't that be just as good? And wouldn't it spare the little spirit the ordeal of the Bane?'

The flame had run to the waiting explosive, which went up in a blaze of glory. The whole assembly greeted the unheard-of novelty with wild acclaim. Pandemonium reigned while Myrddin, as astonished as anyone, tried to think what he could say to set the record straight. But volunteer babies and volunteer parents were shouting from all points of the Circle. The idea was too wonderful for it to be impossible, and therefore taken for granted that the Wands could arrange it.

The Wychy hardly knew whether to laugh outright, or be very worried. The fae wanted a baby fay and would talk of nothing else for days to come. If the Wands refused them, they could sicken with disappointment, which would be deadly in every sense of the word.

Even Gwen and Alder didn't smile.

Then Stella was on her feet running to centre stage where she flung her arms wide with a dramatic suggestion that sealed the whole thing.

'Who else?' she cried. 'Who else but our Liege and his beloved Queen should have the baby!'

The throng rose as one, rapturous with enthusiasm. It was so right, so clear! Alder and Gwen alone should be parents to a little Prince. With the instantaneous rhythm that always affected the fae in moments of deep emotion, they cried out in one voice:

'Please, Wands? Black Wand! White Wand! Please, please, do this magic for us?'

The circle was tense with expectation. The drama bore in on Myrddin with such power; he could not tell them it was impossible. The fae believed their Wands could do anything. Yet to promise it would happen was equally impossible. The Wychy had never been in such a dilemma. Yet, he dare not hesitate. He made himself rise, embrace Stella and kiss her, smiling wisely as if thanking her for her words; and to hold out his hand to his Wych. She rose tentatively but ready, he knew, to agree to anything he might say or do, and he led her to where the King and Queen sat motionless on their thrones, and bowed, drawing her down beside him to curtsey, and said:

'O Beloved Liege and Lady, you have heard your people's plea. Is it your wish that such a miracle should happen?'

Alder inclined his head at once with a smile of such gratitude that Myrddin knew it had never crossed the

King's mind that his Wychy could fail. The crowd gasped its delight and waited for Gwen's reply.

But why did she hesitate? Why did she look so strange? It was clear she was struggling with some strong emotion before inclining her head stiffly to signify consent, and held it there while the faerie leapt and shouted and danced in elation. What happened in those moments before she lifted it again, however, changed her expression into one of glorious triumph. Directed straight at Black Wand, it told him she had won the cake and was going to eat it.

Myrddin could only wonder what had occurred to her, and what had addled their Star Maiden's to utter such a misguided suggestion. He alone knew that if even if the necessary wraith was somehow induced, fabricated or wangled, no simple fay could ever be Alder's successor.

If the Wychy hadn't just found the clue to Merlin's Mount, he would have despaired. Even then, any prospect of success depended on finding the books still there and interpreting them – but what if they were written in Chaldean? It hardly bore thinking about.

When the fae saw their King and Queen agreeing to have the babe, they went mad with elation. They broke the circle and rushed to fall on their knees before the thrones, shouting their joy and mobbing both Wands with hugs and kisses. They knew their Wychies would make the wish come true with the magic of their Wands.

'How long will it take?'

'How small will it be?'

'Will it be wicca or wiccy?'

Which one of us will you choose to be the babe?'

The Wands answered each question the same: they must wait and see.

*

As soon as she could, before the revels were over, Ann took the Star Maiden aside.

'Stella, what a wonderful inspiration! You could have named any wicca or wiccy, such as Pwyll or Loy who are so well beloved or Jean and Clee who are the most perfect of wiccies. Or even Black Wand and myself, to whom magic of this kind would come most easily. Yet you named the two ideal people!'

'It wasn't inspiration, White Wand,' Stella owned innocently. 'I was told to say it. I would have told you earlier if I hadn't been so taken up with the wonder of my first true night on The Wandle.'

Ann remembered her own feelings when she had been set free to remain in the forest at last. She threw an arm round Stella's shoulders, and with it a part of her brilliant Weird to keep whatever the wiccy had to say from being overheard.

'Go on,' she murmured.

'I had a dream the other day – before I became ill. I dreamed I was watching an eclipse of the sun. I don't know how I can describe this, White Wand, but when it became completely dark, I saw a pale gold star come out to shine near the sun, and it seemed to speak to me. It told me that my days as a mortal were short, and that I would return to the little kingdom at the next full moon. It went on to say that when I was present in the Circle of Rejoicing and kneeling at the feet of One of Two, I was to speak with authority and say that The Babe-Who-Is-To-Come would be Royal that he would be from of old and must not be denied. Well, it wasn't until I heard everyone shouting about the baby, that it all came back to me, and I realised it could only mean our King and Queen had to be the chosen parents. I'm sorry I was so excited I didn't get the words exactly right as I heard them – but I know it *is* right that King Alder and Queen Gwen should have the baby.'

'Exactly right!' agreed the Wych with a smile as she remembered the same star of pale gold that had shone like a symbol of hope after the terrible warning of their doom.

She hugged Stella, and kissed her warmly. 'Thank you, thank you, little one. You have set my heart at peace and made me extremely happy!'

She was so uplifted she went to find Black Wand, whom she found deep in thought. 'O wisest of Wands, is it kind to allow your contemplation of the coming babe to keep you apart from your loving ones?'

He drew her close, kissing her fondly before answering in a low voice: 'If I was truly wyché, most beloved of Wands, I would be down on my knees now, coward that I am, demanding the Bane from you. It needs a Wand of the calibre of the one I replaced to engineer this blessed babe. I don't know how to. Do you?'

'O gentlest of liars,' she whispered. 'Can the Heir of Merlyn really expect his Wych to believe he won't find the way when Heaven itself has declared that he will?' And she told him of Stella's prophecy.

'My dearest Wych, I can only say that you have more faith than I have ...!'

CHAPTER 6

THE SILVER BOX

The time following High Moon was almost unbearable for Myrddin as the interregnums began stretching out with the waning moon, and the gnomes lay unconscious for longer intervals each night. Time after time he had to he had to resist the impulse to call Omric and find out how the excavation was going. But he knew they would be working like fiends when awake and that the Master would call him the moment it was finished. Anxiety also plagued him. Was he expecting too much from Merlyn's store of wisdom? Could legend have overestimated its extent and value? Would there be any books at all? And if there were, would they contain the directions he needed to provide Alder and his Queen with the elements of insemination to induce the wraith? And, most important of all, where would the particular spirit come from to inhabit it? He found himself repeatedly thinking how unbelievable and impossible the whole situation was. The forest magic, of which he was a master, was nearly all illusion. The properties of the Wand enabled its holder to will what the fae should see, which was what they saw. To his knowledge, it did not include the scientific manufacture of psychical matter into bodily form.

*

On the day before the new moon, the Master of Gnomes informed Myrddin that he was needed. The summons sounded run-of-the-mill enough for Black Wand not to need an excuse to give to his Wych.

On his arrival at the Mansion, a gnome named Whitegold conducted him speedily and wordlessly through the 76 mortal yard length of excavated passage until they came to a vertical shaft rising above them to the open sky. Here a troubled-looking Master greeted him and explained:

'Black Wand, thousands of moons ago the earth here shook so hard that a furrow split the surface innumerable wands deep at the very edge of the Mound. This is that ancient gap, filled in long ago, that Sandstone dug into from above and found the ring.'

When Omric pointed out the fragments of black crystal and foreign stone in evidence, the Wychy's heart sank as he recognised the mineral as pieces of the same stone that formed the trilithons of Stonehenge, and understood the Master to mean that the Mound itself had fallen into the bowels of the earth.

'O Black Wand, our hearts fail us at the thought that your hidden temple might have been destroyed and the sleeping Queen lost forever!'

Myrddin couldn't tell him there was no Queen. He had managed to get them to increase their efforts because he had provided a simple statement that their minds had seized on with the tenacity of bulldogs. In spite of all their exquisite craftsmanship with gems and jewels and precious metals, they were the simplest of beings.

'Let's get this clear,' he said firmly. 'I take it that you mean that where we're standing is now below the centre of the Mound?'

'Not yet, Black Wand. We are still a little way from that point.'

'Then please continue, Master!' he said, exasperation sharpening his voice. 'Because until I stand below the very centre, I cannot tell if you have been successful or not!'

The gnomes promptly started digging again. If Black Wand believed the imprisoned Queen might still be there, they would not rest.

After an hour of hewing, hacking and carrying, the Master announced they had reached the point Black Wand desired. The Wychy nodded with a brief order:

'Up!'

It did not take long for the tireless workers, standing on each other's shoulders, to open a shaft. At last one cried:

"Tis the foreign stone again, Master, but is only cracked in part!'

'The foundation of the Temple!' exclaimed Omric jubilantly. 'Hew on, brother Feldspar! It should be no more than two wands thick.'

Six inches of sarsen stone! Myrddin thought in despair. Yet when attacked with a tool of the same 'foreign stone', only a short time of hard labour and the six inches gave way to a pile of pink and grey chippings.

'I smell air, Master!' shouted Feldspar. 'In less time than a summer cloud may pass the sun, 'twill be wide enough for one to pass through!'

'What kind of air?' Omric called up with concern.

'Still of under-earth, Master, as of a cavity long overlaid with crusted soil.'

The moment the gap was wide enough; Feldspar came down over the shoulders of his fellows, and doffed his cap to the Wychy.

'There is a chamber half-destroyed, Black Wand. A place so strange, I dare not look on it.'

Without a word, Myrddin climbed on the shoulders of the ladder of gnomes and at last stood in the Mount of Merlyn – or what was left of it.

He was looking around by the light of his Wand at the partial remains of a once circular habitation similar to, but larger than his own. The Wychy was dismayed at the wreckage. To have striven so much for so little. Covering the floor were objects; some intact, others smashed by small boulders, some crushed by earth and overgrown by a sickly-looking fungus. He prowled avidly, and then looked at the segments of what had once been a dome of black crystal, now almost completely spoilt by the amount of earth outside.

After some time, a voiced called up in anguish. 'Black Wand? Beloved Black Wand …?'

Belatedly the Wychy remembered Omric's one-track mind, still in a frenzy of anxiety. Was that lovely figure still lying there, breast heaving gently, waiting to be woken by her Lord?

He couldn't disappoint them, but answered with a double meaning: 'The Queen lives, beloved Master – but it isn't yet right for her to be awoken …'

A huge sigh of relief interrupted him, and he had to wait until its echoing sound had travelled all the way back to the Mansion before continuing. 'There is great mystery here, beloved brothers. I may not explain why, but it must remain secret. So not a word to anyone, until I can release you from your vow of silence.'

It was the best he could do in the circumstances; the fact he had just saddled himself with a female Rip Van Winkle of royal blood, whom he was now honour bound to produce, seemed of secondary importance.

He spent the rest of the day with a borrowed pick and spade, breaking up and removing solidified debris. From time to time, crushed fragments of old parchment came to light that he needed to free with care. He worked on grimly and at last uncovered several scrolls that seemed capable of being restored, and took time off to examine a few of the titles in Anglo Saxon script. He read headings such as: *'Upon Wandling'*; *'Upon the Employment of Magic'*; *'Upon the Secret Springs of the Body'*; *'Upon the Redes of Heaven'*; *'Upon the Nurture of Incubi and Succubi'*; *'Upon the Girdle of Creation'*.

All would need hours of study.

There were other objects, also: a smashed astrolabe of porcelain in a wrecked framework of wood; some kind of curious mathematical instrument, as well as pieces of clay tablets bearing Chaldean inscriptions.

It was when he unearthed a miraculously preserved silver box with a simple clasp, and discovered a sheaf of golden leaves inside, that his excitement became intense - but his heart fell. They were all impressed with the same kind of ancient characters.

He drew them out carefully and on the very first saw the now familiar sequence of symbols Am-Mar-El-Lyn, closely followed by the contracted form of Merlyn. That was all he could understand, but something told him that here laid the clue to the very root of his problem.

With the silver box concealed beneath his Weird, he drew his symbol of the fiery eye across the hole in the stone floor, leaped through it and raced back to the Mansion of the Gnomes.

The thought of having to go cap-in-hand to Gwen was painful, and the Wychy sat in his Retreat a long time musing over his problem. But he could see no alternative. He had to know what the golden wad contained. He decided at last, and not without misgiving, that he would go but wandle the memory of it out of Gwen's mind while she was preparing the translation.

The sun had long set by the time he stole away to the northernmost tip of The Wandle, to glide across the narrow strip of water before turning south towards Alder's Stede, knowing his Wych could not overlook him.

He planned to advise Alder that he needed a private discussion with Gwen when she woke at moonrise. He was therefore taken aback to find her sitting alone waiting for him on the opposite of the two stone chairs.

*

For Gwen, the days following High Moon had been a nightmare. The realisation that had inspired her with so much triumph was that Black Wand would have to come to her to conceive the faerie child with magic, but the Wychy had put in no such appearance.

At first she had felt as betrayed by the revelation as she did by Black Wand who had refused to have anything to do with her. She was also in torment over what she had experienced at the time of the eclipse. *'It was as if something deeply loved but now lost beyond recall because of some wickedness once part of me.'*

But what was the wickedness, and where did it lie?

The sense of guilt persisted, however, and grew until strange memories, visions and delusions began to take hold of her; of war and violence, of children being torn from their mothers' breasts and killed in orgies of bloodlust and horror. These even kept her from the usual faerie oblivion between sunset and moonrise, and became so permanent that sleep deserted her entirely. For hours she wept hopelessly for the blessing of exhaustion, oppressed by the terrible sensations she had felt: anguish, eternal loss, and a terrible guilt for some unknown wrong done aeons ago. She wondered if it was caused by knowing that, deep down, she was not fit to be the mother of the kind of babe that had to be so perfect in origin. She was clearly not perfect herself.

And through it all, she heard no word from Alder, although she knew his presence was near, supporting her. She was sure afterwards that without his being there she would never have recovered, because then it became apparent that it was her love for Black Wand which was the problem. If she could release herself from that mortal desire for him, she could attain the state of being fully born and become a proper Queen to Alder and mother to the miraculous Child. And with her conscious effort and commitment to that end, there came a time of blessed peace and relief. She was able to relax, meditate, and assure herself that this was what she honestly wanted. She spent hours imagining the likeness of the child-to-be. She dreamed of how tenderly she would nurse it and how the fae would never cease to wonder and marvel at its perfections.

But then came the last of the visions – and destroyed her hard-won peace and serenity.

It seemed she was looking into a high-timbered hall, its walls resplendent with heraldic arms and hung with shields. A huge feast was in progress, with Arthur – Alder's mortal counterpart – at its head. An argument, which had broken out among a group of knights at one table, became more and more heated until the raised voices caused the general hubbub to die away. It left one voice, shouting:

'… And I tell you that Arthur's a bastard of unknown origin!'

'And I say he has been proved true King of Britain!' bellowed another, crashing his tankard down on the table. 'He drew the sword from the stone!'

This brought cries of 'Trickery!' and a howl of 'Is Merlin God Almighty that he should decide how kings are chosen?'

Uproar followed as the row spread; hands flew to sword hilts, wine spilled, and meat, bones and bread went flying.

'SILENCE!' Whoever roared then continued more quietly in the sudden hush. 'Prithee peace, valiant sirs, the destiny of Britain lies not in arguments, challenges and blood! I call on Sir Ulfius, who heard the dumb Pendragon speak, to witness that he claimed Arthur as his heir.'

'More trickery!' yelled another voice. 'Uther had no son but three daughters; Margawse, Elaine and Morgan called le Fay.'

'Poppycock!' bellowed a new voice from the back of the hall. 'Poppycock, I say, Sir Accolon, as well you know!'

All heads turned to a large man with green eyes and unkempt ginger hair and beard, in the tattered rags of a beggar who came lumbering up to the top table from the darkest part of the hall, supporting himself on a great ashen staff.

Accolon's hand flew to his sword. 'Begone foul beggar!' he snarled. 'Who gave you the right to speak in the high councils of the realm?'

'The right of God whose prophet I am and of Arthur, our Liege who rules His Kingdom on earth!' answered the beggar proudly, his green eyes blazing, and he spat on the floor at Sir Accolon's feet.

'Sacrilege!'

The knight's sword rasped from its scabbard as he spoke, and wielded a blow that would have sundered the man from crown to crutch. But as it flashed down the ashen staff rose to meet it, deflecting it straight at an escutcheon which it pinned hilt-deep to the wall.

A gasp went up. The sword was thrumming angrily from Sir Accolon's own shield.

'Since when, O King, has it been rule that knights may strike down men of common clay?' demanded the wrathful beggar. 'Fie, for keeping such mongrels in your kennels!'

'The sin shall not go unpunished, Great Merlin,' replied the hitherto silent Arthur. 'But pray have patience. Sir Accolon was not to know that beggary is your favoured disguise. He shall do penance of a vigil full thirty nights upon his knees in our Cathedral of Canterbury and is banished a year and a day from our court.'

When the humiliated knight had bowed and retired, Merlin addressed all the assembly.

'Be warned, all of you, it is Morgan's poison that has undone Sir Accolon. She is no wench but a witch and will beguile to treason and death all who listens to her!'

And it seemed to Gwen that his green eyes looked straight at herself as he spoke, as if challenging her to prove him wrong.

She knew that Morgan le Fay had to be none other than the legendary and immortal Mergyn who was Merlyn's consort of legend, and wondered why Merlin's look should be so hostile ....

The enchanter then called on Sir Ulfius to tell the truth concerning Arthur's birth.

When he had finished, Arthur required his mother Ygraine should come before them with the truth.

Ygraine appeared with her youngest daughter, Morgan le Fay. To Gwen's eyes, the girl had a darkly beautiful attraction – and something else. She could have been looking at a mirror image of Gwen, herself. And Morgan le Fay was staring straight at her just as Merlin had done, but with an odd intensity as if saying: *Look, listen and think about what you are seeing and hearing.*

Arthur called on Ulfius to repeat what he had said, and for Ygraine to defend herself. When her words reached their climax, Merlin vindicated her and stepped back to allow Sir Hector forward to give his testimony. As he did so the magician came almost shoulder-to-shoulder with Morgan le Fay, and Gwen shivered at the glance of implacable hatred that she gave him. The mocking sneer on Morgan's lips said plainly to Merlin: *You know that I know, you're lying through your teeth* to which Merlin's expression of triumph replied: *And you know that I know there's nothing* you *can do about it!*

The vision faded, leaving an astonished Gwen with an awareness that somewhere at the heart of this remarkable sequence was a truth that Morgan le Fay wanted to her to know about Merlin. Gwen was sure the secret lay in that wicked sneer on Morgan le Fay's lips, and a question came to her mind that had never occurred to her before.

Why had Merlin taken the child Arthur from Uther and concealed his origin so long – let alone use needless magic to make him King?

The only way Gwen felt she could reason it out was by analogy. If the modern Black Wand represented Merlin and his Wych equalled Morgan le Fay, then Ygraine must represent herself, Queen Gwen. Hadn't an uninvited child been promised to her? And hadn't Merlin contrived the birth of Arthur by a magical simulation, just as Black Wand was committed to doing. But how could this cause such hatred between himself and White Wand the way it she had just seen it exist between Merlin and Morgan le Fay? And then the truth, clear and simple, dawned on her. *It had been Merlin, not Uther, who had lain that night with Ygraine*! It accounted for everything. Wasn't Merlin the greatest enchanter of all time? Didn't it explain how he could bring King Uther to give him the babe, and afterwards, when the time was right, ensure he would be king – not by his supposed father's right, but by his actual father's command of magic? She had heard Merlin assure Arthur that Ygraine was his mother. She had not heard him similarly assert that Uther was his father!

Gwen's hard-won acquiescence vanished like snow in summer. Her child *would* owe its magical conception to Black Wand after all. And with that ecstatic realisation came the knowledge also that she was no longer Gwen, not even Ygraine but that the spirit of Morgan le Fay, Mergyn herself, the ageless consort of Merlyn had been growing in her since the eclipse. This was the meaning of all she had felt during the eclipse. Then she had passed through a revelation of loss, of terrible guilt, and wickedness. The child to come would be the gift of redemption, which would be hers through love, redeeming all that had been lost through centuries of suffering.

CHAPTER 7

WITLESS WIZARD

It was Alder, who had known that his Queen was recovering the spirit of Mergyn, who advised her of their Wychy's approach. He suggested she might like to be in place to meet him.

Mergyn's relief that Black Wand was on his way at last was tinged with an expression of askance when the King met her eyes with a smile and reached for her hand.

'I do not say our Wychy is the answer you are looking for,' he said gently. 'But I do know he needs our help and that you are the only one who can give him it.'

*

The Wychy sank on one knee before her: 'Hael and wyn, beloved Queen,' he said. The spread of his Weird around him revealed a starlit corner of a silver box under his arm. It was gone by the time he stood up, but the glimpse was enough to intrigue Mergyn. She made a commanding gesture for him to take the opposite chair, and then looked enquiringly at the glittering box when he laid it across his knees.

He opened the lid, drew out the topmost gold sheet, rose and presented it again kneeling.

Accepting it wonderingly, she stiffened when she saw the impressions, and then stared at him baffled. 'Is this something to do with *my* welfare, Wychy?'

'Not yours, O Queen – although who knows? It is mine. I beg you for its translation.'

Mergyn was astonished. 'You mean you don't *know*? That *you* can't read it for yourself – you, who wrote in characters of fire the title of your father in wisdom?'

'They were a copy of something I had seen in a vision. I didn't know their meaning at that time …'

'But you did afterwards – accurately. Now know that *I* am not to be conned like this! You shall tell me – and still on your knees *and* swearing the truth by your Wand – how you discovered their meaning.'

Compelled to obey, Myrddin told of his visits to Sir Edward and Charles Kinney, and the Weir Lord's letter with the translation.

She listened, was convinced, and broke into peals of delighted laughter. 'O Wychy! Knowing nothing at all, you invented that absurd story of Nebuchadnezzar in the despairing hope that somehow, enlightenment would fall on you. O most righteous of Wands!' she mocked, her fingers tilting his chin up to look at her. 'You have broken every canon of your sacred lore. You have deceived your Wych, your King and your Queen beyond excuse and, worst of all, wandled our sacred Weir Ward to boot!' She had taken his chin in her hand, and was holding it firmly towards her as he tried to turn it away.

'I'll do worse if it's the only way of finding the answers my Liege has asked of me,' he said grimly.

She released his face with a deliberate caress that she knew would play havoc with his feelings. Knowing she could demand anything from him, she held back, well aware she could revive the moment again at will, and lowered her eyes to the golden leaf in her hand. '*O heir-That-Is-To-Come*' she read aloud, '*behold around thee the plenitude of wisdom that Am-Mar-El-Lyn of eld that now am Merlin of this age have prepared against thy coming in the dread hour that shall be soon upon thee!*

One hundred mortal years have I laboured in the task fearful that one iota remain unrecorded; And now that my portents of release are nigh upon fulfilment I add this, the Record of my Days, in cipher more anciently familiar to me, lacking which the purpose of my knowledge shall have no meaning for thee ...'

The Queen stopped reading abruptly, dropping the glinting fragment into her lap as if it were on fire.

'Where did you get this, Wychy?' she demanded faintly.

Again, he had to tell her. As he did so, however, Mergyn found herself trembling from head to foot as the memory of such a place and the precious thing it might possibly conceal came vividly to mind.

The Wychy went to raise his Wand protectively over her.

Mergyn reacted furiously. Springing to her feet, she threw her arm between herself and its influence. 'Don't you dare try to wandle *me* under the shield of my Lord's Weird, you traitorous magician!'

'My Queen, all I wanted to do was to save you from the harm of the terror you were clearly feeling,' he said reproachfully. 'In the same way, I am bound to do for any of our people not able to bear such wyché happenings!'

'Not able to bear ...?' she repeated, then rounded on him, 'Are you saying then that I am *un*wyché?'

'You are wyché,' he said, sounding apprehensive.

His admission pleased her, and a little smile played on her lips 'So, being wyché, it must follow that I am gifted with insight and foresight?'

'That could well be, O Queen.'

'Then know this, O mighty Wand, you shall find no way of escaping this doom except by me. You must take me to the Mount, because I see something there that only I can find for you.'

'I can't do that! The Mount is a sacred refuge! Its contents are a secret legacy to me from Merlyn himself ...'

He stopped as she allowed the leaf of gold to slip from her fingers to the ground.

'This is blackmail!' he said.

The lovely head so near his nodded in complacent agreement. Mergyn knew she held all the trump cards with one exception – the Ace. And wherever that lay, she was determined to find and take it before he could.

'You must know that White Wand overlooks the whole of the Weal and the surface of the Wynn. How can I take you there without her knowing?'

'No more than you can bring out the non-existent Queen you have so wickedly misled the gnomes into thinking is sleeping there! O dearest of all delightful wizards, how are you going to wandle yourself out of *that* one without help?'

As if he would rather go it alone than submit, the Wychy put out his hand to retrieve the fallen gold leaf.

Mergyn quickly set her foot on his fingers. 'Pause, childish one,' she said softly. 'Do you really think I am going to allow you to go *that* easily to all our doom? I will be gracious and give you a choice.' She removed her foot and continued; 'You can replace the gold leaf in your box, leave here alone and go and seek all our damnation by yourself, or you can take me with you to read the contents and so ensure the salvation of us all. The choice is yours.'

'And I thought you affected with wilfulness, O Queen,' he said heavily. 'But now I see you are surely afflicted with a diabolical wickedness!'

She laughed, and chided whimsically: 'Whatever lover enticed a maid with such fair words? But now, since you *have* chosen wisely, we shall leave together – not for the Mansion of the Gnomes, but for your Retreat at *Woe Begone!* and complete the translation of these evil writings.'

'Evil? What evil can there be in great Merlyn's wisdom?'

'Doesn't it say in what I have already read that these sheets contain the Record of his Days?' She rose, drawing him to his feet with her. 'O Black Wand, dearest and best beloved of all my days, if you had any wisdom at all you would strew these writings to the wind unread, and listen instead to the love I have promised you. Only love can turn wickedness to good! Won't you try to be wise, beloved Wand, and throw these golden temptations away while time is still on your side?'

'You are the temptress, O Queen. These writings are my heritage. They were written for me and for no one else but me, and I *will* know them.'

'Have it your way then, Wychy. At least in this, Merlyn knew how to wandle so well that not even his dupes should ever guess the fullness of his duplicity. But I cannot read the records here; my lord and liege will hear no evil in his Stede. Therefore – to *Woe Begone!* and to new beginnings!'

'It is the night of the Dark Moon, O Queen. In less than half an hour, the blight of Dragga's breath will be visible on The Wandle and the Scathe thick and deadly in the Weal. It is vital we Wands stand as one at The Wandle's further edge. It is usual to take guard early, and I am already late.'

Mergyn realised this was something she had overlooked in her eagerness, but she wasn't giving up easily.

'There is still time for you to escort me to *Woe Begone!* and leave me there in safety while you keep watch. Besides which, if you say your Wych will be already at her station, she is unlikely to see us. The waiting will also give me opportunity to scan the sheets in readiness for translation when you return – I can then be more accurate in my reading. Come, I will take charge of the precious thing.'

He opened the lid and let her place the sheet inside, before shutting it quickly and tucking it under his arm again

'Don't you trust me, Wychy?' she asked sweetly.

'I do not, O Queen!' he returned bluntly.

'I only wanted to be certain!' she said with amusement. 'It's always a comfort to have one's suspicions confirmed.'

*

They walked across the Weal in silence. Reaching his Retreat in the beech tree, he opened the door for her to enter, then closed it and hurried away to keep his appointment on The Wandle.

As he expected, he found his Wych standing motionless at the far edge looking out at the heaving sea of thick green mist. The session he had just been through with the Queen had left him sore and stripped of precious secrets. It was consoling to think how much Ann's love and admiration would restore his shattered dignity. He took his stand at her side, expecting some gentle reproach for being late, but she said nothing. He presumed she intended to leave the reproach an unspoken one, knowing how deeply occupied he had been of late. He promised himself he would make it up with her and reveal a little – a very little – of the trend his research had taken; a veiled reference or two, a hint that things were moving forward.

He turned to her eagerly with the diminishment of the Scathe, but she stayed him with an icy voice.

'Are you so confident of the favours of your lover, you besotted wizard, that you can afford to wait any longer at the side of your cast-off Wych? Shouldn't you be hurrying back before she creeps away from your Retreat, and trick you of your reward?'

With which she walked off, leaving him speechless. He knew what had happened, though, and could have kicked himself. With his mind so full, he had forgotten she would have called him at their usual hour on this important night and, receiving no reply, would have been alarmed. She would have remembered the previous time he had gone missing, and taken her Wych ball with her to call him the moment his star appeared in it – and so would have seen the Queen and himself travelling from Alder's Stede to the Weal.

He despaired, knowing he had been witless, but what else could he have done?

CHAPTER 8

MERLYN'S DECEPTION

Myrddin had a downy couch in *Woe Begone!* this now held Mergyn. She had removed her cloak and knew she was looking wholly desirable in a diaphanous garment girdled with precious stones. Although she appeared asleep when he entered, they both knew she wasn't – and the intended effect. The Wychy's face was expressionless as she opened her eyes and smiled at him.

'We had an arrangement, remember?' He tapped the box which he set on the small table beside her.

She sat upright, swinging her legs to the floor and patted the couch beside her imperiously. 'Come, timid wizard – if you can summon sufficient courage – and sit beside me while I unravel the contents of your so dreadfully important casket.' She picked it up, fingering it curiously before turning it over and back, undid the clasp and lifted the lid. She noticed the hinge appeared to stick at a certain angle. The inside was lined with cedar wood as fine as tissue. The sheaf of golden leaves almost filled the cavity in length and breadth.

Slowly and delicately she drew out the top three, estimated how many remained and closed the box. She placed it back on the table, making it obvious that she was intending to translate only a few at a time.

Noticing the intensity of his stare she said sarcastically: 'You *are* satisfied I've not hidden any up my sleeves?'

He ignored the remark and waited.

'I will indicate each line with my finger as I translate it, so you can judge if I make an omission. I will start the same way with the sentence I have already read so you may assess its length for future comparison. Is that fair?'

He still made no answer, so she read over the passage she had already given him, and continued slowly: '... *Know then, that I came in that Age of Gold when Fae and Mortal lived in amity and clover; and with me my consort Mergyn, forever the fairest of the fair. But came at last the time when Mortals ravished the Fount of our Life and our Ageless Land perished beneath the waves, so our People wandered homeless seeking refuge. It then fell to the two of us, the Wisest of the Wise, that we should seek the limits of mortality to divert the spreading evil. So runs the song that is sung; yet therein lies a mystery, and no one except you shall know the true manner of our going and the woeful strife it brought between us ...*'

So far Mergyn's translation had proceeded with remarkable ease. She was so fluent that her eyes and mind were ahead of her slow and steady dictation. But now she paused with her finger at the end of the line, quivering with excitement.

'You promised ...' began Myrddin suspiciously.

'I know, I know! But this is unearthly! It is the secret of secrets! Listen!'

'*Knowing by command of Great Mona's Eye that is the all-seeing oracle of our Race that we might not leave our People leaderless, we did between us encompass the coming of He-Who-Is-Alder-Called-King in that I begot upon Mergyn, by virtue of the Girdle of Creation that was hers and the Elixir of Life that was mine, the Faery Wraith that this purest of our Spirits should inhabit. For know that we, the Little Ones of Earth, are but one errant branch from a star-born tree whose roots and branches are infinite ...*'

'Alder is my son!' Mergyn cried, looking up. 'The problem is solved! Merlyn and Mergyn together made Alder. And what has been done once, can surely be done again? Find the Girdle and the Elixir, and – '

'In that wreckage?' the Wychy interrupted dubiously. 'Besides, it says the Girdle was Mergyn's, and you're Gwen – not Mergyn! He might have kept the Elixir and hidden it, but not the Girdle which wasn't his …'

'O-o-o-oh!' While he had been speaking, she had been scanning ahead. What she had learned had made her squeal in rage and horror.

'Oh, the vile, traitorous and wicked devil!' She stabbed a finger at each character as she translated it, practically spitting the words with the emphasis of block capitals: 'BEFORE THE HOUR OF BIRTH WHEN MERGYN'S SPIRIT ROAMED THE HEAVENS SEEKING THE COMING SPIRIT TO INVEST THE WRAITH WITHIN HER WOMB, I TOOK AWAY THE SACRED GIRDLE FROM HER BELLY AND DID HIDE IT SECRETLY–' Mergyn broke off to round on him with blazing anger. 'You said the Girdle could *not* be in the Mount?'

'Because the translation says it was Mergyn's!' he protested patiently. 'I don't know where it is – how could I?'

'I say it *is* in his Mount! It must be! Are you certain you didn't pocket it, O heir to this Grandfather of Thieves and Liars, and later hoard it in the secret cellars of your Wandle Retreat?'

'Seeing that until now I didn't even *know* of its existence how could I?' he returned. 'But even if I had, why would I? I'm the one who has to arrange the creation of the babe between you and Alder!'

'O blind and witless wizard!' She snapped back angrily at his slowness to see what had now become clear. 'Can't you understand? I *am* Mergyn! Alder is my *son*! I *am* the one who should have been *your* Wych.'

'But I am not the immortal Merlyn and you are not my Wych,' he said doggedly. 'You are the Queen – Alder chose you himself.'

'Because he must have recognised me! Do you think one so wise wouldn't recognise his own mother before I knew it myself?' It was some moments before Mergyn could manage her feelings enough to think of continuing the reading. 'It would soothe me at this moment if I could have a somewhat different Elixir before I go on,' she said. 'You are being less than the gallant host you used to be.'

Knowing how impatient he was to carry on, Mergyn could see the way he moved slowly and deliberately to the cabinet, that he was trying to control an intense annoyance. As soon as his back was turned, she looked at the sheet she had been reading and saw a sentence that nearly made her scream it out in joy.

'What will it be?' asked wizard, as he stooped to open the little doors.

'Nothing less, surely, than a Juniper Jolt,' she answered, hiding her excitement. 'I've a feeling I shall need it! Oh, and please, O Sorcerer's Apprentice, do not let your hand slip and lace it with a dash of Bane or drip of Wizard's Woe. My presence *is* still needed by my people and by you.'

She could imagine her sarcasm annoyed him because he said nothing which seemed to confirm that he actually *had* been speculating on the usefulness of one mixture or another because he was taking longer than he normally would in filling two goblets. When he turned round with one in each hand, she had assumed as air of having been watching him with a fixity that suggested she had followed every move.

He handed over the Juniper Jolt. 'Satisfied, O Queen?'

'That you haven't spiked it for me, dear lover? No. How could I be seeing how your ample Weird shielded your arms and hands? How am I to be certain that I'm not invited to a drink that will place me at your mercy?'

He laughed. 'What need, considering you have already implored my love so ardently? If I opened my arms to you now, wouldn't you welcome the embrace?'

'At this moment, no!' she said frankly. 'By that means you could well and truly render me unconscious, and make me read the rest of this without my knowing!' She put the cup down untasted. 'The very thought makes me want to throw up!'

The Wychy picked up the drink and sipped it to let her see it wasn't doctored, before handing it to her again; but she shook her head.

'As if even hemlock could harm you, O Master of Guile!' she said scornfully. 'I said we couldn't trust each other. But enough squabbling. Come, take your place again and I'll continue the dreary recitation.' She carefully counted down the lines on the page she had been reading. 'Here?'

'The end of the fifth line from the top,' he confirmed.

With her finger on the line, she looked at him earnestly. 'It was wrong of me to give way to such undeserved anger, beloved. Will you forgive me?'

'I would – If I believed it was sincere!'

Mergyn shrugged, sighed regretfully and moved her finger to the next line.

'*Now the Girdle and the Elixir have properties and usages that are contained in the treatise entitled The Girdle of Creation –* '

'I have it! I found it in one of the few books still salvageable.'

'How wonderful!' she said, with a pleased glance of admiration. 'Then there can be no more mystery in the matter of begetting the babe!' Then … 'oh, dear, I appear to have lost my place.'

'There!' he said, indicating it accurately.

'*… entitled 'The Girdle of Creation. But of these sacred objects themselves, O heir-to-come, know this; that they lie concealed in the false bottom of an ancient silver box –* '

Both lunged out to grab it, but Myrddin secured it by a split second. He rose and moved away.

'The Heirloom, I remind you, madam, is mine!'

'The box and the sheaf of golden leaves, yes – and the Elixir also, I grant – but not the Girdle,' she said furiously. 'The Girdle is – '

'Not yours either!'

'But it will be! Without it there will be no royal babe! It is *mine*!'

'At the appropriate time,' he agreed. 'Until then …'

'Fool!' she snorted. 'You don't even know how to open the box!'

'Do you?'

She looked down at the script for a moment, then up with a sly smile. 'I do now!'

Myrddin turned the box over while he thought. She saw him note the hairline crack running around it about two thirds down. He opened the lid, shook out the remaining leaves. The cedar wood floor coincided with the line of demarcation, suggesting ample room for another cavity underneath. He pulled, pushed, twisted and even tapped it with his Wand, but nothing happened.

'Well …?' Mergyn mocked. 'Do we make a deal, O wizard without a clue? Shall I open it for you and share the spoils? The Girdle for me, the Elixir for you?'

'Not if there's another way,' he said disdainfully. 'There are hands cleverer than mine who know the secrets of precious things. I shall summon the Master of Gnomes – '

'Do that and I shall summon your Wych to witness what the Master might reveal!'

She saw him hesitate and guessed he was thinking that if Ann saw the Girdle and realised what it meant, she might immediately claim it. But would that matter? She would have to give it to the Queen later for the purpose that their people had demanded.

'But would she …?' asked Mergyn, 'Or would she encircle her own inviting loins and command *you* to drink the Elixir and beget the babe on her instead of me?'

She had a point. She knew his Wych knew where he was and was certain she knew exactly what was going on between him and her, the Queen.

'There are these also,' Mergyn reminded him, fingering the golden leaves he had turned out on the table. 'Do you imagine I'm going to add them to your triumph?'

'If only I could trust you!' he whispered desperately. 'What oath of yours could I accept that you would keep the bargain you have offered?'

'I *could* swear upon the love I have for you,' she said. 'But since you have already spurned my love, the truth of it would have no meaning for you.'

'All right,' he compromised, 'we will share it in the manner you say. The Elixir for me, the Girdle for you, but like this: you read out the secret of its opening and I follow the directions. In this way, I swear by Mona's Eye, I will abide by the bargain.'

She nodded slowly, looked down again and read:

'… and in this manner can the box be opened. Release the simple hasp and raise the lid slowly until the hinge stays your hand for a second, for only at this angle is the concealed device released. Now slide the base to one side and what is concealed therein will be revealed …'

Myrddin did as she directed, and the two compartments separated in his hand, only to leave him staring in bewilderment.

'Well?' asked Mergyn.

He tilted it so that she could see it was empty. When she betrayed no emotion whatever, she saw it dawn on the Wychy what had happened.

'You –! You –!' He was unable to produce an epithet that would do justice to her trickery. 'You read the instructions and opened the box while my back was turned!' He slammed both halves down on the table. 'You devil! Give me the Elixir.'

Mergyn shook her head, noticeably tightened her left hand. He pounced on it and forced it open. It was empty.

Unable to stand her deception any longer, he threatened. 'Listen, I have but to raise my Wand –'

Mergyn raised her right hand and kissed the ring there set with a ruby, calling: 'O Alder, my Liege …!'

The Wychy fell back.

Mergyn knew well enough that no one but he could project a call to go outside *Woe Begone!* equally, though, that he couldn't take the risk she wasn't bluffing. She therefore smiled sweetly and continued: '… our beloved Black One has perfected plans for the inception of the babe and has given me the magic means that will ensure it.'

She waited as if listening to Alder's reply, then acknowledged: 'So shall it be, my Liege.'

She rubbed her wrist unnecessarily at the Wychy's roughness while he fumed in silence, clearly wondering where she had hidden the objects.

Mergyn lifted herself a little from the couch. She had been sitting on them: a flat crystal phial containing a shining blue liquid, and a girdle so light and tenuous it fitted in the palm of her small slender hand. She picked them up and examined them.

'A Girdle so wonderful it is surely not even of Earthly origin.'

'Have you *no* principles? You swore by your love for me you would share the contents.'

'I did not – I said I *could* but that you wouldn't believe me if I did! I would have shared *if* you had allowed *me* to open the box. I made that condition. I would have enjoyed your dismay for a while, but I would have honoured the agreement in the end. But no, you had to have it your way, and that released me from the obligation.'

'I don't believe you! You meant to keep them, knowing I would have given the Elixir to our Liege the King in fulfilment of the pledge made in the presence of our people. I say you lie!'

She laughed. 'Indeed, no, most sorely tried of wizards. Before you ever did that, I would have seduced you into drinking it yourself.'

'You speak treason!'

'I speak common sense, Merlyn's Heir,' she said flatly. 'You are indeed more than heir to magic. I tell you, if you study the lore he left for you, you won't help but take in all the trickery *he* used it for.'

'*You* speak of trickery!' he marvelled. 'You have just informed Alder that the means of begetting the babe is at hand and in the next breath boast of begetting it by me!'

'Don't speak to me of kings and queens and their lawful heirs! Since history must be repeated, this time it's going to be *my* way.'

'And just what do you mean by that?'

'That it was not Uther Pendragon that sired Arthur. It was Merlyn himself upon the unsuspecting Ygraine – '

'Nonsense!'

'Nonsense, you say?' Mergyn laughed. 'I think we'll see the *sense* of it if he keeps this golden Record of his Days as a truthful confession of his deceitfulness as it has been up to now – unless, of course, you've heard enough of his duplicity?'

'Read on,' he said grimly.

Again Mergyn patted the couch at her side. He had no option but to sit and point out the line she had last translated. *'Then made I manikins, male and female in fashion that is recorded in other places and made them to grow in mortal image and stature that in these two our faerie wraiths could live among men. It was then Mergyn asked about her Girdle. But I, having no mind to show my secret intent lied, saying that the All-Seer of the Heavens had commanded it and to his Spirit it had been returned ...'* Here she made a significant pause. The Wychy said nothing, but his surprise, dismay and embarrassment were obvious. She let it sink home before continuing. *'So went we forth into mortal realm and laboured diligently with our faerie arts to stem the wickedness of men, until a time when Mergyn discovered the Girdle by accident still in my possession –'* Here she again paused, letting it sink home before continuing: *'Then was she so wroth –'*

'BLAST!' Black Wand interrupted loud and savagely.

CHAPTER 9

WHITE WAND FEELS WATCHED

While Ann accepted that every wiccy had the right to lay her head on the block at Black Wand's feet if she wished and was not to be wandled from it, the Queen was different. She was committed to Alder, and Ann judged it gross misconduct for her even to think of seducing Black Wand; the more so because she felt certain it was unlikely to be followed by any starry eyed entreaty for the Bane – Queen Gwen was too wyché for that. Ann knew it was being wayward, but felt she had to do something when she returned to her Retreat and watched her partner's star travel back to *Woe Begone!*. She pondered several courses of action while the sun rose above the Weal; rejecting each until an appropriate plan occurred to her, which also involved the Master of Gnomes. The memory of how her partner's storyline of a slumbering Queen had so excited the gnomes persuaded her it was *not* being wayward to find out what he had been up to in his long visits to their underground home. After all, she told herself, she could be misjudging him, so it might even help if she understood his problems ...

She crossed the narrow waters at Weirdsmeet knowing that the fae would come to greet her. At the top of Wandleside she was beset by wicca and wiccy alike for news of the babe. Was it in being, yet? How soon could they expect it?

'It is a matter for deep magical consideration,' she told them gravely, while summoning a certain half dozen to her side with her eyes. 'No such miracle has ever happened before, so my Brother Wand and I are preparing for the Coming with the greatest possible care. I am on a journey even now in quest of certain reassurances in this wonderful concern.'

They heard her with respect, and allowed her to go on her way to the Wynn with the six she had signed to come with her.

Hetty and Stella, Barnsley, Edmund, Pwyll and Loy all wondered where she was taking them.

She beckoned Hetty to walk beside her, throwing her mantle around the wiccy so as not to be overheard.

'You seem sad, beloved wiccy? Is anything wrong?'

'It's Black Wand,' owned Hetty. 'You know how he had me sit at his knee during his first story about Nebuchadnezzar? I thought he had at last heard the desire that is always in my heart. I have loved him so long and sung the Song of Longing to him so often. Yet when he answers, I find myself consoled with another of his choosing. Why is he always so wily, loved Wych?'

Why indeed! Ann thought grimly, while answering, 'Do you really wish to return to mortal life through the passion of his arms, dear Hetty?'

'Of course not! But I still yearn for his love because he is more magic to me than any wicca in the Forest. Why will he not grant me my wish?'

'Perhaps it is because of your own uncertainty over what the end must be, Hetty. You know the law, you cannot love Wychy or Wych and live?'

After awhile, Hetty nodded and said resignedly, 'I think now the doom is worthwhile, beloved Wych, but how can I be certain that Black Wand will respond to my call the way that I want him to?'

'Dear Hetty. Has no one ever told you that the waters of the Wealspring grant wishes? Or have you already frittered away the three you are allowed?'

'No, only two!' cried Hetty in delight. 'Oh thank you, thank you, White Wand, you are so kind!' and she rushed away intent on what she thought of as a glorious doom. And Ann, watching her go, thought: *now try and wriggle out of that one, beloved Wand, if you dare!* Of course, she realised it wasn't the whole answer, but it would at least divert his attention from the Queen. She then summoned Pwyll to her side while she continued towards the Wynn.

'Dear Pwyll ...!' she began remorselessly. 'How long is it since you sang that song of mortality called *Greensleeves* ...?'

For Pwyll it immediately brought back memories of the Gwen he had serenaded in the days before she was Queen, and all the things they had talked and laughed about together. He tried to sing the song now but broke down in tears after the first verse. It was not long before he also was on his way to the Wealspring. The Wych then drew Baddenham to her and revived his latent adoration of Gwen to give her someone else to think about.

With Loy, she had to be more circumspect. He was Black Wand's oldest and stoutest supporter, but he had entrée into Alder's Stede and she could use an ear in that direction.

Barnsley she kept for herself, seeing a future use for him to play off against her partner. So, after playing havoc with his unsatisfied desires, he was at last dismissed with the conviction that he wore her favours openly on his arm and wanted only the opportunity to thumb his nose at the hitherto unbeatable Black Wand.

Last of all, she appealed to her faithful Star Maiden's special affection for the Black One. No harm could come to Stella, for she would be the next Wych, but Ann was in no mind to heed how risky it was to encourage one's successor into developing their latent wychéness before its time.

When she reached the Wynn, she walked alone to discover Omric himself awaiting her arrival at the entrance with

Feldspar and Whitegold. It was a visit without precedent for the Master, and a marvellous occasion.

'Am I welcome?' Ann asked with sweet uncertainty. He assured her she was, adding how deeply honoured they all felt. She took the arm he offered and allowed him to show her around the Mansion's wonders and treasures. However, as soon as she reached the crowded Great Hall and stood in the midst of its marvels, she felt the odd sensation of being watched. She looked around for cause, but could find none although the sensation persisted.

Omric seated her in his own gem studded chair while he described the nuances and niceties of jewels and precious stones, and gnomes ran to bring her examples that showed off their dexterity and skills; cutting, polishing and setting to make exquisite pictures that they wired together with gold and silver thread.

They would have loaded her down with gifts had she allowed them. She knew she had to accept something though if she was not to hurt their feelings. At their insistence, therefore, she chose a necklace of diamonds and earrings to match. And all the time the feeling of being watched never left her. In the end, it became so unbearable; she turned with a disarming smile to the Master asking:

'Tell me, Master, please. I am eager to know what magic presence overlooks you here with such wonderful constancy? Is it some patron goddess of your kind? Or perhaps the spirit of some ancient queen you have enshrined – like the one King Nebuchadnezzar has sent Merlyn to find?'

She only suggested it in humour to induce an explanation and was astounded to see every gnome freeze, and the Master himself staring at her in stunned consternation. Putting Nebuchadnezzar, a queen and their silence all together, along with her partner's unexplained visits, she at last said gently, 'So the Spirits of the Earth have indeed made their vow of silence to the Great Am-Mar-El-Lyn! But was this wise, Master, to so plot and scheme with one Wand to the mischief and bewrayment of the other? Are not my Brother Wand and I as one in all matters?'

The Master cringed at the softly worded reproach, and came to kneel in humble explanation at her feet.

'We were only obeying the Black One's will, beloved Wych. He wanted no word of this was to be said abroad. We believed he wished it so that none would guess the magic outcome of the story too soon. Please, White One forgive us for not remembering this could not have included you?'

Ann smiled her immediate forgiveness, and said penitently. 'O most admirable and gallant of gnomes, it is *your* forgiveness that I crave for using you so cruelly. I meant only to test how well you guard your oath even though I knew how well you would. Most noble of spirits, please forgive your Wych the pain she has so unwisely dealt you?'

All Omric could do was seize her hands and cover them with rapturous kisses, whilst the rest of the gnomes wished they were as privileged to kneel and kiss her lovely hands.

Ann went on endearingly: 'Indeed, dear Master, what else would have bought me here but the wish to satisfy my curiosity? I am so intrigued, I yearned to steal away and come and see the results of your labours and workmanship for myself. You would not grudge me sight of them?'

'Would that I could, beloved White Wand, but alas it is beyond me. The Black One has set his mighty Seal against all access to the ring and to the entrance to the secret Temple.' Which was when the Master rose and drew aside the tapestry to disclose the fiery Eye ...

*

The uncovering of his mystic symbol had caused the Wychy's Wand to twitch against his hand in warning, so he knew at once what had happened, and swore.

'I beg your pardon?' asked Mergyn severely.

'It's White Wand! She's stolen a march on me – she is in the Gnomes' Mansion and somehow wandled the Master into betraying secrets he is sworn never to reveal.'

'What else should you have expected?' said Mergyn unsympathetically. 'Jealousy is the surest way to fire the female mind to action. Anyway, I thought you said your secrets were inviolate?'

'Well, yes, they are, but now she knows there's something there, she's not going to rest until the Master has told her everything he knows!'

'Which is … what?'

'The location of the Mount, even though he believes it to be the ruins of Nebuchadnezzar's secret temple –'

'In which sleeps the ageless queen!' And Mergyn laughed unrestrainedly. 'Oh, Wychy, what a coil of woe you have spun around your feet. Didn't I say –?'

'Be that as it may,' he argued doggedly, raising his Wand. 'I can yet stop the Master – '

She pressed his arm down. 'Don't be witless as well as weirdly, you woman-woed Wand! Your Wych is shrewd enough to know that Nebuchadnezzar's Queen exists only in the gnomes' imagination – and yours. Come, let us get on with this Record of his Evil Days': and she returned to the translation. '*So went we forth into mortal realm and laboured diligently to stem the wickedness of men, until the time when Mergyn discovered the Girdle by accident still in my possession. Then was she so wroth that she conspired with powerful enemies against me, unwisely revealing her true origin. For this she was seized and slain in flame and I escaped. Thereafter, she had to incarnate into mortality for I alone held the secret that fashioned our mortal forms.*

'*She did not always suffer incarnation in human birth but often in her impatience would possess living mortals of their souls and take their bodies the more readily to harass me.*

'And so through aeons we strove; I to perfect, she to destabilize. Knowing the rightness of my design, I would not yield, and so in time I learned the hour and manner in which I could enjoin the perfection of my desire in a Northern Land, and came to Britain with our wandering People led by Alder who was my perfect son. Here in this wondrous forest, I raised The Wandle from the lake; divided the waters and made the pact with Dragga. I selected Wych and Wychy and instructed them with knowledge and magic sufficient to their needs and ends. In this was Mergyn powerless to stop me for I contrived it secretly while she was compelled to follow by seeking natural human incarnation.

'At that time lived Uther Pendragon that called himself King of all Britain holding kings and thanes in thraldom under him and to him I went in many guises foretelling the outcome of his struggles with such sureness that he believed me truly to be the greatest magician in all the world, which I was. And so it came about that by my arts and cunning advice Uther won over his distant barons by duplicity and the sword, and held me in greatest honour amongst men. Then heard he tell of Ygraine that was the virtuous and beautiful wife of he who at that time enjoyed dominion of Cornwall and had him come to his capital bringing her. And lo, I knew that I had met the perfect vehicle for my plan when I perceived within Ygraine the wraith of one of our little People in mortal duress. Yet was Uther so mad to possess her that I saw no difficulty in fulfilling my own desire. To this end I made it appear to the innocent Ygraine that it was her husband lay with her, and caused Uther to believe that it was himself in that disguise which so did. And yet did he not, being only enchanted in a dream to believe this, whilst I begat upon her in darkness with the Girdle of Creation between our bellies ...'

Mergyn paused, 'What did I tell you? Such is your hero from of old, Wychy; a self-confessed thief, liar *and* trickster, to boot!'

'I think not,' said Myrddin obstinately. 'It was Arthur he begat.'

'So, the poison's already at work in you!' she said bitterly. 'I warned you, and I'll warn you again, you want to think well upon your inheritance. You have received it from one to whom the rape of Heaven was a crime as lightly borne as the rape of an innocent woman! He sinned against the Gift of Heaven and disregarded every law that Man in his partial wisdom devised. That is the taint he now passes on to you and deludes *you* into continuing!'

'I can hardly abuse something I knew nothing about, that you have stolen! Whatever taint there is seems more in you than me, even if you *do* use it for the purposes our People need.'

Mergyn could make no reply because she needed him to go on believing she really had informed the King that he had given her the magic means, she therefore resumed the translation: '*And when the Duke her husband was slain that very hour, Uther took Ygrain to wife, and I laid upon him that the reward for my contriving would be the child to be born. So came it to pass that Arthur grew to manhood and to be King of all Britain and a champion of chivalry such as the world has never known; yet did not know his supposed lineage till long after he was King.*

'*Yet in all of this, I sowed the seed of my own undoing for of Ygrain's three daughters by the Duke that were half-sisters to Arthur the youngest was Mergyn called Morgan le Fay. When in time she learned of the begetting of Arthur upon her mother Ygraine by arts of mine she guessed no other could truly have begotten so kingly a man save I, and this by the sacred Girdle that was rightly hers. Being young and unready to match her magic against mine, she plotted Arthur's downfall and death; schemes I tried to avert. But when her knowledge was full upon her, she took upon her the likeness of Nemway and deceived me in such a manner that I conceived an over-whelming desire for her and promised, would she love me, we would beget another as great as Arthur; because in her I saw a wraith of the fae.*

'Yet so plagued she me, pretending and believing in my power, that she would not consent except I take her to the place where the Girdle was hidden and show it to her there. To this I agreed, so besotted I was, and led her to the Mount of my Retreat that I had built years before and stored there the Girdle of Creation with all the parchments yet to be filled with the hidden secrets of my lore.

'Now to enter must I draw the Great Talisman from my thumb, whereat my mortal appearance would dwindle into wraith, and set the ring against a certain place near by where I should enter the Mount and, on return come through the ring and be restored to human shape and height. But lo, when I came bearing the Girdle and the Elixir to pass out again, there was no exit and the ring was gone. Then did the voice of Mergyn cry out terribly but faintly from far away. "Now are we matched, vile lover! You have my Girdle and I have your Ring! Yet neither of us can profit by the exchange for you cannot escape from your Retreat and I am still without my Girdle. Ponder well your everlasting wickedness, Merlyn, once my love with whom I fashioned the only perfection our spirits can ever bear together."

'I heard, yet answered not for I knew of no real wickedness in my ways, having laboured only towards the ennobling of Mankind. Yet in the hundred years that have ensued I have found no malice in my heart towards her and have come to deem it honour that none less than she the Fairest of the Fair should so enthral and overcome me at the last.

'And so having learned at leisure the term of my incarceration, I set myself to leaving you, O Heir-to-Come, the sum of all my wisdom.

'Before I end I lay one solemn charge upon you: that you shall deal kindly with my Fairest of all Fair, if she be still upon this planet; that in you she shall find solace if she will for the rue that has lain so long between us ...'

Mergyn faltered, closing her eyes and dropping the last of the leaves in her lap. They had revived an appalling memory.

She spoke at last in a whisper: 'I see a great splitting of the earth with storms and destruction and a mortal woman, terribly, terribly old, who weeps beside a grass covered mound partly crushed by the trunk of a fallen oak. The old woman speaks and I am filled with anguish.' Mergyn paused, covering her face with slender hands. 'She cries in a high weak voice: *"Woe, woe, that this should prove my dire reward for my hundred years of self-inflicted penance! O lover of my soul, I am come to set thee free, even with thy ring that I stole so long ago, and find thee sped beyond me to the stars! O Mona, Lady of Heaven, intercede …!"'*

*

Black Wand watched her in silence, knowing this was no hallucination; the details were too exact with what he knew to be true.

'The old woman has collapsed … now she recovers … she draws a large ring from a small bag round her neck … It bears a great amethyst that is inscribed AM-MAR-EL-LYN. She drops it into a crevice in the earth and whispers, sobbing '*So be it, Lady of Heaven* …!' she collapses again, but now she is spent … her spirit leaves her …'

A little later, Mergyn lowered her hands. 'O love of my life,' she pleaded, 'don't you see *now* how it is between us? How only we two, you and I alone, can bring the child into being?'

'No!' he replied, stolid and unyielding. 'It's madness! It is ordained that Alder's successor shall be from you and Alder –'

Mergyn got to her feet slowly and majestically and the Wychy, rising automatically in response, saw that her eyes had altered to the shades of night, giving her elfin features a cast of such forceful beauty that he trembled. He had to accept then that she was no longer the wraith of the mortal Gwendolyn Kinney, nor even Queen Gwen, but Mergyn, Fairest of the Fair.

The transformation complete, and Mergyn spoke – vibrantly: 'And who am I, most puissant wizard who apes the wisdom of one long gone?'

'I say that you are possessed,' he said coldly. 'But as far as I am concerned, you are still Alder's Queen, the chosen medium with Alder by whom that this babe will be begotten.'

'By incest?' she demanded. '*You would you have me lie with my own son?*'

'That is enough, O Queen!' he cried furiously, striding to the door. 'Here lies the parting of our ways. You *have* the Girdle *and* the Elixir. Now return to your lord, our Liege and don't come near me again!'

Mergyn looked down at the Girdle and phial in her hand. 'I shall not call you to my couch, beloved,' she said, going to the door. 'It is written that you shall implore me on your bended knees – '

He struck the door with his Wand and it flew open. 'Out!' he ordered.

At the threshold, she paused to turn her head and repeat softly over her shoulder: '*O-heir-To-Come, I charge you solemnly that you deal kindly with my Fairest of all Fair …*'

CHAPTER 10

SLEEPING BEAUTY

The Queen's sudden appearance outside *Woe Begone!* seemed magical to the fae who had gathered there.

'That's funny peculiar.' said Edmund to Baddenham, while the rest of them ran to greet the Queen, Pwyll foremost. 'I mean no one can get in or out of *Woe Begone!* unless Black Wand opens the door for them, so …?'

'He's stayed inside,' said Baddenham firmly. 'Probably something he's arranging for later …'

' … Beloved Queen,' Pwyll was saying, his eyes bright with nostalgia. 'Now you are here, will you stay awhile with us like you used to years ago, when we laughed and talked and sang together? See, I have my lute; and Baddy, you must remember, plays the pipes so well.'

'Please do, loved Queen,' Stella added.

But Mergyn, still caught up in her memories, was only partially listening. She remembered how she had often come among them in the guise of a stranger fay not knowing who she was. She felt proud to have won back the Girdle without the use of magic – which she had forsworn – it made it for a good morning's work. Suddenly aware that the gathering fae were on the point of shrinking away with bewilderment at her strange behaviour, Mergyn quickly reverted to the kind of loving Queen they all remembered, and laughed softly.

'Dear Pwyll, Stella, Mona herself must have inspired you. We'll do exactly as you say, for I've often longed to return to those happy days.'

She put an arm around each, kissing them tenderly, and began walking away from *Woe Begone!* drawing the rest of the crowd after her. 'I remember a little glade on the path towards the Wealspring,' she said. 'The place we used to gather when Black Wand was not on the Weal. We'll go there and we'll sing to our Star Maiden the songs we loved so much. And Loy and Simmo can dance the hornpipe, and Clee and Jean shall lead the dance of the Falling Leaves again …'

The crowd followed shouting and dancing with glee. The Queen had come back to them just as she used to be. The news spread through the Forest and sent everyone racing for the Glade of White Bluebells.

*

Myrddin recognised a thoughtful move on the Queen's part that gave him a clear field of escape: but he was in no mood to be grateful while he preferred to believe she was possessed.

He piled the golden Record back in its silver box, tucked it under his Weird and made for the Mansion of the Gnomes. He arrived to find Ann and the Master in each other's embrace. He knew it was waywardness on his Wych's part because she would have been aware of him the moment he reached the outside entrance. Since it invited serious trouble if she intended tinkering with Omric's romantic inclinations, it annoyed him.

Ann held the kiss until he was a few wands away, before turning to greet him with surprised fondness. 'Brother Wand, how good to see you. Please, will you support me in my assurances to our beloved Master that Nebuchadnezzar's slumbering Queen shall be woken by her prince in time to grace our revels next High Moon?'

Myrddin concealed his frustration behind a look of sober consideration while his mind raced. It was not Ann's fault; it was on the Queen's head he rained his silent curses. She had started all this. All the same, he still had to put his Wych's waywardness in its place.

'That is going to be difficult, beloved Wych.' he said, shaking his head. 'You see, I've made a discovery that alters everything. Look.' And he produced the silver box, which he opened to show its content. Her instant look of consternation at the sight of the characters made him wonder what she had been up to, but turning to the wondering Master, he said: 'Tis the ancient script from great Merlyn himself, and from it I have just learnt that there are certain heavenly portents to be fulfilled before the Queen may be awoken. But be of good cheer, Master – the time will be soon, I promise.'

While they were speaking, gnomic faces had started peering hesitantly through the doors.

Whitegold called pleadingly: 'Master, there is a mighty revel in honour of our beloved Queen Gwen about to happen in the glade of the White Bluebells. Singing and dancing and all kinds of merrymaking.'

'And who deserves a holiday more than our hardworking Spirits of the Earth?' asked Myrddin, with a humorous look at his Wych. 'Will you also grace this phenomenal occasion, beloved?'

'Alas, I am unable, Brother Wand,' she said, which hardly surprised Myrddin, as he imagined the Queen would be the last person she would want to meet at that moment. 'There are needful matters I must attend on The Wandle. But please, dear Master, do go and ensure our brother gnomes are not too boisterous – '

All three were nearly knocked down in the rush. But Myrddin managed to disappear before the last gnome hurtled out, leaving Ann no opportunity to tackle him before he was ready.

*

Left to herself, and after assuring the Master she would far rather he kept an eye on his noisy fellows, Ann sauntered disconsolately in the direction of Wandleside thinking remorsefully of Hetty, Pwyll and Baddenham whom she had so wrongfully despatched to the Wealspring. They would have made their irretrievable wish and sung their Song of Longing for the last time. How could she ever atone for that, or to Stella whom she had encouraged so needlessly? How could she have been so wayward?

She did not get very far before she was aware of another sorrowful soul in the Weal. She called gently and soon Hetty came running to her, crying piteously.

'White Wand! White Wand! I'm already wasting with the Sickness,' she sobbed within the shelter of the shining white mantle. 'I have been to the Wealspring and wished the last of my precious wishes – and all for nothing. I ran to the Meeting of the Weirds and sang my Song of Longing – yet though I waited and waited, he never answered.'

'How could he, my love?' replied White Wand reassuringly. 'He was not there.' She felt shame at what she had to do, but had to see it through. 'You will find him alone in the Mansion of the Gnomes, because every gnome has gone to join the Queen who is having a party in the Weal …'

*

Myrddin, about to descend from the Mount with the scrolls under his Weird, heard Hetty's plaintive song in the Great Hall of the Mansion.

Black Wand! Black Wand!
Be thou my wizard, Wand!
Wyn me my Wychy, Wand,
Anguish is on me.

Woe's in my heart, Wand;
Dread's in the depth of me!
Sped is my happiness;
Joy is gone from me!

Come with thy wealing, Wand!
Love has bewrayed me!
Bless with thy healing, Wand;
Wyn me, my Wand!

He knew it was the kind of summons he could no longer escape. He also realised why his Wych had put Hetty up to it, but could not blame her – in fact, he suddenly realised he should thank her. She had placed the very person he so desperately needed right in his path. Although a Wealspring wish for his love was too sacred to deplore, wandle or avoid, it didn't mean it couldn't be spun out to defer the tragic consequence for a while at least.

He patiently replaced the books beside the silver box, leaped down into the tunnel and walked unhurriedly along it, humming the tune so that Hetty would know he was coming. He barely had time to push aside the concealing tapestry before she was in his arms.

'Oh, Black Wand, surely you are the wickedest wizard that ever was. But it is all right, now, isn't it?'

'As right as a raindrop upon a newly budded rose.' he replied, kissing her.

With a great sigh, she relaxed in his arms.

'Black Wand, how long shall I have with you before I have to take the Bane?'

'Just so long as you continue to look at me with such wonderfully adoring eyes, my love.'

'That'll be an awfully long time, Black Wand.' she promised, then anxiously. 'It will have to be, won't it, after the long, long time I've pined for you.'

He couldn't help laughing. It was in his Book of Wisdom that any fay in this extremity was usually intent on her doom. but Hetty seemed made of sterner stuff as, he remembered, she always had.

When Myrddin indicated that Hetty should precede him back into the tunnel, she hung back alarmed.

'Where are you taking me?'

'All part of the magic, my love. Why, don't you trust me?'

'Of course, I do,'

'Then take my hand and follow closely. The magic you are about to find is known to no other fay in the forest.'

The tunnel was dank and dark, not at all like the clean, well-lit passage from the Mansion's entrance to the Great Hall, and he felt Hetty keeping a tense hold of his hand during the apparently endless journey.

When they arrived at the foot of the shaft to the chamber, he pressed her close to his Weird so that she would not see the fiery Seal above them, before shooting up through it with her unconscious form in his arms. He laid her gently on the mildewed stone in the chamber and smiled benignly.

Now there really is a sleeping a sleeping female in the imagined temple! he thought, and congratulated himself on the neat twist. Everyone would believe she had succumbed to his fatal loving and gone to White Wand for the Bane, and Ann would never have the nerve to deny it. Sitting then on a heap of rubble, he devoted himself to the difficult and uncomfortable study of his crumbling scrolls. It was near sunset when he paused and turned to smile at Hetty's unconscious form. Among other things on the parchments, he had discovered the secret of fashioning an astral form and investing it with a wraith. With care and attention to detail, he could wandle Hetty into a semi-physical creation that could look like Nefertiti and therefore wonderfully acceptable as Nebuchadnezzar's newly-awakened Queen.

He returned to his reading for a long time until his Wand twitched and alerted him that prying eyes had again uncovered the Seal protecting Merlyn's Ring behind the tapestry in the Great Hall.

CHAPTER 11

MORE WAYWARD THAN WEIRDLY

Back in the glade, Pwyll and Baddenham came to sit at the Queen's feet.

'Beloved Majesty,' said Pwyll. 'Baddy and I have a favour to ask.'

Mergyn clapped her hands delightedly. 'Say on, dearest ones, how could I find it in my heart to refuse any request so chivalrously implored? It is granted even before I hear it. Now say on …?'

'It is this, beloved Majesty: we wish – Baddy and I – we wish that you would come more often to this Glade of White Bluebells, and be close to us. We would like a special place to be built for you, covered in flowers, where you may come whenever it pleases you – '

'Hael and wyn!' everyone cried excitedly. 'Please, be with us always, dear Queen,'

Mergyn held out a loving hand to each of them with a nod to the Master of Gnomes who sent his fellows scampering back to the Wynn for materials.

'It shall be ready before Sunné sleeps, dear Lady,' he promised. Like the Black One, Alder's Queen would have her own Retreat in the Weal.

With the gnomes feverishly intent on the construction, and the fae breaking up into groups, Mergyn became aware of Stella on the verge of tears. She called, beckoning the fay close. 'Stella, my love, why so sad on such a wonderfully happy day?'

'It's Black Wand,' Stella answered dolefully. 'I have been to the Wealspring, too, but come back too late to sing him my Song of Longing because Hetty got there first – '

'My poor, dear, lovely, lovely child,' Mergyn exclaimed, rising and taking her in her arms. 'This is terrible, You have been back – what, half a moon-time – and already have the Sickness? Do you really want to leave us all so soon?'

'No, of course not, Queen Gwen. But I have such – '

'Hush,' she was commanded. 'Let's take a little walk together …'

Mergyn walked her to a little track that ran towards Alder's Stede where White Wand couldn't overhear them, and where it did not take long to find the truth of the matter. She had to work quite hard, though, to undo the White One's wandling. Having no magic of her own, but relying on the strength and wisdom of her ancient personality, Mergyn took Stella into her confidence and explained that the Wych, suffering from a spell of waywardness, wasn't responsible for what she said and did at the moment. Mergyn then convinced the fay that she was far too young, dear and precious for sending back into mortality so soon, and in this way enabled Stella to put the deadly longing aside.

*

As it happened, Ann was far too busy trying to avoid any meeting with Barnsley to pay attention to what the Queen was doing. She had to avoid hearing his Song of Longing when he got back from the Wealspring. But where could she go? She couldn't stay on The Wandle, nor go to the Mansion of the Gnomes. And everyone would know where she was if she fled to the Weal. The only place left to her was the Royal Vintner's den – the one other blind spot in the forest besides Alder's Stede.

As she hurried away to the Wynn, her mind returned to the way the Queen had manipulated things in the Glade of White Bluebells. For someone without the least magical ability, the Wych considered the Queen had shown a wonderful aptitude at making things happen the way she wanted them. If Gwen had not provoked Ann to jealousy in the first place, she would never have done the things that she had. If Gwen had never been in the forest before Black Wand's new Wych, Ann, could attempt the Wand; or if Black Wand had only left *Mens Sana* alone and so left Gwen to continue her unlovely existence there, none of this would have happened. But he hadn't, and she had, and all the regrets in the world were not going to undo it.

The Wych sighed. If only the prophecy of The Passing related to the Queen and not to Alder …

No sooner thought than decision followed. The Queen must go.

The intention astounded her for a moment, but she could not ignore the fact that without Queen Gwen everything would be back to where it always had been, and should be, between Wychy and Wych. Of course, it would upset the order of the promised babe, but Black Wand was so wily he could easily deal with that – the fae would accept anything he told them as true. She believed he could even engender it with her, his Wych – which should have been the arrangement in the first place.

She identified Rozyn's Retreat by making a bee-line for the only blank place in her mental map on the Wynn. It turned out to have a concealed underground entrance beneath a slab of stone.

She tapped it with her Wand. 'Rozyn, Rozyn-Who-Knows,' she called softly.

'I am here, Beloved Wych.' His voice came quietly from behind her.

She turned, surprised that any forest entity could creep up on her without warning, and realised for the first time how different he was when he showed no trace of his usual joviality. Remembering there was nothing to account for him in her tapestries, nor anything to say where he had come from, she stared wonderingly into the uncomplicated gaze of his wyché eyes. They had none of the subtleties of her own, or Black Wand's, nor even Gwen's, yet seemed as wise as Alder's own.

'Who are you, Rozyn?' she asked uncertainly. 'And what is it that you know?'

'I am Rozyn the Royal Vintner who knows all the secrets of seeding, flowering and fruiting, O Fairest of Wands.'

'And how old are you, most noble Rozyn?'

'Alder's birth was celebrated with my wines, O Lady of the Wand,' he assured her without hesitation.

'His birth …?' she repeated in wonder.

'Long before the separation of Weal and Woe, and the making of The Wandle,' he said quietly.

'Then who was his mother?' she asked faintly. 'Who his father?'

'Great Merlyn caused him and Fairest Mergyn bore him, beloved Wand, and commanded me to serve him for as long as he remains in this realm.'

The Wych felt a sense of shock. 'I believed Alder to be with us always?'

'Immortality has ascending planes.'

She gave up, and said instead: 'Please, Rozyn, I would like to see your stills and vats and the wonderful blending of things that you do. Will you show me?'

He offered his arm and took her to his secret place near the Brook of Wynn, where he showed her not only a display of kegs and casks, barrels and vessels of all descriptions prepared and labelled, but also vats filled almost to the brim.

'I would like a potion,' she said frankly, 'a potion that will overcome even the wisest of our kind.'

Rozyn looked at her enigmatically. 'A potion …?' he repeated with pursed lips. 'I have many such, but none for those who are already wyché. For that, I would need ingredients not readily to hand, great Wand: ingredients such as Wych's Bane, or Wizard's Woe. How would I come by either of these when their picking is unlawful?'

'But if you had one or the other of these, such a potion could be prepared?' she insisted.

'Without doubt; but the Dwindling Root and the Errant Weed cannot be blended in safety without the addition of Stillbind. Without Stillbind, the effect could well prove fatal to the wraith of the one who drinks it. And I have no Stillbind.'

Ann knew that the Dwindling Root was an ancient name for Wych's Bane, and Errant Weed another for Wizard's Woe, but she had never heard of Stillbind. No matter … 'The fruit of the root alone will be sufficient,' she said bluntly. 'And if Stillbind isn't available, I'll take the consequences. If I give you the fruit of the root, will you prepare the potion I need?'

'This is waywardness, beloved Wand,' Rozyn protested. Such a potion will be deadly.'

'Will you do it or not?'

Rozyn put his head on one side as if listening. At last, he nodded gravely. 'I will help you, Lady of the Wand, if the ingredient is given me.'

'It shall be,' she promised eagerly. 'I will bring it to you at dawn, tomorrow.'

'No, Lady – it must be during the interregnum. None must know of such waywardness, not even your Brother Wand.'

Ann agreed, and then added, 'I need another potion also – at once – a common potion sufficient to bemuse an errant fay.'

Without a word, Rozyn picked up a small skin of wine and emptied into it the contents of a phial containing blood-red liquid.

With this and a goblet concealed under her Weird, Ann returned to the Weal.

She found Barnsley not far from the top of Windaway and guessed he had already sung his Song of Longing with no reply.

'Barney ...' She greeted him with obvious delight, and held out the cup. 'Be a dear and hold this a moment for me, will you? Our Royal Vintner is delayed on his way to Glade of White Bluebells, so I have brought this with me so we, at least, shall have a toast to our union.'

'You mean it worked, White Wand?' he asked, taking the cup. 'You mean you really heard that silly song I sang at the Meeting of the Weirds?'

'Barney ...?' She managed to make it sound an astonished reproach. 'Haven't you noticed I have ears, you thrilling hunk of masculinity? Now hold the cup while I fill it ...'

Before he passed out, she had no shame in wandling his mind so that he would have no recollection of going to the Wealspring, of making his wish, or singing his Song of Longing. It was against every law in the book, but she was trying to undo something she should never have started.

*

Mergyn and Stella came across Barnsley's unconscious form on their way back to the glade.

The Queen hushed Stella's immediate cry of concern. 'All is well,' she said quietly. 'Just find Simmo and Baddy and send them to me here, please.'

Stella hurried off and, left on her own, Mergyn contemplated the hapless fay. She knew what had happened. White Wand had panicked at sending a innocent wicca to his doom, and would certainly have gone even further by wiping his mind clean of Wealspring and Wish. Not just a breach of forest lore, but a dishonouring of the pact with Dragga. She pondered on what was to become of him. Returning him to his past rebellious state of mind would solve nothing; he would only continue to be a source of annoyance to himself and to everyone else. Mergyn had no idea of the cause of his strange streak. It did occurr to her, however, that turning it to some useful purpose might make all the difference to his future happiness – and she knew just where he could find it.

Baddenham and Simmonds came hotfoot on receiving Stella's message, and halted before her in astonishment at the sprawling Barnsley. Mergyn knew they were probably thinking that he must have accosted her or Stella, and that she had summarily dealt with him

'Dear ones, please take him somewhere where he'll be safe from the Scathe this coming night. I seem to remember a nook near the pathway to the Wynn, where two large boulders meet ...?'

They nodded, picked him up, and carted him off in silence. Mergyn returned to the glade to find the outside of her new home complete. A hillock in human terms, but only a fay could recognise or identify the faerie flowers that covered it and grew around the rose-laden entrance.

She accepted the Master's arm and went in to marvel at a domed interior studded with gems and a room furnished with filigree couch, chairs and table artistically arranged on a floor of miniature grass. He then showed her a concealed recess and led her down flight of diamanté steps to a lower chamber forming a bedroom.

The bed blazed with colour under a cascading canopy studded with jewels, and three gnomes were just finishing a carpet of iridescent pile.

Mergyn clapped her hands in delight and wonder at everything the gnomes had done, and thanked the Master with a smile that made him go down on his knees to kiss her hands with reverence. From above they heard the clamour of Rozyn's arrival to crown the day with drink, laughter and dancing. They ascended together, and went out to meet him.

Rozyn stood in the dray, his arms outstretched, greeting the crowd around him.

'All in good time, my loves, I have brought the most potent of brews and distillations by the dozen, designed to wamble the most wayward of innards. But first, I must deliver in humility the ambrosias I have selected for our beloved Queen,'

He leapt from the dray and fell to one knee before her, his head bowed. 'Beloved Queen, I humbly implore you accept the rarest of my offerings – '

He had raised his head to look up at her and stopped, his mouth open, his expression one of awestruck recognition. And yet he shivered a little when she raised him to his feet and embraced him. He whispered quietly so that no one overheard him:

'Lady of Heaven, if I had known – '

'And now you do, beloved Rozyn,' she answered as softly. 'But don't speak here.' Raising her voice, Mergyn continued: 'Come, I am impatient to see your wonderful gifts, fond knower of my heart's delight.'

The Vintner ran to unload a cabinet filled with decanters, bottles and vessels, and brought it into the decorated hillock, refusing all help from eager assistants.

The Queen took him down to see the chamber below.

He looked around and nodded reminiscently. 'The Master of Gnomes remembers well,' he said. 'It is just – '

She placed a commanding finger on his lips and whispered: 'We are secret here, dear Rozyn, and there is much I have to say and little time to say it – '

'Dearest Lady,' he interrupted urgently. 'Please, allow me to warn *you* first. There is another gift to come. I wanted to refuse the commission, but I found no denial. It is a terrible potion that – '

She stopped him with a kiss. 'No more than I expected, my dear son – a potion from which even *I* might not recover. But you, wisest of Vintners, you know the antidote? A measure of Stillbind, and – '

'But I have none!' he cried in despair. 'The great Merlyn alone knew the secret of growing it, and not for two thousand years have I been able to distil it. It does not grow in Britain, or I would have found it. And I cannot stem the ferment of the Dwindling Root without it.' He was wringing his hands in consternation.

She caught and stilled them 'Do not worry, beloved Rozyn, I think I know just where the immortal seeds still lie. If I find them, you shall have them, be assured of that. Now, I have a request to make of you. There sleeps a fay in a nook beside the pathway to the Wynn – '

'I sensed him as I passed, my Queen. His name is Barney, and mine is the woe that led to *his* undoing. But I didn't know then that you were – '

'Hush, dear one, to all intents and purposes I am still Queen Gwen. I want you to retrieve this errant wicca on your journey back to the Wynn before moonset. It comes to me that he will serve you well – most well. You shall instruct him, in all your knowledge. Is this understood?'

Rozyn bowed his head on her shoulder, his eyes misting. 'Does this mean, then, the ending of my age-long service?'

She stroked his head, soothing him as she had in ages past.

'It may well be, faithful one. I can only speak as my spirit guides me. I have no magic now to foresee the things that shall be.'

'Then it shall be as you say, my Queen,' he promised. 'I will take him and apprentice him to all the secrets of my craft as you have commanded.'

*

On their return outside, the celebrations commenced and continued until near moonset, when the gnomes' left for their underground dwelling and Mergyn went with them. There was something special she had commissioned from them that they wanted to give her to as soon as they could, and Mergyn, who needed to find the Stillbind or risk elimination by White Wand, was also looking forward to making a search of Merlin's Mount.

She half-expected to find Hetty at the Mansion, but the gnomes gave no indication of having visitors anywhere, but wanted to present a golden belt, studded with emeralds that Whitegold and Feldspar had spun and set for her, with two matching pouches. All day long she had been carrying the Girdle and Elixir, concealed in one hand or the other, being too precious to put down anywhere. It was an immense relief to insert them by sleight of hand into the pouches, and have them safe around her waist instead.

Her next move was to stand and admire the huge tapestry of the waterfall behind the Master's chair. She told him that such weaving was so impossible for her to believe, she would have to see its other side.

For the second time that day, the gnomes looked terrified, but she reassured them at once. 'Don't be afraid, Master – it is the tapestry I wish to examine, not the Black One's Seal that protects the great talisman of Am-Mar-El-Lyn,' and Mergyn drew aside the covering to examine the workmanship carefully, quite unconcerned by the glowing Eye on the wall.

CHAPTER 12

A NEW KIND OF MAGIC

This time, Black Wand did not say 'Blast!' when he got the message. He listened to the Queen's glowing eulogy on the tapestry, and then her assurance to the Master that she knew all about the secret temple and the sleeping Queen, even telling him in which direction it lay.

None of this surprised the Wychy; he had told her the whole story that sunrise. But he was indignant that she was obviously intending to invade the Mount without his permission. Had she guessed he was there? Or was she trying to find out if he wasn't, with the intention of prying into his sacred parchments?

Well, she wasn't going to do that while he was there. And if she had come to seduce him she would be equally out of luck, because he had a prior engagement.

Deciding he would let her in and enjoy her discomfort, he reached out with his Wand, cancelled the flaming Seal which glared down through the hole in the floor.

*

She eventually arrived at the bottom of the shaft and called up softly: 'Wychy?'

'Enter!'

The casually voiced instruction registered a little black mark with Mergyn. One does not usually tell your Queen that she can jump for it!

She leaped gracefully however and landed accurately on the edge of the opening where she looked at him, at Hetty, and around the drear and uninviting scene with disgust. 'Really, Wychy, you can be the most inartistic wizard of all time when you try. Even my throbbing heart is appalled by such squalor. Couldn't you at least have taken the poor child to *Woe Begone!* or to your lair on The Wandle?'

'And leave you a free hand to rummage here to your heart's content?' he said, looking up from his rolls. And Mergyn saw that he noticed her new belt and guessed its purpose.

'Don't tell me, O Merlyn's studious heir, that you intend to pass Hetty off as Nebuchadnezzar's Sleeping Beauty? It's a great idea as far as it goes, but it won't absolve you from your traditional obligations. Didn't you know it's *you* she wants – not Nebuchadnezzar? Your Wych also cheats *her* lover. But you won't know about that, will you …?' She went on to tell him how White Wand had dosed Barnsley in the forest, concluding: '… Wychies, I don't know what the pair of you are coming to. I warned you this morning, O Black One, that you'd inherit more than magic from your accursed legacy.'

'What I do is needful to fulfil the sacred prophecy,' he said. 'What my Wych does is in accordance with the dooms of her own Weird.'

'But not mine,' she said. 'I am not to be so easily destroyed, if for no other reason than that the babe must be born of me alone. It is promised, therefore it will be – and may Mona blast you if you fail in the duty laid upon *you*.'

She sat beside him on the heap, and he pointedly rolled up the parchment he was reading.

Ignoring it, she picked up the silver box lying nearby instead and played with it in an absent minded kind of way, saying: 'The Wych you so much love has designed a potion to remove me, completely.'

'I don't believe it.'

'Ask Rozyn. She commissioned him to prepare it. I may sometimes deceive, Black Wand, but I do not lie. Tomorrow, she will send him with wine adulterated by the Bane, and I do not intend to suffer such waywardness.'

'Why should you?' he asked carefully. 'If you know what it is – '

'True, but I might mistake the vessel it's in. For safety's sake, I have come for its antidote. I know there is a certain plant that will counter the evil of Bane and Woe.'

'Here?' he asked with immediate interest. 'What's its name?'

'Anciently it was known as Stillbind. Perhaps your writings have mentioned it?'

'Perhaps. But I doubt if seed of such a herb would have survived so long uncultivated.'

'The seed is immortal: it survives aeons.'

'Did Rozyn tell you about it?'

She shrugged. 'It is enough to know it exists and is almost certainly here.' She pointed at the pick and shovel he had used earlier. 'Look for it.'

She knew that if he had not been so desperately anxious to find it himself for his own use, he might not have fallen for her ruse so easily. For it was not a herb but a microscopic fungus that was growing sparsely all around him. She had already plucked an unspored specimen and tossed it through the hole in the floor. Its hundreds of secreted seeds would last whoever owned them more than they would need.

So the Wychy dug with pick and spade for a long time while she sat calmly, lightening his labours from time to time with snippets of conversation to distract him from what lay under his nose.

*

He said nothing, pursuing his search diligently, but she kept up a running commentary. '… By the way, did you know you also have your Star Maiden in the hollow of your hand, most entrancing of Wychys? She has been organised into a second line of cannon-fodder by your doting Sister-Wand – '

'That's enough,' he cried angrily. 'Being wayward is not a crime. If you want me to unearth this infernal herb, stop nagging.'

Suddenly aware of a repressed laugh, Myrddin dropped his tool. She had fooled him. If he hadn't been in such a hurry, he would have thought and consulted the several articles on botany that he had noticed among the scrolls. He sat down again and began running his finger down the parchment nearest to hand.

'May I see?' she asked, leaning forward to look.

'You may not,' he returned, turning away from her. 'Everything in these writings is sacred to me.'

'But you will give me some seeds when you find them?' she wheedled.

'Why should I? I am quite capable of countering my Wych's waywardness by other means, if need be …'

He tailed off, having just discovered the identification of Stillbind that he was looking for – and was keeping the fact to himself.

Mergyn sighed resignedly. 'So you are determined not to help me. I am to be withered and wannioned in retribution for the crime of loving you above all others. Without me all your problems would be resolved, wouldn't they?' She rose. 'Come, I wish to be escorted to my new retreat in Queen's Glade; I will not journey through the Scathe unassisted.'

He sprang up, dropping the roll, and stood between her and the only exit.

'You will go at *my* pleasure, not yours,' he threatened. 'Our Liege has no sovereignty over *my* Retreat.'

He flashed his Wand in an arc before her eyes, and the Queen collapsed inertly to the floor. Black Wand looked down on her with a little smile of triumph. She probably thought he would never dare abuse his privilege in such a way, or she would never have walked so confidently into the trap. He felt justified, however, because he only wanted what was lawfully his. He knelt at her side and opened the pouches of her belt to find ... nothing. Then looked up to realise the Queen's eyes were open and watching him with withering disdain. She had not passed out for a second.

He got quickly to his feet and turned away to hide his vexation that she had doubly fooled him.

Mergyn rose. 'How true it is that good so often comes of evil. We both now know that your Wand has no power over me. Nevertheless, it was well that I took precautions,' and she tapped her empty belt significantly.

He dare not trust himself to answer, but she had not finished with him.

'Am I to make a hasty and ungainly descent alone, O my sorely mortified love? Or will you have the gallantry to descend with me in your arms so that I may land more gracefully?'

He mastered his feelings with an indifferent shrug, but came to her side nevertheless.

She smiled her thanks, and then said gravely: 'Should you not restore your magic Seal, dear one? Or how will you be warned of other inquisitive intruders?'

He hated being reminded, but she was right. He drew the Seal and then, with his arms around her, dropped light as a feather to the floor of the shaft.

*

Mergyn was well pleased. By taking her down with him through his own Seal drawn with a Wand which had proved powerless against her, he had provided her with a way back – unknown to him – at any time she wished. She had also fooled him that she had hidden the Girdle and the Elixir elsewhere before her arrival at the Mount. She had actually returned them to their original place in the false bottom of his silver box whilst he had been so busily digging. It would be the last place he would think of looking.

Myrddin should have realised that Merlyn's Fairest of All Fair, with thousands of years of experience, would have no equal in the art of guile. But she knew he couldn't bring himself to believe that she really had become the Queen, not even when she stooped to recover the minute fungus she had thrown down from above and put it into a pouch before his eyes.

They re-entered the Great Hall together, and passed through it with a courtly word to the Master, who was relieved to see the two together. It appeared to indicate that all was well.

Their unhurried walk through the Weal might have been romantic if it had not been necessary for the Wychy to twitch aside the inquisitive coils of Scathe. Their presence was a reminder of the need for watchful eyes on The Wandle.

*

Myrddin's mental survey of the Weal discovered Ann hurrying to Wych's Lane. Now that he knew her intention, he felt distressed that she was making such a hash of her Weird-weaning, and annoyed that he had to interfere in something that was private to her. But he needed a supply of the Bane himself.

At the door of her new retreat, Mergyn said: 'If you can spare the time, dear Wychy, why not step in and have a look round? No strings attached, I promise. Not this time, anyway.'

'Some other time, perhaps,' he replied tersely, and left her.

*

When Ann found he had followed her into Wych's Barn intent on reaping the Bane himself, she was scandalised.

'Brother Wand, how dare you! You know these trees are a sacred trust of mine alone.'

'Merlyn planted these trees himself *and* grafted in the Dwindling Root that stunts their growth,' he countered.

'It's still *my* province,' she cried angrily. 'Wherever you learnt their origin, it's still the law that the Bane is my prerogative.'

'It is also the law,' he said sternly, 'that it shall be given only to those who earnestly desire it from you – never to anyone who neither wishes nor needs it. I have recently been told that you intend putting an end to our Liege's Queen with a gift of dosed wine. You shall not do this, O wayward One.'

It was impossible for Ann to deny the charge. 'And who are *you* to talk, who have slept with Alder's Queen?'

Knowing the evidence against him made any denial pointless, he ignored the accusation, and went on. 'The Queen has been warned, so it would be better not to try it – someone else might get hurt.'

'Before long, the Queen must come to me begging for the Bane. Even she cannot flout the law forever that to love a Wychy or Wych means the road to mortality.'

'And neither can Hetty, whom *you* so waywardly sent to the Wealspring.'

'That is true – and I am sincerely sorry, beloved Wand,' she owned unhappily. 'But this waywardness is not of *my* design.'

'Nor mine!'

'No? Aren't you being just as weirdly as I am wayward? Who invited Hetty to his feet – and Stella also? You have made these things possible. All I did was to act ahead of time. We are both in error, Brother Wand.'

'Perhaps. But *you* most of all. Who was it went prying into my personal secrets *and* wandled our innocent Master of Gnomes into betraying things he had no right to talk about?' And Myrddin began to attack a spruce with pretended annoyance. With the tip of his Wand he upturned a segment of bark.

She flew at him with lifted Wand. 'By Mona's light, you shall not steal what is mine.'

He turned, lowering his own Wand. 'All right, strike me, I won't defend myself.'

'Then stop what you're doing,' she cried, lowering her Wand, almost weeping.

He plucked out a bunch of the deadly berries before she could stop him, tucked it under his Weird and strode off back to The Wandle where he shut himself away in his Retreat.

He needed time and space to think through all he had gleaned from Merlyn's legacy in the Mount before Mergyn's arrival had interrupted him.

He knew now how to produce babies without the aid of Girdle or Elixir; the material was all around him in the astral forms of plants, trees, birds and animals. By using this kind of plasma, he could fashion a semblance of anything he wanted and even, with the addition of human ectoplasm and certain other materials, the more solid appearance and height of a human being – just as Merlyn had done himself.

Driven by excitement and curiosity, he decided to experiment on two fay sized creations to start with. He would name them Weirdless and Wistful. The former would be his private name for a fay-sized Nebuchadnezzar, with Wistful his sleeping Queen, Aíssa – invested with Hetty's wandled wraith!

He needed to make them in secret, but the necessity of producing the two of them on cue in the Weal made *Woe Begone!* his best choice. He also needed containers for the plant plasma, so he called Rozyn.

How large are your vats and stills, noble Vintner?

Some of them wands wide, wands high, Black One. Our skilful gnomes make them for me as I need.

Then request two more, dear Rozyn, three wands long, two wands wide and one wand high, and ask the Master to deliver them to you no later than noon after the next sunrise. I'll tell you when you can bring them privately to Woe Begone!.

Myrddin was now so obsessed with the wonder and potential of the new magic that nothing was going to be too much trouble, nor deter him from producing the most astounding tableau the fae had ever seen. He ignored the tiny prick of doubt that asked what it had to do with saving them from the doomed forest – he was sure he was doing the right thing in broadening their horizons and preparing them for change.

CHAPTER 13

ALDER GOES SAILING

Myrddin set off for the village a little before dawn. He had decided to visit Sir Edward's comprehensive library for a picture of Nefertiti on which to model the Sleeping Queen. He also hoped to gain some ideas on Chaldean dress for Nebuchadnezzar.

Again, he had no difficulty getting into the Manor. Ivy provided the means of reaching a slightly open top window on the ground-floor to Sir Edward's study and taking a flying leap down to his desk. From that height he had a good view of the bookshelves lining the dark panelled walls to see what there might be on Egyptology.

When he came across the title *Tutankhamen*, he levitated it off the shelf to land squarely on the floor, jumped down and flicked through the pages with his Wand. When he found the pictured bust of the Queen he was looking for, he committed it to memory by imagining how he would mould and delineate the features line by line.

Bounding back up on the desk to look for the next book he was after, his eye caught something he should have seen earlier – a memo pad with a heading in Chaldean characters spelling Am-Mar-El-Lin. He turned for a closer look and found notes on everything that the Weir Lord had discovered concerning the threat to the forest's existence. Sir Edward had left it out in the hope that Black Wand might pay him another visit. Scanning the entries, the Wychy frowned with deepening consternation. The Ministry of Town and

Country Planning appeared to be pushing ahead with its plans far more quickly than he had ever realised. Dated the previous evening, it read:

> *Late afternoon, a party of Surveyors arrived in the village and have put up at The Dragon. As no advice of their coming has been given to me, it is obvious my feelings are not to be consulted, but I shall make it my duty to find out everything that I can.*

The next entry, timed later at 11 pm, read:

> *I have learned from Pop Ashwick, proprietor of The Dragon that the Survey party has now been joined by an architect and several building executives from whom tenders for the work will be invited. This is another severe blow that neither time nor obstacles will deter the Ministry from its objective. This becomes more apparent since I have just received a telephone call from Ashwick advising me that the survey of the Woe will begin tomorrow. Two Land Rovers will carry the gear and equipment into this part of the forest and, providing the weather continues fine, they anticipate completing their check of existing measurements before sundown. Oh, Black Wand, hurry! If I receive no sign from you before morning, I will deposit these sheets in the stricken oak, as I have before. My heart is in anguish.'*

Myrddin placed a small golden tick against the last entry, and was again about to look for the book he wanted when the door opened and Sir Edward gradually entered the study in pyjamas and dressing gown. Seeing the book on the floor, he tut-tutted and lifted it back to its place on the shelf, before taking a seat at the desk. Myrddin then had to wait patiently while the Weir Ward picked up a pen and pulled the memo pad towards him. He reached his last entry and stared in astonishment at the little gold tick. With a sigh of grateful relief, he headed the day's date and wrote:

Mona be praised! But Wizard, are you still here? The most terrible news of all came to me at midnight. Had I known you were coming, I would have entered it straight away. If only I knew whether you are still here –

Black Wand gently struck the pen aside and added a tiny tick to the last word. Sir Edward stared amazedly directly into the Wychy's eyes without seeing him, before continuing with now-trembling fingers ...

Among the surveyors is a certain James Durant, nephew of Sir Angus Durant, the President of the Royal Botanical Society, a man who has repeatedly requested my permission to secure specimens of the reeds that grow in Dragon's Woe. I have constantly refused, but now learn he has suborned his nephew to secure one for him in the course of his official mission. How can I prevent this man from inviting death by drawing the Dragon's Teeth? Only your protective Wand, surely, has power to divert this innocent man from destruction?

Again, Black Wand flicked the pen aside and wrote in gold so quickly it appeared almost instantaneous:

Fear not, beloved Weir Ward; the responsibility shall be mine. Even if the mortal dies, the stain shall be on my Weird, not yours.

Did you come for the book I found on the floor?

I've finished with that one, thank you. Have you anything on Assyrian dress, please?

I have pictures of Assyrian bas relief carving only.

Please!

A few minutes later Myrddin was racing back to the forest, leaving the Weird Lord scratching his head in wonder at how pictures of Egyptian and Assyrian artefacts were going to help him to save the forest.

*

The Wychy felt certain that James Durant would put his professional duties first that morning, and possibly use his lunch break for the attempt on Dragga's Teeth. He therefore made his way to *Woe Begone!* where a crowd of fae followed, eager to tell him all about the events of the previous day when he had been absent during the building of the Queen's new retreat.

'... And below is *the* most wonderful chamber,' said Dina. 'They say the babe will be born there. *Please*, Black Wand, *when* will that be?'

'Everything in its own good time, little one,' he reproved gently. 'There will be other marvels before that day comes; some great, some small, but all never seen in our forest before.'

'Oh, Black Wand, please tell us one of them?' begged Smye. 'Just one – one little one?'

'On the contrary, dear Smye, I shall tell you a big one. The sleeping Queen that King Nebuchadnezzar is seeking shall soon appear to us all in person when I next tell you how the hidden temple is found and opened.'

There was a chorus of: 'O-o-ooh!'

'What will she look like?' demanded Jean.

'I'm glad you asked, dear one, because she won't look anything like us. She is from a different race – but she will be beautiful, I promise you – very, very beautiful.'

When several disappointed fae turned up to report that Queen Gwen was unexpectedly absent from her lovely new residence, the Wychy felt bound to remind them that she could hardly spend all day and every day with them in the Weal. 'Don't you think that the King will be lonely without her?' he asked reproachfully.

Later, when Black Wand was busily organising the glass containers off Rozyn's dray and into *Woe Begone!*, Ann's voice broke in on him privately – although sounding distant in more ways than one: *Brother Wand, our Liege has expressed a wish to be with his people this day, and he and Queen Gwen are sailing towards the meeting of the Weirds in the King's barge. He requests permission to sail on through the Weird that is yours and mine. I have no reason to say not. What say you, Merlyn's Heir?*

I'm coming! he answered as silently and shot off at once in the direction of Wandleside.

Seeing him leave so quickly, the fae streamed after him. Something marvellous must have occurred, they thought, or was about to.

*

When Myrddin arrived at the head of Windaway, the Royal Barge was already stationary at the narrows of Weirdsmeet, and on the opposite side his Wych was deep in curtsey. Enthroned on the Barge, Alder and his Queen smiled up in greeting at their Wychy's rapid descent towards them. The loving smiles on the faces of their King and Queen presented a united message for the fae.

They were taking it that the cherished babe was in being and Alder and his Queen were beaming their thankful gratitude at the magician who had made it all possible.

'Oh, Black Wand ...' cried Dina, and threw her arms round him almost swooning in wonder and reverence. 'Oh, greatest of great Wands – '

He passed her rapidly into the arms of Edmund him. Alder was speaking:

'Beloved Wands,' called the King. 'Your permission to sail upon your Weird over joys me, It would delight me even more if you would both accompany us ...?'

It seemed a natural response on Alder's part, but neither Wych nor Wychy realised just then how near his end the King felt, and that he really did want to enjoy a last sight of his domain.

Ann waited till her partner arrived beside her, then both joined the party in the Royal Barge.

'We would like to go the Wynn,' explained Mergyn. 'Our Liege has never visited the Mansion of the Gnomes. The Master and his Brethren are gathering at the southern point of the Weird to greet us.'

So now was every fay in the forest, since the gnomes were broadcasting the news far and wide. Myrddin could only think how late in the morning it was by then, and near to James Durant's lunch break. The Wychy was grimly glad he had given Sir Edward no guarantee of saving the man's life.

He could see the Queen sensed something was troubling him, but as his habitually veiled expression gave nothing away, she obviously intended nothing to spoil her day with Alder. She was pointing out little details around them for his attention.

'... Oh, my Liege, even the hue of the water is different here to your Weird,' she laughed happily. 'See, the wavelets glint with black and silver as if reflecting the mantles of our beloved Wands. And, look, Magpies, black and white, fly above us, Is it true, dear Wych, that magpies are the only birds that nest on The Wandle?'

'That is true, dear Queen,' replied White Wand. 'Even our spiders and beetles and other insects are either black or white, and of species unknown outside The Wandle.'

Myrddin had not attempted to join in the conversation, but had to reply when Mergyn asked him the colour of Dragga's Weird.

'It is black, O Queen, flecked with green where the fangs of our enemy wait near the surface.' He spoke urgently, wishing she would pick up on some kind of warning. He went on: 'The bed of the Weird is made up of jagged outcrops of black rocks. These are Dragga's teeth and act like jagged knives. Between them and the reeds no swimmer can hope to survive.'

He thought he had succeeded, as his words brought a serious look to her eyes, but then was obviously not the time for questions. The fae were dancing riotously down the descending height of Wandleside to the Wynn, singing, waving, blowing kisses, embracing each other and jumping up and down with joy.

The gnomes expressed their feelings even more lavishly when King and Queen came ashore. On their knees, their faces bright with happiness, they held their arms outstretched in eager welcome.

Myrddin continued to chafe with frustration as the procession moved on into the Mansion. He was also plagued with a fear that someone might say something about the Temple of the Sleeping Beauty. He knew his Wych was itching to find out about it and, in her present state of waywardness; he wouldn't put it beyond her to say something to Alder that would force the Wychy into revealing it.

The last person he expected to raise the subject was Alder himself. But, when invited to choose something he would like from the huge array of treasures the gnomes piled up before him, Alder smiled his bemusement and startled everyone by saying: 'Beloved Master, Brethren and People, I truly find myself akin to King Nebuchadnezzar. I have everything I desire, so how shall I choose anything that will outshine so much?'

Ann seized on it immediately. 'Perchance, my Liege, as happened to Nebuchadnezzar, the Spirits of the Earth have kept a secretly slumbering Queen for you?'

Alder smiled and placed his hand on Mergyn's, who returned him a deeply loving look. 'I have no need of such, beloved Wych,' he replied softly.

And the packed gathering melted into blissful sighs with the added signature and seal to what they all fondly believed – with the exception of Myrddin. He could only think how wickedly the Queen was deceiving their revered King.

Rozyn then arrived with Barnsley aboard the dray. He came forward to present the royal pair with a loving cup he had prepared for them. And Barnsley, in his first official appearance, knelt to present a similar cup to the Wands. Myrddin could appreciate the extraordinary change there was in the wicca. Surely his Wych could be forgiven her waywardness? But she passed the cup to him with a guilty and apologetic look in her eyes. He ignored it and returned the cup to Barnsley.

The whole occasion had become a farce for the Wychy; a hollow hypocrisy organised by the Queen from which he couldn't get away soon enough. Since she had cast the die in the matter of the babe, then babe there would be. But to secure it there would be such wandling as no Wychy had ever performed before.

He became aware of something nagging at the edge of his consciousness – a fiendish sense of razor-edged reeds sharpening their blades for a coming kill – James Durant!

White Wand had turned to him with a shudder. 'Brother, we should go,' she whispered, 'Dragga has been ... disturbed –'

'Too late to need the both of us,' he answered grimly. 'Wait here.'

He rose quickly and went on one knee before the King, 'My Liege, there is an emergency that requires my attention. With your permission?'

Alder consented at once. Whilst Ann watched her partner's departure with an apprehensive expression. Mergyn however, diverted everyone's attention by lightly reminding Alder that he still had a choice to make and held up several of the treasures with admiring comments and the moment of tension evaporated.

CHAPTER 14

DRAGGA'S TEETH

Swiftly back on The Wandle, Myrddin made for the side overlooking the long expanse of Dragga and the treacherous swamp on the far bank, its extent well defined by a stout barbed wire fence and warning notices.

A Land Rover parked on the crest of the ridge above told him that James had arrived. The sight, however, of a lone man in bathing trunks crawling across the marsh inside the barrier made the Wychy almost rub his eyes in disbelief. Although Angus Durant had no doubt warned his nephew to keep the operation secret, it was difficult to credit that the man had come without rope or any kind of back-up support. The only help he appeared to be relying on was a heavy gardening fork, which he was using as a hold, laying across the tussocks in front of him as he went. Every now and then he was lifting himself up to see how far he was from the water's edge. He was already plastered in slime, and the clumps of grass he aimed for were becoming unreliable, the slick, thick, smooth reeds slipping under his muddied hands. The last clump he reached gave way abruptly under his weight plunging him face down in the soft, smelly mud. He struggled up, gasping and spitting, trying to wipe it away from his eyes and pushing now for clear water, still hanging onto the fork like grim death.

Myrddin knew that Dragga's victim had long passed the point of no return before he had arrived. And now, choking and gurgling with the water and slime that rushed into his open mouth, James Durant slid from view beneath the surface.

Myrddin winced at the razor-sharp, knife-like slashes that were scoring across the threshing limbs; while the hands that clutched at trailing reeds were sliced through to the bone. The Wychy watched the black water brighten red, then turned away, thankful that Ann had obeyed him and been spared the sight and felt a sharp, cold anger towards the uncle whose selfish ambition had caused such a wanton and tragic death.

It was the Queen's fault, too, he decided. If she hadn't staged that absurd charade, he and Ann would have been there in time while the young man was still the right side of the fence and could have caused him to forget what he had come for – and to keep on forgetting every time he might remember and return.

He wondered how soon anyone would miss his or her colleague. Indeed, would anyone even know he had gone anywhere that lunchtime? He knew that once the Weir Ward learned that James was missing, he would direct the searchers. The locals knew that Dragon's Woe cast the remains of its victims out from the southern end of its Weir where the Spinner joined the continuation of the River Weir, and that it took twelve hours to wash such leftovers down to shallow water for finding and collecting.

By the time he returned to his Retreat on The Wandle, everyone had left the Gnomes' Mansion to troupe off to Queen's Glade, where Alder was being entertained in the Queen's new residence. Myrddin took advantage of the diversion by making for Merlin's Mount to regain the scrolls he had had to leave there. Hetty was still sleeping peacefully, quite impervious to cold or damp. He dropped a kiss on her forehead.

'Not long now, little one,' he promised, 'and you shall be a Queen yourself.'

In the Great Hall, he took the opportunity of retrieving Merlyn's ring from its hiding place behind the tapestry and hung it over his arm below his Weird. He had not yet worked out just how he was supposed to use it. Merlyn had written of being 'unable to come again through it' to attain his human stature after Mergyn stole it, but even the elf sized Myrddin doubted he could get his head through it.

*

He decided to put it to the test outside his Retreat on The Wandle. Feeling a little absurd, he removed his tall jet crown, placed the ring on his head, and gasped.

The sensation was of being sucked into a vortex, and exploded out at the other end as a giant. He barely had time to register that he was wearing a brown robe tied at the waist with a thick cord, his feet in sandals and carrying a thick staff in his hand before he was back as he had been. The ring lay at his feet and his crown nowhere to be seen. This was worrying until, picking up the ring; he found his jet crown had been lying in its centre. Experiment assured him he had no need to remove the crown anymore than he needed to take off any clothing. Everything vanished in the ring, except the ground on which it lay, which appeared oddly colourless. This was when he realised for the first time that when he picked it up, even his hand and arm must have disappeared through it but, carrying it under his Weird, he hadn't noticed because he could still feel them.

It was clear that Merlyn had enchanted the ring with the human form he had made either with it or for it, and that that form was still there, even if the magician wasn't. It also dawned on him that Merlyn would have worn the thumb ring all the time he needed to appear mortal, and reverted to fae as soon as he took it off. Myrddin hadn't put the ring on his thumb, so had returned to his usual elfin self almost at once, and his crown had only disappeared because the ring had fallen over it.

But how and why the clothes? he wondered. Mortal years previously, when he had wished himself back as a human; the change hadn't included clothing of any kind. He could still remember how sore the bramble scratches had felt all over his naked body.

He tried the ring again with his crown on, became the six-foot-tall monk, found the ring in the grass at his feet and put it on. It fitted his thumb perfectly, and he stayed as he was.

This time he was able to appreciate the difference from the time he had gone back previously to being human. There was none of the red mist and heaviness that had enveloped him then. This shape felt stronger, lighter and easier.

What an incredibly wonderful gift! he thought, his mind so full of it that it was difficult to think of anything else. Looking about him, however, he could see nothing of the faerie world. The density of Merlyn's creation separated him from the faerie vision of vivid colour that glowed in every living thing, although his sense of smell had returned bringing the scents of earth and the sharp clean aroma of the surrounding pines keenly to his nose. Everything around him was also in motion. The wind stirred trees, the swiftness of insects and birds – all verified that he was experiencing it at the speed of mortal time.

Remembering the brambles, he tried scratching himself with a fir-cone – it produced a weal and hurt, but not painfully and soon disappeared. It seemed he had inherited a miracle of the enchanter's art; physical enough to be seen and heard as a mortal but, remembering Mergyn's fate, also subject to disintegration under sustained attack.

Removing the ring brought instant reduction again to the faerie world of towering trees and overhead bracken; melodious sound and vibrant colour, where intoxicating waves of energy surged up from secret springs below and, for him, a new awareness of the discordances radiating from his recent encounters with the Queen and White Wand. Like the faint tremors of a coming upheaval, they were reminding him that time was short. He took the ring with him into his Retreat and sat down to think and study. And further reading of Merlyn's scrolls revealed a possible explanation of the monk's composition.

Whereas Weirdless and Wistful, plus their clothing, could be fashioned from astral plant plasma, the monk's form appeared to have needed the elastic properties of human electoplasm. It seemed the stuff had a miraculous capacity to expand and contract. It further appeared that Merlyn had grown the manikin for his ring from actual human sperm and ova in some kind of ancient IVF program known only to him. Myrddin was grateful not to have to emulate the enchanter in that respect. 'What the heart doesn't know, it doesn't grieve about,' he muttered devoutly.

Continuing to read, he learnt that the magician had also extracted certain of the DNA, replacing it with some other kind, plus an inclusion of Errant Weed, Stillbind and Dwindling Root to ensure its immortality.

Armed with so much new know-how, Myrddin made for *Woe Begone!* in the dark hours of the interregnum to prepare for the creation of Weirdless and Wistful, and called in to see the Master of Gnomes on the way.

It had occurred to him, when White Wand had tried to initiate a discovery of Merlin's Mount that he needed to focus everyone's attention on a temple somewhere else. It would never do to leave Hetty where she was.

Like the Wychy, Omric did not sleep during the interregnum, so they had time to discuss the Wychy's plan without interruption.

The Master was delighted with the idea of excavating a short tunnel leading from the hollow beech tree of *Woe Begone!* to a mound a few mortal feet away. This would allow Black Wand to come and go with all the necessary advice on excavating the mound to accommodate the kind of temple he wanted Omric to build within it.

They agreed certain aspects were be kept secret, but that the Wychy would see to it that everyone was going to know that it would be an exact replica of the Temple of Nebuchadnezzar's Queen and that, when opened, all would be allowed in to witness her miraculous awakening.

Just how the Wychy was planning to transport the sleeping Queen from Merlin's Mount to the new Temple remained Myrddin's own undisclosed business.

Omric promised the work would begin at sun-up.

*

When he left the Master, the Wychy felt satisfied that, with the work in progress and the gnomes diving in and out of the construction like a swarm of bees, speculation would remain at fever pitch and allow him to concentrate on his own occupation in peace. He then harvested all the plasma material he needed during the remainder of the interregnum when there was only his Wych to puzzle over what he was up to on the Weal.

Inside *Woe Begone!* he put the astral substance in the crystal containers he had received from Rozyn and, following Merlyn's instructions worked carefully on the two figures with Wand, will, and some considerable manual dexterity. When it came to clothing, he needed imagination as well. He gave Wistful, the sleeping queen fashioned to resemble

Nefertiti, a full-length ancient Egyptian gown in white and gold, and a folded headdress in blue and gold. Weirdless, the Chaldean King, he decked in a long high-necked gown ornamented in gold, encircled with a gem-laden belt, and scarlet cloak. A three-tier crown topped the Assyrian's head of heavily-waved black hair with its fringe of flat curls, and finished the jaw line with a narrow square-cut black beard. It was then he realised that Nebuchadnezzar would need some attendants.

This didn't present a problem. They would be wraithless automatons – unlike the two lead characters. It simply meant a lot more work.

CHAPTER 15

SAVED FROM THE BANE

When Ann received the plea: 'Am I welcome, Sister Wand?' she responded with joyful thankfulness that her Brother Wand was more than welcome.

Their need for reconciliation made a glorious ecstasy of the time they came together, which should have healed the rift between them, except she sensed something alien in him that had never been there before.

'If I didn't know it to be impossible, Brother Wand, I would have thought you possessed by something mortal.' She said it teasingly, but his immediately veiled look of shock at her intuition was enough, and they were back to square one. 'You *are* hiding something,' she said, her frustration driving her to destroy their new found peace. 'Like a lot of other things lately,' she went on accusingly. 'For instance, the coming Babe? You promised our Liege that we would accomplish *that* magic together because he laid it upon us both. How am I to account to our people for its miraculous conception when I can't even tell them when the birth shall be?'

'All I can assure you is that the whole thing is as much a mystery to me as it is to you, beloved Wych. Ask the Queen; she's the only one who knows the answer to *that* one – and this I swear by Mona's Eye.'

'You mean *you* have no idea of how, when or where this phenomenal conception occurred?' she asked incredulously.

He looked amused. '"Phenomenal" must be about the right word for it. No, I haven't the faintest idea. As I say, you will have to ask the Queen.'

'I will,' she promised, thoroughly perplexed.

'So be it, then. And now I really have to leave, beloved Wych. Sunné's well up and the Master of Gnomes is waiting for vital instructions on building the Secret Temple – '

'That's another thing! You know how unlawful it is to wandle any of our people unbeknown to me. Yet you speak of producing the sleeper *and* Nebuchadnezzar. So who are you using to impersonate these creatures of your mind?'

Black Wand, smiling hugely, took her in his arms and murmured with warm reassurance: 'When that day dawns, O queenliest of Wands, I promise not one of your sacred charges shall be missing from your list of living wraiths. And if I should lie, may Mona wither my Weird and my Wand discard me.' He kissed her fondly again, and left.

She watched his departing figure and wondered why she felt less than reassured.

*

Myrddin found the gnomes busily at work on the tunnel, which meant he could collect Hetty from the Mansion without their knowing and install her in *Woe Begone!*. But first he needed a top-secret session with Barnsley, so strode off to the Wynn where he found the transformed fay at work, his past obnoxiousness gone.

This pleased Black Wand enormously, and he privately paid tribute to whomever it was who had the idea of apprenticing the wicca to the Royal Vintner. It was the last appointment he would ever have thought of making himself.

'Remember, little brother, that you once journeyed to the Wealspring, and drank and made a wish …?' he began.

Barnsley shook his head, remembering nothing. When Myrddin revived the memory, the fay looked troubled and apprehensive. The Wychy could see he felt appalled at having demanded the love of his counterpart, and was now scared that he was about to be punished for the temerity. But Myrddin smiled reassuringly.

'Don't be afraid, Barney,' he said. 'Every fay knows that such a wish is unbreakable. It is the right of every wicca to demand this wonderful form of euthanasia.'

'B-but, B-Black Wand,' stammered the wicca, terrified. 'I don't. It is not my True Wish, anymore. I should never have made it at all. I love our Lady of The Wandle, as do we all, but I have no *wish* to go back to mortality. I might have done once – but not now.' He fell on his knees, pleading with clasped hands. 'Oh, Black Wand, mightiest of all mighty magicians, please, please, save me!'

Black Wand let him think that he was giving the matter serious consideration, before replying regretfully. 'Neither my Wych nor I may set a Wealspring wish aside, dear Barney. Once uttered, it must be granted.'

'Then I shall take the Mortal Sickness,' moaned the wicca. 'I feel it already upon me. Oh, is it so wicked that I should be afraid to leave the little kingdom?'

'I spoke only about the granting of the Wish,' replied Black Wand with deliberation. 'Whether or not you then take the road to mortality will be a decision only you can make. The doom *can* be averted.'

Barnsley clutched at the straw. 'That's right,' he cried. 'You lived on, didn't you, after – after …?'

'The circumstances are hardly the same, little brother. I was already destined to succeed to the Office of the Wand, and couldn't be allowed to depart. And yet …' He allowed another thoughtful pause, 'perhaps there *is* some similarity. Tell me, if it was possible for you to escape the full finality of the doom, would you go more happily to fulfil the Wish?'

'I would indeed, Black Wand. What must I do?'

'What I am going to tell you must be secret between us, little brother – very, very secret. It needs a great enchantment that only I can do. However, providing you follow my *every* direction to the letter, I promise that you may love my Wych *and* live.'

Barnsley seized the hem of the wizard's Weird, kissing it passionately while promising incoherently to do anything and everything as instructed.

'One thing will still be necessary, little brother,' warned Black Wand. 'After leaving White Wand you *will* take the Mortal Sickness and return to her for the Bane – no, don't be worried. Have I not promised I will be on hand to deliver you? The Bane will wither you a little, but I will rescue you, and you will wake up to another new and wonderful existence still within our faerie kingdom. Perhaps you won't look quite the same as you do now, but you will have great honour, and love and respect among our people. This I promise on my sacred Wand.'

Black Wand waited in Rozyn's Retreat while Barnsley went running through the Wynn to Weal. Then, as soon as the wicca was on his way down Windaway, the Wychy made off to the empty Mansion of the Gnomes.

He brought Hetty's unconscious form down from Merlin's Mount, through the tunnel and into the Great Hall where he erased all previous memory of the tunnel from her mind, so that she returned to consciousness exactly where he pinpointed.

'Have you found it?' she asked, opening her eyes.

'Found what, Little One?'

'What you were looking for when we came here? You said – '

'So I did, Bright-eyes, And no, it isn't here, after all. But I know now that I shall find it at that certain fairyland that

Never-Was but which by my magic I shall bring into being especially for you, my love …'

*

When White Wand saw her partner and Hetty walking in the Weal together again, and heard the astonished cry at their appearance on the forest telegraph, she was equally surprised. But she had little time to think about it as she was watching Barnsley's approach with concern, but heartfelt relief. The guilt she had felt at betraying his Wealspring Wish had plagued her unmercifully. It was obvious from the purity of his star, however, that he was now a very different wicca. She could only attribute the miracle to Black Wand, and be grateful to his kindness for easing her path. So when Barnsley sang his Song of Longing as sweetly and plaintively as the most well-bred wicca might have done, she very lovingly translated him to The Wandle and guided him to her.

*

Inside *Woe Begone!*, Myrddin enfolded Hetty in his Weird and whispered: 'Are you ready to enter the Fairyland of Never-Was, beloved?'

She nodded, closed her eyes and became lost in the long, ecstatic and seemingly unending kiss he gave her.

When she opened her eyes, she gasped: 'This is a palace …'

'The Faery Palace that Never-Was but now most surely is,' he corrected.

'It's a dream,' she cried. 'It can't be real.'

She wasn't to know how right she was, for he was projecting into her mind the rose-marbled palace with its colonnades and engraved domed ceiling that the gnomes would be building. It seemed a good way of preparing her for what she would see when she woke up as Nefertiti.

Later, when she lay content and radiantly happy, he mesmerized her even more deeply with the continuation of the story and how she would feel and act on wakening in the Secret Temple, and what she must do when she left his couch.

He ending his instruction on a firm note. 'Now listen, Hetty. You know that we have loved in accordance with the eternal law, don't you?'

She nodded. He pressed on, 'And in consequence, you are afflicted with the Mortal Sickness?' Again, she nodded.

'Now you must go weeping to White Wand and implore the blessing of the Bane?' Another slow nod.

'Then go *now*,' he ordered. 'And, for Mona's sake – and your *own* – don't *dare* forget the other instructions I have given you – or else you will never see me again. Is that clear?'

He watched her go with some anxiety. It was vital that as many fae as possible should witness her meeting with Barnsley returning from The Wandle in the same bemused condition. There could be no argument then as to where they had gone or what had happened to them.

When the two met above Wandleside, they came to a halt, recognising each other's suffering, embraced, and wept copiously on one another's shoulders before, after a doleful kiss of commiseration, they resumed their ways.

The watching fae noted it with dismay and apprehension, and duly spread the news.

*

Hetty's mournful cries at the meeting of the Weirds aroused White Wand from the keen remorse she was feeling over Barnsley, to find another cause for spiritual agony. She had answered such cries before, but it was always harrowing.

She translated the distraught fay across the water and guided her to her Retreat. As soon as she appeared, White Wand took her in her arms, and tried to reason her out of the desire. But Hetty was too morbidly hysterical to listen. She sobbed repeatedly: 'The Bane, the Bane, the Bane, beloved Wych. It is my right; you cannot refuse it. Give me the Bane, dear Wand. I cannot bear the anguish. Please, the Bane, the Bane, the Bane …'

If Ann had had more experience, and not been so distressed herself, she might have been suspicious. According to her Rune Records, a fay came seeking the Bane starry-eyed and dying for mortality. But Hetty snatched the berries avidly from her hand, gobbled them down and then ran away as fast as she could for the Circle of Rejoicing, leaving White Wand to marvel at the awesome effect that her partner's loving had had on the distracted victim. But what greater and more passionately inspired lover was there than her own so deeply adored Wychy? And she wept afresh because all this sadness and woefulness was down to her own wayward wandling.

*

It was traditional that the eater of the Bane would make for the Circle of Rejoicing. Whether they dwindled away to a speck before they arrived there was too painful for either of the Wychies to ever to want to find out. A moment like that was sacred to the departing wraith.

In Hetty's case, she ran on blindly and seemingly in circles, whimpering all the time for Black Wand. Something terrible was happening to her. Very distantly, she heard his voice calling: 'this way … this way, Hetty …' only it seemed to be coming from all directions. He was there – but where? Her diminishing wraith tripped over her robe and fell on a bed of pine needles that looked larger than huge brown spears.

She struggled up and fell again. Enormous spiders almost as large as herself trampled by like great white mounds.

*

Black Wand, crouching beyond his side of the Circle, was nearly as desperate as she was. He called and called between barely-opened lips for fear his Wych would hear him. When he saw the shrivelled form at last staggering towards the opposite side of the Circle, falling and rising, it was all he could do not to dash across and rescue her. Had he done so, White Wand would have seen him and that would be … well, 'catastrophic' did not seem too strong a word for what she might say or do to him,

He had to will the minute scrap across the last few yards, then reach out and whisk the tiny thing up to quickly press the Stillbind into her mouth. Hoping it wasn't too late he then raced for his Retreat, where he laid her reverently on his jet-black table top.

It was some moments before he could be sure she had stopped shrinking.

Then he had to wait for Barnsley.

*

When the wicca arrived at White Wand's Retreat, his condition was almost as bad as Hetty's had been, and the Wych tried even harder to reason with him. But Barnsley was unresponsive. He just shook his head and repeated his request for the Bane, the bleak look never leaving his eyes. Unlike Hetty, he didn't take the berries at once but stared at them fearfully awhile as they lay in her palm, then looked at her and burst into tears. He took them with trembling fingers but put none in his mouth, shaking his head as if unwilling to distress her further, and walked dejectedly away.

Seeing him begin to wander dazedly, she realised he would never find his way to the Circle, so she went with him, gently guiding. When they arrived, she waited at her side of the perimeter while Barnsley walked on and went to Alder's throne. He bowed before it on bent knee, sobbing as if his heart would break, and then did the same before the Queen's throne, as if begging both for their understanding and forgiveness. It was so moving that White Wand wept.

Nothing in her records described such a thing happening. She decided she would need to incorporate it into her weaving, so that future Wands might know what to expect. Barnsley went to bow to Black Wand's seat, and then to White Wand's, where he began to place the berries one by one in his mouth. When they were gone, he laid his head on his arms on the seat and cried. White Wand could bear it no longer; she turned and ran for her Retreat to agonise with herself all over again.

*

Myrddin had seen her and, knowing how long it would take before she got there, dashed into the Circle, swept up the diminishing wraith with one sure hand, pressed the mould into the tiny mouth, and bore the now unconscious form away to join Hetty's.

*

The Wychy waited until the interregnum before taking both to *Woe Begone!*. Only the all-important and delicate process of joining the still-unconscious wraiths to their new forms remained, and it was nearly noon before he had completed the instructions given in Merlyn's thesis entitled '*On the Investment of Manikins*'.

He had just sat back to admire the results and near panic engulfed him when there came the sound of a sharp rap on the outside entrance and an imperative summons from his Wych to 'open up!' She had to speak to him.

CHAPTER 16

WHITE WAND'S VISIONS

When Mergyn appeared at her residence in Queen's Glade, White Wand had gone to meet her. 'Hael and wyn, beloved Queen,' she said, curtseying. 'I have heard so much about your new residence here in the weal, that I have come to ask if I might also be allowed to see its wonders? I would have come earlier, but my duties have kept me until now.'

Mergyn rose, extending her hand. 'Of course, dear Wych,' she said warmly. 'I would love to show you all that our brother gnomes have done for me. Come.'

The two went inside, where Mergyn began pointing out in fond delight some of the less obvious details, although she said nothing about one of the most artistic pieces in it – a silver cabinet containing an even wider selection of Rozyn's concoctions than the Black One was said to have. She was not being malicious. For Ann, it was a subtle way of indicating it held no murderous potion. If there had been, she would have needed to point it out. In an illogical fashion, this convinced Ann that the Queen knew that she had come to ask about the babe; which became clear enough when Mergyn took her to the lower chamber. Showing her the bed and Mergyn remarked in an appropriately awed tone, 'I am told, dear Wych, that its design is identical with another so old that none would know its age – if it even still existed.'

'Upon which Mergyn bore Alder our Liege the King,' guessed White Wand.

'So, you know that secret, too?'

'Rozyn told me, O Queen.'

'Ah!' The exclamation suggested that that explained everything. 'It is fitting then, dear Wych that the coming Babe should be born here thus, also?'

The Queen appeared so assured of the event, White Wand had no idea what to say. Her partner had said he had no knowledge of it. Could it be possible he was deceiving both herself and the Queen?

But Mergyn was turning to her as if having suddenly made up her mind to share something. 'Listen, most beloved of Wyches.' She whispered her excitement, drawing White Wand down to sit on the bed beside her. 'I must tell you this because I can no longer keep it to myself. Two most wonderful magic things have become known – gifts from our Lady Mona that have been hidden until now against this time of dire need, when she has at last revealed them, a faerie Girdle and a celestial Elixir. I recognised them at once to be the same heavenly devices by which Merlyn and Mergyn conceived Alder, and so – '

'But where?' White Wand interrupted with astonishment. '*Who* found them where and when?'

'It was a secret box that came into our beloved Wychy's hands, dear Wych? He knew nothing about them, being more interested in certain ancient writings – '

'Golden sheets inscribed with wedge-shaped characters in a silver casket?' the Wych said quickly and, at the Queen's nod, went on: 'I was also shown them – briefly.'

'He needed their translation, dear Wych – but don't ask me what they meant, for that is your Brother Wand's business, not mine. I have it on my conscience, though, that I took advantage of his preoccupation with the records, and removed these two heaven-sent devices I've told you about, without his knowledge. It was a selfish and unthinking act, for which I am very sorry indeed. It has robbed him and yourself of the joy of presenting them to Alder and myself for the wonderful purpose for which they were made. Please, dear Wych, dare I ask *you* to tell your Brother Wand of my waywardness?'

And White Wand was more than willing, mainly because it gave her the second of two legitimate reasons for disturbing her partner in *Woe Begone!* and hopefully discovering what he was up to.

*

Of all times for gate-crashers to come pounding on the door! Myrddin thought with guilty alarm. Whatever it was his Wych had on her mind it was unlikely she would be prepared to discuss it on the doorstep, so he ditched the crystal baths he no longer needed into his end of the tunnel which the gnomes had already excavated before putting the two sleepers more carefully out of sight there also.

The noise it all made sounded chaotic, but he shut the trap to the tunnel, covered it with a rug and made sure there was nothing else visible of his handiwork before opening the door and allowing his Wych to enter.

He watched her eyes searching everywhere to find some account for the fishy-sounding delay, but seeing the simple furnishings showed nothing out of place, she launched into an opening salvo that his delay had given her plenty of time to think up.

'Brother Wand, from what I have just heard you are the simplest, most easily-beguiled wizard that eternity, in all its dubious wisdom, has ever fashioned from its inexhaustible fund of futile experiments.'

Myrddin relaxed. It didn't sound quite the kind of thing he would have expected if she had found out what he had done to Barnsley and Hetty.

'Beloved Sister Wand, I am delighted with your visit,' he said courteously. 'How can I help?'

'I bear an apology from Alder's Queen.'

'I'm speechless,' he said truthfully. 'I would never have said she would so readily admit to such a deception.'

'Then you knew?' she answered, equally astonished. 'I was told you did *not* know the secret of how to beget the babe.'

Myrddin frowned. One or other of them had hold of the wrong end of the stick.

He answered guardedly: 'I refer to the way that the Queen chose to make it apparent to our people that that the child was already conceived – when, to my knowledge; no such thing has yet happened.'

Ann returned a patronising smile. 'O deluded wizard, that's *exactly* the matter I have been asked to raise. Our beloved Queen apologises for not telling you of the existence of a magic Girdle and celestial Elixir by which the miracle will happen.' And added witheringly: 'She stole them secretly while you were studying certain other – er – secrets that night when she and you were here alone together.'

As if I didn't know, thought the Wychy. He had to give Mergyn full marks for table-turning, though. He must either tell White Wand the truth and raise a rumpus, or remain silent and look a fool.

His sister Wand went on to grind it in with both heels. 'Therefore, I say that you are surely the most easily-beguiled wizard that ever was. You have made fools of us both, since our Liege charged us with making it happen. Instead of which, if you had succeeded – which you have not – you wanted all the kudos for yourself.'

'When have I condemned you, Sister Wand, for any of your manifold wayward acts?' he asked gently.

The reminder went home, destroying her triumph and anger. She should have known that his weirdliness had been the cause of his blindness.

She reached out to him contritely. 'Forgive me, my sorely stricken brother. If I hadn't been so unhappy over Barney and Hetty, I would never have dreamed of chiding you like this. What is done, is done, and has to be accepted with good grace. What really matters is that the prophecy of the Coming is made to happen.'

He allowed his tender kiss to imply what he dare not admit – that he had no idea himself how the blessed event would ever become a *fait accompli*.

They spent a while making up, before White Wand broached her second subject. 'Dear Brother, Dragga sounded disturbed again this noontime, so I went to see what was happening – '

'Without calling me?'

'I know, it was wrong,' she said regretfully. 'But I wasn't very pleased with you for shutting yourself away so much from our people and anyway, after what has happened, I felt I could deal with it just as well as yourself – '

'You win,' he said fondly, thinking how well his Wand had weaned her Weird and become his equal. 'What was it?'

'There were mortals just beyond the fence that guards the marsh – there are now two policeman on guard at the top but they did not stop these men from coming to the fence because their officer – '

'Must be the Superintendent from Corsham,' guessed the Wychy.

She nodded. 'He came with three other men, one of whom was addressed as Mr Minister and Sir Thaddeus – '

'Lovejoy?'

'You know of this visit, then?'

'No. Only that he is the mortal most concerned with the most recent design that threatens the existence of the forest.'

'*As* I learned from their talk.' Her tone became reproachful. 'O Brother Wand, why did you keep this news from me? Am I a child, or am I your Wych?'

'Beloved, I was only hoping to get around it with my own arts. I thought it had to do with the third prophecy of the Desolation of our Lands and Weirds but, as I wasn't certain, I didn't want to say anything until I was sure.'

'So this has been the cause of all your weirdliness?' she asked. As this was what he wanted her to think, he said nothing and she went on. 'Oh, Merlyn's Heir, aren't we intended to be as one on such things? If I had only known – '

'You were not weaned – '

'I am now. And from now on, I am standing beside you against this threatened woe. Promise me?'

'I hear you. Now, please, say what you heard. I assure you it is urgent.'

'It is! Sir Thaddeus Lovejoy had come to see the deadly Weird for himself. I gather there seems to be a great outcry about it – some demanding the scheme be discontinued, others insisting it should go ahead. Great men, including Sir Thaddeus, are threatened with the loss of their position and power. There was talk of Parliamentary opposition and attack on the Government. It is clear that our forest has now become a big issue among mortals.'

'What else?'

'Sir Thaddeus is a strange mortal,' she said slowly. 'He is wilful, and does not listen to advice. He insists the draining of Dragga's Weird is a matter of urgency. He wants a dam built at the northern end of The Wandle to divert the river into King's Weird and ours only, allowing Dragga to run dry.'

'I suspected as much.'

'But how will our people come back to us without Dragga?' she cried passionately. 'Sir Thaddeus can't do this.'

'Such a man can,' he assured her grimly. 'His powers are great. He will wait until the hubbub has died down, and then secretly ensure that his plans are carried out before objectors have a chance to mount further protest – '

'But he has the wraith of a fay himself,' she interrupted.

Myrddin almost whistled his surprise, and demanded more information. Ann was able to tell him that Lovejoy was so determined on the project that he had arranged to stay at the home of a friend near Corsham until the fate of the forest was sealed.

'Daughter of Mergyn, you know it is against the law for Wands to wandle mortals …?' he proposed hesitantly.

'Of course I do. But when a mortal has an immortal wraith …?'

He sealed their tacit understanding with another kiss, and then chuckled. 'Light of my eyes, are you wayward, or am I weirdly?'

'I don't care,' she answered softly. 'So long as we act as one, you and I, I will happily submit to whatever vengeance Mona may devise in her wisdom.'

'So be it, beloved,' he murmured, kissing her again in fervent triumph. Any time in the future that he needed to take a trip to Three Weirs, or anywhere else, he would be able to do so as openly as he wished, with 'Lovejoy' as the password between them.

'Tell me, beloved,' Ann wheedled. 'Who will be the principal actors in your story when it appears?'

'They are privately named Wistless and Weirdless,' he confessed without hesitation. 'But they will be known to our people as Queen Aíssa and King Nebuchadnezzar.'

'Wistless …? Weirdless …? These names speak of magic, Brother Wand. Enchantment without limit.'

'That's right, Light of my Eyes! Limitless enchantment for our people. My magic has grown somewhat these past days, so there will be no difficulty beguiling our people's eyes with simulations such as these.'

'Simulations ...?' she repeated wonderingly. 'But why? To what purpose? I will certainly be attending this pageant,' she warned. 'And shall require a personal introduction to these "*simulations*".'

'I wouldn't have it any other way, Beloved. It would be most unfortunate if you were absent from an occasion at which our Liege and his Lady will be present.'

'But that would make it a state occasion!' Ann sounded incredulous.

'And necessarily so. We have a foreign monarch coming to seek a hidden treasure within our Kingdom.' Then he saw it begin to dawn on her just how much she had underestimated the seriousness with which he was treating the whole business. To go to such lengths made it no longer a story to delight the fae, but a factual presentation of such importance that Alder himself had to be drawn into it.

Clearly it was all too baffling for words so she reverted to a more legitimate subject. 'In the matter of Lovejoy, Brother Wand. Will you slay him with the Woe?'

He smiled. 'I ask you,' he teased, 'could any Wychy ask for a more fully weaned Wych of The Wandle than one that would dare ask such a question?' And speaking of questions, I think it is more than time that I introduced you to the Oracle of our people and let you ask of it what you will.'

*

She followed him to the Circle of Rejoicing and to the great throne of Alder draped in its rich scarlet covering.

'It was the Last-Wych-That-Was that showed me this, my love, and now in turn, I reveal it to you,' said Black Wand, folding the drape reverently to one side, before drawing his Wych down to kneel at his side before the crystal block.

'What do you see?' he asked. To his surprise, she answered at once:

'A most awesome-looking eye.'

He could only suppose it had come so readily to her because he was there with her, yet he could see nothing try as he might. He realised it might well be because he had not come prepared with any overwhelming question. Beside him, however, White Wand gave a startled gasp.

'Oh! I see a monk sitting at a rough oak table, writing,' she said, and went on: 'It must be a long time ago because he's using a quill and there's a odd-looking earthenware pot of ink … I can't see what he's writing, though … now it's gradually fading and something else comes … Oh!' she said again, after a moment's silence. 'It's an owl – a pure white owl. It's very still, though,' she added, frowning, 'I don't think it's a live one – but it isn't stuffed either. Now that's fading away and – Ah! This *is* alive. It's an otter and it's dripping wet so it looks dark in colour but silvery grey at the same time –'. She broke off with a little laugh to clap her hands in delight. 'Everything is in is motion here. It's lovely, the river sings, the leaves of the willow trees twinkle and their branches sigh …' She sighed herself as the vision faded and a new one took a steady form. Once more, she gave a little cry with a quick intake of breath. 'It's a pure white unicorn. It races gracefully over the grass, nodding its horn. It turns now and is galloping towards a hill. But it is changing – melting – turning itself into one of those chalk effigies of horses – Oh!' she ended. Instead of fading unhurriedly away, the vision disappeared with such abruptness that she started back with shock. 'It's gone,' she cried turning to her partner. 'Everything's gone.'

From his own experience, Myrddin knew the Oracle had spoken. There would be nothing more to see.

'You must have asked a question?' he prompted in wonder. 'Something you wanted to know very much? Can you remember what it was?'

'Why, yes,' she answered at once. 'When you said it was the Oracle of our people, I took it for granted that it would show us how we should expect help to come. I'm sure it has shown us, but I don't understand what the pictures mean, or *how* they can help.'

'They are symbols,' he assured her. 'Their meaning will become clear with time. We'll recognise them when they happen.'

He stood, drawing her to her feet, and kissed her. 'I confess you more wyché than I am, Sister Wand. It would never have occurred to me to ask such a wonderfully simple and obvious question …'

CHAPTER 17

THE BOOK OF AMARANTHUS

Back in his Retreat on The Wandle, the Wychy felt he couldn't wait to visit Sir Edward in the guise of Merlyn's monk and learn more of what was happening in the outside world. He also wanted to know where Sir Thaddeus lived.

This time, he warned his Wych where he was going – although not how – and that he might be away some time.

*

The appearance that evening of the outlandish-looking, sandaled monk with a large amethyst ring on the thumb of a hand holding a stout staff sent a flustered maid at Weir Court rushing to the Weir Lord. Myrddin followed to hear her gasping:

'Oh sir, There's ever such a strange man asking to see you. He looks like a hermit or something. He's in the hall now, sir. I said you were at dinner. He said to say "Augustus Autrey" – but he doesn't *look* like Mr Gus, at all – not as I remembers him.'

'Good heavens,' exclaimed Sir Edward, dabbing his mouth with his napkin and rising. 'Show him in at once, please, Edie.'

It was hardly surprising that the Weir Ward should blink at the strange man he saw entering his dining room.

'All right, Edie,' he said, dismissing the wide-eyed maid before greeting his visitor. 'Autrey?' he said doubtfully, offering his hand.

The Wychy shook it firmly, pleasantly surprised to see the difference that mortal time made to the speed of Sir Edward's speech and movement.

'Black Wand actually, beloved Weir Ward, Better than having to write down a conversation between us, wouldn't you say?'

His host blinked again 'Good heavens, Black Wand? Gracious me. Forgive me – I had no idea – this is extraordinary.'

'Of course – how could you? It's a new line in magic for me, too. I could use some decent clothing, though. I think I can truthfully say this robe is some hundreds of years old, But, please, I was forgetting mortal habits. Do finish your meal.'

'I have,' the other said, indicating his almost empty plate. 'What about you? Spot of cold chicken? Ham? Salad perhaps …?'

'Kind of you, but no,' Myrddin said, not knowing what food or how much of it Merlyn's form could cope with, and not feeling hungry either – unlike the time he had returned to his own human body eighteen years previously.

'Then come upstairs and we'll see what we can find for you.'

The Weir Lord gestured the wizard to precede him into the hall again. 'Humphrey's more your size than I am,' he went on conversationally. 'He's married with children of his own now. He and Diana have a place in Esher. Humphrey's practice is in London so I don't see a lot of him – especially since Margaret died.'

Black Wand heard no criticism in the comment, just a simple observation of Sir Edward's son's way of life, and remembered very well the grief-stricken Weir Ward's previous visit to the forest to tell its inhabitants of his wife's death, and to express the hope that she was with them and near him still.

Black Wand's silence spoke for itself. He could almost feel his host's shoulders sag with disappointment, so he turned and looked at the weather-lined, kindly face in its frame of silvery fronds, and spoke compassionately.

'Be assured Sir Edward, those who are not with us in the little kingdom have other, higher destinies.' Myrddin could only speak in faith from what he believed himself. For that time, however, they straightened the old man's shoulders and brought a new light to his eyes. He nodded brightly ahead of them to a door on the landing.

'Humphrey's spare things are kept in there.'

In the small room, the Weir Ward rummaged busily through a wardrobe.

'Ah, just the thing,' He turned with some clothes to find his guest staring at himself in a wall mirror.

The reflection had taken Myrddin by surprise. He had had no idea that the gaunt frame he had inherited had a mane of ginger-gold hair and green eyes, and was even good-looking, but the almost translucent skin had a strange grey-blue tinge to it. From the magician's writings, the wizard realised it was due to ichor, the watery fluid said to have run in the veins of the Greek gods instead of blood. It probably accounted for the stronger, lighter feel there was to the whole body.

Sir Edward left his guest to change, inviting him to join him in his study when he was ready.

When he had changed and looked in the mirror again, Myrddin was thankful to note that his appearance seemed at least a little more normal in shirt, slacks and sandals.

As Myrddin rejoined his host, Sir Edward laid down a large book on his desk, waved his visitor to an armchair and went to his cabinet.

'What will you have?'

The Wychy answered cautiously. 'If you don't mind, I'd rather not until I know what I can, or can't, eat or drink in this form?'

'Of course. Quite understand. But you know,' the Weir Lord continued, 'it really is quite extraordinary, you turning up like this – apart from the obvious, of course. Only this morning I received a parcel from an old college acquaintance of mine, the Marquis of Rules. We weren't close friends, you understand, so we didn't know too much about each other's families. But he heard about my campaign to save Weir Forest and very kindly sent me this book, which he says has been in his family for two hundred years – written by a monk by the name of Amaranthus. Did you know it was fashionable for wealthy families to keep a recluse, or 'holy man', on their estates in the eighteenth century?'

'Vaguely,' Myrddin answered, wondering how he was going to experiment with eating and drinking. 'Did yours?'

'I rather think we had enough on our plate with the forest,' said the Weir Lord dryly, returning to his desk. 'Patronage like that in those days could attract all sorts – charlatans; itinerant tramps and vagabonds, anyone who wanted a regular supply of food, clothing and shelter. There were genuine hermits, of course, and it seems the Rules picked a winner. When he died, they found some sheaves of manuscript, which they had bound and kept in honour of his memory. I'm sure you, of all people, will find the content somewhat interesting, to say the least.'

He picked up the bound manscript he had laid on the desk. 'The whole thing is a treatise rather prosily entitled: *"The Faerie Realm. A veritable account of all the so-called faeries, pixies, sprites, elves, pookas and other curiously named denizens of the otherworld inhabiting these shores anciently called Brython, together with a description of their whereabouts and how they may be known to the intelligence of those that have the inward illumination of seeing. All culled from a secret manuscript written down by a learned brother of the Abbey of Larne in the eleventh century according to the chronology of this world"'*

'Good heavens!' exclaimed Myrddin, who had sat upright and was now reaching out to read it for himself.

'Please?' Sir Edward drew back. 'Allow me the pleasure of sharing just a little of it with you? You can then have it to yourself for as long as you like, I promise.'

The wizard leaned back in his chair, resigning himself to wait while the Weir Lord turned to where he had inserted a marker. 'Listen,' he said, 'the reason the present Marquis has entrusted me with this is that it refers with astonishing accuracy to our own people. Here they are spoken of as the Weirdfolk. Amaranthus writes: "*And of these southern English Faeries, none is more perfect in form and amiability of disposition and unrestricted nobility of mind than the Weirdfolk who are to be found in the Forest of Three Weirs in Sussex adjacent to the town of Corsham. Most blessed also are these in that their kingdom is forever warded against mortal intrusions by their puissant Guardians, the scions of the house of We'ard, who exercise the right of life and death against all unlawful intruders into their sacred domain. And it is here that the most fearsome of all the netherworld nemeses holds his age long sway, the Green Dragon of the South, one of the four great mystic Guardians of the faerie. Even mortals when the moon is new retire into their habitations, fearful lest the vengeful wreak from his nostrils lure them into his fatal domain.*'" He looked up. 'There is more in the same vein, Black Wand, but I think I've quoted enough.'

'You most certainly have, beloved brother,' said Myrddin firmly, holding his hand out for the Record. 'Time is running short, and it's these *other* branches of our race I most urgently need to study. So, please …?'

'You know, there's something that's troubled me for a long time,' said the Weir Lord, handing it over. 'Ann Singlewood

– she wrote to me just before she died bequeathing me *Wizard's Woe*. She believed she was going to be with you in the forest. I've always wondered if she actually did?'

'She did indeed, Sir Edward,' the wizard answered. 'And only just in time. And yes, she and I have watched you walking in the forest. Our people are not afraid of you, nor of Diana and the children when they visit. We have seen them grow from babies with great delight.'

Sir Edward looked thankful. 'I'm relieved,' he confessed. 'Ann's death was such a terrible tragedy on top of young Autrey's, and I felt somehow – well, responsible, as if there was something I could have done, although what, I don't know. But the manuscript you left was an enormous help. It confirmed so much of our family history …'

Myrddin was hardly listening. He had just noticed a newspaper with banner headlines concerning the death of James Durant, along with a report of Sir Thaddeus Lovejoy's personal visitation to Dragon's Weir to inspect the scene of the appalling incident. He pointed to it.

'I'm sorry, I just couldn't prevent that,' he said a trifle bitterly. 'Reminds me, though. Would you happen to know where Sir Thaddeus Lovejoy is staying while he's in the vicinity?'

The Weir Lord nodded. 'It would be nice to think Angus Durant has the grace to recognise his criminal responsibility in the matter. Of course, it's added fuel to Lovejoy's campaign. You'll find him staying with the Frenshams, at Dyke's Hall near Corsham, They're friends of his.'

He looked back at his visitor curiously. 'Think you're going to be able to persuade him to back down on this scheme of his?'

'I have every expectation of so doing,' replied the Wychy truthfully. 'Oh, and by the way, your maid, the woman who –?'

'Edie Adams?' Sir Edward interrupted, mildly surprised. 'Why do you ask?'

'I used the intro' "Augustus Autrey" without thinking. If she says anything in the village …?'

'I see, yes. So what name would you like to use?'

'How about Black – Myrddin Black?'

'The Welsh form of Merlin, eh? Apt enough, I would say.'

The Weir Ward tugged a bell-pull by the fireplace. 'Edie,' he said when the maid appeared. 'I'd like you to meet Mr Myrddin Black. He was a friend of the young man who died eighteen years ago. You seemed to remember August Autrey …?'

'Oh, yes, sir,' she said, beaming joyfully at her employer's strange visitor, while he suddenly realised why her stocky form and cheerful face had appeared familiar. 'I remembers Mr Gus, He wrote stories for me and my cousins Stella and Johnny – Johnny used to call him 'Uncoo Wug.'

Sir Edward looked astonished. 'Good heavens,' he said faintly. 'Of course – the little chappie who once went missing in the forest for a couple of hours?'

'Yes, sir,' she answered. 'So I knew this gentleman wasn't Mr Gus.' She took Myrddin's proffered hand with a simple curtsey. 'Pleased to meet you, Mr Black, sir.'

'And I – you, Edie,' he said, cutting himself short just in time of saying 'remember'. 'Talking of stories, Sir Edward,' he went on when she had left the room. 'You have reminded me – and now that I have the means …' He held out his hands, spreading his fingers '… I'd quite like to write a "catch up" on the forest for you. I can round off *Wizard's Woe*, too, with an account of how Ann came to join me there. What do you think? Do you know where I could beg, borrow or steal a typewriter?'

'My dear fellow, what a splendid idea. Use mine, it's electric.'

Myrddin spent the rest of the evening alone, absorbed in the book of Amaranthus. It was enlightenment beyond his wildest imaginings. Scholarly, orderly and comprehensible, it set out the division of Faerie England into four strictly-defined quarters; first, by a line from the Severn to the Thames that segregated the whole of Southern England, then by vertical division separating east from west as far as the Ribble and the Humber: above which the remaining region was the North. Each of these major divisions held several federated communities linked by one general description. Each had a ruler or overseeing body, and each a spiritual guardian Dragon. The great custodian Dragon of the North was black: that of the west, which included Wales, red, the east blue and the south green.

The fascinating details listed the generic name for the faerie of the north as the Mabyn. In the west it was the Kin of Beauty; east were the Denefolk and in the south the Weirdfolk.

The Mabyn were accounted a sober folk, wise and aloof, who lived in mounds and hills with a stone effigy as their oracle. They seemed to be the most ancient of all four divisions, just as the Weirdfolk were accounted the most recent. What made the Wychy sit up and whistle, however, was their use of a white unicorn to communicate between their kin – the fourth image of White Wand's vision. What was it she had said first? '... *A monk sitting at a rough oak table writing. It must be a long time ago because he's using a quill and there's a odd-looking pot of ink ...*' Then '... *an owl – a pure white owl. It's very still. I don't think it's a live one – but it isn't stuffed either ... An otter dripping wet so it looks dark in colour but silvery grey at the same time. Everything is in is motion here. It's lovely, the river sings, the leaves of the willow trees twinkle and their branches sigh ... a pure white unicorn. It races over the grass, its horn nods gracefully. It turns now and is galloping towards a hill. But it is changing – melting – turning itself into one of those chalk effigies ...*'

Myrddin thought hard: if Amaranthus equated with the monk she had seen first, then the otter and the owl *had* to be messengers of the others,

He turned to where Sir Edward had inserted the marker, and quickly scanned the remainder of the passage the Weir Ward had started to read. Sure enough, the crystal block was mentioned as being the oracle of the Weirdfolk who, like the other three kins, also had a messenger in the form of a white dove.

This was one of the strangest statements to Myrddin, for only he knew that there once *had* been exactly such a messenger. A brief reference in his Book of Lore – a single sentence following the description of the great catastrophe that had devastated Wynn and Woe: '*And no more was known to us the White Dove, the heavenly messenger of our kind.*'

It was a confirmation that spurred him on through the lengthy passages of flowery English to read the descriptions and occupations of the other races. The Denefolk of the east, a people of the hollows and hills, were apparently the least substantial of all the Faerie Kins of Britain. He learned they possessed a chameleon-like ability to blend with their surroundings. Not surprisingly, their oracle was the artful reading of wind and rain, and by this means, nothing was unknown to them. It jolted him to read that their messenger was a grey otter.

The Kin of Beauty in the west, ruled by Gwynn the Son of Nudd, were idle, living a rich and elegant life in vast palaces both above and below ground, where they continued all the pleasures they had known in mortal life. Their messenger was a snow-white owl, and their oracle none other than Gwyn, the Son of Nudd himself, magician and astrologer.

Discovering that the fae of the forest were part of a great family of Fae, and not alone in the world after all, had a profound effect on Myrddin. On the face of it, he reflected, there seemed more than one possible refuge among their cousins, and therefore the next logical step would be to contact them. Never mind that the Weirdfolk didn't have their White Dove messenger anymore. Wasn't it wonderful that he could now make three of them to send as messengers – rather as Noah had sent his birds. One of Myrddin's might also return with an olive branch …

While he was about it, he thought jubilantly, a suitable spirit from among the new-found Kindred might well be willing and happy to inhabit the promised babe, What could be better? And while he was waiting to find the right spirit, the wraith-less babe he intended making for the Queen would make a good stand in for the one that his Nefertiti lookalike, Aíssa, would also be revealed to be expecting.

*

He returned to the forest in his elf-form, leaving Humphrey's clothes in a small suitcase hidden in an outhouse on the estate. The key to the backdoor that he had been given, he dropped under a loose floorboard along with the ring. Sir Edward had suggested the arrangement before he had gone to bed. This gave the Wychy the freedom of any convenient interregnum to come and work, and the library's upper window would not need to be left open for him.

His mind still in a whirl, he spent the interregnum making three white doves: sending them to the north, the east, and the west.

With sun's rise he was busy. He needed the gnomes to set up the temple to his specification; then he had to secretly rehearse Barnsley and Hetty in their new characters until they were word-perfect, and compose his own introductory speech. During the following interregnum he also made a small dragon – a singular 'special' effect, which needed only his Wand to animate into appropriate action. It was all a tremendous amount of work in a very short time but the gnomes worked tirelessly and Myrddin felt he was not only getting somewhere at last, but marvelling at his story's appropriateness to what he had just discovered.

CHAPTER 18

A COURT APPEARANCE

At sunrise, the forest woke in a frenzy of excitement. Black Wand had promised that King Nebuchadnezzar would be arriving that very day. Everyone now knew that Alder, his Queen and the entire royal household were to be present on the Weal – an unheard of event. The fae went running to *Woe Begone!* where they pointed out to each other the awesome array of six golden seats set out to face the temple mound the other side of the clearing. They chattered incessantly over what was to come until they realised that the Royal Coach was already in the Weal and travelling at walking pace towards them so ran to greet the cortege and escort it triumphantly to its destination.

White Wand arrived just as Myrddin was secretly explaining something to the gnomes. He left them at once to greet her and in time to welcome the Royal Coach.

With everyone in place, and Alder and Mergyn sitting with a vacant seat between them, Black Wand went to take the stand for his address.

'Beloved Liege, beloved Queen, I know that the story of Nebuchadnezzar and his Quest is already dear to you both. But even I did not know how intimate a connection it had with this our own little kingdom when I started. Unknowingly, I wove a fable that had roots in a reality that has only recently come to my knowledge. Merlyn himself placed the history of King Nebuchadnezzar in the first ever

Black Wand's Weird, but kept its interpretation secret until the right time came for it to be known. That time has come. I have learned that Nebuchadnezzar was not a figment of my imagination but a living personage – a King told by Am-Mar-El-Lin to seek his sleeping Queen here in the little kingdom.'

He paused to allow the significance to sink in. It was the first implication the fae had ever heard that there were others like themselves somewhere, and an awed whisper ran through his listeners.

Black Wand continued. 'I would now like to ask our noble Master of Gnomes to relate to our Liege and Lady the wonderful part the gnomes have played in this incredible discovery.'

The Master came forward, relieved to be able to tell the secret at last; how, at Black Wand's command, they had dug a secret tunnel in the Wynn to enable the Wychy to explore an ancient and terrible place where he had found the slumbering Queen, and sworn the gnomes to secrecy.

Black Wand then broke in diplomatically to explain that that was when he had magically discovered that King Nebuchadnezzar not only existed, but would arrive in the forest in due course to claim his Queen. However, astonishing as all this was, time and disaster had taken its toll on the hidden Temple in the Wynn. Knowing that Alder would be distressed to have his Royal Visitor find his Queen of Beauty lying in such sorry surroundings, he had asked the gnomes to rehabilitate her in a restored Temple exactly similar to the one she would expect to wake up in. They had done this willingly, and constructed it within the mound before them and, by his arts, he had transported the Sleeping Queen into it.

Black Wand fell gracefully on one knee, spreading wide his flowing Weird with a slow but commanding gesture, and addressed Alder in a low, tense voice.

'O Lord Immortal of our Ancient Land, the hour is come. Even now, the great King Nebuchadnezzar and his followers walk within your domain. I go now to fetch the great Am-Mer-El-Lyn himself, and beg you, my Liege, to send your Royal Chamberlain and Herald to greet the King and his party and guide them here.'

Fascinated, thrilled and not a little apprehensive, the crowd watched the two officials walk away through the trees in an easterly direction, and then heard the distant sound of the Chamberlain's voice:

'Oh Great Nebuchadnezzar King of the ancient land of Chaldea, we come by command of our Liege King Alder, Lord of all the Fae, to greet you and guide you most lovingly into his presence.'

While the rapt listeners heard Nebuchadnezzar's reply and other courtly speeches, Black Wand quietly disappeared.

*

Mergyn leaned towards Alder. 'Our Wychy tells a wonderful tale, my love,' she said in a low voice.

'For which he has asked our support, dearest Mother,' returned the King as softly. 'It has become necessary for our people to learn that there is more than one branch to our race.'

There was a gasp from the crowd as the Royal Herald appeared with the Chamberlain, accompanied by a crowned figure carrying a sceptre, and looking resplendent in crimson and gold. Four bodyguards came behind him, mailed, booted and equipped with bows, swords and lances, followed by servants carrying burdens on their heads.

*

Alder rose with the Queen and White Wand to receive the King's presentation by the Chamberlain, who began a courtly introduction to which Mergyn paid scant attention. She was too engrossed in trying to account for the visitor. Nothing in his obviously mortally-fashioned face was familiar and yet – and this raised her hackles – the plasma body of the bogus king held the wraith of a fae, and she remembered: *Then made we manikins, male and female, and nourished them to grow in human image ...* Now recognising the meaning of Black Wand's recent activities, she was alarmed. It was one thing to fashion simple astral robots, but to have so profited from the Enchanter's wisdom as to repeat the miracle of investing one of them with wraith and spirit – and for far less logical reason than that of the misguided Merlyn – was worrying.

When Nebuchadnezzar had taken the chair between herself and Alder, he summoned his retinue with a lordly wave to come forward with their burdens, and to unfold and display the treasures he wished to present to the King.

Nebuchadnezzar then told the story of his travels, delighting the fae with an account from his own lips that none had heard before, adding even more authenticity.

'... And now, most noble and mighty King,' Nebuchadnezzar said, turning to Alder, 'I crave to be allowed to know the whereabouts of the Temple that Am-Mar-El-Lin has told me that I shall find here?'

Alder inclined his head, and gravely held out a hand towards a newly arrived figure at the back of the crowd as the person that the other needed to ask.

Everyone turned to see a stranger in a tall conical hat, robed in a mystically spangled gown and cloak which were half hidden by a nearly knee length white beard. Holding a long staff he came forward and faced the fae, half-bending with a finger to his bearded lips that invited their silence and co-operation for this part of the proceedings. It puzzled them for a moment until he went to the centre ground and called loudly in all directions:

'O ye Spirits of the Earth to whom all secrets of the Earth are known, I command you appear and reveal the ancient Temple you were bidden to find!'

Then it made sense, because everyone there, apart from the newly arrived King and entourage, already knew where it was. So it was fun, and right and proper that the discovery be re-enacted for the sake of their visitor, and the fae hugged themselves with the glee of inside knowledge as the gnomes jumped up and entered their part with gusto.

They ran busily all over and around the clearing, scrutinising the ground and looking into bushes and between blades of grass, miming to each other as if arguing or debating; some picking up imaginary stones or unearthing specimens of rock and metal, poring over them then flinging them away to search for others.

Then Sandstone, who had been digging hard at one particular spot, jumped up, holding aloft a glittering object. The others came running to see he had found a golden sandal, then ran with it to Am-Mar-El-Lin who placed it on the ground, waved his staff over it, and everyone saw it rise and turn and point directly to the crest of the mound.

The gnomes raced over and scrambled to its top where they pretended to start digging. As they did so, the head of a dragon shot up, belching fire and smoke in anger at being disturbed. The gnomes at once scattered and fled in mock terror, while everyone else shrank back in real astonishment and alarm as the huge beast levered itself out of the mound, rearing up on its back legs to fix Am-Mar-El-Lin with wrathful red eyes.

Mergyn whispered laughingly to Alder, 'I do think our beloved Wychy has excelled himself, my love, don't you?'

'In truth,' agreed the King with one of his rare smiles. '"T'would be a disappointment if such a marvellous-looking beast were destined for destruction.'

It looked for a moment, though, to have reached that end when it staged an attack of fire on the magician which was so realistic Nebuchadnezzar's guards came rushing forward to defend him. Coming at the dragon from all sides at once, they plunged their swords and lances into its body, causing it to hit out right and left with forelegs and tail, knocking them away.

The fae, who had all retreated to a safe distance, watched the spectacle a little apprehensively before Am-Mar-El-Lin stepped forward, and touched the now-dizzied creature on the nose with his staff. They saw it collapse, no longer blowing fire but folding its wings submissively and laying its head on the ground at his feet.

The magician placed a golden chain around its neck and led it to the royal party. At his command, the great beast then sank to the ground before Nebuchadnezzar, raising and lowering its head three times in homage. Am-Mar-El-Lin then passed the end of the chain to one of the guards, bowed to Alder and Nebuchadnezzar. The way to the Temple was now clear.

Everyone rose to follow the Royal Party into the mound, where Am-Mar-El-Lin opened a huge entrance in its side, and all went in with 'oohs' and 'ahs' at the rose marbled interior with its fluted columns, arching traceries, fountains and statues.

The Queen lay in a smaller golden inner chamber on a stand overlaid by a sheet of gold reaching to the floor, where only her lovely head, its sleeping features outlined by the folded blue and yellow Egyptian headdress, was visible.

Mergyn and White Wand could only gaze in wonder at the perfect features of ancient Egypt's Queen Nefertiti.

'Behold, O Mighty One of Yore,' Am-Mar-El-Lin said in reverential tones, 'before you is your dream come true. The moment of choice has come. Will you revive this ancient Queen, or will you draw back?'

Nebuchadnezzar assured him that nothing would keep him from his chosen one. 'Only tell me what I should do?' he begged.

'Then say this, great King: *O fairest of Queens, Aíssa I, Nebuchadnezzar, have travelled through aeons of time and over countless mortal miles to claim my love. Awake, Aíssa, and behold your longing lord.* Then you shall kiss your chosen Queen, great King, and she will wake and love you ever more.'

Nebuchadnezzar repeated the words with adoration, then slowly bent his head and crossed his lips with those of the Queen.

At once her golden eyes opened and looked straight into his and everyone near enough to see caught their breath in wonder and satisfaction.

Nebuchadnezzar smiled, took her hand and reverently helped her to sit, before assisting her to her feet from the rather uncomfortable bed on which she had apparently lain so long.

Aíssa looked around her in wonder and then back at him, before opening her arms and welcoming him with a kiss.

Only Mergyn could guess why 'Am-Mar-El-Lin' had quietly disappeared before Aíssa opened her eyes. Aíssa's form also held a faerie wraith and spirit and would have recognised him as her creator.

*

Behind the mound, Myrddin quickly removed his disguise, and was waiting as Black Wand when the ecstatic fae began reappearing.

Sylvie and Dina flew to him, covering him with kisses. 'Dear Black Wand, you are the greatest of all magicians whoever were,' declared Dina, nearly swooning with love against him. 'Never, but never has there been such a wonderful happening before.'

'Black Wand?' Sylvie said, 'Do you think King Nebuchadnezzar and Queen Aíssa will stay with us for a while before he takes her away to his country?'

'I would think so,' said Black Wand, judiciously. 'He will need a rest after all his searching – and you'll have the dragon, too. He is wonderfully tame really, and no more dangerous than your beloved Dreadful. See how disconsolately he sits waiting for someone to love him.'

The Wychy was right. The dragon made a willing pet and playmate and was as gentle and obedient a companion that any of them could wish for. He did exactly as asked, even when in constant demand for flying trips around the forest. The only proviso Black Wand laid on them was that their new Dreadful had to return to the Temple before the Interregnum. It was still the dragon's duty to keep watch over his Mistress, the Queen Aíssa, he told them – which was true. He had programmed the beast as an early warning system should anyone take an unauthorised interest in his creations.

With the faerie thoroughly immersed in their new entertainment, Myrddin hurried away with Omric to the Mansion of the Gnomes where he asked the Master to accompany him to Merlin's Mount.

'I have a request – if you are minded to hear it, Master?'

'Say on, most excellent Black Wand, it shall be done.'

'It concerns the black crystal of this mound. It is telescopic in character and I need to use it as such. Could you find an unspoilt piece and set it in such a way as I could look through it in comfort?'

'Like mortal spectacles, Black Wand?'

'More like mortal wrap-around-shades made of one lens to fit across both eyes, Master?'

'It shall be done, Black Wand, even as you describe.'

Myrddin then returned to *Woe Begone!* where he shut himself away for some serious study of some still unread scrolls.

He made a spot check every now and then that all was well in the forest, and saw the fae were coming every waking hour to marvel over the fantasy that had become a reality before their eyes; watching and talking with the new arrivals in wonder.

The Wychy therefore relaxed and relied on his Weird to alert him to any need for intervention, and on Dreadful to sound the alarm if there was any meddling with Nebuchadnezzar and Aíssa. He also spent the next two Interregnums at Weir Court, working on his manuscripts

If he had typed quickly enough on his old manual typewriter, his fingers flew even faster over the electric keys. By each dawn he had typed around fifty thousand words, which gave him great pleasure to leave for Sir Edward to read.

The second time he returned to the forest, he found the Queen and Aíssa waiting for him outside *Woe Begone!*.

'Did I not promise that he would appear at my summons?' the Queen said with a sweet smile to her companion.

CHAPTER 19

MERGYN REGINA

Mergyn had been happy to take a back seat for two days while the fae came every waking hour to watch the new arrivals and ask them endless questions. On the third day, however, the Queen gently suggested that they should perhaps respect the privacy of the visiting King and his Queen, and give the happy couple time to be alone. There would be plenty of time to worship their new demigods because Nebuchadnezzar would never think of subjecting his adored Queen to the rigours of the long journey back to his own country until his heir had been born.

They understood at once, and begged Nebuchadnezzar and Aíssa for the loan of some of their attendants instead. They wanted to show them around the wonders of the forest with Dreadful, who was allowed to be with the fae during waking hours.

Mergyn was sure that this was not what the Wychy intended but, as he put in no appearance to stop it, she certainly wasn't going to prevent it either. Mergyn's purpose was to interview the two royals privately within the Temple, well aware that Black Wand had sealed it off from any eavesdropper. She knew that White Wand was also waiting for just such an opportunity to visit and interrogate the King and his Queen for herself. Loyalty to the absent Wychy, however, meant keeping a vigilant eye on the gallivanting puppet attendants.

*

Mergyn listened courteously enough to Nebuchadnezzar's mythical stories about his far off-kingdom – which she could have corrected a dozen times or more – and the adventures he had had on his timeless wanderings. These tales had held no flaws for the fae but Mergyn recognised them as vintage Black Wand.

However, when the king rubbed his hand across his eyes, frowning as he tried to recall a wayward memory, and said: 'Somewhere, I remember, I was once shown many wonderful secrets of herbs and magical mixtures of potions, concoctions and remedies ...'

And Mergyn was shocked and scandalised to realise the Assyrian King held the wraith of their erstwhile new Vintner – Barnsley. Clenching her hands, she fumed in silence over the outrage. Their beloved Rozyn about to be taken from them and her own appointed understudy kidnapped for a charade like this. *Just wait!* she promised herself inwardly and vengefully. *Just wait!*

She realised the Wychy must have thought that when Barnsley took the Bane, it would have left him no memory of his former life in the forest. It appeared, however, that the wizard had failed to take into account how much of Rozyn's potions and wyché instructions had already affected his erstwhile apprentice. Consequently, in spite of the Wychy's spellbinding and detailed rehearsal of the King in his new role, Barnsley's confused memory had begun to surface.

For Mergyn, it went without question that if the King was Barnsley, then his Queen had to be Hetty and, under Mergyn's careful questioning, it did not take her long to establish that Aíssa's hangover memory from her previous existence was her passionate love for Black Wand.

Contriving a private talk together with the Queen, it became even more evident that Aíssa was also confused between past and present. Mergyn soon learned that Queen

Aíssa believed herself to be pregnant, but she wasn't sure who the father was. In order to explain this, Aíssa confessed to an ancient misalliance with the Court Magician, Am-Mar-El-Lin, which had brought down the wrathful retribution of her royal husband at the time. But Am-Mar-El-Lin had saved her in a deathlike trance until he could wake her again. Yet here was a *new* husband and lover: Nebuchadnezzar, speaking and acting as if the babe-to-be was his. And Nebuchadnezzar had told her how the Great Am-Mar-El-Lin had guided him to her, so she couldn't understand why her ancient lover hadn't woken her himself and claimed her as he had promised?

Mergyn tried to bring a little order to the puzzle by explaining that the fae accepted Black Wand (whoever he might be for the time being) as Merlyn's Heir, and that he had declared that Am-Mar-El-Lin and Merlyn were just alternative names for the traditional magician: '... who is long passed beyond the stars, dear Aíssa,' she said. 'Black Wand only called on his *spirit* to help Nebuchadnezzar to find the sleeping Queen he had been promised – the Queen who would give him an heir.'

'Nothing assures me, nothing reassures me,' said Aíssa sadly. 'You say my lover is gone beyond recall – and yet, I *know* he lives. My love for him is old, yet new. Who is *your* Black Wand?' she begged. 'He sounds so familiar. What does he look like? Why haven't we seen him? You are very blessed, dear sister,' she went on impulsively, laying her hand on the Queen's arm. 'You *know* the father of your coming babe. How shall I discover the truth of what really *has* happened?'

Feeling as angry she had over Barnsley's abduction, Mergyn could have wept over Hetty's tragic bemusement between fact and fiction. 'By hearing it from the lips of the perpetrator himself,' Mergyn said, coming to an abrupt decision. 'Come, dear Aíssa, we shall go to his Retreat and summon him to answer you. And if he *won't* answer, I shall ask the One he dare not disobey to order it.'

*

So it was that Black Wand found himself confronted by the two Queens on his doorstep.

As he went down on his knee in acknowledgement of their presence, Mergyn said mockingly: 'This, dear Aíssa, is our mighty Lord of The Wandle, Merlyn's Heir, the wisest of the wise, Black Wand to whom little in heaven or on earth is not an open book.'

'O most gracious and beloved Queens – ' began the Wychy, rising.

'It can't be,' interrupted Aíssa, pressing a hand to her breast. 'How should I *not* know *you* for my lover. And yet you are he who – oh, I don't know what to say …'

'The facts are,' Mergyn cut in brusquely, 'that at the time this trusting and faithful Queen suffered the vengeance of her kingly lord, a certain magician convinced her he had got her with child himself. Now say, wizard, would his seed have remained as timelessly suspended as was its mother in her age-long sleep?'

'The laws of magic are not to be ridiculed, beloved Queen,' the Wychy answered evasively. 'But since you ask my poor opinion, I would judge that, since the royal sentence was upon Aíssa herself – '

'That the babe she may be carrying is of recent conception?' finished Mergyn shrewdly.

'No, no!' moaned Aíssa. 'I swore I would survive to bear the one conceived upon me by Am-Mar-El-Lyn, *whatever* I suffered.'

'You hear that?' Mergyn hissed at him. 'Now speak the truth or I promise in Mona's name …'

'These events are shrouded in the mists of time, O Queen,' he said.

'In the mists of your wicked imagination, you mean, you liar!' Mergyn fumed. 'Down on your knees, you charlatan you, and confess your devilish impersonation.'

'No, no, I beg you,' said Aíssa. 'I don't care who he might pretend to be now, for I *do* know him.' And she held out her arms to the Wychy, crying: 'I know you as my lover – as my master – my maker, Even when I danced with you before I became as I am to walk and talk at your command – '

Myrddin twitched his Wand and Aíssa sank unconscious. Catching her instinctively as she fell and boiling with vexation, he demanded: 'Where are the Queen's attendants?'

'Enjoying a vacation in the forest, Merlyn's Heir,' Mergyn said coolly, taking the unconscious Aíssa from him. 'I shall be having further words with *you* later, you blackest of wizards.'

Myrddin watched her go, glowering and thinking bitterly how it was that every time he was on the brink of some great discovery or achievement, the Queen had to interfere and leave him squirming.

He was about to move on when Dreadful, now aware that some disturbance was threatening the person he was created to serve, came raging back through forest breathing fire and slaughter.

His creator, however, was in no mood to appreciate his concern. 'Scram!' he snarled.

The confused beast halted in its tracks, its fiery breath evaporating into thin air, then turned and fled as fast as it had come.

'Why the hell do I bother?' Myrddin groaned, and went off to join Sir Edward at breakfast. It was all that promised to lift the black mood he was in.

*

There was no one around when he emerged from the outhouse as Myrddin Black, and Edie greeted him with a bright smile when he reached the house – having no idea of his visits during the small hours.

Sir Edward accepted his appearance with pleasure, waving him to a seat opposite him at the breakfast table.

'So glad to see you, Myrddin, But what will you have?'

'A piece of dry toast, perhaps, and a cup of sweet warm water will be fine, thank you,' answered the wizard quickly. 'I wonder if I could have another look at that manuscript of Aramanthus, please …?'

Myrddin had been reading for two hours or more when something tugged urgently at his consciousness for attention – his presence was required in the forest. Something was wrong.

*

Silence lay everywhere in the Weal, and Myrddin found the Master coming to meet him.

'O Black One, your return is welcome beyond measure,' he said, with an expression that was anything but joyful. 'You know what has happened?'

'Tell me, Master.'

'Our Liege Alder is gone from us. We are bereft. What are we to do? Woe is on all of us …'

The Passing. And him not there to help ease the shattering blow.

The rest of Omric's sentence was lost in hearing a distant summons, calm and imperative:

Errant Wand, your presence before me – at once!

Black Wand stiffened. Emergency it might be, but galling beyond measure to realise that if the Queen now held Alder's Wand she also called the shots.

Making no immediate move, he spoke to the Master.

'How go the proceedings I left with you, Master?'

'All is well, Black Wand, I – '

I await your coming, tardy Wand, he was interrupted again. *Our people are distraught and your return is long overdue.*

He gave up and obeyed. As he hurried through the Weal and on towards Weirdsmeet, aching misery lay everywhere. Not a fay ran to greet him, although each knew he was there.

Even White Wand had sent him no word of greeting.

The moment he discovered the Queen sitting on the opposite of the two stone chairs with Alder's crown on her head and the powerful golden Wand across her knees, he realised he was up against it. This was not Gwen the fay, nor even Gwen the wilful Queen, but an ageless spirit whose darkness vibrated with the same mortality he had taken into himself through Merlyn's Ring. If she commanded the begetting of the babe between them now, he had no power to refuse her.

But she didn't. She said instead: 'Know this, Wychy. The destiny of this our little kingdom has passed to my hands, and I shall not suffer anyone, be it you or your sister Wand, to interfere. You have presumed too much in such affairs of late. From now on you will therefore devote yourself solely to those duties for which Merlyn properly designed your Wand.'

Myrddin made no reply and, since she had not gestured for him to take a seat, stood in as dignified a manner as he could while she continued.

'I am already aware of some of your manifold wrong-doings, O errant Wand. I shall be lenient, however, provided each is set right and pursued no more. Our beloved Vintner, Rozyn-Who-Knows, is gone with Alder. The wines, the vintages, the nectars and ambrosias are woefully diminished after comforting our people's sorrow. So tell me, Wychy, where am I to find a Vintner with even one particle of the knowledge needed to replace our beloved Rozyn?'

Her tone told him the question was rhetorical, that there was no doubt in her mind concerning the problem. 'Hear me then, I know you have interfered with the sacred obligations of your Sister Wand, yet again I am disposed to be lenient because I believe that that Prince of Fools, whose dupe you are, beguiled you. You shall therefore destroy the mortal aspect of this fay, O Misguided One, and restore him to his understanding of Rozyn's teaching. It can, and shall be done.'

Once more, Black Wand had to swallow the rebuke and all that it implied in silence. He knew she was right; the fae were the concern of them all and they needed a Vintner. Belatedly, he began to realise what a prize tangle he had got himself into, and there was more to come.

'Then there's Aíssa – O Black One! Black One!' She shook her head despairingly, 'May Mona forgive you, for I find it hard. You will release her also, and put that scheming imagination of yours to work to soften her departure for our people.' She paused, still holding him with her gaze, as if pondering the wisdom of bringing up another point at this time.

He braced himself, waiting. But she finalised the interview by saying briefly, 'You have until sunrise tomorrow, Wychy.' With this she rose, and stalked away, leaving him to seethe with rage at the situation, knowing it was all of his own making.

For a moment, he wondered if the Queen had been right from the start when she warned him against Merlyn's magic. Then he told himself, no, she was simply jealous of his increasing magical ability. She was afraid he would become powerful enough to control *he*r – hence she had seized the present opportunity to browbeat him into temporary subjection – and cleverly, too, he had to admit. Rozyn must be replaced and if Nebuchadnezzar went, Aíssa must have her baby and go also.

He could only hope to make it enough of a pageant to off-set yet another cause for woe, and somehow find an alternative focus for the fae's affections. On top of which, there was now the problem of how he was to deal with the Queen. Now that she possessed this undeniable royal authority, disobedience was out of the question. While she held the supreme Wand of power in her hand she could destroy both himself and White Wand simply by withholding its blessing from theirs – and if that happened, there would have to be a new Wych and Wychy.

'Perish the thought!' he muttered to himself. But the thought wouldn't perish, because it brought another to mind. The Queen had said nothing about the problem of the promised Babe, which she had sworn he must get with her. Did the omission mean that, in view of all his 'wrongdoings', she no longer thought him worthy of the honour?

The idea piqued his vanity. Even if he didn't intend to concede, the idea of her finding someone else was so outrageous that by the time he returned to Weirdsmeet he was in turmoil. This Queen, possessed by Mergyn's spirit and so compellingly lovely, had become a challenge to his sovereignty. He drew his Weird closely around him. If his Wych caught any sense of his emotions, there would more cause for upset. But the thought that she alone was his one true, faithful and appointed love comforted him as he turned to glide across the water to where he saw she was seated, engaged in weaving a Runic tapestry.

He was determined to explain everything in such a way that would convince her – which didn't mean it had to be *entirely* truthful – and win her co-operation. Apart from which he needed to tell her the even more urgent news contained in the manuscript he had not long finished reading.

On his arrival at her side, however, his sister Wand did not even look up. Her hands flew on without stopping as if too immersed in her work to notice his belated homecoming.

He got the message. His beloved Wych was not just trying out a new line in reproach. His closed Weird meant concealment and that was not the way of an innocent approach. Her presence there was also a mute reminder that at any moment some other distraught fae would be coming down Wandleside to sing their last Song, and so would be aware that she was there to receive them. Let Black Wand take warning from this meticulous attention to Wandle duties they should be rightly sharing together,

The Wychy passed on. He was feeling an additional exasperation as he became aware for the first time how deep the rift was growing between them. What had the prophecy said? *And all three of ye undone ... one-and-one-and-one.* The King had left them. And White Wand and he, himself, who should never be disunited, were being parted like windblown apples from the bough. In the solitude of his Retreat, he sought mental and spiritual recuperation, while thinking hard on how he was going to deal with Nebuchadnezzar and his Queen without causing more wholesale misery.

*

When the fae became conscious at sunrise, they were aware of an unusual sense of urgency that sent them hurrying through the Weal in the direction of Nebuchadnezzar's Temple.

CHAPTER 20

NYZOR

The fae agreed that something astonishing and wonderful had happened, although no one knew what it was. On their arrival at the temple, all were astounded to see a beaming Nebuchadnezzar with an equally happy Queen Aíssa sitting at his side holding a small bundle in her arms, and their own Queen flanked by her Wychies waiting to greet them.

Welcoming everyone on her fellow monarchs' behalf, Mergyn lovingly congratulated the pair on the arrival of Nebuchadnezzar's longed for son and heir and, in honour of the happy event, declared it would be a day of universal rejoicing. At evenfall, her royal barge would then convey the family and their attendants as far as the limits of the little kingdom allowed on their journey back to Nebuchadnezzar's own realm.

The fae were ecstatic. The occasion was just what they needed to restore their spirits, and Edmund and Baddenham who, since Rozyn's departure had taken on the task of eking out the ambrosias, went to fetch the remaining stocks from the Wynn.

With Mergyn ordering the contents of her own cabinet into circulation, meant Myrddin could do no less than open up his own reserves.

At the end of a day of games and dancing, Mergyn again took over. She swept in with Nebuchadnezzar to lead everyone in the measure of a well known and much loved dance, sent Edmund and Baddenham back to drain the barrels and vessels to the last drop, and dispatched Loy and Simmonds to Alder's Stede to prepare her barge for its journey. The final scene was as wonderful as any ever seen and one to remember when the fae followed the royal party down Windaway to the barge that glittered below. The last rays of the sun gave a ceiling of orange and grey, saffron and purple clouds that, reflecting in the long stretch of water, appeared to suspend the waiting vessel between heaven and earth; and made a glorious backdrop for the departing family into their unknown realm.

When the head of the serpentine procession reached Weirdsmeet, Black Wand turned to take his leave of Mergyn with a bow, since he was accompanying the barge. To his surprise, however, Nebuchadnezzar seemed to have forgotten the pre-arranged protocol for the occasion and instead of pronouncing the farewell address as the Wychy had instructed him, begged Mergyn to accompany them to the limits of her Kingdom to help cheer them on their way.

Mergyn accepted happily. The King handed her aboard, with Aíssa, where Loy took over to conduct the monarchs to their places of honour. This left Myrddin to find a space in the stern with the attendants but being concerned as to how far Mergyn intended to go with the family, he never thought twice about it.

With cheering and singing from the bank following them like a wake of sound, the rowers sent the boat skimming up the centre of King's Weird, the myriad facets of spray spangling air and water alike with rainbows of colour.

Despite the jubilance of the send off, however, Myrddin began to sense a certain trepidation beginning to fill the rowers as the barge neared the limits of the royal Weird. The sun had set, but the moon in her first quarter lit a clear sky on their arrival where the river became divided by The Wandle.

He was pleased to see that Loy and Simmonds appeared to have regained a spirit of adventure, which reassured the rowers when they found themselves between the Weal on the right bank and Woe on the left where they had never been before.

When Myrddin directed Loy to pilot them to the Woe side of the river, it was obvious that the Pilot's self-confidence had begun to inspire the rowers to overcome their alarm as they nosed into a space where the bank was less steep.

At the Queen's quiet command and pointed Wand, the Wychy understood he was to leave his crown and tell-tale Weird in the barge so that none would know of his return to the forest by a different route. Holding his Wand disguised as an ashen staff, he was first ashore to hold the silvery rope from the bow and to signal the attendants to join him and assist Nebuchadnezzar and his family to disembark.

Myrddin had no objection to the King's taking farewell of the Weirdfolk's Queen with a kiss, which assured him that she was coming no further. It was her whispered instructions into her guest's ear that made him feel apprehensive.

He cast off the rope as soon as his victims were ashore, and watched the barge leave until, rounding a bend, it was out of sight, then led the group upwards to level ground. As they walked, he gave directives to the two 'royals' under which their erstwhile characters gradually disintegrated.

He freed Barnsley from Nebuchadnezzar, allowing the wicca to retain all his memory as Rozyn's assistant, and the naked fay shot back into the forest so fast, the Wychy hardly saw him go but that was as it should be and didn't worry him. It was Hetty's memory that he needed to erase completely. She must return as a newly arrived half born without even the recollection of a name.

To his utter astonishment, however, instead of racing back to the forest she rubbed her eyes as if she had just been woken from a deep sleep and looked about her with a frown.

Then her eyes lightened, her chin lifted proudly, and she stared at him haughtily. 'Where am I?' she demanded and, before he could say anything, regarded him more closely: 'You look to be of the Weirdfolk. Who are you?'

'I *am* Black Wand of the Weirdfolk,' he said, wondering what had possessed her. 'And that ...' he indicated over his shoulder, '... is the Forest of Weir where you should be.'

'I think not,' she interrupted with a scornful laugh, and called: 'Windfleet!'

To his further amazement, there came an immediate response. Out of nowhere, with a thud of hooves and an answering whinny, came a white mare, side-saddled and bridled. 'Hetty' caught the reins, and stroked the animal lovingly before taking down a voluminous blue cloak that lay across its back and covering her nakedness in its folds. Mounting the horse to sit sideways with the ease of long experience, she held the animal in check for a moment whilst eyeing the Wychy with another frown:

'I expect I'll remember you, too, in time, O Black Wand of the Weirdfolk,' she said, and nudged her mount forward. 'On Windfleet,' she said, and was gone.

It left Myrddin slack jawed in astonishment until he remembered the differences she had always exhibited that should have marked her out as a stranger fay. If he had known earlier of the existence of the Kin of Beauty, he felt he could have recognised 'Hetty' as one of them. He realised that in removing all memories of her later existence, he had enabled her to remember her true origins to which she was obviously returning.

Reducing the robot attendants and the now wraith-less forms of king and queen back to plasma was short work. The babe he hid in a bundle and then it was back to the forest himself, an entry that should have gone unnoticed but didn't because he came across a naked Barnsley standing by the entrance into Wychies' Lane.

In response to the Wychy's kindly: 'Hael and wyn, little brother.' The apprentice Royal Vintner drew himself up and returned anything but the witless stare that Black Wand expected. He looked the Wychy up and down a moment then said kindly: 'Hael and Wyn, stranger. I see you are burdened. Have you come far? Come, I will gladly take you into the little kingdom. It will be bad for you to be abroad when our Lady Mona has gone to rest.'

Dumbstruck for the second time that night, Myrddin watched the wicca move off until he found his tongue with a brusque: 'And you can stop right there, Barnsley.'

The figure turned to face him. 'But I am Nyzor the Knower, son of Rozyn the Wise who is no more. And you are …?'

'I am Black Wand, little brother,' he answered crisply.

The wicca clearly disbelieved him and shook his head consolingly. 'Surely, you are wandled, misguided one. Black Wand of The Wandle is cloaked and crowned and uses no common ashen staff like yours. He has an ebon Wand – '

'Which you will feel about your naked buttocks, if …' And Myrddin stopped, stifling his anger even as he lifted the stick. It wasn't Barnsley's fault. He was obeying that last whispered instruction from his all-powerful mistress. It was Mergyn reminding the Wychy that she was the one with the upper hand. Even the threatened gesture with his staff had failed to make an impression.

There was only concern in Nyzor's voice, as he begged. 'Stranger, I do urge you to come with me. The Breath of Dragga's Scathe will soon be everywhere, and neither the Wychies of The Wandle nor their Queen would thank me, if I allowed you to fall victim to its power.'

'Indeed!' said Myrddin. 'It's more likely *you'll* be the one to be the victim, you poor idiot. Only a Wand can walk alone when Sunné and Mona are absent.'

'As you like then, poor wandling,' Nyzor said. 'Come, we'll walk together and put your contention to the test. You will doubtless be met by one or other protecting Wand to aid your failing feet.'

'From which unlikely event, may Mona preserve me,' said the Wychy. The last thing he wanted was White Wand to discover him returning to the Weal side by side with Barnsley's tell-tale star.

He thought providence had heard his prayer when Loy came running up the lane towards them bearing clothes. But was disillusioned when the Pilot bowed to Black Wand, and held out the garments to Barnsley.

'Hael and wyn, Nyzor the Knower,' he exclaimed. 'Our Queen has commanded me to bring these vestments of the Royal Vintner's office, and to conduct you into her presence.'

Myrddin noted with satisfaction how completely unfazed Loy appeared at being sent beyond the Veil of Illusion and said nothing while he watched the reclaimed Nyzor being clothed in the distinctive Royal Livery.

When fully dressed, and to the Wychy's intense annoyance, the Vintner addressed Loy: 'I thank you, messenger, for your help, and will come with you without delay. But I am worried by the plight of this poor wandling, here, whose disordered spirit believes he is none other than Black Wand of The Wandle.'

'Do not worry, dear Nyzor,' said Loy and turning to Black Wand, announced: 'Her Majesty instructs me to tell you will find your Weird nearby for your comfort and protection.'

'And where is the Queen?' asked Myrddin, keeping his temper with difficulty.

'Her Majesty awaits us in her royal barge beside the river here,' answered Loy, not disrespectfully, but apparently under orders not to acknowledge the Wychy's identity.

Myrddin found his Weird and crown lying beside the path, and boarded the vessel. With the craft being taken down King's Weird by the current, Myrddin gave vent to his feelings – or tried to: '*Was* that little episode really necessary, O Queen? And what will our people believe of this sophisticated change in Barney?'

Mergyn quirked an eyebrow. 'Barney?' she said, 'But it is Nyzor, the Son of Rozyn-Who-Was –' '

'Mona preserve me,' Myrddin said irately. 'You might fool our people, O Queen, but not my Wych. His star will be apparent in its true likeness in her Wych ball, no longer hidden by his late form.'

She laughed. 'Is it not known to you then that faerie generations are far, far shorter than those of mortality? How long is it since our Rozyn-Who-Was went from us?'

'The moon has waxed only little,' he answered pointedly. 'But you cannot hope to convince my sister Wand that Rozyn generated an heir in such a brief space –'

'Why not, when I shall prove it to her *myself* in the same amount of time to her complete satisfaction?' returned Mergyn.

'How can you?' he said disbelievingly. 'You have not yet conceived.'

'As you truly say, not *yet*.' She didn't press the point, and continued: 'But that is not my intended explanation for Nyzor. You shall inform your Wych that when Rozyn-Who-Was left us, his spiritless *wraith* was left wandering, and so it chanced that the departed *spirit* of Barney-Who-Was which was also wandering –'

'That's preposterous – '

'It is entirely logical *and* it will then become apparent to White Wand that one of your reasons for being absent so long was to seek out and magically weld the errant wraith of the one with the forlorn spirit of the other.'

'My sister Wand isn't going to fall for that for a moment.'

'But she will – for two very good reasons, most obstinate Black One. First, *I* will confirm the fact. Second, *you* are going make certain alterations to the newly returned wraith to conform to the outline of Rozyn-Who-Was. Now you shall do this at my Stede, and later transport him secretly to the Brook of Wynn, where he shall rediscover all the magic of his craft.'

Despite himself, Black Wand had to agree her plan answered every need of the fae, his Wych and the new Royal Vintner.

*

So it was that when he eventually presented the result of his efforts only a little later to Mergyn, she scanned the restructured Nyzor carefully with a wistful expression, before saying softly: 'For this gift may Mona bless you, beloved Wand. Even *I* can believe that our immortal Vintner is with us once again. For such service I shall extend your permitted hours until sunrise, O Wychy unparalleled. Now take him swiftly to the Wynn by the Weirdside path, while your Wych, whom I shall summon, takes the forest path …'

The extension of time was not something Myrddin had anticipated, but was prepared to put to good use so, having escorted the now respectful but still self-possessed to the Nyzor to the Wynn, Myrddin betook himself to the Mansion of the Gnomes.

CHAPTER 21

'AND SO BETWEEN US …'

Omric was delighted to see him and brought out the shades he had made from the black crystal. Although earth and rubble covered Merlin's Mount, one of Merlyn's scrolls had described the difference between the crystal of Black Wand's Retreat on The Wandle and that of his own Mount. Whereas, a Wychy could see only what was happening within the bounds of the forest from his Retreat, Merlyn had written of his Mount as an observatory of the heavens and for fields afar, which was what Myrddin was after – although he could not have said exactly why.

He found the shades comfortable to wear but had to thank the Master in faith for he could see nothing through them from within the Gnomes' Mansion. However, when he lay stretched out on his back in the Wynn to gaze up into the heavens, it was as if he was inside space capsule detached from earth.

Field upon field of starry constellations filled his vision everywhere he looked. Large and brilliant as they appeared, he knew he must concentrate on what lay beyond them. Filled with an impression of speed as if he was hurtling out of himself, everywhere became nothing but light; an intense chaotic sea that glowed from end to end of the heavens. Within it, coils and spirals of even more brilliant formations took shape – just as he had read in Merlyn's ancient screeds which also warned that this was only a beginning, and an illusionary threshold. If he did not overcome the hypnotic effect, he could lose his mind. He was thankful for the warning; for he soon found it was an intense effort to concentrate. The glare was mesmerizing and absorbing; drawing him up and away from his earth-bound wraith, until it all went black and a speck of golden light like some small sun out of orbit came rushing towards him, threatening a collision that would blast him into eternity. In sheer agony of terror he cried out:

'*O Spirit of Eternal Merlyn, save me, Help me, Lord of the Heavens, for I am powerless.*'

An answer came, not in words but in star-studded understanding that swirled around him dizzily, chiding him and rebuking:

Said I not, O weakling of the wastes, to deal kindly with my Fairest of All Fair ...?

Yet he was saved. A conviction of power and confidence enveloped him; a certainty that the spirit of great Merlyn himself had rescued him. Words, phrases, sentences from the records exploded with new meaning in his mind until they reached a climax so personal its meaning was inescapable.

'*And so between us did we encompass the coming of He-Who-Was-Alder-Called-King ...*'

The Wychy's consciousness alternately floundered in understanding, yet thundered triumphantly: *The Weird of Merlyn is now mine for I know his power, his mind, his very being.* And into his mind, it seemed, came a vision. He was kneeling at the feet of a figure whose form and face he could not see, but from whose long delicate fingers hung the mysterious wonder of the sacred Girdle of Creation.

*

Ann took the forest path as instructed to meet the Queen, and was satisfied with the explanation she was given for their new Royal Vintner. She received the news with joy and thankfulness that the babe, to be conceived at sunrise, she was told, would be born three sunrises later.

*

Assured that all was well, Ann returned to her Retreat on The Wandle, where her Wych ball showed Black Wand's motionless star in the Wynn, which seemed odd. But when it began to move in the direction of the Weal, she anticipated the truant was on his way to The Wandle, and this time she was not going to let him pass unnoticed. To her surprise, however, he was not on his way to her. Her bewilderment increased to see he was cutting across beyond Wandleside, bound by the Royal Road to the Queen's Stede. And then another surprise. Pwyll's star had left the Stede and was travelling outwards along the Royal Road. This was a relief when it explained the why and wherefore of Black Wand's change of direction.

She wondered though at the strangeness that this purest and finest of all wiccas was conscious, let alone *abroad* during the interregnum – quite apart from what he had been doing at the Stede in the first place. Even if the Queen had somehow rendered him wyché during his stay there, he still couldn't expect to survive the Scathe without a Wand to protect him. It was a consoling thought that her partner was aware of him until, as she watched, she saw the two pass each other as if neither were conscious of the other's existence. She could hardly credit her eyes that Black Wand had not stopped to save a wraith that was now in deadly peril.

She flew across Weirdsmeet and raced up Windaway as she had never done before, hurling angry recriminations after the now distant Wychy's black mantle but was too late to save Pwyll. By the time she reached him, he lay quiet, already wrapped in a sickening tentacle of Scathe that was sucking the life out of him. She slashed it furiously with her wand, agonised by the memory of another occasion when she had found the previous Wych in the same plight.

Pwyll looked up serenely, smiling at her as if his circumstances held no terror for him. She knelt to cradle him, wrapping him in her Weird.

As she did so, he said: 'Sore wounded I was, and near death, when I was borne away. And now, as then, carried westward to an Isle forever blest. And when I come again, and shall come again, the fates that bind us all shall be made anew ...'

She had no idea what he was talking about, and was too deeply concerned with getting him back to The Wandle in time for the Bane.

*

As for Mergyn, there was now no going back. The only reason she had kept Pwyll virtually imprisoned in her Stede was that she knew his was the chosen spirit to invest the babe she was about to conceive. Releasing him, she had committed herself. With the Sacred Girdle now fastened around her hips, she awaited the coming of her lover, certain of the issue – although his ardent haste was presumptuous. He had no right to come unbidden by the Royal Road. He must be compelled to make the more correct approach by the Weirdside path; a journey now hidden from White Wand due to her preoccupation with Pwyll.

When Mergyn then became aware that he was standing in the Great Hall of the Palace waiting for *her* with his Weird drawn closely about him, she felt intrigued and mystified. He was enclosing a secret, and that disturbed her.

When she called sharply: 'Approach, Wychy,' no answer came. *What new magic had he now discovered that he could dare such effrontery?* she wondered, but the enigma tantalised her so much that she at last rose up and walked as sedately as she could into the Palace.

Finding him still where she had divined him to be, she went up to him; head erect and stared into his eyes challengingly. But only for a instant for her gaze was met with a smile of such radiant and all embracing love it melted her completely. Then he sank to his knees before her offering a cup, and whispering:

'… and so between us did we encompass the Coming of He-Who-Was-Alder-Called-King …'

*

Sometime later, when White Wand was sufficiently composed once more to watch her Wych ball after Pwyll's passing, she was mystified to see Black Wand's star once again still and unmoving in the Wynn. It seemed he must have returned while she was saving Pwyll. She naturally wondered what had taken him to the Palace, but comforted herself that the Queen would have given him a dressing down for his disrespect in approaching her by the Royal Road. In the same way, she also intended taking him to task for his terrible neglect of Pwyll.

At about dawn, she realised with quickened interest that his star was in motion again. This time she sighed in vengeful relief to see it turn aside halfway to approach Wandleside. But instead of descending Windaway, it turned north again along the forest path to the royal Stede. It made her so angry she started up intent on following him, but Mergyn's voice stopped her, commanding her to stay where she was.

*

The sky was brightening as Black Wand arrived to keep his appointment at the place of the two stone seats. There was nothing in his bearing, however, to suggest that he was dutifully fulfilling any command of the Queen.

Mergyn sensed in him a sudden, new urgency so that even when she smiled most lovingly at him as he knelt and gave the traditional greeting 'Hael and wyn, Beloved Queen.'

She said nothing beyond: 'Hael and Wyn, O beloved Wychy,' to remind him of the secret now fulfilled between them.

For his part, he scarcely seemed to notice the Sacred Girdle encircling her hips, before commencing: 'Beloved Queen, the secrets of the heavens have been revealed to me at last, and I have learned in what direction our people must leave here and find refuge in another place.'

Mergyn nodded gravely. 'And where, Merlyn's Heir, shall our people look for their peace and wellbeing?'

'This is hidden from me at present because the world and its people's have altered so much from the symbols that Merlyn attributed to them.'

'Describe these symbols, Wychy, I might be able to help,' she offered, and wondered why her soft tone appeared to take him aback, as if he not expected her to defer to him.

'The Triad of Mona, the starry symbol of the faerie, is no longer fixed, O Queen. It is visibly moving from its ancient position –'

'In which direction, Wychy?'

'Westward, O Queen.'

'Westward …?' she mused. 'Due west from here lies the Tor of Glastonbury in ancient Avalon where Arthur lies –' She broke off, and bid him rise and be seated opposite her.

'In Avalon,' he agreed, his tone was cautious, and he looked taken aback. 'The isle to which, according to legend,

Arthur's body was taken by three Queens after the tragedy of Lyonesse – one of whom was Morgan le Fay?'

'Taken in body only, Wychy,' she corrected mildly. 'Fae was his wraith and to the Fae it returned. But I doubt this can be the place for our people now – it has become too public. More westward still lies the Kingdom of Gower where King Uriens reigned –'

'To whom Morgan le Fay was given in marriage,' he interrupted pointedly.

'So runs the legend,' she returned calmly, and went on: 'In Wales there lived – and perhaps still live – the very core of our Kin. Indeed, beloved Wychy, in Wales there could be more than one place for refuge.'

'There was another singularity in the heavens, O Queen,' he went on quickly. 'The ancient Triad not only moves, but one of its stars has changed. According to the great Merlyn, the constellation comprised a gold star northward, and a black and a white star together in the south but now, although the black and the white remain unchanged, the gold shows as a speck within a larger *blue* star, What can this mean, do you think?'

Mergyn laughed triumphantly. 'The stars of the Lord of the Heavens do not lie, Wychy. Doesn't this herald the coming babe? The blue star is mine and the golden speck is the seed of the new King I now bear.'

'You mean then, O Queen, that by some magical means unknown to me, the babe is already in being?'

'*Unknown to you,*' Mergyn's tone was incredulous. 'Beloved Wand, is this the moment to pretend such arrant absurdity?'

'Pretend?' Black Wand looked stunned. 'If there's any pretending, it's yours, O Queen, not mine.'

'Are you daring to say that you *didn't* come to my Stede during the Dark?' Mergyn was so angry; she practically spat the question at him. 'Or are you so beguiled, you think you wandled me into believing it was someone else – just as your wicked Father in Evil of old did upon the innocent Ygraine?'

'I neither came, nor tried to wandle you into any kind of unknowing. Until this very time, I have lain in the Wynn – albeit my spirit was adrift among the stars –'

'Liar! Liar! Liar!' she screamed. 'You came to me by the Royal Road and lurked here in my Great Hall, where I found you. You went down on your knees before me, beseeching me even as I said you would, and reminded me of what was written in the Record of Days – "*And so between us we did encompass the Coming of He-Who-Was-Alder-Called-King.*"'

She saw an alarmed and startled recognition in his eyes, and was triumphant. *You do know and remember*!

But he said: 'If there's been any wandling, O Queen, then it's down to you. Or this accusation is a trick. For I tell you this – as I have learned more deeply the secrets of our race – we are a barren people for a reason. There is no power that can give me or any of our wiccies seed. It was forsworn to Dragga so that we should remain a secret people and live by the renewing of our race in *mortal* cycle. I have read Merlyn's treatise on the *Girdle of Creation*, also, and am even now on my way to ask my Wych to inform you that, with the Girdle upon you, *you* must *drink* of the Elixir *yourself* – not me. You don't have to believe me – I can show you the words as they are written.'

Mergyn was more than confounded, she was dumbfounded, for his words brought vividly to mind the 'loving cup' of the Elixir her lover had shared with her.

Abruptly she rose, bringing him to his feet also. 'Hence, Wychy!' she said imperiously, struggling to keep her composure under control as the wonder of a new revelation dawned on her.

Only when she had turned her back on him and was walking quickly away, did she allow her face to show the overwhelming joy that flooded her. It had not been Black Wand but the very spirit of Merlyn himself had come to her in the Black One's wraith, and she needed to be on her own now to savour and relive the memory repeatedly – a truly heavenly secret she could confide in no one – least of all the Wychy.

CHAPTER 22

WYCH'S WEAL

Myrddin waited respectfully until she was out of sight before turning himself to make for Weirdsmeet and his Wych. It was even more necessary now that the pair of them were reconciled.

Filled with every good intention of contrition and apology, the Wychy crossed the narrow neck of water and came to where White Wand sat sewing her Runic tapestry.

'Hael and wyn, beloved Sister Wand – ' he began.

'Don't you 'hael and wyn' me, Brother Wand,' she interrupted furiously. 'What of that poor wight last night whom *you* allowed to wannion of the Scathe?'

'I'm not with you, Sister Wand,' he answered blankly.

'You know very well what I'm talking about. Our most beloved Pwyll. You passed him on the Royal Road and never stopped to put him in a place of safety.'

'Pwyll?' he said, astonished. 'I met no one on the road when I escorted Nyzor to the Wynn.'

'When you were going *from* the Wynn to the royal Stede,' she said sharply

'I returned from the Wynn by the Weirdside path,' he said steadily.

'I'm not talking about *that* journey, which was your second. I mean the one where you ignored Pwyll. I had to fly to save him, calling to you. You took no notice and I was too late to save my poor wicca from the Scathe. There was just enough time to bring him back here for the Bane – or he'd have gone entirely.'

Myrddin was shocked and baffled. It seemed to confirm what the Queen had said and yet he knew had not left the Wynn.

'You must be wandled, poor Wych,' he said earnestly. 'At no time did I leave the Wynn to go to the Palace by the Royal Road. I wouldn't. It's against all protocol.'

'Can my Wych ball lie?' she asked.

The Wychy gave up. It was pointless to attempt any kind of reconciliation faced with an impasse like that.

*

Back in his Wandle Retreat, the Wychy put the puzzle behind him and instead summoned with will and with Wand the return of the three dove messengers he had sent abroad. When none appeared, it occurred to him that, simple astrals as they were, they could be flying around outside the forest. He decided to check. Fortunately, there was enough going on in the forest to keep anyone from missing him. From sun-up to zenith, Nyzor had kept the fae happily occupied with scouring the Weal for the supplies he needed. Then Mergyn had arrived to take up residence in her Bower, and called on White Wand to announce the arrival of the Royal Babe in three days time, on top of which they still had Dreadful. Black Wand had seen to it that after careful priming, Aíssa had bequeathed the dragon to the fae in token of her gratitude for the refuge they had provided for Nebuchadnezzar and herself.

Myrddin made his way out onto the main road, and scanned the skies for white doves. There were none. However, the further summons he made with the Wand brought an astonishing answer. A white owl appeared on the uneven ridge of a nearby barn. Even at that distance, he could tell it was no bird of bone, flesh and feather. For one reason, it was flying too swiftly, and for another, although mortal in size, was astral in composition and therefore could only be the messenger of – which race …? He thought hard. *The Mabyn?* This had no sooner registered with him than a flight of birds, approaching rapidly over the open field, distracted his attention. Their flight was purposeful and appeared concentrated on the owl. He knew it was in the nature of rooks and crows to attack owls that showed in daylight. Nevertheless, the speed at which these flew revealed they were also astral and similarly of mortal size.

As if sensing danger, the owl took off. At once, the approaching group spread out to encircle it; which was when Myrddin recognised they were neither rooks nor crows but – of all things – black falcons! Yet not only were black falcons foreign to the northern hemisphere, no falcon he had ever heard of hunted in company; and there were seven of these – all swift, black and deadly. When he saw the seven raiders swoop as one to seize the owl in midair and begin tearing it to pieces between them, he realised he was witnessing something entirely alien to mortal nature, and had to look on helplessly while the owl was destroyed. In moments, it was gone and with it whatever message there might have been for the Weirdfolk. It explained White Wand's words when she had said of it in her vision that it had appeared to be dead. Watching the seven falcons fly off to the west, he asked himself what it could mean, and found the answer disturbing.

Only a fae intelligence every bit as knowledgeable as himself, could have fashioned such creatures, and Gwyn the Son of Nudd was not only just such an enchanter, but had refused to acknowledge the rule of Arthur. Wasn't it logical, therefore, to assume that the King of the Kin of Beauty had received Myrddin's dove, destroyed it and then set out to destroy any other messenger he found heading for the

Weirdfolk, such as the White Owl of the Mabyns? It was a sobering thought to find the Weirdfolk had an enemy and, although it also revealed that the Mabyn were friendly, it was straight into the danger in the west that the Triad of Mona was moving, Hetty had also raced away to the west. Supposing she had taken back news of the little kingdom where its wizard had so wronged her?

He returned to the forest wondering why there was no mention of enemies in the Wychy's Book of Lore, nor had Amaranthus referred to the Kin of Beauty as enemies – only that they had refused to acknowledge Arthur as King.

Thinking of the owl's merciless annihilation, he castigated himself for being so thoughtless as to send his messengers into the blue without thought of any possible hostile reaction. It put a new complexion on everything. He supposed he could be thankful that the Owl had *not* flown into the forest, and could only hope that the little kingdom's exact whereabouts was still unknown. He realised he was going to have to do something about guarding its approaches for returning fae. The thought of what it could mean if those falcons returned did not bear thinking about.

He wrestled with the problem and possible solutions for some time until he realised he was approaching it from the wrong angle. Surely, the best way he could protect any returning fae would be to remove the menaces themselves. Providing he was bigger, stronger and even more savage than they ...

All he needed was an appreciable amount of human ectoplasm. He would have set off on the job at once, if the Queen hadn't commanded his immediate presence before her in her Bower.

He debated a moment whether to beg off from where he was, or to go and do it in person. Deciding his actual presence could carry more weight, he went dutifully to kneel at her feet, much to the joy of the attendant fae who were always delighted to see him.

'O Queen,' he begged. 'Matters attendant upon our Lady of Heaven command my immediate presence in the world of mortality.'

'On the contrary,' said Mergyn evenly. 'Your Lady of the little kingdom commands your continued presence here in immortality. I have summoned your Wych, beloved Wand, that we three may discuss matters attendant on the welfare of our people here. You have recently been presuming a responsibility for their destiny that is not yours to take.'

Was it a warning? Was it a threat? It sounded like both to Myrddin, although her tone appeared temperate and reasonable.

Yet it was neither, as he later realised. Time was running out and Mergyn knew that the Wands had to be reconciled to each other. It had therefore seemed clear to her that, unless she did something about it, it wasn't going to happen.

When White Wand appeared the next moment, Mergyn rose, dismissing her attendants, and placed an arm around the Wych's shoulders.

'Dearest of Daughters,' she said to the Wych, guiding her to a seat, 'our beloved Brother Wand here is going to take us into his confidence upon everything that he has discovered of our destiny, and how it all came about. And it seems best, beloved Wychy, if you started with how you first came to learn about the great Am-Mar-El-Lin …?'

Myrddin was trapped. She was asking for a full confession, which it would have to be because there was little that she had not already learned or guessed in the meantime. If he left anything out, she would only remind him, and that would look bad. It wasn't that he had any radical objection – he had tried to confess some of it to White Wand himself previously. What nettled him was the need to take precious time out now to tell it – *and* to tell all. He saw no way of getting out of it. He therefore decided to pull no punches and held nothing back.

Speaking quietly without trying to excuse his behaviour, the telling took a long time because he covered it in minute detail, including the Queen's first avowal of love at the previous High Moon. And later, and equally dispassionately, of the fateful interregnum in *Woe Begone!* where the Queen had translated the golden leaves, and robbed him of the Girdle and Elixir when his back was turned, and then sworn she would not part with even the Elixir until he came to implore it on his bended knees and beget the babe with her.

He paused here while White Wand, who had sat with downcast eyes listening, looked up questioningly at the Queen, who nodded confirmation. It was all part of the cure – White Wand's cure.

When he reached the most crucial confession of all, the wandling of Barney and Hetty into asking for the Bane, White Wand started up in righteous indignation.

Mergyn stayed her with outstretched hand, reminding her: 'No more in essence than what you yourself had had started, dear Wych.'

White Wand crumbled at once. She threw herself on her knees at Mergyn's side, burying her head in the Queen's lap, crying her woe. On hearing her Brother Wand's measured words on how he had subsequently revived each wraith; Mergyn had to forcibly restrain her, commanding her attention while her partner's voice described the new living he had provided for the wraiths he had so illicitly preserved.

At that point, Mergyn interrupted him with a gesture. Looking down at the Wych, she said movingly. 'Dearest daughter, how can I make it plain to you that in all this wrong there is the will of Heaven? Were it otherwise, wouldn't Mona have punished them?' She shook her head admonishingly as the Wych looked up to argue. 'No, dear

Wych, listen to me. Are you and I so blameless that we can condemn our brother's weirdliness? Is there any canon of our ancient law that not all three of us has broken? *Myself* more than either of you? I longed to win a love that wasn't mine but yours alone, dear Wych. Whereas your Brother Wand has worked only to find a way of preserving our people from the promised doom.'

This support was a surprise for Myrddin, already conscious that without the Queen's goodwill his quivering Sister Wand would never have stood for even a tenth of what he was being forced to confess. So when he carried on to tell of his self-introduction into Weir Court, he felt much like a criminal already proven guilty and asking for other offences to be taken into consideration.

He did gloss over the manuscript that had come into the Weir Lord's possession, however. That, he felt, belonged to White Wand. It confirmed her visions in the Eye of Mona and something for her to hear first in private.

He then told of his disposal of Hetty and Nebuchadnezzar, including the latter's return as Nyzor the new Vintner, and Hetty's departure west – which they might need to be aware of in time to come.

After that came his survey of the heavens during which it appeared, Pwyll had made his last journey.

He paused, seeing the Queen lower her head to whisper something in White Wand's ear which he could not overhear but clearly startled her. The Wychy continued then with what he had told the Queen of the portents of the heavens, and ended with the row that followed when he rebutted the Queen's assertion of his visit to beget the babe. During it all, Mergyn continued to stroke White Wand's hair, expressing all the love and sympathy she could.

When Black Wand fell silent at last, Mergyn reminded him: 'You said this morning that matters attendant upon our

Lady of Heaven commanded your immediate presence in the mortal world?'

But Myrddin felt he unburdened himself sufficiently by then. He still couldn't entirely trust the Queen, and was still obstinately determined to retain some degree of independence over their emergency. He therefore said nothing of the Owl and its destruction but answered:

'It is important that the Weir Ward be advised of the portents, beloved Queen. It is important to seek such guidance as he might be able to give us about the west. It is important that he also knows where to find us.'

She nodded and dismissed them both, saying: 'Beloved Wands, I'm sure you are aware that during our time here, Sunné has set and Mona also will soon be down. I think it wise to allow you to be about your forest duties and see that all are safely under cover.'

*

Both Wands were keenly aware that Mergyn had given them a new lease of life together and, having ensured that every fay was safe, they sauntered side by side to Wandleside whisking away the thin early tentacles of Scathe which approached and then receded as if hesitant to pursue the two of them.

'It seems Dragga is less eager than he used to be, brother,' remarked Ann.

'And so he should be,' said the Wychy. 'His continued existence depends on us. We cannot allow him to be destroyed. Our time in the forest is coming to an end.' He sighed. 'I shall have to begin releasing those of our people who are in mortal incarnation – '

Ann was horrified. 'You can't do that.'

'I have to – a few at a time,' he said quietly, adding: 'How else am I to ensure they are not left behind when we leave?

If they return to the forest and find we're gone, where will they go?'

'Then I will come with you, Brother Wand,' she insisted. 'It is a burden we shall bear together. We will act as one.'

He touched her Weird gently in acknowledgement. 'I would welcome that, beloved sister, but this work is *my* Weird. Yours is here. On top of everything else, the Queen needs your support and our returning people need to be met and clothed. Now, during the interregnum, I must go and bring Sir Thaddeus in and when I get back I have some very important information for you …'

CHAPTER 23

THE GREEN DRAGON OF THE SOUTH

Dreadful came in use as the quickest means of transporting Myrddin to Dyke's Hall, where Sir Edward had told him he would find Thaddeus Lovejoy. With the dragon able to fly him through several open upper windows, it was not long before the Wychy found the sleeping Lovejoy into whose open mouth he trickled an overdose of Wizard's Woe. With little time to spend hanging around, he needed quick results.

The moon was still well below the horizon when the Wychy freed the unconscious wraith from his mortal body and delivered him into Dreadful's care while he got to work on the elastic properties of the astral ectoplasm.

Anyone but Dreadful would have been scared witless by the towering Golden eagle that the Wychy's Wand conjured from the material and shaped into being. Having immersed himself in Merlyn's books even more by now, Myrddin knew how to shrink and draw the bird into his own wraith – the magic of it being that he could as easily project the shape outwards again when he needed to be an eagle. It seemed to account for wizards' renowned ability to turn themselves into animals, birds or even fish in the twinkling of an eye.

He performed a similar action on Dreadful with some more of the stuff. The dragon made a good pupil; obediently swallowing everything that the Wychy fed him. In moments, he learned how to increase his length from four feet to forty and in that form, Myrddin turned the dragon's scales to a particularly virulent looking green. The Wychy was pleased with the result. He wanted the enemy in no doubt that the Great Green Dragon of the South was still alive, kicking *and* up to protecting the Weirdfolk.

It then only remained to get the beast back to his foot long, golden coloured and lovable self before mounting him with the unconscious fay in his arms.

On his way back, he dosed several villagers with lesser but still lethal dosages for their return to the forest and, once back himself, he left the unconscious Thaddeus with Dreadful for company in the now vacant Temple, and hastened to The Wandle where he humbly asked White Wand if he could see her.

She rose to meet him as he came to her Retreat. There were stars of adoration in her eyes, and a new wisdom crowned her manner. The relief and warmth of their wordless embrace sealed the healing between them. It had been so long since they had come together; it was some time before the Wychy could bear to bring himself back down to matters that needed their urgent attention.

Imminent sunrise meant finding someone to meet and reassure Thaddeus Lovejoy before the newly arrived minister woke to discover himself alone with a dragon – even if small, golden and loveable – and Myrddin still needed to tell his Wych what he had found in the manuscript of Amaranthus.

*

The moment they woke, Edmund and Baddenham were inspired to race each other to the Temple in time to rescue a new and terrified half-born from the dragon's friendly advances, while Myrddin started telling his partner of the discoveries he had made concerning the Faerie Kingdom.

Ann's absorbed interest was shattered to hear a distraught, urgent and tearful summons from the Queen:

Anguish of ages
Now is upon me
Mona has struck me
Down in the Darkness

Gone is my ageless pride,
Gone is my wisdom!
Come with your healing, Wand!
Come with your Bane!

White One!, White one!
Why won't you hear me?
Daughter of Mergyn
Why do you desert me?

And Stella's voice also, calling the Wych secretly in the way White Wand had taught her:

White Wand, White Wand, Come quickly. Our lady Queen is stricken and needs you.

Already on her way in alarm, Ann returned: *I come, beloved Queen! I come!*

Stella was standing at the entrance to the Bower quivering with enough anxiety to rack the forest.

Please, Brother Wand, Ann called silently. *Our people are becoming aware of their Queen's distress. If you would reassure them …?*

At the entrance to the Bower, Stella clutched her in terror. 'The Queen! The Queen!' she cried almost incoherently, as White Wand manoeuvred her quickly inside. 'I found her just now at daybreak. She was moaning and calling for you. I don't know what's wrong. She won't say –'

Striking the wiccy gently into unconsciousness, Ann flew down the staircase to the chamber below.

The Queen lay face down on her bed, weeping.

Throwing her Weird across her distraught monarch, the Wych gathered her in her arms with astonishment. This was no longer the proud, invincible spirit of Mergyn, or even the aloof consort of Alder, and nor was she miscarrying, as White Wand had first thought. This was simply Gwen the uncomplicated fay of moons ago.

For a long time the Queen clung to her like a child, sobbing and sniffing, while the Wych stroked her hair, now fair once more, hushing and soothing her while wondering at the cause of the distress. When Gwen at last looked up at her, White Wand saw the Queen's eyes had become as clear and honey coloured as any of her subjects.

'I-I'm s-so frightened,' she said brokenly. 'I don't kn-know what h-has happened or been h-happening to m-me – I feel so lost. It feels like I've been in a most awful and terrible dream and yet somehow it was wonderful and unbelievable at the same time, and I don't know what to make of it all – I even dreamed I was with child, And that I miss most of all, because I know it's impossible ...' and the tears began streaming anew.

It took White Wand a moment or so to think how she was going to help Gwen to realise what had happened and to come to terms with being possessed by the spirit of Mergyn. The effect on a fay that was now as simple and unsophisticated as any fully born, could be an immediate demand for the Bane.

She began by asking gently: 'You know that it is no dream that you are our most beloved Queen, dearest Gwen, don't you?'

'Am I really and truly so, dear Wych?' she pleaded. 'For Alder was one of the dearest and most wonderful persons in my dream – and then, it seemed, he was gone.'

'That is all true, dear one. And true it is also that you, and he both, asked us, your faithful Wychies, to perform for you both the miracle of a babe –'

Sudden hope lit Gwen's questioning eyes. 'You mean that *that* is true as well?' she asked, as if scarcely believing it could be.

For answer, White Wand took the Queen's hand and laid it on the tenuous Girdle of Creation around her hips – and both gasped. The marvellous thing was alive! There was no other way to describe the tiny tremors that quivered within it.

'Oh Gwen, beloved Queen!' cried the elated Wych. 'Why it didn't occur to me straight away, I'll never know. But you became yourself again the moment your babe quickened at dawn this morning. For his coming, the spirit of Mergyn lived in you and now that Arthur lives in you, *her* work is finished. He will be born the day and at the hour that *she-who-was-in-you* declared he would be.'

Gwen could only gaze at her with abruptly shining eyes, so full of joy she couldn't speak, and then burst into tears again with the happiness that filled her. 'O White Wand, thank you! Thank you, thank you!' she cried. 'I am so happy because a terrible part of the dream was that I had loved Black Wand and wanted to take him from you –'

The Wych laid her fingers on the Queen's lips, and kissed her. 'Not so, dear heart,' she said, almost in tears herself. 'It was just part of great Merlyn's magic that made it appear so.'

Ann could not immediately leave the Queen. All Gwen wanted to do was laugh, and talk endlessly about the approaching miracle and the wonder of its accomplishment. The most White Wand could do was to restore Stella to her senses and send her to Black Wand to reassure him that all was now well.

The next thing that concerned the Wych was how much Gwen intended to tell Black Wand next time she saw him. In view of her completely altered appearance, he would be astonished and perplexed. So what did Gwen want White Wand to tell him?

The question quietened the Queen at once. It seemed she remembered well enough that the Wychy did not believe she could be with child, and be even more convinced when he saw her.

'I will tell him,' she decided after awhile. 'I will tell him – no, I will *confess* to him – that I have been wandled in my mind all this time, just as he was sure I was – and that is no more than the truth, dear Wych,' she added quickly, at White Wand's stiffening with sharp objection. 'I have *not* been myself, And I shall ask his forgiveness for deceiving him like that. And now that I am now whole and well again, as he will see, it will make him glad and willing to forgive me.'

'Forgive you –' began White Wand, incensed at the idea there was anything to be forgiven, then stopped. Perhaps it would be better that way. She knew her partner had been irked enough by Mergyn's overwhelming rivalry in knowledge and authority. 'But the babe, dear Queen?' the Wych reminded her. 'He is quite convinced there is none.'

Gwen spread her hands helplessly. 'When the babe comes, he will question me, and I will not be able to lie. But I doubt he will believe me even then – ' she broke off to look earnestly at White Wand. 'O wisest of White Ones, we both love him dearly. How *can* we spare him such doubt and torment? Isn't there *anything* we can do?'

White Wand thought of her Brother Wand's proud spirit and the effect it would have on him if he thought the Great Enchanter had used him against his will.

She smiled as a possible answer came to her. 'If that is what you want, dear Queen, then I rather think my Brother

Wand is going to provide a babe the same way as he provided one for Aíssa. He will doubtless ask me to smuggle it into you during the Dark before dawn the day after next, but I shall take and hide it in my Retreat, and you shall present Black Wand, and all our people, with the real one.'

Gwen clapped her hands with delight. 'Oh, yes, dear Wych,' she exclaimed with relief. 'Yes – that is the answer.'

'Then, if I may leave you with Stella …?'

'I shall be all right with Stella, dear White Wand, and thank you again for *all* the comfort and joy you have been to me.' And she hugged and kissed the Wych warmly in gratefulness.

*

As soon as he received White Wand's message via Stella that all was well, Myrddin was thankful that whatever the trouble had been, it appeared to be something and nothing. As three of the wraiths he had freed in the night were safely back, met and clothed, and knowing another two should be on their way, he was anxious to reconnoitre the situation outside the forest.

First, however, he called Dreadful to come to him on the Woe side of The Wandle where the Wychy instructed him to blow himself up into the new leviathan shape that he had made for him in the early hours that morning and to go and wait on one of the highest trees of The Wandle.

With Dreadful positioned and primed to appear the moment he called, Myrddin soared away into the sky as the golden eagle. The sensation of flight, of powerful wings bearing him up, filled the Wychy with exhilaration. *Why, in Mona's name, hasn't this occurred to me before?* he wondered.

Breaking through the Veil high above the forest and circling away to the north he spotted two of the black falcons doing a wide patrol of the barn on which he had seen the owl.

From Merlyn's scrolls, Myrddin had learned that whatever creature you made, you endowed it with all the instincts of the image it bore. If pigs didn't fly, neither did astral ones. Therefore, although a falcon could be fiercely courageous, it would think more than twice about challenging another bird of prey superior in altitude, weight and endurance, and these two falcons needed no instruction regarding their appropriate action when a golden eagle plunged down on them at speed. He guessed this would send them westwards but, as they could not cross the Weal, they had to go south skirting the forest first before turning to the west.

He found he was already looking, foreseeing and reacting with all the elemental purpose of the bird he was supposed to be. He was going to catch those falcons, rend them, rip them and feast on them as if he and they were the real things. The two fled south, edging closer and closer to the forest boundary as he herded them in that direction. It was not long, however, before they dived and tried to turn again, but his sudden plummet from a greater height forced them to go south. Harrying them like this, they came to the junction of the Spinner with the outlet of Dragga's Weird. There he changed tactics, and rushed at them so fiercely they turned abruptly north skimming low over the Woe. With no cover in sight, they were like a pair of sitting ducks when the magnificent form of Dreadful roared down on them in a great swoop from above The Wandle tree-tops over the boiling surface of Dragga's Weird. Recoiling from the dragon's gaping jaws, they became ready victims to both assailants who savagely avenged the White Owl's destruction with beak, talon, tooth, and claw between them.

Dreadful snapped once and swallowed his meal whole, increasing his length by another inch, but the eagle minced his meat in more leisurely manner, not only because it was an eagle's nature, but because Myrddin needed to savour every gobbet of information it carried. In this way, he hoped to ingest the memories which this particular marauder had acquired during its time near Weir Forest.

He learned little yet much. There was a vision of their creator; a handsome, tall and proud, cold-eyed and cruel individual, who exuded power that spoke of an oppressive and unscrupulous ruler, and from the bird itself a succession of mental images of malformation, subjugation and slavery that was the lot of the whole of Faedom beyond the forest. He also digested a session of furious words spat at the falcons by the unknown magician. Myrddin didn't know what he expected, but what he received felt like a shock of cold water:

'You blind scourers of the skies. What use is it if you bring me the essence of all but one of the returning messengers from my ungrateful vassals? Where is news of my ancient enemy? I find none of its treasonable poison in your villainous crops. And this above all, I will have. Go, you craven sparrows and cringe not again before the magic of my enemies. The bird must still be on the wing. Get after it and bring me the guts of this mangy Owl that torments my peace.'

He had hoped that, as the falcon had eaten some of the owl; it should also carry a trace of its message. However, its owner appeared to have wiped it clean on receipt but left the bird in its remembered state of terrorised obedience.

The Wychy dismissed Dreadful back to his usual form, before taking to the skies again to make a vigilant round of the forest but found it clear of menace for the returning half borns due that afternoon.

Stella came flying to meet him as he entered the forest. 'Black Wand, Black Wand!' she cried. 'The most wonderful thing happened just a little while ago. A great green Dragon suddenly appeared and sat on the top of the trees of The Wandle, Everyone was terrified because we couldn't find Dreadful anywhere, until White Wand said it was Dreadful after all, only very grown up all of a sudden because he was guarding us – and then he disappeared and we thought he had left us forever.'

'Instead of which he returned only minutes later looking just like his usual golden self,' Black Wand finished for her, while wondering how his Wych had recognised the beast, and why he hadn't thought to warn her. 'Well, you must be prepared for all sorts of things like that now, little one. Remind me to tell you and everyone of the story of the Great Green Dragon of the South – it's quite exciting, only first I must find White Wand –'

He broke off because a crowd of happy fae that moment were coming towards him with his Wych. He opened his arms to her.

'O my incomparable one,' she sighed before their lips met. 'I love you so much and have so much to tell you –'

'And I you, joy of my heart,' he said, drawing her aside. 'Things we should speak of together on The Wandle. But how is the Queen?'

'Still within her Bower, my love, and I must warn you, she's no longer the same as she has been lately.'

Myrddin could only think things had become worse, and concern sharpened his voice 'Sister Wand, what is it? Your message from Stella said all was well. What has happened now?'

Within the shelter of his Weird, she spoke in low tones of how Gwen had become unconscious during the interregnum and was now herself again. Myrddin pressed her head to his shoulder in sympathy to spare her further admission of the disillusionment he imagined she must be feeling, while his own thoughts were triumphant at its implication.

A round to me, at last! he thought. Mergyn had so signally failed to wandle him with her arts; she had finally admitted defeat and was gone. What more could he want? There remained only to present the Queen with the babe.

He kissed Ann tenderly. 'All will be well, my love,' he murmured. 'In the interregnum before Mona's rise tonight, I will meet you outside the Bower with the babe. Then you can place it in our Queen's arms for her to find when she wakes.'

'O incomparable Wychy,' she said softly, shaking her head in thankfulness that she had read him so well. 'I love you.'

'Joy of my heart,' he said softly. 'You know that there will be more new arrivals today, but I cannot be here to meet them. Will you see that they are met and clothed? I am going now to see our beloved Weir Ward, and will bring him back myself this night.'

He did not tell her that he was also looking for their previous Black Wand. He had just about visited every eighteen year old boy in the village, but there remained one more.

CHAPTER 24

THE BIRTH OF ARTHUR

'Impy', so named because of his thin, lopsided features and long, almost pointed ears, was a retarded young man who lived alone with his grandmother. As Myrddin had hardly expected to find his predecessor incarnated in the village idiot, Impy had been left until last. The Wychy was only visiting him now because he felt honour bound to leave no one out.

No one in the village doubted that Impy had the gift of seeing the faerie, but teased and bullied as he was, he had long stopped saying anything about it except to those he trusted.

Myrddin found him sitting on the grass in Wisher's Mead, his knees drawn up to his chin, staring straight ahead, and was startled to hear him say:

'I 'members thee, Mr Fairy.' His voice sounded low and drawn out, and the way held his head, moving it so as not to look directly at him, made the Wychy realise Impy was seeing him in his peripheral vision. The child had no faerie wraith, but did have a pure and simple spirit that shone like an elfin light in his blue eyes when he was happy – as he always was whenever he was 'talking to the flitteries' as he called the fae because they moved so quickly.

'What do you remember, Impy?' asked the Wychy in astonishment.

'I 'members wearing black, like thee, and had a magic Wand, a'well.'

Myrddin was stunned. He had found his predecessor! The greatest Wychy of all time, who had somehow been able to turn the human Augustus Autrey into an elf and back again to mortal. A wise and kindly Wychy whose Wych had been at his side to rescue a rebellious half born from the might of Dragga; a Wychy whose Weird August had then seen withered; his Wand casting him away, who had gone to pay his debt to Dragga.

'Impy – Black Wand!' he cried eagerly, forgetfully trying to bend round to look him in the face, 'I've come to take you back to the forest – '

'Can't go back.'

'You can,' Myrddin said. Then asked: 'Why not?'

'My Nan says I bain't fay no more – I's a baptised Christian now.'

The Wychy was incensed. 'We'll see about that, Impy,' he promised. 'I'll come and give you something tonight when you're asleep –'

'Won't work, Mr Fairy,' Impy said, shaking his head.

And neither did it, although Myrddin administered enough Woe to have killed a horse. Impy simply woke just as usual and none the worse.

'Tol' you t'wouldn't work, Mr Fairy,' he said with a bright smile. 'My Nan says I bain't fay, no more.'

*

Before calling on Sir Edward with the Woe, Myrddin conducted another aerial reconnaissance. Hungering for any sign of the black falcons, he flew a figure of eight but found nothing that might have indicated their presence, which was disappointing.

He was about to turn for Weir Court when a speck of white below him caught his eye. Plummeting down, he had to check and swerve aside, startled at discovering a mortal sized white dove flying straight for the forest.

Not wishing to spook it, he hung back, before remembering the guardian he had set in place in the forest, which meant diving across the Woe at speed with a screaming yelp at Dreadful to tell him the bird was peaceful and not to be hurt.

He was only just in time. To the astonishment of the throng outside the Queen's Bower, the dragon had started to heave himself aloft with a bellow of rage and a change of shape that caused everyone to shrink in alarm, before reducing itself to normal.

High though he was, Myrddin could still hear Stella's reproachful: 'Dreadful, dear, we do wish you'd give us a *little* bit of warning before you show off this new trick of yours.'

There was a long drawn 'O-oh!' of amazement from all present when the dove, the size of a physical bird, landed in front of the Queen, and stood beside Dreadful ruffling its breast feathers.

Gwen looked askance at White Wand, who shook her head, and both looked relieved to see Black Wand appear and come to kneel between Dreadful and the bird.

'Beloved Wand,' cried Gwen, taking his hands in hers. 'It is so good to see you.'

The Wychy, stunned by the change in the Queen's appearance, could only stare in awe at the vision she presented of sweet gentleness and trust.

His sister Wand, delighted by his amazement, broke the spell reluctantly, saying: 'Dear Wychy, do you know the meaning of this?' She indicated their visitor.

Myrddin was almost thankful to rise and dismiss Dreadful before laying his hand on the dove's shoulder. The bird stilled itself to attention.

'O Queen, O Wych, O Master and all who are gathered here,' he said addressing everyone clearly and solemnly. 'In the beginning when The great Merlyn made Weal and Woe,

Weird and Wandle, he also made a dove that was to be the emblem and messenger of our Race. But one day there was a huge storm and an earthquake. It caused great damage and since that time, our dove has been lost to us. But now, if this enchanted bird is our own then it will have a message for us.'

'But how shall it give it, dear Wychy?' asked Ann looking puzzled. 'Will it speak?'

'O Queen, O Wych,' he said. 'I suggest we three place our Wands together beneath its beak. It will then give its true origin, or betray itself as false.'

White Wand followed his example and placed her Wand tip with his under its bill and together they led it forward to Gwen, who reached out and added her own. What they each then heard silently made them look at each other in wonder; Gwen especially. She gazed from one to the other of them clearly mystified.

Myrddin spoke: 'Beloved Queen, if you will repeat the message aloud, we shall know if we all heard the same?'

Gwen's unclouded eyes remained wide with awe as she replied: *'Hael and wyn to you, Weirdfolk of old who have waited so long for me to return. Sad though the numbering of your days in the forest may seem, I bear tidings of refuge far away where neither fae nor mortal shall oppress you. Go to Glastonbury, most blessed of Queens, you and your Son-to-be, and all your people. Go to the nearest of your kind, the Kin of Beauty that do dwell in Glastonbury's Tor whence the remains of Arthur, the King-Who-Was, who shall be King-Once-More, were taken. Your kinsman Gwyn Son of Nudd and Lord of Avalon waits to welcome you and take you to Annwyn.*

'Before the waning of the next moon he will send an escort for your journey that you may come in safety. Until that time, most gracious Queen of the Weirdfolk beware all other messengers who come no matter how fair they look, or how sweet their words.

'Rejoice and be merry, O Folk of the Weirds.'

As soon as Gwen reached the end of the message, the bird took wing and flew off. It was so unexpected, Myrddin was alarmed – those black falcons! 'Beloved Queen,' he said urgently. 'It is imperative I leave immediately.'

The words were a formality. This Gwen was not going to raise the least objection. As for his Wych, she had her hands full with the number of newly returned half borns as well as dealing with the general clamour for an explanation of the dove's message. Who was this new King? Was it another story like the one about Nebuchadnezzar that had turned out to be true? Where did he live? When were they going on this journey?

It took precious moments before the Wychy could race away for the privacy he needed to take to the air again and when he did, there was no sign of the dove.

Has it been attacked? he wondered, while feeling strongly that there would have been some indication if it had. All was peaceful, the Sussex landscape mottled only with wind-chased shadows of drifting cloud. Coasting on the wind, he thought again about the dove's message. The three Wands had confirmed that the bird was genuine, yet it had come from the Kin of Beauty whose magician King he now suspected of being the enchanter who had made the falcons. The message of the dove had referred to Annwyn which, as far as his sketchy memory went, was the Celtic synonym for hell. Were hell and Glastonbury Tor the same? Either way, it hardly sounded inviting and he remembered the dove had *not* been among the visions that White Wand had seen in Mona's Eye when she had looked for help. Supposing it *was* their dove and been in the possession of the black falcon's King all this time? What if *he* had sent it when his falcons had brought him the white owl's message? In addition, *if* the dove was their messenger, why had it flown away?

He felt he would have given a lot to see the dove again at that moment and, genuine or not, would have killed and eaten it without compunction to discover who had really sent it.

In the end, he turned for Weir Court, transforming out of his eagle shape before entering the outhouse to find Merlyn's Ring and get dressed in the shirt and trousers the Weir Lord had lent him for his appearance as Myrddin Black.

After commiserating over the death of Lovejoy's nephew, Sir Edward greeted the news of his own coming demise with relief.

Myrddin gave him careful instructions on when he was to drink the Woe which he mixed with a small glass of water. '… It's getting dangerous out there, and I want to take you back safely myself.'

'That will give me time to make last arrangements,' said the other agreeably. 'I'll leave a note for Humphrey that you've always been welcome to use the typewriter whenever you want. Is that what you're here for now?'

'Thanks. But I'd like to catch up on some news first, please, if you have any papers? I'd also like to study a map or two of the British Isles?'

The Weir Lord indicated the pile of periodicals and papers he kept updated in his study and Myrddin settled down to catch up on the political and social repercussions regarding the forest.

To Myrddin, James Durant's drowning seemed like weeks ago, so much had happened in the forest. But here the banner headlines of that tragedy were still reflecting a furore which was further inflamed by the news of how Sir Thaddeus Lovejoy had succumbed himself following his personal visitation to Dragon's Woe to inspect the scene of the appalling incident. It was a coincidence cleverly underlined by inference and not by word. The authorities, bombarded for news, were evasive; neither confirming nor denying the possibility that Lovejoy might have caught the bug when he visited the fatal Weir. The media had not taken the brush-off kindly. Why so much mystery regarding the exact cause of death? The uproar had increased with the still breaking news of a spate of deaths in Three Weirs and the adjacent villages. One reporter had thrown in a bombshell by asserting the cause was unknown to medical science as yet, and raised another crisis on that point alone. It forced the Government to take action and hammer the medical experts for a clearer statement, while clamping down on press releases.

The Opposition were rejoicing at the opportunity to slap the Government's jowls for aiding and abetting an attempt to hold back vital news, and the whole country was rocking with indignation over the affair. The Ministry of Health had reached the stage of refusing to be wheedled any more by government policy and was coming down with a heavy hand; throwing a cordon around every village affected, and rounding up and segregating every known contact with those affected.

It was obvious that it had almost certainly put paid to the plans of the Ministry of Town and Country for any kind of housing development in the area but did that mean the forest was safe? Myrddin doubted it; they were bound to drain Dragga so that they could be seen doing something.

After sunset, and before moonrise, he took leave of the Weir Lord, reminding him of his instructions. Leaving as he had arrived, he flew in ever widening circles for an hour or more before he saw anything amiss, and that came in the shape of ferocious looking wolves not of mortal size but large enough in fae proportions. They were racing south. Hanging back out of sight, he followed them, knowing they were making for the village of Three Weirs. On their arrival, and to his relief, they showed no sign of trying to get into the forest, but simply patrolled its confines, endlessly searching highways and fields for non-existent prey.

Having watched them for a while, he wondered if he should call out Dreadful and make an end of them, but decided against provoking an inevitable retaliation for which he was not prepared. Their behaviour appeared controlled and purposeful, as if directed by an unseen presence especially when a moment later they just as quickly changed tactics and disappeared away to the west. It seemed safe then to visit a now sleeping Impy. It had occurred to him that there still was a way in which something of the child could live on in the forest.

Just as he could harvest plasma from living plants without damaging them, he could also take a little of Impy's ectoplasm to make the babe without harm to Impy and, if the babe had to be something special, then who better than Impy? It *had* to work, he reasoned. Surely *something* of the greatest Wychy who had ever been must still reside in the astral make-up of his mortal ectoplasm. With this in mind, Myrddin went to work reverently and carefully on the sleeping youth. Then it was on to Weir Court to collect Sir Edward's now unconscious wraith. Whilst there, the Wychy tried to find the book of Amaranthus to check on the origin of the White Owl, before remembering that the Weir Lord kept the manuscript locked in his safe.

This time, he returned to the forest with Sir Edward's unconscious wraith and the tiny piece of Impy in his talons, while carrying Merlyn's thumb ring in his beak.

He dropped the ring into a small hole by a fence post in Wych's lane, became himself and took the Weir Lord into Nebuchadnezzar's Temple past Dreadful on guard at the entrance.

*

Outside the Queen's Bower Myrddin duly handed over the tiny bundle he had lovingly fashioned from Impy's astral material and had carried closely hidden beneath his mantle. The minute scrap was still without a wraith or spirit to animate it, but it was a babe and would behave like one, which was all that the fae had asked for.

Nevertheless, they both knew that it fell well short of the truthful heir of perfection that their people would believe it to be.

'A magical beginning indeed, Beloved Wand,' Ann said. Then added enigmatically: 'What could be a more fortunate omen than that he should pass from your Weird to mine before he ever wears the one appointed for him?'

'Extremely fortunate,' he admitted, feeling a flood of gratitude for her apparent willingness. She had done so much else, too, shouldering his responsibility for the returning half borns on top of her own duties without complaint.

Before he left the vicinity he flew a circuit of the Forest and to his surprise could find no wolves anywhere. He searched literally high and low before coming to rest in a tree to think. There seemed as many reasons for it being a bad sign as there were for good. So he flew off to find them. He discovered why they had gone missing when he found the pack streaming eastwards chasing a diminutive but voluminously-cloaked female figure riding a white mare.

He at once recognised the erstwhile 'Hetty', and saw that she appeared quite capable of defending herself. Despite having the reins of her own horse and those of a fae-sized but massive black charger in her left hand, she also held a whip in the other that streaked out in a flash of fire to claim any wolf that came within range. The wolves nearest the collapsed beast fell on it, tore it to pieces and devoured it, while the rest caught up to continue the chase. Seven times he saw the streak of fire take a wolf before the rider got through the village of Three Weirs. To his alarm, however, she crossed the road separating the village from the forest and rode into it.

Diving in ahead of her, he watched her slow to a trot as if knowing she was out of danger. Morphing back to himself, he stepped out from beneath some bracken just as Dreadful's vengeful form came hurtling down the track. He stayed the creature with his Wand and turned to face the rider, who had came to an abrupt halt but close enough to put him in range of her whip.

'Ah-ha.' she said curtly. 'So we meet again, Mr Black Wand of the Weirdfolk.'

'Also titled Merlyn's Heir, and a guardian of this Forest of Weir. And you, Lady …?'

'And that sorry beast?' she asked mockingly, ignoring the question and looking beyond him to Dreadful. 'Is he the other guardian spirit of your kin, wizard?'

He knew the question implied that she recognised it as a fake. 'No, he isn't, Lady,' he said evenly. 'But he can deal just as harshly with any four-legged scarecrows as your own scourge.'

She nodded casually, while continuing to study Dreadful like a huntress examining the points of a passably good horse. Then with a movement so fast he barely saw it, the fiery leash streamed out at him. If he hadn't already seen the lash in action, he would have been defenceless. But he countered with his Wand, which returned the whip to its normal appearance.

She raised an eyebrow, laughing. 'Heir to Merlyn, indeed, O wizard of the Weirdfolk. Had you been any other, my magic would have destroyed you, for I am Nemway, that Lady of the Lake whom Legend says led your father Merlyn to his doom.'

Nemway! It was hard to believe that such a powerful sorceress could have been concealed in Hetty. Yet he of all people knew that they were the same wraith. He knew something else, also: Nemway was *not* the sorceress who had imprisoned Merlyn in his cave.

'And who but Merlyn's Heir would know that?' she returned with a mysterious smile, when he voiced the revelation. 'But my mission is not to talk with you, warlock. I have come to see Mergyn of whom immortal Arthur is to be born this day.'

It was his turn to smile enigmatically when he thought of the surprise in store for *her*. Friend or foe, Nemway would have to betray her true colours when she discovered that neither Gwen nor the babe were who they were supposed to be. And sooner than he realised, for as the sun rose they became aware that the Weal was ringing with golden notes from Kye's trumpet.

From the door of Gwen's Bower, the Royal Herald was summoning the fae with cadences of joyous sound that danced a jewelled response from every dewy twig and leaf and blade of grass.

CHAPTER 25

EXCALIBUR

With Nemway riding at walking pace beside him, the Wychy directed the way with Dreadful bringing up the rear.

Everyone was running in a torrent of excitement to Queen's Glade. From Nebuchadnezzar's Temple, the bewildered new arrivals rushed to join the throng, asking what it was all about. Nobody knew, but when they poured into the glade it was to see a gathering of the Court Officials before the entrance to the Queen's Bower.

Kye did not end the prolonged fanfare until every fay was present. Then the Chamberlain stepped forward, scroll in hand, and read: *'O my people, with loving greetings to you all, know that I, Arthur, King of all Brython, summoned by you one and all, am come again.*

'Great is this day, O my people, yet greater still shall be the day when I shall lead you to realms afar and possess my Kingdom, for this is the Weird woven long ago for my wearing. Hael and wyn, O my people. Hael and wyn.'

Listening on the outskirts of the crowd, Myrddin hardly knew what to say or think as the Chamberlain fell silent. *Preposterous!* might be a good word he decided as the Bower opened and Gwen, with White Wand at her side, came out to take her place on the throne before it. In her arms she carried the tiny babe they had waited so long to see.

The hundreds surged forward in awed gentleness, each eager to pay homage to the miracle. They came, and looked, and cried their gratitude and wonder; touching and kissing the hem of Gwen's long robe in tearful thankfulness; then sat before her to continue to look and sigh with gladness and to hug each other with joy; pointing out all the wonderful perfections of the baby King.

Stella ran to White Wand, crying out how grateful they all were for the magic that she and Black Wand had done on their behalf. But why wasn't their Wychy there so they could tell him how much they treasured his wonderful magic?

White Wand turned the fay around with a smile, directing her attention to where her black-cloaked partner stood and beside him an imperial-looking lady in a blue cloak, and wearing a white wimple, who was holding the reins of two horses.

Heads turned at Stella's startled cry and an avenue cleared for their approach. Nemway stayed back, allowing the Wychy to go first and introduce her. Myrddin knelt, without even a glance at the babe.

'The Lady requests an audience with you, Beloved Queen,' he explained. 'She is titled Nemway, Lady of the Lake.'

He looked searchingly into Gwen's face for any effect it might have on her. It had occurred to him that there could be little love lost between the two, which might spell trouble – but as Gwen no longer looked like Mergyn, and the babe was not Arthur, who knew what the witch might do?

'Nemway?' Gwen's surprise was innocent. 'Wasn't it she who befriended Arthur …?' She broke off, her gaze going to the Lady standing beyond the crowd, but no recognition showed in her eyes.

Myrddin stood, turned and bowed, indicating to Nemway that the Queen would receive her.

Leaving the horses, the visitor passed regally through the wondering fae, staring keenly at the Queen until she stood before the throne.

It was enough. She turned her head and shot a look at the Wychy that should have slain him on the spot. This was not Mergyn! Nevertheless, turning back to Gwen, she slowly and gracefully curtsied. 'I bow before the grace and sweetness of the Queen of the Weirdfolk.' She spoke loudly and pointedly, as if addressing everyone there except Gwen, before rising she said more gently: 'I am Nemway, gracious Queen.'

Gwen's face lit with joy and admiration. 'Welcome, Nemway, Lady of the Lake. I give you hael and wyn and the gladness of us all this wonderful day.'

Nemway stepped back a pace, glanced at White Wand, shot another look to kill at the Wychy while her fingers played with the handle of her whip as if half minded to use it on them all. Then, for the first time, she looked at the infant.

No one moved or spoke while she stared intently, a little frown deepening between her eyes as they went from the babe to Gwen and back again. Myrddin prepared himself for the worst – which never came.

Sinking on one knee, she crossed whip and hands over her breast, to say softly: 'Hail to you, King-who-was and shall again be King again! Hail to you Arthur, mortal and immortal, hope of our world. I dedicate my arms to you, and with them bring your own that I have hidden so long, waiting for this moment.'

Myrddin was astounded. If this stranger spirit had seen that Gwen wasn't Mergyn, why had she accepted such an obvious fake of an infant?

Nemway returned her attention to the Queen, saying: 'Gracious lady, have I your permission to speak with my sister in magic? The King's arms and armour that I bring for him need to be safely stored.'

Gwen agreed at once. But it sounded ridiculous to Myrddin – and ominous. If she was in the employ of the enemy, what kind of trick was she planning? He had to warn White Wand, who should herself know that Nemway's reaction was all wrong. But Gwen chose that particular moment to reach out her hand and lovingly draw his attention to the child he had not yet acknowledged.

Forced to kneel, he found himself jolted by a miracle. From somewhere the child had attracted both wraith *and* a spirit. It shouldn't have happened.

No wonder Nemway had recognised the babe as real! he thought, and decided it had to be the magic in Impy's ectoplasm. It could have attracted a wraith even if it wasn't Arthur's. There was so much he still had to learn from Merlyn's scrolls – and half of them were missing …

Clearly touched by his wonder and surprise, Gwen laid her hand on his and thanked him gratefully for the babe's marvellous origin. Myrddin could only take her hand and kiss it, not daring to look up for fear he would betray the guilt he felt at the deception he and his Wych had passed on her and the whole of Faedom who would now believe the real Arthur had come.

Very well, he thought with abrupt determination. *I'm just going to have to be the greatest magician ever to make it so – and, come to think of it, I haven't made a bad start, either!*

*

While White Wand was leading Nemway back to her horses, the elfin worshippers found themselves torn between sighing over Black Wand's adoration of the little king, and following the two sisters in magic, for a peep at the promised gifts.

It wasn't such a dilemma for the gnomes, however. Arms and armour were always of immediate interest to them. Feldspar, Sandstone and Whitegold pressed eagerly forward.

'White Wand, Lady from afar,' Feldspar appealed. 'Please, we gnomes are workers in every kind of gem and metal. There cannot be a safer place to store them than in our underground Mansion ...?'

'We would be proud to guard them with our lives,' put in Whitegold earnestly. 'We will keep them so polished, their brilliance will dazzle everyone. There really isn't *anywhere* as suitable as our Mansion.'

'Sister of the Wand,' Nemway called sharply, 'these are not Weirdfolk. They look more Mabyn – or my eyes deceive me.'

Ann said quickly: 'These are gnomes, Lady. They have been with us always – although their ways are different to ours. We love them equally, and they build and make wonderful things for us.'

Still ruling they were Mabyn nonetheless, Nemway turned back to the gnomes: 'Sincere ones, you shall see and admire the gifts I bring and, with permission of your Lady Wych, I see no reason why you may not keep them in your stronghold until the hour that our Liege has need of them.'

She threw off the covering from the black horse to reveal the pieces of an entire suit of faerie armour – lance, sword and battleaxe – each adorned with jewels, all securely fastened to the great saddle.

'You see!' she exclaimed. '*I*, at least, am true.'

Taken aback, Ann said: 'I don't understand. What do you mean?'

Nemway looked her up and down. 'Your brother of the Black mantle titles himself Heir of Merlyn. How are you called, sister Wych?'

'White Wand's title from of old has always been daughter of Mergyn, dear Lady.'

'Then tell me, Mergyn's daughter, where is your mother, that witch, that Fay supreme who betrayed the great Enchanter in my likeness?'

Belatedly, Ann realised the need to wandle the suddenly hushed and wondering gnomes and gathering crowd away from them. With the slightest twitch of her Wand and a mental direction to Nyzor, she sent them running back to the Vintner to find him already drawing out his celebratory mixtures.

'Is it not enough that the infant Arthur himself is here with us?' the Wych begged, seeing Nemway's eyes narrow at the departure of the gnomes.

'It will be enough when I know what trickery has been played on me by Merlyn's Heir,' Nemway retorted, turning back to her. 'That is not Mergyn who holds my foster-son so fondly in her arms.'

'There is no trickery – least of all by Merlyn's Heir, O Lady of the Lake,' the Wych answered vehemently. 'There is mystery, yes. But no trickery. This I swear in Mona's name. I saw the child born this morning. And she who bore him is our Queen, spouse of Alder-who-was.'

'And still I ask – and shall not ask again,' Nemway persisted threateningly. *'Where is Mergyn? Her* messenger summoned me to the Coming of the King?'

'I swear it is a mystery not mine to tell – '

'You swear too easily,' said Nemway, turning abruptly and throwing the cover back over the armour. Remounting her own horse, she said: 'You can hide your mother in the filthiest of pig-pens – which is where she belongs – but I *will* find her. *And* have my revenge ...'

White Wand ran in front of the moving horses, raising her Wand protectively, knowing she had to stop Nemway from leaving.

'Don't wave that piece of straw at me,' Nemway warned wrathfully, although she reigned to a halt. 'Merlyn's Heir might ward my stroke, but I very much doubt that yours will. I tell you, stand aside. I have no quarrel with the Weirdfolk – only with my enemy.'

Ann lowered her Wand, but stayed where she was. 'And I have no quarrel with you, Lady, though you mistake me,' she said quietly. 'Please, think a moment. You have acknowledged that Great Arthur is come again. You have solemnly pledged the return of *his* arms and armour. Why are you suddenly so insistent on throwing the whole day into shadow just because of Mergyn? I don't understand you.'

'Two things I have set my heart on for a thousand years,' replied the other fiercely. 'First, to cherish these sacred arms of the King, who will restore the freedom and happiness of our kind – second, an oath of vengeance on the one who not only brought about Arthur's downfall but that of Merlyn also, *and dared to do so in my name!*'

'Yet you came at her bidding – your enemy?'

Nemway was scornful. 'Not at her bidding. I came believing she had repented, and made atonement by bringing back the one deliverer of our kind to whom we could both pay united homage and in him find reconciliation.'

'And that is *exactly* what has happened!' cried White Wand in anguish.

'What?' said Nemway incredulously. 'You still insist on lying to me? You have already sworn in Mona's name that the babe was born of that simple fay that is your Queen. Do you take me for a moron? Out of my way before I forget the laws of hospitality and ride you down.'

White Wand took hold of the white horse's bridle in desperation, her voice an urgent whisper.

'Lady Nemway, listen to me, *please*? Mergyn *has* come, and if you will only come with me somewhere where we will not be overheard, I will tell you everything I know ...'

'It didn't escape my notice that you were well able just now to prevent our exchange from being overheard,' said Nemway coldly, but agreed to follow Ann to Nebuchadnezzar's empty Temple. As soon as she stepped through the entrance, however, the witch froze.

'There is nothing to harm you here,' said White Wand quickly. 'This place is as secret as the Queen's Bower.'

But Nemway was frowning. 'What *is* this place?'

'It was built by the gnomes to illustrate the story of King Nebuchadnezzar and his Queen Aíssa that my Brother Wand was telling our people.'

Nemway hissed 'Nebuchadnezzar. Aíssa. I *know* those names.' She walked slowly round the great hall, staring at every detail of its furnishings. At last, she took a seat on the edge of one of the fountains and beckoned the Wych. 'Come; tell me all that you promised ...'

White Wand obeyed, beginning with the prophecy she had heard at the eclipse. From there she went on to tell of Mergyn's possession of Gwen; the Passing of Alder, the coming of Nyzor, and the loss of Hetty's wraith, for which her partner had been unable to account. Then the revelations she had heard in Myrddin's confession in the Queen's Bower the day before – including the wandling of Barney and Hetty.

Nemway listened in silence until she heard how with the quickening of the babe, Mergyn had forsaken her possession of Gwen, and then put her head in her hands. 'Sister, I am ashamed,' she said lifting her face. 'My behaviour towards you has been inexcusable, yet you refused to allow it to stand between us. And now your words have healed a wound so deep; I don't know how to thank you enough.'

'Yet there *is* more, dear lady, My partner Wand was so against Mergyn, he could not believe she had conceived the child, and so fashioned a babe himself from plasma so as not to disappoint our people. The Queen and I then witnessed another miracle this morning when we placed it beside the real one, for wonder of wonders, the two merged into one being. For a moment, the Queen was fearful of what it meant, but I was able to comfort her, reminding her how protective Black Wand always is and has been and that this, although my Brother Wand might not realise it, is surely a most fortunate provision for Arthur's future safety.'

'That may well be true,' Nemway said thoughtfully. 'The babe does possess a shell of mortal composition.'

Ann was filled with wonder. 'Then prophecy is truly fulfilled – mortal *and* immortal both!'

Nemway nodded and, gazing at each other, they wept and laughed together with the love and joy that filled them before Nemway rose, holding out her hand. 'Come, sister, let us return at once and make the day also rejoice for our infant King.'

'Willingly, dear Lady – we have been too long already. My Brother Wand will be wondering what we have been up to. I see he mistrusts you?'

A frown replaced the happiness of Nemway's expression. 'For some reason he hides a guilty conscience, dear sister, so he doesn't trust me.'

'I fear it's his continual journeying into the realms of mortality that plague me,' White Wand sighed. 'I fear for his sanity every moment that he's gone.'

*

Ann's guess at her partner's state of mind was true. He was nearly beside himself with anxiety while the two of them conferred in the temple. For all his desire to rush off and eavesdrop on their meeting, however, he could not escape from Gwen's side. Her elemental delight at having him near her was something he dare not wreck by leaving her, especially with the Wych absent and the babe developing so quickly before everyone's delighted eyes. Myrddin had given Nyzor a recipe for the Vintner to provide for the fake infant's well-being, not knowing Mergyn had already primed the Vintner on what to feed the real Arthur. The babe was thriving on the liquid Gwen was spooning him from a silver cup. By noon he was so lively, he was already sitting up on her lap like an eighteen month old, drinking from the cup itself and watching everything with solemn wisdom. His eyes shone with a grey purity that in days to come would unerringly recognise friend from foe; a discomforting experience which Myrddin had already discovered. But then the Wychy's veiled eyes were an exception which Arthur would never question.

*

When everyone became aware that White Wand and Nemway had left the temple and were walking the horses back to the Glade, they ran off to greet them and to marvel at the kind of animal they had never seen in the forest before. Myrdddin could see them thinking what noble pets they would make alongside Dreadful!

Gwen exclaimed her delight at the sight of the chargers and when told that the black one, Windflame, was to be Arthur's own, she lifted the child up to see the gift.

Reasoning that if the horse came from the same place as the arms, armour and wolves the result could be too disastrous for words, Myrddin intervened. Pretending to misinterpret her action, he took the infant and stood aside as if to allow her to examine the horse unimpeded. Gwen seemed to see it as a paternal desire on his part to hold his child himself, and was delighted to allow him.

He saw White Wand shoot a look of apology at Nemway, who smiled back reassuringly.

Amid loud gasps of wonder, Nemway then displayed the glittering objects that the black charger carried. Along with the lance and battleaxe came a golden helmet with a plume of feathers; a suit of golden armour inlaid with jewels; and a great war-shield embossed with a dazzling design of black and silver stars.

Nemway presented each diminutive astral counterpart of their great earthly originals to the child in Myrddin's arms, before handing them to the Master of Gnomes for safe-keeping. The Master and gnomes were in a state of bemusement over every piece of it.

'By whose hands, O Lady Nemway, were these perfections fashioned?' asked the Master in whispered awe.

'Who else but Wayland, noble Master?'

'*Wayland.*' Every gnome echoed the name with a kind of fearful wonder, and started swapping legendary examples of the Norse god's craft and prowess at weapon making.

'These are wonderful gifts, Lady,' said Myrddin. 'But what of Excalibur?'

'I have reason for leaving *that* until last,' she said, unfastening an embroidered cover from the charger' side. The scabbard of the sheathed sword she lifted from blazed with jewels. 'You will remember Arthur's first sword was embedded in stone and only he could free it, thus proving him King. However, it broke in battle, and *I* gave him this ...' She held the weapon up for all to see. '*This* Excalibur is the astral of that earthly weapon with one important difference. Like the sword in the stone, only the King of all our kind in Britain will be able to draw it.' She looked straight at the Wychy as she spoke, adding, 'So who should be better entrusted with its keeping than you, O Heir of Merlyn who was always Arthur's closest friend and counsellor?'

Myrddin was nonplussed. What deep treachery did it serve to give him charge of it when he could so easily annul any contrary magic she had put into it? It didn't make sense, but he certainly wasn't going to refuse the offer. He returned the babe to Gwen, and received the sword across the palms of his hands, in one of which lay his Wand. He looked for a warning response from it, but none came. It seemed to him, however, that Nemway's smile was enigmatic, as if by this act she had crowned some dark and artful scheme.

'Lady, I accept the trust, and will take it at once to place of safety.' He bent his knee to Gwen, for her to admire the scintillating hilt and scabbard, then disappeared with it through the throng.

*

In the secrecy of his Wandle Retreat, the wizard spent half an hour wrestling with the sword before discovering that neither brute force nor the power of his Wand would loosen it from its sheath. It was such a blow to his pride; he convinced himself that the construction was the simplest of all tricks. If he, the very Heir of Merlyn, could not separate the two parts, then the whole thing was a revealed as a single piece that even a real Arthur could never release, let alone a false. It would therefore discredit the king at the very outset.

No wonder Nemway smiled, he thought wrathfully. How diabolically she had contrived its fulfilment, too. What were a few slain wolves so long as they gave substance to her story? The dove's message had been true: *beware all other messengers who come no matter how fair they look, or how sweet their words*.

The only option was to meet cunning with cunning. He must get the gnomes to fashion an exact copy. He would need to pitch them a story to account for it, but that wouldn't be too difficult. Hiding the sword closely under his Weird, he set off for the Gnomes' Mansion while its inhabitants were still engrossed with the events at Queen's Glade. He planned to leave the sword there, return to the glade and make his explanation secretly to the Master.

He no sooner arrived at Weirdsmeet than he spotted an animal's head moving swiftly down King's Weird towards him. As it left no wake behind it, it had to be an astral entity. Instantly alert, he moved quickly under cover to watch. To his astonishment, the flat, sleek crown and foreshortened nose revealed a fay-size otter. It came out of the water and hurried on its four short legs to the foot of Windaway to begin bounding up its winding path.

Beware all other messengers ... But this was one that Mona had shown his Wych.

CHAPTER 26

GARETH AND THE HOLY GRAIL

Myrddin was in a dilemma. He needed to hear the otter's message, and there was no time to take the sword back to his Retreat. He laid it at the foot of the nearest fir tree, and floated back across Weirdsmeet in pursuit of the otter, calling it to stop. It paid no attention. He raised his Wand and commanded it. The otter ignored him. This was infuriating; especially when throwing dignity to the winds, he had to run after the animal to catch up with it. He was so incensed; he failed to think of Dreadful's reaction.

It caused a near riot when it appeared in the glade. The dragon lunged at it, Nemway came to the otter's rescue with her whip, and Myrddin arrived just in time to prevent Dreadful's destruction.

The fae thought the otter was another pet to play with, and pandemonium broke loose when the poor creature, now thoroughly frightened, began snapping and barking at the multitude of hands stretched out to fondle it.

As the Wychies restored order, Myrddin saw the animal streak off again, straight for Gwen and the babe. White Wand flew to interpose herself and the otter fled to Nemway instead where it lay at her feet and took no further notice of anybody.

White Wand explained to Nemway how she had seen the animal in their oracle, and believed it to be a messenger.

Nemway nodded. 'You saw truly, dear sister, it is the traditional messenger of the Denefolk, a people skilled at interpreting wind and water and the movement of all natural things.'

'Then, if you will allow us, dear Lady, my Brother Wand and I will lead it to our Queen …?'

Considering its previous behaviour, Myrddin doubted its obedience to their Wands, so was thankfully surprised when it cooperated. Joined by Gwen's Wand under its jaws, with Arthur sitting up on her lap, the Queen spoke its message aloud:

'Greetings to you, Queen of the Weirdfolk. Greetings from the people of the Hollows and the Hills. Our hearts are heavy with the news of the coming desolation of your Kingdom. We sorrow also that we have no sanctuary we dare offer, being fugitive ourselves from the dread Usurper who holds our realm in bondage. Yet great is our rejoicing that the Coming foretold so long, is now at hand. Hail to you, Mergyn and hail to your son-to-be and to his strength that shall surely deliver us all. May he lean upon our wisdom and be guided by our oracle, which shall ever be at his service and command.

'Be pleased, O gracious Queen, to allow the homage of our secret messenger that he may return to us with early tidings of our King.'

Gwen looked at her Wychies in bewilderment. 'Who are these people of the Hollows and the Hills that call my son their Deliverer?'

Myrddin explained, adding a caution: '… I would not advise any open discussion of their oppression or the Usurper of whom the message speaks.'

With her eyes on the Wychy, Nemway added a warning of her own: 'The Denefolk are also Knowers and Seers of all events past and present that have happened in these isles, and cannot be beguiled by friend or foe.' He later learnt she meant him to know that it wouldn't do him any good to have imposed a fake animal on them. But to Myrddin, her words sounded like a carefully veiled threat.

In the meantime, the fae were waiting for his reassurance and interpretation of the message, especially Sir Edward We'ard – whose name the fae had quickly shortened to Redweird. Myrddin knew that with his mortal memories still strong within him, things must be appearing vastly different to the way they had been portrayed in *Wizard's Woe*.

The Wychy drew himself together and spoke: 'Beloved Queen, beloved people, it is no longer secret from you that beyond this realm of yours, there live many other immortals who have also waited for the wonder of this day. The great Merlyn separated us from them for this very purpose. He kept us hidden so that in the fullness of time when Arthur was come again, he would be safe from his enemies until, overcoming their enemy and his, he could bring us all together once more in joyful unity. Our Lady Mona has decreed that before long, our Weirds and theirs shall be one, and the name of Arthur is the magic which will bring this about.' He paused a moment to let this sink in. The thought crossed his mind that he was doing even better than the Chamberlain had at sunrise, before continuing: 'I have to tell you, though, that not all our distant kins have been able to enjoy the same perfections and protection that we have here. Most of them have no loving mortal guardian to keep them from safe as we have had, and so they need our help. But I know you will willingly welcome any who come to join us here.'

Gwen and White Wand were listening with expressions of surprise, and Nemway even nodding approval. It told him he had managed to gloss over the harsh truth by appealing to the fundamental principles of the Weirdfolk's nature, so that they would long to help these distant cousins. It seemed he won full marks again when he then put another idea to them. 'It may well be that when our King is grown, and sees how much you long to help these less fortunate than ourselves, that he will want to see for himself how his far off subjects live.' He turned to the gnomes. 'O bravest of spirits and most skilful of all, would you have our King go out on such a mission unattended and alone?'

Just as he expected, the response was immediate. They clamoured for permission to make armour for themselves and to become a personal bodyguard for the king – although whether they had any idea of what it entailed, other than parading themselves for the admiration of the wiccies, was hard to tell. But it played neatly into Myrddin's hands. While they were doing all that and using Arthur's armour as models, they could reproduce a dozen Excaliburs if need be. He therefore gave his gracious consent.

Immediately, one gnome took everyone aback by running to Omric and imploring on his knee: 'O Master, I claim an ancient privilege. I remember now, how my true name is Gareth. Allow me to make arms like those I once bore?' It was Sandstone, he who had found Merlyn's ring, and now not only appeared to have gone out of his mind, but his features had subtly altered. Nemway remarked the difference at once.

'I said these gnomes were Mabyn.'

Myrddin ignored her. Going over to the still dumbfounded Master, he spoke to the gnome at his feet. 'Rise, Sandstone,' he ordered kindly. 'Tell us what you mean.'

'It was the sight and touch of Arthur's magic armour that affected me, Black Wand,' he said, choking with emotion. 'It brought it all back to me. I remembered similar arms bearing a device of a hart of ten[1] that are my own and remembered that I, Gareth, fell at Lyonesse in the Great King's company.'

---

1 Heraldic term indicating a male deer of five years or more, with ten points or tines to each antler

'What do you make of this, noble Master?' the Wychy asked. 'If this brother *is* Mabyn in origin, then you must all be Mabyn.'

'Not all, Heir of Merlyn,' Omric answered almost defensively with an air of embarrassment. 'I, the first of Gnomes, have always been Gnome and was of Merlyn's company while we were still wandering in different lands looking for sanctuary. When we came here, I asked Merlyn for the company of spirits kindred to my own to share the crafts I love – for there was much to do. So Merlyn brought to me such Mabyn as were in the southern part of this realm, saying they were close kin to me. And so I loved them as my brothers, and told them nothing of who they really were for fear they would pine and leave me. I have heard nothing of Sandstone's history 'til now – which is a mystery.'

'No mystery, really,' Nemway said. 'It is plain that Sandstone is Mabyn in spirit and not of the Master's original company. He was most likely released from his last mortal body so near this forest that its magic drew him here instead of to his more distant kind.' With a glance at the Wychy, she went on significantly: 'It is not an uncommon happening, Master. I know of at least *one* other spirit who did the same and returned to the Weirdfolk here, instead of her own kin.'

Ann raised an eyebrow of shocked enquiry at her partner, clearly asking if this could be the missing 'Hetty' whom he had said he had last seen going west.

Myrddin was more concerned with what Nemway implied. *Heaven help me if she remembers her internment as Aissa!* he thought. 'Dear Lady,' he said quickly, 'perhaps it would be better if we discussed these mysteries apart? Beloved Queen,' he turned to Gwen, 'I hope you will you permit me to speak in private with the Lady Nemway?'

Of course, she would, so the two walked away together through a throng of the faerie so bemused by the day's events, that neither they nor their great ones noticed that the otter had quietly disappeared – until they remembered and looked around for it.

*

Myrddin would have preferred to take Nemway to The Wandle but, as he had abandoned Excalibur there at Weirdsmeet, had to take her to *Woe Begone!* instead.

The place brought back vivid emotional memories for Nemway. 'I loved you here,' she said frankly.

'And now you hate me?'

'I could,' she said with a shrug, 'save I've better things to do.'

'Such as?'

She looked incredulous. 'Like being thankful that I was here in time for Arthur.'

'You have Mergyn to thank for that.'

'So your Wych told me.'

'And what else did she tell you?'

She smiled thinly. 'Enough to tell me that you have such a corkscrew mind, it's a congenital impossibility for you to see anything that's as simple and straightforward as that baby.'

'Meaning precisely what?'

'If you can't believe your own eyes – how shall you believe mine?'

'By what sign do you recognise this infant of ours?' he asked curiously.

'Sign?' she returned scornfully, seating herself on the couch. 'Why should I need a sign? I *know* Arthur, remember? His coming is also expected immanently throughout the faerie realm.'

'Even by that evil Enchanter of the black falcons?'

'Him especially,' she said sharply, looking surprised.

'You had best guard Arthur well. Like Herod of old he will destroy his rival, if he can.'

'And sends you, his chief emissary, to ensure the deed.'

She looked astounded, and answered with asperity: 'Mortleroy wouldn't choose Nemway to run his meanest errand.'

The Wychy pounced on the apparently gratuitous slip, and sneered: 'Yet you know his name?'

'And why not?' she snapped back. 'The Seers, Knowers and Readers of the Denefolk know all things above the earth.'

'And they would tell *you*, of course,' he said derisively.

'As they must, if I ask.' She rose lithely and faced him trembling with anger. 'Learn this, you witless fool! The Sage of all the Seers was born of me. And may Mona rack you eternally for your witless wizardry if *you* fashioned that likeness of his sacred messenger today.'

'Witless yourself! *I* didn't fabricate it – it was your master Mortleroy.'

Nemway looked so furious, he thought she was about to strike him with her whip and raised his Wand in readiness to counter. But she unleashed it against the door instead, blasting it in a sheet of flame which left a gaping black hole through which she stalked.

Staggered at her magical dexterity, he followed quickly thinking that in her present mood she might disregard the subtle plan to discredit Arthur and simply slay the child out of hand. At least his and his Wych's Wands together would be sufficient to protect the child against her. As he went, something like a shudder went through him when he thought of what he had learned. Mortleroy – Death the King – or more succinctly, King Death. And Nemway had made no bones about the devilish magician being intent on removing *any* rival.

*

He was hard on Nemway's heels when they arrived back in the glade where they found Gareth holding everyone spellbound with the story of the Holy Grail.

Nemway paused at the edge of the circle to listen, so Myrddin was able to get to Gwen's side ahead of her. He tried to catch his partner's eye, but his Wych was looking enquiringly at Nemway who smiled back rather ruefully before going to sit at her side.

*

'This is most intriguing, beloved Lady,' White Wand whispered softly as the other joined her. 'Our new-found brother Gareth has been telling us how, after the field of Lyonesse, he returned in spirit to Caer Leon to mourn the passing of Arthur in company with many of his comrades. And that Perceval had come and told them of a prophecy that Arthur would not come again until the Holy Grail was found and returned to Britain.'

'I have heard this, also,' Nemway whispered back. 'I heard, too, that certain knights went seeking it –'

'Among them Gareth,' said White Wand.

'… and ages long was our search.' Gareth was saying. 'We sailed at last for France – Percival, Peredur and I – since prophecy seemed to direct us there. Yet though we travelled many miles for many years, we did not find it. But it was always like that. Kings and Princes pretended to know where it was to secure the services of knights like us, and held the knowledge back to be given only as reward for services in arms that allowed them victory over their enemies. And when they had no more need of us, they would say they had heard tell that the Grail was in this or that far distant place, where it never was, yet we dare not stop searching. From end to end of France we went and fought, suffering terrible wounds and hardship …'

Ann could see that part from Redweird and other new arrivals who remembered similar tales, the fae trembled and the gnomes shivered as the narrative went on and on throughout the afternoon, yet none left the glade. Normally they would have asked endless questions but, with the exception of Arthur now equalling an inquisitive four year old who was displaying an insatiable curiosity about anything and everything, no one voiced any. Gareth was too earnest and carried away for them.

White Wand whispered again to Nemway: 'I wish I knew the end to this, beloved Lady. Do you know if the knights ever succeeded in their Quest?'

'I have never heard that they did, sister Wych. And not even the Seers of the Hollows and Hills have known where the true vessel is hidden. I can imagine a great many false chalices were made to allow their owners to claim retirement.'

'But how will it be for Arthur, if the Faerie Grail can't be found? Gareth doesn't seem to have been successful.'

Nemway was firm. 'I'm certain the Knowers and Seers would have known if he had returned to Britain with it.' she said.

It was such a hopeless prospect, White Wand felt a sense of dread. Gareth was carrying everyone away with his tale; and it began to seem vital to find the vessel.

And an idea occurring to her, she rose quietly and walked away.

*

Ann was astounded find the abandoned sword under a fir tree when she reached the other side of Weirdsmeet. She took it with her to the Circle of Rejoicing and, removing the royal mantle from the throne, she laid the sword across the arms. As she did so, it seemed fitting. It was if she had found the magic weapon for that very purpose.

Calm and reassured, she prepared herself to see the answer to her soft question: 'Where is the faerie vessel now from which the King must drink to fulfil the prophecy?'

She expected to see the likeness of a jewelled goblet exquisitely moulded and chased, not the simple gold cup no different from a dozen others that the Royal Vintner had in his possession. It was so unexpected she was incredulous and, being anxious to discover if there was some identifying mark on it, she reached in for it without thinking. The crystal stopped her hand and the vision was gone.

*

She returned to the Weal as anxious as she had been when she left, to find Gareth reaching the end of his story.

'… and so the three of us perished in Hindustan …'

'And never found the Grail?' asked White Wand.

'Nor had sight of it, White One," he answered. Then, with sudden resolution and quiet dignity, he got up and approached Gwen. Sinking on one knee, his head bowed, he cried: 'O Royal Mother, in the name of him you have upon your knee, I ask a boon.'

'Say on, dear son,' she invited.

'It is this, that as soon as my arms are forged, that I may be allowed to go again on my immortal quest that the ancient prophecy may be fulfilled.'

Myrddin closed his eyes with a groan of complete exasperation. The very idea of Gareth resuming his quest seemed idiotic enough. Not only was it unnecessary and absurd, but what chance of survival had the Mabyn got outside the forest as things stood?

But Gareth was drawing back a sleeve of his jerkin to show a deeply lacerated and scarred forearm. 'Grant me this boon, and I swear upon these unhealed wounds that I shall not rest nor be made whole until the Grail is in my hands, and I can offer it upon bended knee to the spirit that is my eternal King.'

Gwen wept as she gave her consent, and looked in mute appeal to the Wychy for his comfort and guidance for this brave being.

He had to bow his head in mute assent, wondering how he was ever going to get around this latest and alarming development.

As soon as the Master and Gareth and the rest of the gnomes had gone to start work on the armour, Myrddin found himself approached by Ann and drawn aside for privacy.

'Dear Brother Wand, I have an idea that our brave Gareth has no need to journey so far and so dangerously after all.'

'Tell me, dear heart,' he replied, gratefully clutching at any straw.

'I consulted our Oracle – which reminds me,' she broke off reproachfully. 'I found Excalibur lying on the ground at Weirdsmeet. It's safe now, though. I laid it across the throne and then was shown the vision of a ordinary plain gold cup like many that Rozyn has –'

'An unmarked goblet!' her partner exploded in frustration. 'O Lady of Heaven, preserve me! With such a sign of deceit and treachery placed above the oracle, how could there be any truthful answer? O you poor misguided, yet ever beloved helpmeet, the sword is false. The thing is all of a piece; the image you evoked confirms the betrayal. The Eye, which can only see truth, was too angered by your simplicity to reveal the secrets of the Holy Vessel – if such a thing even exists.'

Not wishing to wound her more, he turned and left her. The show had to go on no matter what his feelings. He summoned Nyzor to come again with his dray and pointedly chose the Star Maiden to lead the Wandlewile dance with him in honour of this remarkable day. It was a studied insult to his Sister Wand, but he needed time to think.

*

White Wand could only watch and mourn. Circumstances were driving them apart again. One and one and one – would there never be an end to it?

'White Wand …?'

It was Redweird. The Wych had been aware of the Weir Lord's return, having seen him from time to time among the new arrivals, distinctive in the green and gold costume he had chosen, and knew his change of name. She had meant to find a moment to welcome him personally for he seemed an eternally lonely soul.

'White Wand, am I allowed to ask for a dance?' he said with the same unworldly courtesy that had characterised him as a mortal. He had not recognised her as the mortal girl he had once known as Ann Singlewood.

Realising how unwisely she had allowed her dejection to show, the Wych smiled at him, noticing for the first time how wyché his own eyes were and responded gladly: 'Redweird, thank you! Of course, you may. Come,' she said, rising. 'we will tread a Wandlewile of our own.'

She had never led the dance with anyone other than Black Wand before, but found the ex-Weir Lord quick to foresee her direction and intention as he copied the pattern she wove through the complicated swirls of the main dancers. Together at first and then in widening spirals, she found a fresh exhilaration each time he anticipated her and met up at her side. It also caused a new kind of bafflement in the already bewildering twists and turns taken by the Wychy and Stella as the Wiccas naturally turned to follow White Wand the more they became aware of her presence.

Knowing of old, her Wychy's signal that would herald the race to end the dance at the foot of Gwen's chair, she had no difficulty in matching the moment to catch Redweird's hand and fly with him to the finish line alongside Black Wand and Stella.

'Touché, sister Wand,' Myrddin said softly, as they acknowledged the Queen and a delighted handclapping Arthur. But only Ann saw the twitch of his Wand that made Redweird pass a hand over his brow and exclaim in bewilderment:

'The Lady Nemway! I must ask a dance with her.'

'That was a weirdly thing to do, brother,' said the Wych reproachfully when they were alone.

'But necessary,' he answered crisply.

CHAPTER 27

THE WOLVES OF WAR

Leading the dance with Stella, Myrddin's mind had worked at all the problems that appeared to be multiplying by the hour. In addition to producing a magic sword, which would work, he now had to produce a Holy Grail for the comfort of a spirit possessed by an age old Quest, and ensure Gareth's safety and success into the bargain. It was only the thought of how much a cup, lending weight to the sword he would have to have made to give Arthur credence, which spurred his imagination into having three brain waves.

Brainwave number one was using Dreadful as transport to solve the problem of how to avoid Gareth becoming dogs' meat as soon as he showed his nose outside the forest. As for the cup, this became brainwave number two when he suddenly remembered where he would find one that would suit exactly; which left problem number three: Nemway. He dare not leave the Queen and Arthur alone with her, and he needed to know how the gnomes were progressing with Gareth's armour. Likewise, the only time he could leave the forest to get hold of and plant the cup he had thought of, would be during the interregnum. Brainwave number three wasn't as breath taking as the previous two, but it served. He wandled Redweird into requesting the Lady Nemway for a dance, while he took Ann aside and asked her to take the witch to The Wandle.

'Our Wandle?'

'Why not? She knows most of our other secrets. It would be proper to show her the Circle of Rejoicing and the care we are taking of the Magic Sword. You could also introduce her to Dragga.'

"Brother Wand, this is getting even more weirdly. If it's that important, why don't you take her there yourself?'

'Because, beloved sister, if *I* stood with her on the brink of Dragga, I would be tempted beyond endurance to cast her into his maw.'

Ann looked at him appalled: 'In Mona's name, why do you hate her so?'

'Hate? How could anyone hate such a lovely creature? No, it's politic. Better her death, than have our people slaughtered by her allies. So will you take her to our Wandle, please, dear Wych?'

'I'll do anything to preserve her safety,' White Wand answered defiantly. 'But what has she done that makes you so sure she is an enemy?'

'Remember the warning – *beware all other messengers who come no matter how fair they look, or how sweet their words?*'

'And you want me to take her to our Wandle *now*?'

'As soon as she's free – and take all the time you want.'

She nodded. 'Before I go,' she said diffidently, 'could I ask how Gareth is ever going to find the Grail in readiness for Arthur's coming of age in three days time – quite apart from surviving to tell the tale?'

'O ye of little faith,' he admonished. 'This is why I need your help. I need time to arrange it, dear Wych. No harm is going to come to Gareth, I promise you, and the vessel *will* be found by him.'

She looked astounded. 'You mean, you know where it is?'

'I do. But it's secret. Not a word to anyone – not even to the Queen – or all my spells will be ruined.'

'Very well,' she agreed. 'If that is what you want, I will do it.'

As soon as the dance had ended, she went to Nemway. 'Beloved Lady, I have found the cause of my Brother Wand's distrust of you. If you will come with me to our home on The Wandle, I shall be able explain everything properly …'

*

White Wand took Nemway first to the Circle of Rejoicing where the witch nodded her satisfaction and approval at seeing Excalibur safe beneath the throne's covering. Then, sitting together on one of the polished seats around the Circle, White Wand explained the cause of her partner's mistrust.

Nemway was rueful. 'It seems your Wychy is too strict with this 'other messengers' interpretation, dear Wych. I am merely the appointed Keeper of Arthur's possessions – *not* a messenger. As I remember, you said Mona's Eye had shown you three messengers: the Owl of Gwyn; the Otter of the Denefolk and the Unicorn of the Mabyn. What other messengers are there?'

'If there are any other than these, then they must be the ones to be disregarded,' White Wand suggested logically. 'There was a dove that my brother said was ours. It told us to go to Glaston –'

'No!' Nemway interrupted, looking horrified. '*That's* the false messenger! Glastonbury was taken from Gwynn by Mortleroy –'

'Mortleroy …?'

'It's a foreign name for a King who rules all Faedom. Death comes to all out there – even your fae die from time to time.'

'No, that is pact with Dragga,' Ann said firmly. 'Without it we could have no existence here.' She then voiced her curiosity. 'How does the cycle of incarnation occur then among our distant kin?'

'Out there death comes by war and wound and all kinds of mishap and maiming; if not by spear and sword, then by tooth, by claw, or talon – and another difference. When born anew our wraiths are not whole and mature like the Weirdfolk, but must incarnate among each kind as babes – which is why the Coming of Arthur is so miraculous. The Weirdfolk are barren, are they not …?'

There was much to talk about and time flew.

*

When they returned to the glade, Black Wand was winding up the proceedings as if he had never left the scene. While they had been away, however, he had found the gnomes passionately at work on arms and armour, and not very happily so, either.

'O Black Wand, how pleased we are to see you,' Whitegold greeted him with relief. 'Our brother Gareth tells us that all we have made so far bears no comparison to the steel of the Master Wayland or even the craftsmanship of the faerie smiths of Damascus – '

'… He says there's nothing *we* know that can render it as tough as the arms *he* used to bear,' put in Feldspar.

'… Aye, and proved it by cutting this lovely breastplate clean in two with one single stroke of the first sword we made,' another gnome said, holding up the two halves.

Myrddin was secretly delighted to hear it. Anything that would delay Gareth's departure from the forest until everything was in place had to be a good thing.

He was examining a number of pieces while they were deploring their lack of skill. 'Be at peace, brothers,' he said firmly at last. 'The problem is not an impossible one. Continue your work but don't hurry it. When the entire mailing is complete, I will tell you how it can be hardened and tempered. The fashioning appears excellent enough to my untrained eye – but let Gareth be your guide in every detail except the hardening. Then I will bring to it the virtue of my magic.'

He had no idea what he was talking about; but was playing for time until he had trawled through Merlyn's scrolls again. He then found Omric and Ironwright anxiously watching Gareth's critical inspection of a lance.

'… The head still lacks strength, brother Ironwright,' Gareth was saying. 'The point also is too tapered to withstand the judder of a horse-borne charge. Oh, how I wish I knew the secret of Damascened steel.'

'Don't be so worried, Gareth,' said Myrddin kindly. 'The perfection you want is magical – as I have just explained to the others. When everything is shaped to your need and satisfaction, I will then add my touch of magic.'

Relief shone in all their faces.

'O Son of Merlyn, forgive me,' said Gareth, contritely. 'In my fervour I had forgotten your wisdom. It shall be as you say and I will be patient.'

With that hurdle behind him, Myrddin asked to speak to the Master and Gareth alone. 'It is a matter of vital privacy, so nothing is to be said to anyone' he warned as soon as the three of them were apart from the others. 'I have learned of a wicked plot that only you, Gareth, will understand in whole. There are those who are intent on stealing Excalibur from our very midst.'

The Master looked appalled, but Gareth took it in his stride. 'I remember there were designs on the sword during mortal Arthur's reign, Heir of Merlyn. Morgan le Fay had it stolen once and given to that traitor Accolon to bring about the King's death in tournament –'

'So runs mortal legend also, Gareth,' Myrddin interrupted, impatient to get to the point. 'And this plot is just as bad ...' He went on to explain that he had learned that Mortleroy wanted to ambush the Weirdfolk as they left the forest, and to discredit or destroy his newborn rival with a false Excalibur '... but you, Noble Master, will make another. I will bring the false sword to you secretly and you shall make a copy so exactly like it no one will know them apart. Then we three will see that the trick one falls into the hands of the hands of the evil monarch's emissaries.'

The stratagem won their applause, but Gareth spoke anxiously: 'How shall *I* be able to help, Black Wan? I don't know how long my quest will take ...'

'Another half-score centuries?' Myrddin said gently. 'Or have you been blessed with some heavenly vision never given before?'

Gareth looked chastened. In his obsession, he had given no thought to direction or guidance, so confessed his plight and begged for advice

'Rejoice,' said the Wychy simply. 'The secret of its hiding place has long been known to me and if you had not remembered your quest, I would have ensured its return myself. But I would not cheat you of an honour you have so suffered so much to gain.'

Overcome with emotion, Gareth fell on his knee and clasping his hands together, pleaded to know where the sacred relic was.

'It is no great distance from where we are now, Gareth,' Myrddin told him. 'But it is not right for you to know until you are ready to set out on the Quest. Is that understood?'

*

Myrddin had returned to the glade well ahead of White Wand and Nemway, which made it look as if he had never been away. He then ensured that Gwen and the still avidly curious child retired first, and exacted a promise from his Wych that she would stay at the Queen's side until dawn.

White Wand accepted the duty philosophically. 'And where shall our Lady Nemway retire?' she asked.

'Anywhere she likes – except the Bower or The Wandle,' he answered indifferently. 'In *Woe Begone!* if she wants.'

'But surely, Brother Wand, that's very private to you? And unless you escort her there, how shall she open the door?'

'Oh, didn't you know?' he said casually. 'She's already destroyed the entrance with her whip.'

'No!' With Ann's expression so thunderstruck; he believed she must at last begin to realise the extent of danger in their midst and pursued the advantage. 'It's the reason I don't intend leaving the false Excalibur a moment longer on the King's throne. I had intended taking it to the Gnomes' Mansion, which I was on my way to doing when the otter appeared. I had to abandon the sword as I needed to pay attention to the creature.'

'You mean, you didn't invent the otter? That it was the true messenger of the Denefolk?'

'More like a spurious invention sent to spy on us *and* mislead us. I will trust no one who enters this forest uninvited. Now while I leave you to guard the Queen and her son, I must be about my business.'

*

More perplexed than ever, Ann watched him stride away to Wandleside, before she went to find Nemway, who had been collecting her horses.

'Lady Nemway, I have learned that the otter was no subterfuge of my Brother Wand's, but an artifice sent by Mortleroy to spy on us.'

'Whose magical doxy he believes me to be,' said Nemway bitterly.

'Only because he thinks you're a messenger,' said the Wych apologetically. 'Could the otter have been as he believes?'

'It *is* possible,' Nemway admitted regretfully. 'Mortleroy had a very able magician, and the otter could have been a move in a very subtle plot. It seems we two need to talk together a lot more deeply –'

'I am sorry, beloved Lady. I am commanded to stay with the Queen for fear of your designs on her and the babe.'

'Satan seize him,' swore Nemway wrathfully. 'And, pray, how does our lord and master decree that *I* pass the interregnum?'

'He said in *Woe Begone!* if you wish, since you destroyed the entrance.'

Nemway's anger turned to laughter. 'So be it, then,' she said with a chuckle. 'It will provide excellent stabling for Windfleet and Windflame. They need sheltering from your Scathe ...'

*

After taking Excalibur to the Master of Gnomes, Myrddin made a routine telepathic survey of the forest from his Retreat, saw what Nemway had done and fumed with anger. *How dare she turn the sanctity of Woe Begone! into a common stable.*

If he hadn't been so pressed for time, he would have done something drastic about it. As it was, he had to assume his golden eagle shape and fly off over the Woe in a very unpleasant state of mind.

He started with a circuit of the forest before flying to Three Weirs, and discovered immediately that his worst fears were realised. The adjacent countryside now teemed with packs of patrolling wolves. Solitary scouts roamed between each with the clear intention of keeping news as up to date as possible. Nothing leaving or entering the forest could go undetected. Within minutes, the entire force could be concentrated for a kill the moment one of them raised an alarm. It was even more disturbing to find they had spotted him although he was flying high. It suggested that Mortleroy having learned of the eagle's existence had instructed a worm's eye look-out. The only answer was to fly low and take advantage of every bit of cover.

He plunged into the nearest wood and, as soon as the foremost of his pursuers were well into it, streaked out again at a tangent for the next cover, then shot back into the forest skimming low over the foreground that the wolves had just vacated.

Screaming a warning to Dreadful to stay put, he wove his way northward through the trees, dived low again over Wychies' Mead and hedgehopped the fence in the hope that the main road might be clear. But it wasn't. The enemy had quartered reserves in the village itself so that he almost cannoned into them as they came charging down a lane. He reflected ironically that what they lacked in size, they more than up for in speed, well out running the night time traffic of cars, lorries and other transport. Soaring away to the north of the village across open country, he made a tantalising descent into another wood and waited until he saw the horde come swarming after him. He left at its northern end and dived down to the surface of the River Weir. After half a mile of strenuous effort, he flew into a copse and waited. He heard them howling to each other while they searched the wood and then poured out again in twos and threes in every direction.

Their thoroughness was frightening. Now thoroughly roused, it was obvious they would not rest until they sighted him.

He took off again, eastward this time towards the thickest cover he could find; and discovered a discarded cardboard box that had been thrown into a bush. It was large enough to shield him from below, so he changed back to his normal form for a rethink. The wolves searched the wood from end to end and took a long time doing it.

Fortunate they have no sense of smell! he thought, but then, neither had he any scent. So how did they track? Astral vibration, of course! The answer made him extra wary as he cautiously changed again. Rising out of the trees, he kept low and made for the village expecting a warning howl at any moment. But his tactics seemed to have evacuated the garrison there.

His objective was Joe Harmer's cottage. He flew in through an open top window and landed on the bed alongside an ancient inlaid bedside cabinet. On top of the cabinet on a circular velvet covered pedestal, and enclosed in a small glass dome was a legendary Fairy Cup, the treasure of old Joe's living.

Joe had once shown it to the late Augustus Autrey, then known as 'Mr Gus' to the villagers. 'Mr Gus' had recognised it for what is was because he had an uncle wealthy enough to have a private collection of unique pieces of gold and silverware, and had recognised a similar tiny medieval miniature. A little research in village gossip revealed Harmer Senior had found Joe's example of a silver chalice only half an inch high in the draw of a battered old cabinet. But Joe grew up firmly convinced it was a fairy cup given to his father by the forest fae in return for some service he had done them. It seemed providential to Myrddin that Joe had not already returned to the forest being in the region of eighty-something years old by now.

He got to work on giving the sleeping mortal precise instructions. He inspired a dream in which the fae came to Joe, and begged him to give the cup back to them as their new King had come, and they needed it for him. Joe must therefore get up, dress, and take the precious relic to a young oak tree by the entrance to the track he knew as Wisher's Lane and press it into the crevice formed by the junction of one of the limbs with the trunk.

*

Although the vicinity was clear when Joe got up and set off with the extra agonising slowness of any elderly mortal. Myrddin didn't go with him for fear of attracting unwelcome attention. The Wychy's caution paid off because when Joe returned, only one solitary wolf was following him down the dark deserted lane to his home. It waited until Joe had gone in and closed the door before loping away out of sight.

It was disturbing all the same, Myrddin thought. Would a lonely mortal abroad in the middle of the night have aroused any interest? Yet even if it had, he was persuaded there was nothing to link it to the eagle they had been chasing and, if he could make a silent get away …?

He waited until Joe was back in bed, gave him an over dose of Woe and waited for his demise before making his bid to return for the forest. But time as well as luck had run out on him. No sooner had he leapt from the windowsill and become airborne with an unconscious wraith in his talons; than a warning howl from almost underneath him told him that this part of his plan had gone for a Burton. Now he really had to hurry. If they had seen anything significant about old Joe's action, the cup would be lost. So, throwing discretion to the winds, he sped directly back into the forest leaving a howling havoc in his wake.

CHAPTER 28

THE WEALSPRING

Much later Myrddin learnt that the wolf monitoring Joe Harmer had seen nothing of significance until the eagle had emerged from the cottage after the mortal's return. The wolf then howled its message of a connection between the bird and the mortal's visit to the oak to hide something in it too high for the wolves to get at. The item, retrieved by a nearby magpie, was flown to the Baron of the Southern Wold, who had it taken via hawk to the Lord of the Western Marches, and so on to Mortleroy.

News of the destruction of his precious black falcons by a mysterious eagle in tandem with a green dragon had reached the King much the same way. The trees held many of his messengers, and the one he had already received, via his falcons' destruction of Gwyn ap Gwyn's white owl, had also warned him that something was beginning to stir in the long silent territory of the Green Dragon of the South.

He had wolves put to patrol all approaches to Weir Forest and had personally sent the long held captive white dove of the Weirdfolk to tempt them out of it. He had already found the forest's protection too strong for any creature of his own to enter.

Nemway's sudden reappearance also had taken him by surprise and concerned him deeply. Having thought her long ago accounted for, he at once diverted all available wolf packs to reinforce those in the forest's vicinity with orders now to capture or kill anything or anyone seen going in or coming out of it.

He would have sent his Royal Falcons to supplement their efforts if he hadn't been rather proud of them and didn't want to lose any more.

He learned of the eagle's lair in two successive communiqués, one informing him that the bird had come out of the forest and led the wolves on a wild goose chase but had shown no sign of attacking; the second reporting its sudden reappearance in Three Weirs village in connection with a mortal who had hidden something in a tree. Mortleroy at once sent mobilisation orders to his entire resources in the South of Britain. Every baron, every knight, every man-at-arms must be alert to this unexpected threat from the forest. He wanted a round-the-clock surveillance maintained for the eagle's re-appearance, and issued orders for its destruction. As for the object secreted by the mortal, the Baron of the Southern Wold understood he could either get it into the royal hands by sunset or be held fatally responsible.

Mortleroy spent a long time patiently analysing the cup when he got it before arriving at the same conclusion as Myrddin had regarding Excalibur; it was a fake without a minim of magic in it. In fact, he concluded wrathfully, it was more than a fake – the eagle had tricked him by successfully diverting his attention away from whatever it was that it was up to.

*

At sunup in Gnomes' Mansion, everyone woke to start working at fever heat, with Gareth involved in a meticulous criticism of every item.

Where before the Wychy had wanted to slow things down, he now needed to speed them up. On his return with Joe Harmer, he had spent the rest of the interregnum going through Merlyn's scrolls on tempering metal. 'These must now remain as they are, Gareth,' he insisted firmly. 'If you are not on your quest by noon or earlier, the Grail will be beyond all power of reclamation.' He turned to Omric, 'Noble Master, have your brethren dig trenches straight away by the Brook of Wynn, and have them filled with deadwood twigs and branchlets as large as you can bear …'

The principle had barely altered down the centuries. Soften the metal with heat while controlling the temperature, before quenching each piece with cold water to harden it.

The gnomes worked with a will. Happy to be free from the pernickety knight, they dug industriously and scoured the forest for fallen wood. Myrddin then set it alight with his Wand to burn slowly and produce the necessary bed of red-hot embers. With the pieces inserted and raked over evenly with more glowing charcoal, the wizard waited until his Wand and instinct told him the moment was right, before having them lifted out and doused swiftly in the brook. The end product stunned even him. When the first piece was passed to Gareth, it was apparent he felt the same, for he fell on his knees sobbing with joy.

'O mighty son of Merlyn, no gift from Wayland could be more perfect …'

With no time to waste, the Wychy had them buffed and polished by a team of gnomes and fitted until Gareth stood completely encased, and glittering from head to foot.

'Come,' the Wychy said briskly. 'We go to Queen's Glade at once where you shall take leave of the Queen and set out on your errand.'

'But, most noble son of Merlyn, I have no horse.'

'*The* most wonderful steed in the world is champing at the bit waiting for you,' Myrddin assured him. The noble knight had shown himself to be so stiff-necked in the matter of tradition, the wizard wanted no time left for any argument that knights slew dragons; they didn't use them as aerial chargers.

With shield, mace and lance borne proudly behind him by the hard working gnomes, Gareth clanked martially into Queen's Glade at Myrddin's side. Even so, he only came second in the day's marvels, because the fae arriving at the Bower had found Arthur already a youth still asking endless questions and smiling wisely on them all.

The splendour of the knight was a novel sight for the excited fae, among them the newly returned Joe, renamed J'armer, and wonderful it was to see Gareth arrive to kneel at Gwen's feet with Arthur behind her richly arrayed and wearing a gold and purple cloak.

Gareth rose and bowed deeply to Arthur. Before Myrddin could give the knight his final instructions, however, the boy king spoke:

'Sir Gareth, my lady mother has explained to me the perilous adventure you are set upon, and I feel concerned for your safety. Please don't go before you have drunk at the Wealspring and prayed a wish.' He turned his uncomplicated eyes on the Wychy, adding: 'A Wealspring wish *is* inviolate, isn't it, Merlyn's Heir?'

'That is the unbroken law of our forest living, my Liege' he answered, unable to explain that the granting of the Wish was only possible because one or other of the Wands would ensure that it came true. As it was certain that Gareth would wish his mission was successful, and Myrddin had already done everything he could to ensure that it would be, he fretted at the unnecessary delay.

Arthur courteously offered his arm to his mother, and the Weirdfolk almost cried with joy at the sight, and the way he was so thoughtful for the knight's welfare.

Myrddin could only wonder where Arthur was getting it from. How the kind of plasma babe he had fashioned could have grown so wyché and king-like, he had no idea. Could it *all* be down to Impy's astral and Merlyn's recipe that he had given Nyzor? They were questions he had to leave unanswered because everyone was on their way to the Wealspring.

*

With Arthur and Gwen standing one side of the bubbling font in the grotto, and the Wands and Nemway on the other, Gareth approached and knelt before the spring, and set his helmet beside him. The Master handed him the goblet from where it stood on its crystal plinth. Gareth filled it, rose, bowed to his sponsors and drank the contents in silence.

When the silence extended to what seemed an eternity, it became one of growing anxiety for Myrddin.

What is the matter with him now? he wondered in frustration, as Gareth stood motionless, eyes to heaven, the goblet clasped to his breast. The Wychy found it difficult to believe his ears when the Mabyn spoke at last.

'O Master, please, un-mail me.'

'Un-un-mail you,' stammered Omric, as stupefied as everyone else.

Nemway came to her senses first. 'A Wealspring wish is inviolate, Heir of Merlyn, is it not?' she asked looking from the Wych to him with a ghost of a smile.

Before he could answer, Arthur stepped forward and began removing the arm pieces himself, which set Omric hurriedly helping to remove helm and breastplate. It took a while, and Gareth remained unmoving except when they took his gauntlets while he kept hold of the goblet, passing it from one hand to the other. When he was down to his normal dress, he held out his right arm.

'Master, please, bare this arm?' he said quietly. Omric drew up the sleeve and revealed it clear of any stigmata, as were all other parts of him that they could see.

None was more astonished than Myrddin; not only that Gareth had chosen such selfish wish, but that the wish had come true without any assistance from him. Yet there was more to come, for Gareth after refilling the cup sank to his knees and offered it with trembling hands to Arthur. 'Behold, beloved Liege from of old, the Sacred Vessel is found and, as I swore to do, I present this to you on bended knee. My age-long quest is over, and your long-told need fulfilled.'

Myrddin could not believe it, until White Wand, overcome by the miracle, knelt at his side and kissed his hand. 'O incomparable Wychy! How wonderfully you kept your secret so that Gareth could find the vessel without coming to harm. Despite your pretended wrath, you *knew* Mona's image did not lie. This *is* the very cup that Mona's eye revealed to me.'

He dare not disillusion her. But the effect of the goblet on Gareth was baffling. Why had had it never been apparent before that it was not the Wealspring water but the *cup* itself that held the healing. A draught from any spring would have the same effect if drunk from this vessel.

Arthur took the brimming cup from Gareth but instead of drinking from it himself, presented it to his mother and she drank; although what she desired not even the Wychies knew for Arthur already had a growing magic of his own.

Now that Gareth's obsession was resolved to everyone's satisfaction, and J'armer the most wonder stricken fay of all, Myrddin's credit stood higher than ever. Only he now knew what a first class hash Joe's 'Fairy Cup' would have made of it all. It did not change his mind about Excalibur, however. It just went to prove that Mona's Eye remained true above all unseemly surroundings.

When everyone went off to Queen's Glade for renewed jubilation, Myrddin set about the next part of his plan. He gave Gareth and Ironwright the job of taking all the knight's arms and armour to Nebuchadnezzar's Temple, and took the Master privately aside, reminding him of the copy he had made of Excalibur.

'I would like to come with you to temper the blade you have prepared, Omric. We will build the fire at the foot of the shaft under the ruined Mound, and use the water from the underground spring inside the Mansion ...'

With the job done, he sent the Omric to find Ironwright and Gareth, with instructions to fit the Mabyn into his armour in the privacy of Nebuchadnezzar's Temple, and then to give a performance on Dreadful to entertain the crowds in Queen's Glade.

'I want you to explain to Gareth that it is part of my stratagem to outwit the thieves,' Myrddin told Omric. 'He shall mount Dreadful and demonstrate charges with the lance for everyone's entertainment. Then he will hear me secretly calling him to fly around the glade once or twice before making a bee-line for Wychies' Lane where I will be waiting with the false Excalibur ...'

*

With Omric on his way, Myrddin took the two swords from the Gnome's Mansion to The Wandle and laid the newly tempered one on the throne. Returning to the Weal with the genuine article suspended from a baldric under his Weird, he made his way to *Woe Begone!* trusting that Gareth's presentation was keeping everyone's attention well occupied. He then sent a silent instruction to Gareth to start flying, and mounted Windflame, Arthur's charger, because it had a male saddle, and sped off for Wychies' Lane calling Gareth to follow.

There was only mild surprise when Gareth and the Dragon disappeared from view, as everyone expected their return at any moment. But it was Nemway's white mare, Windfleet that came at a gallop into the glade, straight to her Mistress's side which caused alarm.

Nemway leapt to her feet and mounted the animal, Ann started up in apprehension. 'What's happened, dear Lady?'

'That fiend your partner – who else?' Nemway hissed in a low voice. 'He has taken Windflame.'

'But where to?' asked the bewildered Wych. 'Why?'

'Where?' repeated the Lady of the Lake. 'Nowhere – because I've have already commanded Windflame to stop. The 'why' I shall find out for myself – and Mona, has his excuse better be good …'

CHAPTER 29

THROWN TO THE WOLVES

Myrddin had reckoned on Nemway's pursing him through the Veil of Illusion. He hadn't expected the charger to be checked in full flight, jettisoning him between its ears to come to rest spread-eagled in the lane. He sprang up immediately, but although he called, exhorted and waved his Wand, the horse careered back up the way it had just brought him.

Dreadful and Gareth had disappeared through the Veil, and he would have to run to catch up with them. He might have chanced taking off as the eagle and carry the sword in his talons, if he hadn't heard approaching hooves.

It was Nemway on her mare thundering down on him with the charger and reigning in as they came level: 'Explain yourself!' she cried.

'Emergency!' he said quickly making sure that his Weird fully covered the sword. 'I needed speed – there are wolves out there.'

'What emergency? And where is Gareth, and where the dragon?'

'They're already diverting the beasts. Without a horse the whole plan is going to end in disaster.'

'Plan?' she said scornfully. 'Some fool plot, more like. By now the wolves will be in dozens.'

'Hundreds, actually,' he corrected. 'Must I really go it on foot, or will you lend me the horse?'

Nemway released the thong of her whip. 'Not until I know what you're up to.'

'There is a sacred Talisman – the Ring of Merlyn that I had to hide out there a while since. If the wolves find it, and dig it up – we're lost.'

'Mount, then,' she said, wheeling round and bringing Windflame to his side. 'But I'm coming with you. My whip slays better than your Wand.'

As they raced towards the end of the Lane, he shouted: 'The Ring is cached some mortal ells further than the forest boundary. I planned Gareth should draw the wolves down the road westwards while I dashed for the hiding place before reinforcements arrive. This delay will have made things worse. If you will ride and help Gareth, there might still be time to get the Ring –'

'To hell with the Ring! I'm doing this for Gareth's sake …'

*

When they broke through the invisibility veil, Myrddin saw they need not have worried. The knight was having the time of his life, spearing wolves left, right and centre along the grass verge with Dreadful charging to and fro scorching their hides off. The wolves were game, though. Their orders were to kill, but the combination of fire and lance was holding them off for the moment. Ten lay dead, transfixed by the lance. Twenty more, maimed by fire, were howling their woe. With reserves pouring in between the passing traffic, however, it seemed the situation was becoming critical.

Myrddin and Nemway sped along the roadside in opposite directions, and she was well distant by the time he came to a halt and slid to the ground beside the post.

It didn't take long to retrieve the Ring, and plunge sword and scabbard into the gap. The tiny jewelled hilt was just visible above the earth. He had barely done so before a stray band of wolves came howling towards him. He just had time to mount and gain a lead on them when Windflame threw him again and bolted to Nemway's aid where she was in dire trouble.

In spite of his own danger, Myrddin found time to smile. There wasn't a hope of the lady getting away alive. Blowing a derisive kiss of farewell in her direction, he ordered Dreadful to take Gareth back to the forest, then dealt with his own plight. There were two ways out. He could take wing and fly back, or transform himself into Myrddin Black.

As flying would reduce pressure on Nemway by distracting the wolves, he slipped the ring over his head, picked it up from his feet and sauntered back down the lane with it on his thumb. His sudden appearance caused the prolonged blare of a horn from a passing car that faded quickly into the distance.

The afternoon, warm, golden and alive with movement invited relaxation; to lie down and wallow in the scent of earth, grass and flowers, but he had no time for the luxury. While it was poetic justice to have the cohorts of Nemway's paramour, Mortleroy tearing his own spy to pieces, he still had to account for her. And only the truth, more or less, would satisfy his Wych. He would have to tell her that he'd gone to recover the Talisman, and that Nemway had insisted on accompanying him, but that once free of the forest she had deserted him, taking the horses, and left him in a mess he was lucky to have survived.

He walked on down to the inlet to Dragga's Weird before taking off the Ring and, transforming into the eagle, winged his way to The Wandle with the Ring in his beak.

From the safety of his Retreat, he sat down to review the situation in Queen's Glade through the crystal of his dome. Gareth would have long returned and be entertaining everyone with an enthralling description of the best fight of his life. But the moment the scene came before him; the Wychy bolted upright in shock.

Neither Gareth nor Dreadful was present.

He jumped up to make a wider inspection. Neither of them were visible anywhere – not even in the Woe. He shot out of his Retreat and took to the air practically in one movement. Flying to the northern end of The Wandle, he passed through the Veil of Illusion. Not a wolf in sight, although the roadside was liberally scattered with dead ones, especially around the spot where he had last seen Gareth and Dreadful.

Where, in Mona's name have they got to? he wondered frantically. It was unthinkable that the wolves had annihilated them. Yet there was Gareth's lance abandoned in the grass and near it, his new and magnificently blazoned shield. Myrddin soared high, making a painstaking search of the entire area in ever widening circles, but found nothing.

How am I to explain Gareth's and Dreadful's absence back in the forest, now? he wondered desperately, dropping into the uppermost branches of a tree to gloom. If the wolves had torn Nemway and her horses to pieces and left no trace, that was understandable; but they could not have done that with Gareth's tough armour. The only conclusion left then was that the enemy had somehow captured the gallant knight, and destroyed Dreadful.

*

Back in the forest, White Wand had to invent her own story by saying the Lady Nemway had gone on an urgent journey to do with Arthur's welfare and that Black Wand, Gareth and Dreadful had gone with her to protect her.

When none of them had returned by dawn, and the awakened fae came running to her for news, Ann had to act fast. She beckoned the dependable Redweird to her and suggested he might involve them all in discussing and planning the kind of celebration they could arrange for the wanderers' return.

She then left, saying she needed to renew her stock of secret herbs. It prevented anyone following her as she made herself walk slowly down Wychies' Lane until she came to the Veil of Illusion.

She had never been back through it since she had arrived, and now found it took some faith to do so. Her horror and dismay at what she found was overwhelming. No one had warned her such terrible beasts existed as the remains she saw littered everywhere along the verge. When she realised that Gareth's lance and shield were lying among them, she ran to pick them up weeping, before collapsing on a small stone with her face in her hands. The heavy, ponderous and noisy slow rumble of passing traffic made it almost impossible to think what to do next.

'White Wand!' called the unexpected and astonished voice of Nemway above her. 'What are you doing here? Such a terrible sight as this is not for you.'

The Wych looked up in amazement to see Nemway, with the two horses, plus Gareth and Dreadful, all looking down at her. She got to her feet, crying now with relief and happiness to see them, and looked for her partner.

Nemway was surprised. 'Is he not with you in the forest?'

'Not since he left yesterday afternoon – when you went after him,' said the Wych. 'O beloved Lady, you promised to safeguard him for my sake – '

'Safeguard my would-be assassin!' Nemway interrupted, nursing a badly injured arm. 'I think not! I fell for a story that he wanted to collect some sacred Talisman he'd left out here not knowing it was to lure me to my death. Having got us out here, he disappeared, leaving us to our fate. And *you* reproach *me*! Gareth and I are both badly wounded, as were Dreadful and the horses – except I was able to mend them – '

'He may be weirdly, but he is not wicked – '

'Look,' Nemway indicated the post along the path with her free hand. 'Gareth, brave knight, you see a jewelled hilt there *just* above the ground? Please, get it and unsheathe it – *if* you can.'

Gareth obediently retrieved sword and scabbard from the hole. With all his knowledge of arms, however, he could not release the one from the other. He inspected the thing minutely, then said: 'I cannot be mistaken, Lady. You brought this sword – Arthur's sword here to the forest, yourself.'

White Wand stood mute, stunned into silence.

'More than that, fond lover of Merlyn's Heir,' Nemway continued. 'In order to make certain of my destruction, he summoned the sacred Dragon of the South in all his immensity –'

'Dragga!' White Wand exclaimed incredulously.

'Yes – that enormity that lurks beneath the waters of your Woe: a great green dragon full forty times the size of this golden imitation here – '

'No, no, beloved Lady! It's something he has taught Dreadful to do – to magnify himself –'

'Then how happened that I slew it with my whip "Lightening"?' demanded Nemway. 'I dealt the apparition such a blow, it disappeared ...'

*

Piecing it all together between them, they managed to make sense of what had taken place. It appeared that when the dragon had responded to an order from the Wychy to get back to the forest with his rider, he had whisked around to free his tail from half a dozen wolves before, soaring into the air, it had banked dangerously at the same time so throwing Gareth to the ground. As soon as the dragon had got into the forest and realised he had lost his rider, he had reacted to the danger by blowing himself up to full size. When it then came charging back to the rescue with a bellow of fire, it had sent the wolves howling for shelter. After picking Gareth up, Dreadful had gone on to attack the pack surrounding Nemway.

Too desperately engaged in fighting for her life, Nemway hadn't seen what was happening behind her. A wolf had leapt onto Windfleet's back and gripped her whip-arm in its jaws. It was when she changed the whip to her left hand, and Windfleet reared at the same time to dislodge the wolf, that this forty foot long virulent green monster came out of nowhere looking as it if it was about to destroy her. She lashed out at it rather wildly but missed contact. Dreadful, startled by the angry red flash, stood on his tail in midair to avoid it – spilling his rider to the ground for the second time in as many minutes retaliating with a furious blast of fire.

This time, Nemway didn't miss. With both horses screaming beneath the contact of Dreadful's breath, her whip curled like a ring of fire around one of his huge wings and a foreleg with the result he crashed on his side some distance away writhing in pain.

The respite for Nemway seemed miraculous. Not a wolf in sight, and Gareth struggling safely, if dazedly to his feet. She had no idea how he had got there, but told him to mount Windflame and follow her. The wolves had maimed both of Nemway's horses, and seriously wounded her. With Gareth in a state of concussion, she needed to get them all under cover before the wolves came back – and cover did not mean looking for it in the forest,

It was when she looked back, before turning the painfully hobbling horses northwards, that she saw Dreadful lumbering awkwardly in her rear.

Intent on staying with Gareth, the poor thing had reduced itself to normal size the better to manage its wounds. Nemway, having no idea that it was Dreadful who had attacked her, was indignant at the sorry state the beast was in and wondered just how callous the black magician could get than involving an innocent pet in his disastrous schemes.

She told Gareth to stay where he was, while she got hold of a wolf corpse and with a knife and one hand, fashioned the astral remains into a likeness of the dragon's foreleg. She then copied the shattered wing: but when she approached him to attach them, Dreadful belched so angrily, she had to raise her whip, feeling regret for the way it cowed him. If it hadn't been that Dreadful was programmed to stay by Gareth, he would have lurched away. But Nemway talked soothingly, explaining what she intended to do and at last, he allowed her to do the grafting.

This magic Lady had soothing powers, and clearly loved him the same way that that the fae did, so Dreadful began transferring his loyalties to her without a qualm. Nemway then attended the horses in the same way, but could do nothing for herself and Gareth – they would have to wait for the Wealspring Cup.

As she was becoming anxious that the wolves would return before they had found shelter, she did what she had seldom done. She whispered on the wind the secret name of her son, the Sage of all the Seers of the people of the Hollows and the Hills asking his help to hide them.

When the light of a small green will-o-the-wisp appeared, they followed it to an abandoned fox-earth. It provided a roomy shelter for them and the horses through the night, with Dreadful on guard at the entrance. She tried to discover how Gareth had got himself in such a state, but he was in no condition to give a coherent reply. He was wandering in mind and rambled aloud of his interminable adventures. Hoping to find a clue in them, she provoked, prompted and encouraged him until she at last got to a vague account for his being outside the forest.

'It was Black Wand he said, shaking his head. 'A villainous plot of an evil king ...' and then suddenly: 'The sword! The sword! The false Excalibur that thieves must take ...!'

It took time to piece the disjointed sentences together and make sense of them, but when she got the picture, Nemway was beside herself with frustration and anger. If Mortleroy possessed Excalibur, it could account for the sudden absence of the wolves. He wouldn't need them with the Sword of Power in his hand.

As Gareth become unconscious with moonset, she was desperately tempted to leave him securely hidden with the dragon on watch, and race back to the forest alone, hoping against hope that the sword was still there. Then felt forced to admit she might never get back again to rescue the knight.

Going to the entrance to keep the lonely dragon company for a while, she was relieved to sense a familiar presence.

'Hew,' she whispered. 'Does my son know of the Sword?'

'He knows, mother,' came the ghostly reply. 'He says it still stands where the Heir of Merlyn pushed it into the earth, and you need have no fear for its recovery. When the Usurper heard that the Weirdfolk magician had put it there, he ordered it left where it was, declaring that he would never fall for a trick like that again. And when he then heard that *you* had slain the Guardian Green Dragon of the South – he issued a decree that the Lady of the Lake shall have the right of free passage anywhere in his realm and nevermore be molested by man, bird or beast under his command. In this way, then, you will certainly succeed in restoring the sword to its proper place.'

'Except that its proper place is in the heart of a forest where my whip is useless against the magician when he stands on his own ground,' answered Nemway, while thankful for the news of safe conduct.

'Have no worry, mother. The Heir of Merlyn will have gone to his doom before you arrive in the forest again. Within this hour, the enemy will avenge you with his death – '

'No,' cried Nemway in anguish at what it would mean to the Weirdfolk, his Wych and to Arthur. 'Hew, he needs to be taught a lesson, yes. But not to die.'

'The reverend Sage shall be so informed, revered mother,' answered the invisible whisperer dutifully. 'Now I go. Await the north wind's coming. And may wind and water ever bring you joyous news …'

Gareth seemed to have recovered most of his normal senses when he became conscious again at daybreak. She helped him into his armour and onto Windflame, before mounting herself.

The signal came at last; a firm ghost-breeze from the north. As they galloped away, it grew stronger, appearing to lift their mounts off their feet while Dreadful glided ahead of them without any need to beat his wings, and so returned to find White Wand weeping on the verge near the forest with Gareth's lance and shield beside her.

CHAPTER 30

THE SAGE AVENGES HIS MOTHER

The explanation that the 'Great Green Dragon of the South' was only Dreadful after all, made Nemway explode with laughter, although she apologised sincerely to the dragon for hurting him. She was not convinced, however, that the wizard hadn't deliberately ordered it, and Gareth's memory was still too hazy to reassure her.

A sudden roar from the dragon, however, broke up their discussion, alerting them to a distant group of wolves with a mounted knight bearing a white cloth on his lance. They had arrived on the opposite side of the road, a fair expanse away to them. They could see, though, that the knight's shield bore the device of a bloodied sword.

Gareth immediately urged Dreadful into the air, but Nemway cried out an urgent: 'Hold!'

The knight's visor was up and the wolves stationary, some even sitting on their haunches, their tongues hanging out. Dreadful subsided.

'Gareth, you know this knight?' asked Nemway.

'The blazon on his buckler tells me he is Accolon, Lady – the dupe of Morgan le Fay who for love of her, brought Arthur nearly to his doom long before she did so at Lyonesse,' was the unpromising answer. 'Lady, please, I beg you let me run him through.'

'And I say hold,' Nemway reminded him as Accolon began an effortless weave to speed through the intervening cars and lorries towards them. 'We are less than two mortal ells from safety. I want to hear what he has to say. Ask him to give account of himself.'

Retrieving his lance and shield from White Wand, Gareth obeyed and met Accolon at the edge of the wolf-strewn verge. 'Greetings from the noble Lady Nemway, Accolon of the bloodied sword,' he said frostily. 'My Mistress would know your mission?'

'Greetings to you, also, Gareth of old,' Accolon answered easily. 'I bear greetings from the High King of All Britain who hears of the Lady's prowess in slaying the great Dragon of the Weirdfolk. It is his desire that she ask freely whatever she will of him in return for the inestimable service she has done for the justice of his cause. Such is the royal message borne by me, Accolon of the bloodied sword.'

His voice carried clearly, and Nemway was about to dictate an incensed reply, when White Wand whispered. 'O Lady, if you love me, don't be headstrong, I implore you. *Please* ask if there is news of Merlyn's Heir and, if he is in danger, that the King deliver him?'

'I would rather bite out my tongue,' she returned acidly in a low voice. 'But for you, dear Wych, I will ask.' Raising her voice, she called back: 'I accept the safe conduct, Sir Accolon. As for the boon, I ask the same safe conduct for the Heir of Merlyn, the wizard of the Weirdfolk – should he be found.'

Accolon looked astonished, but the terms of the boon appeared to be wide enough for him to agree. 'The King's word is law, noble Lady. Although if it is to be ensured I need to know where the Heir of Merlyn can be found, and how he shall be recognised?'

Nemway hesitated, not knowing the answer, which Accolon seemed to interpret as mistrust. 'I swear by my holy doom, Lady,' he said, coming closer. 'No Weirdfolk magician has yet been met. The only denizens of this forest

– other than yourself and Sir Gareth – that are known to have come out of it, were the mighty Dragon that you slew and a great golden eagle.'

Nemway looked at White Wand who shook her head. The bird was a mystery to her, too. 'We know nothing of any eagle, Sir Accolon. I want the Heir of Merlyn found and restored to his sister Wych. I will ride with you in search of him.'

'How will you find Black Wand, if this knight knows nothing about him?' asked the Wych with alarm.

'I shall find him, dear sister, don't worry.'

When Gareth discovered that neither he nor Dreadful were accompanying the party, he condemned it passionately. 'You cannot do this, beloved Lady. Sir Accolon is falsest knight to King Arthur that ever disgraced the Round Table –'

'But *I* have safe conduct, dear Gareth,' she said sweetly, '*you* do not. And you *are* needed in the forest where your anxious fellows are waiting for you. Come now, let White Wand take Windfleet, while you return on Dreadful the same way as you left, and all will be well.' She kissed the Wych, and rode to join Sir Accolon, as Gareth glumly but dutifully mounted Dreadful and returned to the forest with White Wand.

When they were alone, Accolon inclined his head courteously. 'Which way, noble lady?'

'Wherever the golden eagle was last seen,' she said firmly. 'I have an idea that this bird is an emissary of Merlyn's Heir. Perhaps the wolves you have with you have news of it?'

'They have indeed,' said Accolon unhappily. 'They have not long told me that an eagle was slain at daybreak by the archers of the Baron of the SouthernWold, and afterwards devoured by the Royal Falcons which had lured it from its Retreat.'

'Slain!'

'The wolves do not lie, My Lady – '

But Nemway was not listening. Hew had told her that the Heir of Merlyn was destined to meet his doom at the hour of dawn. Her plea that his life be spared appeared to have arrived too late.

'Where did this happen?' she asked. He described the locality, and Nemway recognised the woods being the same as those which she and Gareth had sheltered in for the night. It was clear the attack on the eagle had coincided with the time that Hew had insisted she must be on her way.

'Then that is where we ride,' she said, and galloped off. It was in her interests as well as the White One's, to know if the wizard was really dead or alive.

*

Faced with Gareth's apparent capture by the enemy, Myrddin had perched high in the tree the previous evening for some time going over every possible course of action until the idea of actually getting in touch with the people of the Hollows and the Hills hit him like a revelation. If he wanted to know what had happened, they were the ones to ask and with Nemway gone, he was free to look for them. He would fly north-east towards London, then east into the traditional realm of these mysterious people.

He had so long ago dismissed Nemway's claim to kinship with the Sage of all the Seers as a lie designed to put him off ever trying to make contact with the only source of truth he was ever likely to find outside of Mona's Eye, he put aside the possibility of a truthful connection.

Even when a steadily increasing gale caused him a laboured flight, he still didn't get the message. Not a physical leaf was stirring anywhere, yet the rising astral pressure against him was great enough to bring down chimney stacks. He tried to get above the current but it pressed him down. Struggling on a further hundred yards was like swimming against a torrent of water and he gave up. Aggravated and alarmed, he turned back, thinking to return to the forest and try again on the morrow. With the force at his back, he reckoned to be there quite swiftly. The wind at once boxed the compass and blew against him from the opposite direction. Startled, he then laughed.

They're waving me down of course, he thought delightedly. *There'll be a messenger below waiting to give me directions.* He gave in and plunged into a large wooded area which he recognised as the one in which he had taken refuge earlier that evening in the cardboard box, and landed in a squirrel's dray. The wind dropped.

He turned into himself, stood up in graceful pride and called: 'Fair enough, O people of the Hills and Hollows, I am here where you have led me to rest. Please give me your message.'

He didn't know what he expected, but nothing happened. No apparition, no voice, no quiver of a leaf or crackle from the twigs and straw beneath his feet. He tried again. 'O people of the Hollows and the Hills to whom all Destinies are known, the Heir of Merlyn waits on your kindly guidance …'

Still nothing.

Annoyed and irritated, he transformed back into the eagle and vaulted into the air. A savage buffet of wind hurled him straight down again. He would learn later that to the Sage of all the Seers, it appeared only right and just that the wilful spirit who had so nearly brought his mother to her death should be the sacrifice to ensure her continued safety. Myrddin was therefore pinned down until allowed to fly free at dawn

The moment he broke cover, there came the scream of a black falcon alerting its brothers. It was just what Myrddin wanted. He had a score to settle with them and a whole night's frustration to get out of his system. If he managed to get his murderous beak into only one of them it would make his day – provided the cowardly things hung around long enough.

To his surprise, they did. All five closed in on him and at the last moment averted their attack. He dashed after one but it darted into the trees – only to come up on his tail the moment he went for another. The chasing falcon got a couple of his tail feathers before he could turn and give battle then dropped like a stone beneath him. The feathers felt like having a couple of teeth yanked out without anaesthetic and so enraged him that he charged recklessly at another tormentor to be treated to the same tactics which maddened him still more. When he finally caught one of the falcons and sank the hook of his beak into its neck with satisfying ease, he became more eager to serve another the same, except by then the remaining four were all streaking away to the north screaming like mad. Too late, he realised the purpose of the piecemeal pecking they had given him, and the dawning truth of Nemway's claim to motherhood that had resulted in the ambush. The Denefolk were on the side of the enemy, also, and had betrayed him.

'The plan works,' he heard the Baron of the SouthernWold cry. 'The Royal Falcons have lured him down to the very points of our lances –'

'Not a hope, Lord Baron,' muttered one of his archers taking presumptive aim. The first arrow whiffing through his feathers came as a shock and Myrddin sensed rather than saw the others about to follow it. He swerved, banked and tried to climb upwards. But the Sage of all the Seers did not intend to let him off so lightly despite his mother's plea. Myrddin found himself blown back with a sudden gust that had him spread-eagled against the outline of the trees long enough to ensure three other arrows found their mark. The first smashed his left wing, the second slammed through his thigh, and the third clouted his head. He flopped sideways and thrashed madly for the safety of the woods by which time the falcons had wheeled around and were coming in for the kill. With little hope of escape as he was, he ejected his avian form. It crashed to earth where the Baron's wolves tore it to pieces, while he fell into a tree to hang helpless over a thin branchlet with a broken arm, a crippled leg, two missing toes and a blinding headache before blackness engulfed him.

CHAPTER 31

THE SAVING OF DRAGGA

Myrddin became conscious of swallowing water and opened his eyes to find himself cradled in White Wand's arms. She was holding the Wealspring Cup to his lips and looking at him with such concern he nearly laughed.

'O beloved, you're alive,' she cried.

'Of course I'm alive,' he answered, feeling almost insulted and looking around in astonishment at finding himself in the Great Hall of the Gnomes' Mansion. An austere looking stranger, richly attired, and having a thick gold ring encircling his black curls, sat in the Master's chair with Omric standing beside it. 'But I must be dreaming. Who's this?'

He got to his feet, helping Ann to hers, and looked enquiringly at the Master for an introduction.

The stranger spoke for himself: 'I am Amyas, King of the Mabyn, O Black Wand,' he said quietly. A horse-like snort and a silvery jingle of metal behind made Myrddin turn quickly. A splendidly caparisoned white Unicorn was sharing the Hall with them, its harness ringing softly as it tossed its head.

'Truly the Unicorn of my vision that vanished into a hillside, beloved Wychy,' whispered White Wand, squeezing his hand.

'Icefire,' said the Mabyn with a small smile, before continuing: 'To the people of the Ancient Mounds there are Underways straight and true than any paths used above.

So I was able to bring you even to the underground door of your forest upon which I had to thunder seven times before the Master here opened it – '

'I opened only when this Mabyn of Mabyns gave me his ancient name and said that he had you with him, O Black One,' Ormric cut in hastily.

'I never knew there *was* an underground passage,' said Myrddin

'There is now,' said Amyas. He bent down and hefted a heavy chain attached to large equally weighty spiked ball into view. 'Meet *Moldwarp*; slayer of armies; hewer of tunnels,' he invited. 'The Master here told me where his Mansion lay and *Moldwarp* did the rest – '

'Were there wolves or falcons about to observe it?' Myrddin's tone was abrupt.

'Plenty of dead ones,' said White Wand with a shiver.

Talk of the wolves reminded the Wychy what he had been doing. He turned to White Wand. 'Dear Wych, I have sad news,' he said. 'I believe Gareth has been taken prisoner by enemy forces – '

'No, dearest Wychy,' she said happily. 'He is sitting with our people in Queen's Glade this very moment, telling them of his wonderful adventures with the Lady Nemway – '

'Nemway!' exclaimed Amyas, starting to his feet with delight. 'My sister has returned already?'

'Not yet, most noble Amyas,' said White Wand, carefully. 'She brought Gareth and Windfleet back here to the forest early this morning. When she heard that that my partner was not here, she went off immediately in search of him.'

Myrddin swallowed hard, shaken at the prospect of what might happen to him if Amyas learned all he had done trying to get rid of his sister. He then listened in silence to White Wand's account of the mix-up with Dreadful and the mistake Mortleroy had made in thinking Nemway had slain the great green guardian Dragon of the South. She said nothing about finding Excalibur, however, and managed to keep Nemway's recriminations of the wizard out of the telling. '... the Lady Nemway had no idea where this green monster had come from,' Ann explained sincerely. 'She was mortified when it turned out to be Dreadful – so wounded that she had to find shelter for the night to repair him and her horses. She met me beyond the Veil of Illusion at daybreak when she returned with Gareth. The enemy's envoy followed them. It turned out that the King, believing she had slain his worst enemy, was granting her safe conduct and any boon she cared to ask. She was going to refuse it, but I begged her to think again and to use it to pledge *your* safety, beloved,' she turned to her partner earnestly. 'The envoy asked how he would know you, and where you could be found. But as we had no idea where you were, the Lady Nemway said she would go with the knight to look for you. That was early this morning, and there's been no news of her since.'

With Nemway after his blood, and in collusion with the Sage of all the Seers to make an end of him, Myrddin was hardly surprised she had not returned. It was ironical, that his rescuer should be her brother,

But Amyas was nodding. 'She is well – I have seen her. When you spoke of her, I had hoped it meant that she had had second thoughts about Sir Accolon escorting her to Mortleroy.'

Myrddin changed the subject quickly: 'Great Mabyn, these Underways you speak of, do they lead to the halls of Glastonbury where King Gwyn is said to rule?'

'He rules from the Halls of Annwyn, which are vast and deep in caves and ways so old that even we don't know their origin,' Amyas answered factually. 'For the most part, they lie in the West of Britain although they do reach far beyond their proper confines. This is how Gwyn Son of Nudd can reach his old enemy whenever he likes. But he does it for himself,' he added dourly. 'He serves none else.'

'Yet our messenger brought news that he will offer refuge –'

Amyas laughed scornfully. 'Don't believe it, Heir of Merlyn.' Then leant towards him solemnly, saying: 'But now *I* would like to pay homage to my King.'

Myrddin wondered what the Mabyn would do when he found Arthur to be a sham. Yet what could he do …?

*

Black Wand's reappearance in the forest at noon with White Wand, and the Mabyn of Mabyns on a fabulous beast like the Unicorn, initiated a new round of wonder and celebration. The fae streamed off to greet the entourage as soon as it was realised it was on its way from the Wynn. Crowding around the Wands, they nearly overwhelmed them with love, kisses and excited enquiries. Even the business-like spiky ball that swung gently from the great Mabyn's hand failed to deter them from touching and stroking his lovely mount.

When they arrived in Queen's Glade, Myrddin was surprised to see how much taller Arthur had grown in the space of the previous interregnum. The serene and steady regard of the youthful grey eyes made the Wychy veil his own eyes in confusion and annoyance. Merlyn had a lot to answer for by not warning him of the effects of the special elixir that Nyzor had made from the recipe – or maybe Nyzor had added something special of his own. Myrddin had never expected the babe to grow, let alone behave like this youth with such alarming self-assurance and composure.

He knelt to Gwen. 'Beloved Queen, I bring Amyas, the Great Mabyn King of the North who has journeyed …'

But Gwen was already acknowledging the Mabyn's bow with a warm smile. The Mabyn gave Arthur one searching look – then fell on his knee and mutely kissed the youth's hand.

Again Myrddin did not know what to make of it. Everyone except him, it seemed, accepted the bogus youth without question. Either they were all blind or he was the mightiest magician ever. So why worry? It would certainly help matters for the counterfeit King to play the part well. Myrddin would need to watch he didn't get a swollen head, though, because of all the adulation. If he deferred to his benefactor, the pair of might get along quite well.

Without need of words, the Wychies wandled their fae's attention away from the royal party and back to their own amusements, to enable Gwen, Arthur, the two Wands, and Omric and Amyas to sit and talk together on their own.

In an aside to the Wychy, Omric confided that the enemy had not picked up the false Excalibur as expected and White Wand had brought it back into the forest.

Myrddin accepted the news philosophically thinking perhaps that it was just as well to be in control of the thing himself. It could come in useful if and when it ever came to proving Arthur false if ever the true turned up.

It was noticeable that the dour and powerful Mabyn King and Omric had taken to each other like long lost blood brothers, and when the Master requested leave of the Queen and Arthur to invite Amyas back to his Mansion, Arthur wanted to go with them, still as curious as ever. He wanted to listen to Amyas bringing the gnomes up to date on what was happening outside the forest. When Gwen retired to her bower beckoning White Wand in with her, Gareth, Feldspar and Whitegold all hurried after their departing figures, which left Myrddin free to get hold of the false Excalibur again.

*

Omric proudly showed Amyas the progress they had made on their arms and armour with Black Wand's magic, and

Amyas was impressed. He also inspected and tested Gareth's shield, and marvelled. He marvelled so much that he laid it on the floor and before anyone guessed what he intended, whirled *Moldwarp* down on it. All were in awe when the flail came back to his hand without as much as a dent on the shield or damage to any of *Moldwarp's* manifold spikes.

From staring down at the impregnable buckler, the Mabyn's eyes went slowly and steadily to the Master's and around to each one watching. 'It is legend, my brothers, that no child of Wayland can ever hurt its brother.'

'Then Merlyn's Heir has truly inherited his magic,' said Omric in hushed tones.

*

With everyone occupied, none knew of the Wychy's visit to the empty Circle of Rejoicing where he collected Excalibur, after testing it that it was still impossible to un-sheath the weapon.

Hiding it beneath his Weird, he was about to recover the Crystal Throne when he almost casually realised the Eye of the Oracle was visible – undulating gently at the bottom of several Wands' depth of water reflecting the orange blaze of a inferno that raged above Wandleside. It was so unexpected, he gasped stepped back and the vision vanished. Fire and flood spelt out the foretold destruction of the forest which meant it would happen after the next full moon. And a flooded Wandle meant the joining of the three surrounding Weirds – which must not happen with Dragga still in his. Saving their enemy was suddenly priority number one.

He left the Sword in his Retreat and hurried to the edge of the Woe.

Looking down at the faceless surface of the Weird where he had so often stood to defend their Kingdom against the lethal menace lurking beneath its dark waters, Myrddin spoke aloud:

'Hear me, Dragga! If I am to save you, I must know the secrets of your depths.'

This I know, came the ghostly reply. *The roots of your destruction are already loosened in their sockets, and unless they are saved my strength shall be gone forever and your people's road to mortality and back shall be no more. Go therefore to the northernmost tip of my Weird. Dive there and you will see and know without further guidance from me.*

On his way there, the Wychy summoned Nyzor to bring his dray and two large containers as quickly as he could to the Woe's northern end. Contemplating the jagged reeds at the northern tip of Dragga's Weird brought back vivid memories of James Durant's death. The thought that he was about to plunge willingly into the grim depths seemed tantamount to consigning himself to the tender mercies of a seething volcano. Putting it from his mind, he stripped naked, and dived in as gracefully as a salmon leaping.

He found it rather like flying in a new dimension, and was immediately aware that the physical flow of water entering the Weird had increased several-fold. It was now moving fast enough to start uprooting the reed beds. An unprecedented surge was tearing Dragga apart before his eyes. He hung back out of reach of the streaming reeds as he looked for seed vessels, and saw the spiky things growing at the reed tips; some already torn away and speeding recklessly down the Weird. Then he saw that there were two types of reed, and understood that these seed bearing kind were harmless; the rubbery parent growths that scattered fresh seeds every season to renew the lethal variety which were sterile and needed replacing with young and vigorous scythe-like blades. Even as he watched, he felt rather than heard another agonised groan of despair as the current tore a couple more of the unnatural growths from their ancient holds, and swept them away into darkness.

His decision to salvage what he could of the rapidly departing bulbs seemed to communicate itself to his enemy for when he left the water to look at the containers Nyzor had brought up, Dragga let him go.

Nyzor unloaded two large stoppered containers from the dray and helped the Wychy with them to the water's edge. He then waited while the wizard dived in for the second time.

Slashing the parent reeds with his Wand, so they were carried away by the current, relieved the weight on the roots which were then easier to tug out and get into the containers. Yet even while he worked, he felt the presence of being watched; a presence that drew at him, licking its lips; avidly craving to slice him neatly to pieces. But none of the scalpel like reeds that were sharpening their blades was near enough to touch him, so he was safe for the moment. It was a long time since the old enemy had enjoyed devouring its last Wychy, and Myrddin could sense Dragga drooling at the prospect of the next. The entity was reaching into his mind, intruding its sense of delicious and exquisite pleasure at the thought of shredding him to ribbons the better to enjoy each living, quivering morsel to the full, so much more succulent and tasty than mortal remains – and so rarely enjoyed.

'... And there's me with no idea you had such a vivid imagination, Dragga,' he said to himself, with a moue of revulsion. 'But I still have my Wand,' he added, slashing viciously at another clump of rubbery reeds. 'So you can pack it in, you old fiend.'

Reasoning that seven was the mystic number of numbers, and that one for luck made a perfection of eight, he put four into each jar and wedged them tightly between other roots until full. He was taking no chances that Dragga wasn't merely waiting until sure that even one root was safe before swirling the Wychy into the nearby bed of reeds as a last meal for some time to come.

When he got the roots back to the bank, he called to the Vintner that if he saw the Wychy disappear beneath the surface at any point, he was to throw both containers straight back into the Weird. With these words, Myrddin had the satisfaction of feeling the evil presence slide angrily away from beneath him, baulked of its very intention.

Safely ashore, but feeling unimaginably filthy and mentally stained, it made sense to agree that Nyzor should take the heavy containers back to the Vintner's place in the Wynn. Before leaving, however, Nyzor took a small thin bottle from his pouch and removed the stopper, presenting the phial to the Wychy.

Myrddin sipped and then drained the fresh, cold Wealspring water in full, allowing it to penetrate like fire, cleansing and invigorating every part of his being.

'Thank you,' he said. 'That was rather necessary. How did you find time to collect it?'

'Rozyn-who-was taught me to fill many containers from the cup at the Wealspring – which I did when I had to replenish all my stock.' said the Vintner.

Myrddin clapped his shoulder thankfully. 'Rozyn found a worthy successor, Nyzor.'

CHAPTER 32

A NEW WAND AND A NEW BEGINNING

Standing with White Wand at Weirdsmeet at High Moon, Myrddin thought of all that had happened since the previous. Mergyn's possession of Gwen had come and gone; the finding of Merlyn's Ring leading to his Mount and the discoveries he had made there that had so altered everything, and the Book of Amaranthus ...

The fae's excited chatter echoed across to them from down the packed winding path of Wandleside. The brave new appearance of the gnomes mailed cap-a-pie, each bearing across his breast the Green Dragon of the Weirdfolk surmounted by the crown of Arthur seemed to epitomise new expectations and readiness of all now to venture beyond the Veil of Illusion. It seemed the time for leaving was closer than ever.

The Wychy caught hold of White Wand's hand, and she turned to him in glad surprise. He wanted to tell her – ask her – so much and found he couldn't. Hidden as they were in the trees, all he could do was embrace her wordlessly, before they wrought the magic that brought delicate tracery of the crystal bridge into being between them that never failed to bring long drawn gasps of 'oohs' and 'aahs' in appreciation and delight, especially from the new arrivals.

When there came rhythmic shouts of 'Gwen! Queen! Queen Gwen!' 'Arthur! King! King Arthur!' the Wands knew that the royal barge had been sighted coming down the upper Weird.

When they stepped forward from the cover of the trees to await their guests, however, Myrddin was mildly surprised to see two barges sweeping down to Weirds-meet. The first was Gwen's in which she sat still wearing Alder's crown and blazing mantle; in the second was Arthur resplendent in his armour and wearing a mantle of crimson, gold and purple quartered with the four dragons of his kingdom, the Red, the Blue, the Black and the Green. With him, were Amyas and the Master of Gnomes mailed and armed after their different fashions.

The significance of it only dawned on Myrddin when Arthur stepped ashore, and Kye, the Queen's Herald greeted him as High King of all Brython, guest of the Queen of the Weirdfolk, and not just their own particular ruler as Alder had been.

It seemed to Myrddin that his next step had to be Arthur's proper regulation. Their self-appointed 'King' had to be told of his true origin and recognise his coming dependence on the magician if he was going to be revealed to the outside world.

The fae were thunderous in their applause as he stepped ashore. Queen and Wychies curtsied and bowed before him – though Myrddin did so grimly as he endured the acknowledgement for the fae's sake.

When the royal party disappeared into the trees, the two Wands received their individual greeting from the fae, then followed after them to the Circle of Rejoicing where Gwen and Arthur had taken their thrones.

The Wychies took their own black and white thrones while the jubilant throng settled into its usual places – with the exception of the newcomers, whom the Lord Chamberlain marshalled at the far end.

Another fanfare from Kye, and the Chamberlain beckoned the newly returned fae of the Weirdfolk forward to present them first to Gwen as their immediate Queen, and then to Arthur. When all had retired back to their places amid general rejoicing, the Wychies rose, approached each other and glided side by side to Gwen's throne, where they knelt. The Queen touched the tips of their Wands with her own to evoke the unifying flash of light between the three.

The pair returned to their stations and faced each other, Wands poised in readiness to repeat the High Moon's ritual, so loved and welcomed by the Weirdfolk, who began the traditional chant until every voice became as one:

'Wed the Wands, O Wychies! Wed the Wands!'

As usual, the Wychy mutely signalled the exact moment his Wych should launch her Wand so that they would meet at the centre before the Queen. They had done this so often; they had even learned a certain skill that provoked an even more awesome display of fireworks from their Wands' union, delighting the fae.

When Black and White met high at their usual point, the Wychies had a shock. One Wand fell inertly to the ground.

Myrddin stared and stared, unable to believe the terrible truth. His was the Wand that lay there – not his Wych's. Her Wand had returned to her hand after a brief gyration. His Wand had had enough of him.

The Wychy hardly heard the hushed whispers of shock and dismay that followed the stunned silence:

'The Black One's Wand has cast him away.'

'But my Weird is *not* worn!' he muttered in horrified amazement to himself, remembering how grey and lifeless his predecessor's cloak had hung the at same moment. He could see his own was still brilliant around him. *What does it mean? It has to be a mistake! What am I supposed to do?*

He forced himself approach the spot where the bright Wand of his erstwhile power lay. For a moment he was tempted to hold out his hand for it to rise to him, but it had been a part of him too long not to know that that wasn't going to happen. Finis. It was the end. Whatever might follow was no longer any concern of his. Last acts of relinquishment must be performed.

He made himself remove his crown, placing it gently at the Wand's side, then removed his bright Weird, handing it to the Chamberlain.

He looked for an instant at his weeping Wych before going to kneel for the last time before the Queen.

He rose without a glance at Arthur – let alone obeisance – and passed swiftly out of the Circle while Kye strode to the centre of the arena and the cries hushed with a fanfare that vibrated in tones of reassurance and hope …

*

And where does a Wandless and Weirdless magician go from here? Myrddin wondered. Certainly not to Dragga! He had not worn his Weird and Dragga owed *him* – not vice versa. Nyzor had charge of his enemy's roots. The Vintner would know what he must do when the Weirdfolk reached whatever new destination lay in store for them.

He made his way to his Retreat thinking himself into a new persona. There, he crushed the grey and silver hose and tunic he had always worn under his Weird into its astral essence. It was a reminder of a past to which he no longer belonged. But if August the elemental had gone, and Myrddin the forest magician was no more, he was still Merlyn's Heir, and still entitled to call himself Am-Mar-El-Lyn, and think of himself in great Merlyn's form as Myrddin Black.

He quickly reformed the plasma with knowledgeable fingers into a man's loose white salwar trousers and long embroidered tunic. Then fashioned a carrier into which he piled Merlyn's ring; the crystal shades made for him by Omric; a container holding all his scrolls and the sword he had taken from the throne.

He paused for a final look through the walls that had been his home for so long. In the Circle of Rejoicing, just as he had known it would, the Wand had risen to Redweird as his successor. What widened his eyes with surprise, however, was the distinctly reddish sheen that now lay in the black brilliance of the Weird as it enveloped the new Wychy.

In the Weal, all was quiet and empty with only a patient Dreadful keeping lonely watch. The dragon looked in his direction as if sensing him there and Merlyn's Heir smiled, thinking of all the ways in which the creature had served him and brought so much delight to the Weirdfolk.

Well, long may he go on doing so, thought the magician, then remembered the words of prophecy: *Before Mona's light thrice more has waned, there shall be a passing and a coming, and a desolation within your lands unknown since their beginnings, and Wands all three divided one-and-one-and-one and Dragga, too, undone, 'til the One who comes is seen and known by all.*

Two High Moons passed already. Two mortal weeks remained before the forest was destroyed.

Did he, himself still have a part to play in rescuing the forest's inhabitants? He had no idea. It seemed fitting, though, that now he *was* on the outside, he was ready for the true Arthur – *and* had the sword on hand to disprove the one he had left in the forest!

In Wychies' Lane, he slipped the ring over his head and made for Weir Court as Myrddin Black to meet the new Weir Lord, Sir Humphrey We'ard, for the first time. The Baronet should be asleep at that time in the early hours, which promised Myrddin time to do catch up with his manuscripts …

NOT THE END

WIZARD'S WOE

Writer and journalist August Autrey arrives in the village of Three Weirs to cover the story of the Forest of Weir. The villagers have long believed the forest to be the home of a wizard and a dangerous dragon. When August disappears leaving only his empty clothes draping the seat of a chair, many believe he has paid the price for being too curious.

His landlady's niece, Ann Singlewood, dreams that she meets the missing journalist living in the forest as a nine-inch high elfin wizard.

Two weeks later, however, August is back. He types for three days without stopping, then sends a long manuscript to Ann.

As Ann reads, she realises that the magical world she dreamed of is real - but that August has come back because he is in love with her. Yet how can they ever be together when August is found dead the next morning ...?

ORDER FORM

Price: £6.99 each or 2 for £12

Delivery: UK: £2.25

To order please complete the form below and send with your payment to:

YPS, 64 Hallfield Road, Layerthorpe, York, YO31 7ZQ
(Cheques made payable to York Publishing Services Ltd)

☐ *Wizard's Woe* ☐ *Merlyn's Heir*

Name: _____

Address: _____

_____

Postcode: _____

Tel. No: _____

Email: _____

No. of copies: _____

P&P per book: _____ £ _____

Total £ _____

I wish £2.50 from the £6.99 I am paying for this book to be donated in support of

☐ **ELF** - Exeter Leukaemia Fund;   ☐ **Cancer Research**
☐ **Save the Children Fund**   ☐ **ACORNS**
(Children's Hospice)

☐ **Parkinson's UK** (Parkinson's Disease Society)

Order online at www.ypdbooks.com or
Telephone 01904 431213